Time Slider

Time Slider

Alan E. Todd

Library of Congress Control Number: 2011963282

ISBN:	Hardcover	978-1-4691-4316-3
	Softcover	978-1-4691-4315-6
	Ebook	978-1-4691-4317-0

This is a work of fiction. Names, characters, places and incidents either are the product of the author's imagination or are used fictitiously, and any resemblance to any actual persons, living or dead, events, or locales is entirely coincidental.

This book was printed in the United States of America.

To order additional copies of this book, contact:
Xlibris Corporation
1-888-795-4274
www.Xlibris.com
Orders@Xlibris.com
101705

Contents

Part II—Time for Change

Part III—Time Has Come

For my daughters and wife.

May our lives together,

slide joyfully through time forever.

Nameless Curse

I am cursed with a nameless curse.
No water can quench this undying thirst.

Still I observe you from afar,
An ever-present, but distant star.

As time flies by, I go from place to place,
And I dream of you, your beautiful face.

The rules keep us apart, but how can this be?
Like a ghost in your world, you can not see.

Suddenly you're gone . . .

All that I know, all that I am, is the clock ticking away.
I scream out your name, but all I hear are my own helpless cries.

The happily ever after you dreamed of doesn't exist.
The dream is gone and dead like leaves in the winter.

I am cursed with a nameless curse.
No water can quench this undying thirst.

Eden Spigener—Age 12

MY THANKS AND appreciation goes out to my family and friends who have given me support and encouragement in the creation of this book. Specifically, thank you to my wife, Elaine, for her thoughtful critique, ideas, and editing. Thank you also to Cyril Cal, Steven Cardimona, and the Spigener Family for their insightful guidance, encouragement, and review. And finally, thank you to the Creator of Heaven and Earth, for whom time is already written.

Prologue

THE YOUNG BOY leaned over the edge of the babbling creek with his knees pressing softly into the small rounded pebbles. He could see his reflection in the water. The image of his lightly tanned face and brown hair reflected back to him in the gentle ripples on the water's surface. He focused past his own reflected image, down to a creature that had just wriggled itself under a rock beneath the water. It was a fish, only about three inches long, with dark smooth skin and whisker-like hairs that protruded from its face.

In two smooth, coordinated movements, the boy lifted the rock with his left hand, sunk an inverted glass jar into the creek, and landed the opening over the catfish. Then he flipped the jar and lifted it up to examine his catch through the clear glass prison. The boy smiled. It was one of the biggest catches he had made since first finding this stream in the woods behind his eastern Oklahoma home.

"Whacha doin'?" a small voice surprised him from behind. The boy jumped, dropping his jar onto the forgiving pebbles at his feet. He recovered quickly and caught it again before it tipped over.

The boy hadn't heard the girl glide up silently behind him. She wore a white button-down shirt, a pink skirt, white tennis shoes, and short white socks. She looked way too clean for playing in the woods, the boy thought. She had blonde hair, fair skin, and the most brilliant blue eyes the boy had ever seen. She looked younger than him, but his inner desire for a friend overtook his natural instinct to pretend that he was too old to talk to such a child, even a girl child.

"Catching catfish," he answered coolly.

"What for?" she asked.

"I dunno." He shrugged, "'cause they're for catching."

"Oh," she agreed, nodding her head but not sure if he really had answered her question. She decided it didn't really matter. "Can I look?" she asked.

The boy nodded yes, and she knelt down beside him. He handed her the jar with the new catch. "Ahh," she sighed with wonder, putting the jar up close to her face and peering through the glass. He was impressed that she didn't seem afraid at all as the catfish turned around on the bottom of the jar, pumping his gills. "It's so neat!" she said with quiet excitement to avoid scaring the creature. Then she furrowed her brow and turned to the boy. "Will you eat it?" she asked, concerned for the well-being of the little fish.

The boy smiled. He could have lied and tried to worry her more but decided not to be mean to the little kid. "No," he said reassuringly. "I don't hurt them. I just catch them, look at them for a while, and then let them go."

"Good!" She smiled as she gently tipped the jar to see the underside. "I think he has a family he'll want to go home to." She paused and then said, "My family lives up the hill back there."

The boy frowned. "You mean the white house with the sale sign?" There were only two houses up the hill in that direction, his and another that his friend Jeremy had moved out of a few weeks ago. He had prayed every night before bed that a new boy his age would move in.

"Yeah," she said, still amazed at the long, prickly-looking hairs that twitched and the tail that flipped back and forth. "We just moved here. My mom and dad said to run off and explore while they unloaded the truck. They said I was too small to help and would get in the way."

"Do you have any brothers?" the boy asked hopefully. He wasn't sure what he thought about a girl living next door with no brothers. What a waste of a house.

"No, just me." She smiled as if she sensed his disappointment but didn't really care. He frowned again. Jeremy had been nine years old, like himself. This girl looked to be only six. She was like a baby.

"Can I please try?" she asked politely, setting the jar down gently next to him.

"Guess so," the boy muttered. "Here," he said handing her another empty jar. He wasn't ready to let his catch go. They both peered through the water, both their faces reflecting side by side. "What you got to do is . . ."

"Got one," she squealed, faster than he could finish his instructions. He looked in disbelief. Hers was even bigger than the one he had caught; maybe she wasn't such a baby after all. Maybe having a girl neighbor would be okay. Maybe they could be friends. Maybe she wouldn't act too much like a girl.

"Wow, he's pretty." The girl giggled excitedly.

The boy changed his mind. She was definitely a girl.

PART I

Time of Discovery

Man cannot remake himself without suffering, for he is both the marble and the sculptor.

—Dr. Alexis Carrel

Not until we are lost do we begin to understand ourselves.

—Henry David Thoreau

Chapter 1

A CHANGE IS COMING

Wednesday, May 10, 1995

TIM WOKE UP outside at 12:13 a.m. on his twenty-third birthday, wearing only his red boxers. He knew it was 12:13, because he always woke up at 12:13; thirteen minutes after midnight, every night for as long as he could remember. This time, he noticed the shimmer of orangish light around him even before he was completely conscious. "Tiki torches again," he thought as he slowly blinked his eyes to try to clear the film that had formed on them during the last half hour. His eyes felt dry and swollen as usual, and he knew it would take another minute or two before he would be able to see clearly. "Happy Birthday to me," he said sarcastically.

A warm breeze caused the small flames to flicker. As Tim's vision began to clear, he confirmed to himself that he was outside his home in the woods just beyond his short suburban yard. He was one of the fortunate few in the sprawling city of Houston, Texas, to have undeveloped property so close by. The flat coastal landscape and frequent heavy rain made it necessary to leave some land open as floodwater retention zones. Having this so close to his home meant dealing with lots of mosquitoes, snakes, and even the occasional alligator. But it also meant he had several hundred acres to escape to when the city life was too much, or when Natalie, his girlfriend, was nagging him.

One of the Tiki torches was on fire around the bamboo straps that held the canister of citronella in place. "She always overfills them," he grumbled to himself, then quickly looked around again to see if she heard him. She wasn't there. "Must have given up her exorcism attempt again and went to bed," he thought. His girlfriend was only 5′ 5″ and barely over 115 lbs but somehow she could drag him out here and still have the energy to do her voodoo mumbo jumbo. They had been together for almost two years, and she had made it her "mission" to cure him of his "curse."

What that curse really was, he didn't know; and neither did the doctors, psychologists, priests, or any other healer he had tried to find answers from. One scientist thought his mind was being taken over by aliens from the Vega System, as they tried to gather intelligence about the human race. Sadly, that explanation was as good as any he had heard. He had had countless tests run on him when he was eighteen after he wound up in the hospital, but even those failed to make sense of his condition. Tests could measure the symptoms but couldn't give any rationale for what happened to him each and every night.

A neurologist he had called "Doc" probably could have figured more out if Tim had let him. Doc Bruin had run the tests after his accident. But just when he started to uncover some of the mysteries, Tim panicked and decided he didn't want to know more. Maybe someday he would go back to Doc, but for now, he had found peace with just accepting the abnormality. And as he learned to use it to his own advantage, he found himself questioning it less and less. He just wished Natalie would leave it alone. After all, he was twenty-two, no twenty-three now, and very rich. So what if his success wasn't completely legit. He might as well use his condition, his "zone" for himself.

Tim left the torches burning as he hiked out of the woods and climbed up the small hill that led to his home's rear entrance. It was a large home, but nothing too fancy since he didn't want to draw attention to himself. He didn't work, at least not regularly, and when he did, it was usually just for fun so the pay wasn't much.

When anyone would ask how he afforded to live, he'd just lie about inheriting a fortune from his parents. It was a lie, because they weren't dead yet, although it had been almost five years since he had spoken to them. Even if they had been dead, they weren't rich and didn't have much money to pass down.

When Tim reached the back door, he found it unlocked. "At least she didn't lock me out again," Tim thought as he slipped in quietly and closed the door behind him. He would have been quite angry if Natalie had done that yet again. "It's my house, not hers."

He often wondered why he even put up with this. He had lost count of the number of times she had messed with his limp and lifeless body while his consciousness was in his zone. She had dragged him outside several times, pricked him with needles, poured "holy water" onto him, and tried a multitude of other half-baked schemes to rid him of the curse. Twice, she had even thrown him into the bathtub and filled it with ice water! He was a little surprised she hadn't tried to burn the demons out of his body with gasoline and matches.

"Why do I put up with her?" he thought again as he topped the stairs and turned into his bedroom. Light from the moon poured into the room from the open window and fell onto the goddess-like form of Natalie's naked backside as she slept contently on her stomach.

"Oh yeah, that's why," Tim sighed as he admired her long-legged perfection. He crawled into bed next to her and ran his hand up her thigh, across her rounded buttocks and rested it at the small of her back. She didn't stir from her content slumber. He was always in awe at how soundly she slept. "She sleeps just like a baby," he thought. "At least, like most babies."

Chapter 2

IN THE BEGINNING

1972: 23 Years Earlier

TIM WASN'T LIKE most babies. From the day he was born, he would wake up crying, and his mother would rush into his room at 12:13 a.m. She'd pick him up out of his crib and nurse him to calm him down. She was amazed at how consistent his schedule was for feeding in the middle of the night. She had no way of knowing that it was his dry, burning eyes which caused him to cry out and not hunger pangs. Regardless of the cause, his crying effectively rewetted his eyes and soothed the burning, allowing him to fall back into a normal deep baby sleep.

"Sarah, you have to give him 'tough love,'" his mom's friend, Mary, told her. "Babies need structure and consistency. If he thinks you'll just come running in there at every hour of the night, then he'll always expect it."

"But he needs to know I love him and will always provide for him."

"Of course. And you do show him, when his requests are reasonable and not at one in the morning."

"I'm supposed to just let him cry?"

"Look, just try it for a week. Trust me, he'll stop waking up in the middle of the night and will love you just as much during the day."

Other friends gave her similar lectures. They said he was just spoiled. Even their pediatrician said all kids would sleep through the night once they accepted that that is what night was for.

John, Tim's dad, was an intellectual kind of person. He didn't like to just trust advice unless he could find it in books. So he borrowed some books from the library and poured through them one at a time. It seemed to him that half of the books said, "Show your child you love him by meeting his needs immediately" and the other half said, "Show you love him by teaching him when it is appropriate to have his needs met."

Sarah, tired from months of 12:00 a.m. feedings, decided to try the teaching approach. It was very difficult for her at first to hear him crying and not go to him. But he seemed to calm himself down and go back to sleep after just a few minutes.

After a couple of weeks of letting him cry when he woke at 12:13 a.m., Tim's mom was convinced that they were right. He did stop crying every night, and she got to have her full night's rest. However, for six-month-old Tim, nothing had changed. He still woke up every night at thirteen minutes after midnight. And since he wasn't crying now, it took a little longer for the burning to go away and for his eyes to be clear and comfortable enough to go back to sleep.

Tim never complained about waking up each night to others, since by the time he was able to talk, he had accepted it as a normal part of the night. As far as anyone knew, he was just a normal kid like any other. Even *he* thought that, or at least he hoped he was normal.

1984

By the time Tim was twelve years old, he was doing well in school, had lots of friends, had crushes on classmates, and played various intramural sports.

Tim almost told his best friend Lexie one afternoon while they were exploring the woods behind their house. She was his next door neighbor, and the only other kid nearby on their rural road.

A new subdivision was being built just down the street, but their houses remained relatively isolated.

Tim and Lexie's parents enjoyed the quiet isolation so near the city of Tulsa, Oklahoma. Tim and Lexie enjoyed the freedom of playing and exploring. She was two-and-a-half years younger than Tim, but they were both only children, and their parents had become good friends. It was only natural that they would find an effortless friendship.

"Did you hear that storm last night?" Lexie asked as she flipped some wet leaves with a stick.

"Nope," Tim replied absently as he tried rolling over a soggy log. "Guess I slept through it."

"I got up because the thunders scared me, but Daddy told me to go back to bed. I sat by their door for a long time until the thunders stopped." She laid her stick down over the leaves, and then pulled her shiny blonde hair back into a pony tail to keep it out of her face while they played.

"Guess that is why it is so wet out here." Tim grunted as he continued pushing on the large half-rotten log.

"Then," Lexie continued as she walked over to Tim to help with the log, "after the storm was over, I went back to my room, and my clock said it was ten minutes after midnight! I've never been awake that late!"

"I'm always awake after midnight," Tim started to brag to his younger friend.

"Why?" she asked puzzled. He started to answer, but then hesitated, wondering if she would think it was weird that he woke up at the same time each night.

Suddenly, the log they had been working on finally budged unexpectedly, causing them both to lose their balance and fall into the soggy leaves. Lexie fell into the muddy spot where the log had been, and both kids began laughing as they tried to get up before their clothes got too soaked. Their previous conversation was forgotten as quickly as it had started.

Another year went by and though Tim still awoke each night, he continued to keep it to himself. He had started to realize that it was abnormal, but at thirteen, the last thing he wanted others to think was that he was strange.

Keeping it a secret seemed like the best plan. But secrets have a way of coming out, and it was Lexie who first noticed that something very strange happened to Tim each night.

Chapter 3

BEST FRIENDS

Saturday, August 10, 1985

"READY TO HEAD out?" John bellowed from the driver's seat of their brand new blue 1985 Plymouth Duster. Tim and Lexie grinned at each other in the back seat, accepting his dad's enthusiasm at the start of their annual camping trip. They enjoyed the trips each year, as did Tim's mom; just not as much as Dad always did. He was a true camper. Give him a sleeping bag, some trail mix, and a pretty view, and he was in heaven. He didn't like tents since they blocked the view of the stars at night, but he accepted them as a necessary evil since his wife, Sarah, refused to camp without as many comforts as possible.

She had threatened to never camp again two summers ago when her air mattress was punctured by a sharp rock sticking up through the bottom of the tent floor. Halfway through the night, she found herself not only lying on a mostly deflated mattress, but also with that same sharp rock pressing into her side. Since no one else used a mattress, she was forced to spend the rest of the night fighting for space in the small four-man tent away from the rock.

John realized quickly that his joy of family camping was about to end if he didn't act quickly. Heading back into town from their lakeside campsite on Eufaula Lake in Oklahoma, he found and purchased the thickest, most durable, multichamber air mattress he could find. He also bought a second tent to use for the kids. It made sense to split into two tents now that the kids were getting older and taking up more space. John had often joked, "Whoever called this tent a 'four-man capacity' tent must have only known really small men!"

John's quick reaction had quelled Sarah's protests. Now, two years later, John was smiling and whistling as they pulled out of their driveway near Tulsa and headed this time to Skiatook Lake. Tim was thirteen, and Lexie, ten. Lexie would be eleven soon and was always annoyed at Tim for calling her a baby in the four months between his birthday and hers.

Lexie had been part of the Caston's family camping trips since she was six. Chris, Lexie's dad, couldn't get much time off work so her parents usually drove out for only a night or two. Lexie happily stayed with the Castons the rest of the trip.

This time, her parents couldn't come at all, since Lexie's aunt had just had her second baby. Gracie, Lexie's mom, had decided that they were going to visit them over the weekend, even though her sister had specifically said that she preferred to have time alone with her new baby and family.

Lexie was kind of glad they weren't coming. Her mom had been acting somewhat strange for several months—getting angry about random things or forgetting she had already done something and doing it again and again—things like that. Lexie was glad to get away.

This arrangement suited the Castons fine too, since Lexie seemed like part of the family anyway. With no other kids nearby, the two children spent all of their time together. Lexie was a regular guest at their dinner table, and Sarah often laughed that it was just like having two kids, except they got along better than normal siblings! They rarely fought unless one would pester the other for too long, and they got into trouble more often for laughing too loudly than for arguing or fighting.

The drive to Skiatook Lake was fairly short from Tulsa. The two kids played games in an activity book while they rode north along highway I-75. Tim won the first four tic-tac-toe games in a row. Then Lexie stopped letting her older friend win. The next few games ended up as a draw until Tim made an error when he was distracted by a suped up red corvette speeding past their Duster. He was a little upset by his loss and decided it was time to change games.

"Let's play Dots and Squares," he suggested.

Lexie thought for a moment and then said, "I don't know that game. How do you play?"

"It's easy," the confident Tim bragged. "We take turns drawing a single line on a grid of dots to form boxes. Each time you finish a box, you get another turn, and the person who completes the most boxes wins."

"Sounds good," Lexie agreed, though she wasn't exactly sure yet how to play.

They played five rounds with Tim narrowly winning the first two times. The third match, however, Lexie figured out his strategy and collected most of the boxes for a big win. She won the fourth and fifth rounds as well, taking the best of five.

"Why do you always win?" Tim said frustrated that Lexie figured out how to beat him yet again.

"You win a lot too."

"Only at new games that you've never played before. Then you figure them out and beat me."

"Maybe you are just a good teacher," she said, trying to soothe his hurt ego.

Tim envied his young friend's gift to learn so quickly. Everything came so easily for her. She could scan a page just once or twice and then remember it as if she'd taken a photo with her brain. With games, she'd follow the rules but swiftly figure out ways to take the upper hand.

"I think you are just too smart for your own good. Boys will never want to marry you if you always beat them at stuff."

"Eww, why would I want to get married to a boy?" Lexie responded instinctively. She knew that girls and boys their age weren't supposed to like thinking about stuff like that. "But if I do get married someday," she said, realizing it was silly to just reject something so likely to happen, "I want him to be brilliant. If he is dumb, I won't have any respect for him. How can my prince and I live happily ever after if he is dumb?"

"What you gonna do, give him a test if he proposes?" Tim grinned.

"No, but I might make him sit down with me and play some games. If he can't give me a good challenge, then I'll just say, 'Sorry, you are dumb. You can just go back to the store and get your money back on that ugly ring.'"

"I'm glad I'll never propose to you, then." Tim laughed. Lexie didn't laugh.

John and Sarah were content in the front of the car with their own thoughts. Sarah was already thinking of the chores and shopping she wanted to do when they returned home after this yearly escapade. John had visions of campfire chats, s'mores, hikes, and lakeside lounging. He hoped Sarah and the kids would enjoy it as much as he would. He always spent much of the time trying to make Sarah comfortable and the kids happy, but he also took enough moments out for himself. After all, this vacation was his way of unwinding each year from his stressful oil field job.

After pulling into the campground, finding the "perfect" site, and then helping Dad unload the tents and cooking equipment, Lexie and Tim snuck off to explore the lakeshore. They had always been trustworthy, so John and Sarah allowed them substantial freedom to be kids. Most of their time was spent riding their bikes around the trails and campground roads. Sometimes, they'd meet other kids and strike up conversations or play at the playground. Most kids assumed Tim and Lexie were brother and sister, and often the two let that remain a private joke between them.

At night, the four Castons, including Lexie, would take turns telling stories around the fire. Each had their own style. Sarah's stories were usually short and lacked much detail. She never could get her heart into it. John, on the other hand, would go on and on with so much detail that often the other three would forget what the story was supposed to be about by the time he wrapped it up. Tim's stories usually involved fast cars or He-Man type action heroes. His stories almost always ended with, "And the hero saved the day yet again!"

"You always tell hero stories," Lexie teased.

"That's because my boy wants to be a hero someday," John said, ruffling up Tim's hair. Tim thought the action was slightly demeaning but accepted it as his dad's way of affection.

"Are you going to be like the heroes in your stories, with muscles so big that your arms are the size of tree trunks with ugly veins popping up through your skin?" she teased again.

"Yep, I'll be the strongest hero of them all," Tim mused. "Bad guys will shiver at the sound of my voice and the size of my muscles."

"I'm shivering at the size of your head," Lexie laughed cutely. Tim knew she was making fun of him but couldn't help laughing as she puffed up her cheeks with air and pretended her head was growing.

Lexie, although the youngest of their crew, was the best storyteller of all. She would think up and weave together some great adventure. And if there was a hero in her stories, it was always a beautiful woman instead of some sweaty muscle-laden jock.

After storytelling, the s'mores would come out. John could always find the perfect stick for cooking eight to ten large marshmallows at once. He would occasionally share them with others but usually smiled and said, "Get your own stick and cook some up." He wanted everyone to enjoy the thrill themselves.

Sarah didn't want to get dirty, and marshmallows heated up over a fire and then squooshed onto melted chocolate was just about the messiest thing she could think of. Not to mention cooking them on a stick. "I don't know where that stick has been!" she would say. She usually just ate the marshmallows cold with a cracker and no chocolate.

Lexie carefully cooked just one at a time, slowly turning it around and around in the fire until it became the perfect shade of toasted brown. She then gently placed it on her cracker under a square of Hershey's chocolate. She savored each bite until it was time to make the next one.

Tim really didn't like marshmallows. He just put them on the stick for the fun of it and burned them one at a time. He liked watching the blue and green flames shoot off the marshmallow as it puffed up twice its original size. Then it would fall from the stick and land in the red-hot glowing coals. "Guess I need another one," he would say with a laugh.

John and Sarah always sent the kids off to bed by 10:00 p.m. They'd stay up another half hour or so to make sure the kids went to sleep and then would try to be romantic enough to spark a roll in the double sleeping bag. Usually though, they were so worn out from the day, they too would quickly fall to sleep having only been romantic enough to kiss for a few moments before rolling apart.

On the second night of their camping vacation at the lake, Lexie woke up a few minutes after midnight, needing to go to the bathroom. As she slowly unzipped the tent's door, she glanced toward Tim to see if she had woken him up with the noisy zipper. In the dim light that was filtering in from the moon, she could see his form next to where she had been sleeping. He was on his side with his head toward her and the door. His sleeping bag covered his body and some of his face, but it looked to her like his eyes were open.

Apologetically, she whispered, "Sorry I woke you up. Gotta pee really bad!" He didn't respond, so she finished opening the door far enough to slip out. "Guess he was still asleep after all," she thought.

It took her a few minutes to find a place secluded enough to go where she thought she was hidden from view but also not too far from the safety of their campsite. When she crawled back into the tent, her flashlight shined near Tim's face for a moment. She saw that his eyes really were open. "You are awake!" she whispered louder this time. Tim still didn't respond. She deliberately pointed the light at his face this time. Then she screamed.

Chapter 4

DISCOVERY

IT SHOULD HAVE taken John less than fifteen seconds to tear open his zippered door and dive into the kids' tent. He was already partially awake from hearing the zipper open and close just moments before on the smaller tent next to his. But the zipper on his older tent was sticking. He only got it open a couple feet when the worn fabric along the zipper caught. He struggled with it for another moment but in his haste to open it quickly, it was stuck much worse than usual.

Sleepily, Sarah asked, "What's wrong, what's happening?" She hadn't heard the scream but was annoyed at John's frantic movements as he continued working on the zipper. John glanced back at her for a moment, then made the decision to just crawl through the small opening he had managed to make. "I don't know" was all he said, as he wormed out through the opening.

When he reached the other tent and crawled through the still mostly open flap of their door, he saw Lexie sitting against the wall of the tent in the corner farthest away from Tim. Tim was rubbing his eyes with both hands. Lexie's flashlight was still turned on but shown mostly onto the floor where she had dropped it. John could hear her crying but couldn't figure out what was wrong. Realizing he hadn't remembered to grab his own light, he picked up Lexie's and crawled over to her.

"Lexie? I'm here. What's wrong?" Lexie continued to sob but quieter now as John put his fatherly arm around her.

"Are you okay?" His mind was alert from the adrenaline rush his body produced at the sound of her scream. He mentally raced through possible scenarios for what could have happened.

"Did someone try to hurt you?" he asked as he thought about hearing the zipper of their tent.

"No," she sighed apparently calming down now.

"Then what? Was it a bad dream?

"No, it's Timmy!" she sobbed again. John pointed the light back toward where Tim was now sitting. His sleeping bag was partially open as he sat with his legs still covered but torso out. He was rubbing his eyes with the sleeve of his pajamas. John couldn't see anything wrong with him.

"Tim, what's going on? Are you all right?"

"Yeah Dad." Tim yawned. "Just sleepy."

Wondering what time it was, John looked at his wrist only to remember that he had taken his watch off in his tent when he and Sarah had gone to bed. Noticing his Dad's look to his wrist, Tim spoke up.

"It's 12:13, Dad."

"Oh okay." John's mind flickered for a moment on the question of how his son knew the time without looking at any watch or clock, but then fell back on the bigger question of the moment.

"Why is Lexie upset, Tim? What did you do to her?" John knew his son wouldn't hurt Lexie, but his mind was still grasping for answers. For the first time, he wondered if thirteen was too old to be in a tent alone with a girl.

"He didn't do anything to me," Lexie quickly defended Tim. "It was just . . . his eyes!"

Lexie described what she had seen to John and Tim listened. He was sick inside knowing how much he had frightened his friend. But he was also curious. No one had ever seen him just before he awoke.

"His eyes were black," she said. "I shined my light at his face, and his eyes were black."

"Dark you mean? Like in a shadow?" John probed.

"No it was like a *Twilight Zone* show! There was no white in his eyes, just black. And they weren't moving at all, just stuck open."

John looked over at Tim again. "Were you trying to scare her?" Tim was in shock from Lexie's description so didn't answer right away. He had never considered that the reason his eyes hurt so much when he woke up after midnight was because they were stuck open. It made a lot of sense. It would explain the burning, dry sensation that hurt so much each night. But now he also realized how strange it was, and he didn't know what to say.

"I asked you a question, son. Were you trying to scare Lexie?" John said again with a raised voice. Then, remembering where they were, surrounded by sleeping campers, he whispered, "Why would you do that?"

Still thinking about what had happened and what Lexie had said, Tim stammered. "I, uh . . . I don't know."

"You don't know why you did it, or if you were trying to scare her?"

"I just . . . Um. Uh . . ." Tim decided it wasn't the right time to tell his dad everything. He didn't know what to tell Dad even if he wanted to. "Sorry, Lexie. I am sorry I scared you."

John looked at Tim carefully for a moment. He sensed that there was more to say, but he was tired and worried about the other campers getting upset if they kept talking.

"Ok, we'll talk more about this in the morning. Lexie, are you okay now?"

"Yeah, I guess so." She knew Tim wouldn't have wanted to scare her so much on purpose. She also realized that Tim didn't want to tell his dad something. "I'm ready to go back to sleep," she assured John.

"Tim, you going to go back to sleep now?" John questioned, still unsure of the whole situation.

"Yeah, Dad. I will." Tim lay back down in his sleeping bag and started to zip it up around him again for emphasis. John sighed and shook his head, still confused at what was going on. Saying goodnight to the kids he slipped out through the door and started to zip it closed.

He paused one more time and said in his best fatherly tone, "Tim, your eyes look really red. Guess that is your punishment for trying to scare Lexie."

Tim nodded in agreement. His eyes *were* red. He could still feel the familiar discomfort.

The kids listened to John's steps as he wandered away from the tents to use the bathroom, and then lightly pad back to their own tent to check to see if they were sleeping. Hearing nothing from the kids, he headed back over to his tent.

Tim and Lexie listened to him walk back over to his own tent, struggle through the stuck zipper, and finally force the zippered door close. They could hear the parents exchange a few words and then nothing. Lexie looked over at Tim who was looking back at her. Stretching out her sleeping bag a little closer to him than usual, she kept her eyes on his face.

After lying down in her bag with the opening facing Tim, she whispered as quietly as possible, "What was happening to you? I don't think you were doing that on purpose."

Tim was a little surprised she wasn't angry at him. "I wasn't doing it on purpose. I don't really know what I was doing. I only remember waking up and hearing you crying over there. Then I heard my dad coming into the tent."

"So you were asleep when I went outside and came back in?"

"Yeah, I guess so."

"But your eyes were opened the whole time. I thought you were awake at first, but you didn't talk when I talked to you. Then I pointed the light at you and saw your eyes. They were so . . . scary!"

Tim was expecting her to say his eyes were weird. He was oddly relieved that she said "scary" instead of strange or weird. "Thank you for not being mad at me." He sighed.

"Why would I be mad? I know you didn't do it on purpose. You are my best friend."

"KIDS!" John groaned from the adjacent tent. "GO . . . TO . . . SLEEP!"

Tim smiled at Lexie, and she smiled back. He felt relieved to finally have someone to talk to about his nights. He knew now that she would listen and not judge him. Maybe she could even help him figure out what was going on. Without thinking, he leaned over to her and kissed her cheek. She smiled again, and they both closed their eyes and quickly fell asleep.

Chapter 5

THEIR SECRET

JOHN WAS UP early the next morning as usual. He loved getting up at dawn and enjoying the quiet time on his own. "Morning just smells better" he was fond of saying.

He found a comfortable spot under a tree and sat. Leaning against the trunk, he listened to the birds singing their morning songs, watched the squirrels leap from branch to branch as they gathered up food, and enjoyed the unspoiled solitude.

The morning was starting off cool, and he pulled his jacket close and then leaned back against the tree and closed his eyes. The dry breeze felt refreshing on his face. As the sun began to rise up behind the large pine trees on the opposite shore of the lake, he thought again of the previous night.

"What was that all about?" he mumbled to himself. He had watched the two kids play for years and knew how well they got along. Tim had scared her before many times, but she usually laughed afterward, not cried. Maybe it was because she had been asleep?

John thought about it a while longer as a squirrel picked up an acorn just a few feet from where he was sitting. It stopped for a moment and looked up at John as it pouched the nut in his cheek. Turning, it hopped off and climbed up the trunk of a tree a few yards away.

The squirrel got all the way up, scurried across a large limb, and leaped to the next tree over. Upon landing, he took out the nut to reposition it in his mouth. The nut slipped out of his little bony hands and fell back to the ground.

John laughed as the squirrel quickly climbed back down the tree to retrieve his nut and repeat the process. The squirrel didn't question his world; he just lived it and let nature lead him.

As he smiled to himself, John decided to leave the kids alone. He'd watch them and make sure there were no serious issues to deal with. But they were natural friends and nature would take care of itself. He got up and decided to start cooking breakfast.

"Tim, Lexie . . . Want some bacon?" he called to the kids forty-five minutes later. Sarah and the kids were still sleeping. Sarah didn't usually eat breakfast, so he didn't call her name. She'd hear the kids and roll out of the tent when she was ready.

Tim heard his dad call out but didn't respond. He sat up, yawned and stretched, and then looked over at Lexie. One small bare foot and tiger-striped pajama leg was sticking out of a hole in the bottom of her sleeping bag. She had slid toward the wall of the tent and the escaped leg was up on his backpack. Her head was completely in the bag, and he assumed she was still asleep judging from her lack of movement.

He felt very relaxed and couldn't suppress the smile on his face as he thought about her knowing his secret. "Lexie?" he asked quietly. She didn't answer, so he unzipped his bag and slid over to her across the slick plastic tent floor.

"You wanna have some bacon? My dad is cooking it."

"Bacon?" came a small, yawning voice from inside her bag. He saw movement and then her head popped out of the top. "I can smell it." She unzipped her bag a little more and started to crawl out. Her hair was disheveled from the sleeping bag's static electricity.

"Good morning, touslehead," Tim greeted her.

She felt her hair and then looked at him and frowned. "Touslehead? Your hair is just as messed up as mine."

"Mine's just the way I like it," he smirked.

Lexie stuck her tongue out, and they both laughed. Then changing the subject back to breakfast, she whispered, "I wonder if he made the eggs in the bacon pan again."

"I hope so!" Tim said raising his eyebrows and smiling at her. "I like the brown bacon chunks!"

"Ewww. I hate those chunks! And the eggs always look dirty and greasy."

"Just come on." Tim pushed her on her shoulder. She grinned at him and jokingly leaned to the side as if she would fall over, before bouncing back to her sitting position like a wobbly weeble.

After breakfast, the two kids talked about Tim's "zone." Lexie had made up that term after thinking about how his eyes had reminded her of an episode of the *Twilight Zone* that she had watched with her dad just a few days before their camping trip.

After lunch, they slipped away from Tim's parents again.

"Does it really happen every night?"

"Yes. Every night," Tim answered.

"Why didn't you ever tell me about it?"

"I haven't told anyone about it. Not even my parents. I just . . ." Tim trailed off and put his head down. The two were sitting on a large fallen sycamore tree next to the lake. Lexie had a stick in her hands that she was using to poke at a floating lily pad in the water.

"I'm sorry," she said when he didn't start talking again.

"It's okay. I'm used to it."

"No, I mean, I'm sorry I cried last night when I saw you. I'm sorry for screaming."

"What? Why are you sorry for that?" Tim felt bad that he had scared her. He wished now that he had told her a long time ago so it wouldn't have been such a shock to her.

"I think that if you haven't told anyone about it, you must have a good reason. Maybe you are scared that people will think you are different." Lexie checked the expression on Tim's face. Confirming to herself that her intuition was correct, she continued. "I'm sorry because you're my best friend in the whole world, and as soon as I found out, I screamed and made your dad come over. Then I cried like a baby. I didn't mean to make you feel bad." Tim listened and was again shocked at her response. She stopped poking the lily pad and looked up at him again. He was still looking down at the water.

"But I'm not scared now," Lexie went on. "And I don't think you are weird."

Tim finally looked up and saw Lexie smiling reassuringly at him. How did she understand him so well? "You really don't think I'm weird?" he asked.

"Course not, silly. It's like a mystery. A secret, nameless mystery for just us!"

"More like a nameless curse," Tim sulked.

"Don't be so dramatic." Lexie laughed. "Will you tell me more about it?"

Tim told Lexie everything about his zone he could think of. Most of it didn't make sense to either of them. But some things, like his dry eyes, did make sense now.

"I never knew my eyes were open during it. I always just wake up and they hurt."

"I can't even hold my eyes open for more than a few seconds. See?" She opened her eyes up big and looked into Tim's eyes like a staring game. He smiled and played the game back. Lexie blinked first and then laughed as she blinked quickly and repeatedly while Tim tried to keep going.

"At least I can beat you at some games!" Tim laughed.

Together, the friends played and laughed the rest of the afternoon. By dinner, they were hungry and ate the hamburger and vegetable stew that John had whipped up. John was relieved to see the two of them back to their normal happy and carefree play. Still, he couldn't help but wonder what had happened.

Later that night, all four of them sat out late watching the stars. It was a beautiful, clear night, and the yearly Perseid meteor shower was in full swing. They counted as light after light shot across the sky, reaching over one hundred in less than an hour. Finally, Tim said, "I'm tired. I want to go to bed now."

Looking at his wrist and finding his watch this time, John responded, "Well it is almost eleven o'clock. Guess it's time to turn in."

Sarah and Lexie went off to the restroom building while John and Tim stepped into the woods to relieve themselves. Tim got back to the tents first and started to step in.

"Tim?" John called as he came back toward the tents himself.

"Yeah?" Tim stopped and turned back toward his dad.

"I just wanted to say that I trust you, and I know you kids will go straight to sleep tonight, right?"

"Yeah, Dad."

"I just mean . . . don't give me any reason not to trust you."

"Ok, Dad."

"You are getting older after all, and boys and girls . . . And maybe it's not appropriate . . ."

"Dad, I get it. No way! Okay?!" He paused to see if John was going to say anything else, then stepped into the tent to change into his pajamas before Lexie returned.

When Lexie did come into the tent a few minutes later, Tim was already in his pj's and had crawled into his sleeping bag. She had changed in the bathroom, and so crawled into her bag.

"When did you say it started, Tim?"

"I think around 11:30 p.m. or 11:40 p.m. I haven't figured out if it's the same time."

"But you said you had tried to time it."

"Yeah, but a lot of the time I think I fall asleep first, and other times I just can't remember what the last time on the clock was before it happened."

"Well, let's time it tonight."

"My dad said he wanted us to go straight to sleep."

"Why'd he say that?"

"Dunno," Tim said with a yawn. "I think he may be worried that we might . . . Well . . ."

"What?"

"You know. Boys and girls. That lesson in school I had to have last year, and that thing your mom got all weird about when she told you about it."

"Ewwww! No way!"

"I didn't say that, I just thought maybe that was what he was thinking since at first he thought I had done something last night."

"You wouldn't ever do that."

"Well duh! But I just . . ."

"Ewww," Lexie said again. "Let's stop talking about that."

"Good." Tim smiled.

"All right, let's lie down, so I can watch when it happens." Tim had already been lying down but had sat up when the conversation got "ewwy," so he lay down again.

"Here," Tim said as he took off his watch. "Hold this so we'll know what time it starts." Lexie scooted her bag over closer to him by wiggling inside it like a worm. Taking the watch, she settled in and got comfortable on her pillow with her face just about a foot from his.

"Do you think they'll hear us if we whisper?" she asked as she finished adjusting her sleeping bag under her body.

"Not unless you scream again," he joked back with a grin. Lexie smiled too. This was kind of exciting for both of them. She moved the flashlight to point between them so that she could see him without the light blinding him. "I think they are already in their tent. I heard the zipper."

"Yeah, and your mom said she was really tired and . . ."

"Lexie?" Tim interrupted. He looked nervous.

"Yeah?" She scooted even closer now.

"I think it is going to happen soon. You sure you want to see this?" Tim checked his watch and saw that it was 11:31 p.m. now. He usually felt a little strange just before it happened.

"Do you mean, will we still be friends? Of course, silly."

They were both quiet now. It was a little strange just looking at each other like this. Tim's dad really did have nothing to worry about. Tim hadn't yet discovered any true desire for girls. He recognized that some were more pretty than others. He had noticed that some of the girls his age were growing breasts and wearing makeup. But those thoughts hadn't yet transitioned from an innocent boy's observations into teenage lust.

As he looked into Lexie's blue eyes, he started to actually look at her for the first time. She was small and young. There were no signs yet of the womanly characteristics he was seeing in the girls his age. But as he lay there looking at her, he started thinking for the first time how pretty she was.

That was the last thought Tim remembered as Lexie's eyes suddenly got bigger, and he heard her whisper his name. The next moment, his eyes were burning, and the light had changed. "Lexie?" he whispered. He wanted to rub at his eyes, but something was on him, pinning his arms down. He couldn't yet see through the blurry film covering his eyes. "What's on me?" he asked. "Did it work?"

Lexie had been looking into Tim's eyes just as intently as he was looking at her. She had always had a secret crush on him. He was, after all, older and much more interesting than all her friends at school. Plus, she had known him much of her life and felt extremely comfortable with him.

As Lexie watched Tim, she noticed that he was looking at her differently than before. Usually they were playing and moving around. His eyes only saw the little girl next door and seemed to look past her most of the time. But this time he was looking at *her* and not at everything around her.

Then, without warning, his eyes slowly shut. "Tim?" she whispered, a little surprised. "Tim? Are you going to sleep?" She reached her hand out of her bag and touched his head. "Tim?" she called again.

He lay still next to her. A small white down feather that had worked its way out of the sleeping bag was lying a few inches from Tim's nose. The air from his breath caused it to gently dance between them.

Once more Lexie said "Tim?" as she now put her hand on his shoulder and gently shook him. She looked at his peaceful face again and reached up to touch his cheek. The moment her fingers touched his right cheek, his eyes flew open. They were completely black.

Lexie jumped back. The suddenness of his eye movement startled her. Actually, it scared her. But she held in her scream this time.

Lexie sat mostly out of her bag now, leaning up against the side of the tent. Tim lay perfectly still, exactly as he had a few minutes before when he gazed into her eyes. Only now, his brown eyes were black and large.

His stare was completely blank, and his eyes didn't move. The initial fright caused by Tim's eyes and the unexpectedness of their opening lessened as Lexie watched him. She moved along the side of the tent around to Tim's back. Having his gaze away from her was far less frightening.

At first, she just sat still next to him. Then she remembered that this was sort of an experiment, so she should try to learn stuff. "Timmy?" she whispered directly into his ear. "It's me, Lexie."

There was no response. She wasn't sure what to expect. "Oh, I forgot to look at your watch," she whispered mostly to herself. Realizing now that she had left it on the other side of Tim, she started to reach over him but couldn't see it. Her sleeping bag was opened up and partially dragged toward the side of the tent. The watch must have gotten caught up in the jumbled fabric during her startled escape.

Tim's face was still the same when she looked over him from behind. His black steady eyes were still frightening, but at least less terrifying since he was looking away from her. Deciding to act quickly before she lost her nerve, she started to crawl over Tim's limp body. She noticed that he rolled a little from her movement, and his right arm that had been lying on his side fell down in front of him.

Lexie paused, halfway over Tim, to see if he was waking up. His eyes were still scary black, and she suddenly noticed that he wasn't breathing.

A chill shot through her, and she jumped back off him. Was he dead? She knew from watching and holding her dog, Alphie, at home that breathing slowed down during sleep. She'd hold Alphie on her lap and pet the fur on his little chest. The rise and fall of his chest would become lighter and lighter unless she moved suddenly. But Tim's chest seemed completely still.

Pulling together enough courage, she crawled back onto Tim and then rolled him onto his back. She watched his chest closely. Was it her imagination, or did she see very slight movement? "Tim, please wake up!" she uttered into his ear. "I'm getting scared."

Then she remembered something. "The feather!" she called out almost too loudly. At first she didn't see it since she had rolled Tim over and the feather had stayed with the bag. Then, finding it, she held it to his nose and waited. At first there was nothing; then a slight quiver in the little hairs of the white feather. As she watched, the feather would alternately flutter out and in with his almost imperceptibly light breathing. She felt relieved that he was breathing, even if only slightly.

Calmed, Lexie laid her head onto Tim's chest with her arms hugging his torso. As her own heart stopped racing and slowed down, she started to hear Tim's heart beating rhythmically but slowly within him through his thin pajamas. She felt silly that she had panicked so easily. Surely he wouldn't die the first time someone watched him in his zone if he'd been experiencing this all his life.

Lexie listened to Tim's heart for several more minutes. She began counting the slow steady beats. She no longer was afraid and was instead thrilled to share such a secret with her best friend. Her own breathing slowed now. Feelings of comfort and happiness filled her head. Thoughts of experiments and observation never found their way back into her mind as her eyes closed and she fell asleep.

"What's on me? Did it work?" Tim said again as he tried to move the object on him. There was something warm and soft against his right arm and hand. He could feel his left hand being held by a smaller hand, and he realized it was Lexie.

"Lexie, are you okay?" He pulled his right arm out from under her and stroked her hair gently. "Lexie?"

"Oh Tim!" she woke quickly and hugged him tight. "I'm so sorry. I guess I fell asleep." Feeling embarrassed for falling to sleep right on him, she sat up and then moved more to his side.

Lexie filled him in on the events she had witnessed and apologized profusely for forgetting about the watch and then falling asleep before he woke up. Tim assured her that it was okay and that he was still grateful to have someone to talk to even if the first experiment hadn't been completely successful. The strangeness of the situation left them both weary, so it was agreed that they would talk more in the morning. Lexie and Tim fell asleep at about the same time with their backs against each other and Lexie's hand in his.

Chapter 6

THE STRANGE STRANGER

THE NEXT DAY started off like most Caston camping mornings. John made breakfast, fed the kids, and then gently started the wake-up process for Sarah.

It wasn't possible for Tim and Lexie to break off from his parents that day and talk about the previous night, because John had secured a boat for them to use for the day. Apparently, the elderly RV campers, two sites over from their own campsite, had come out expecting to meet their daughter, son-in-law, and three grandchildren there at the lake. The older couple brought along their Starcraft Tri-hull boat, and instead of their normal fishing equipment, Jerry bought a new set of water skis and an inflatable tube.

After arriving and setting up camp, their daughter called and spun a tale of child illness and work deadline excuses to get them out of camping. Jerry tried to convince them to still come for the day but to no avail. She had done this to them before and would do it again.

Jerry and Thelma hadn't brought any of their fishing equipment and had no interest in skiing themselves. So when Jerry ran into John early that morning while he was watching the sunrise, Jerry offered John and family the boat for the day. John surprised the kids with this news that morning while they were eating breakfast. Even Sarah seemed thrilled with the news. She was ready for a change of pace and was glad not to have to spend the day hiking or sitting at the crowded swimming beach.

They threw on their swimsuits as soon as breakfast was cleaned up. Jerry was pleased to see how excited John's family was to use the boat. He handed John the keys and helped lead them to the boat dock where it was ready to go. Several other boaters were getting ready as well. In the slip next to them was another family. All were very overweight and were climbing into a Bayliner ski boat. It was a wonder that the boat could hold them all.

Across from them on the other side of the dock, a tall single man in a large brand new bass boat sat looking at them. He stared oddly at the four Castons and Jerry. John looked away and over at another boat where three young women were taking off their T-shirts and shorts revealing their colorful bikinis beneath. As they adjusted their suits John felt a poke in the ribs and looked over at Sarah who was giving him a face.

"Just looking around," he said sheepishly.

"Sure," she said with an angry smirk on her face.

As Jerry began running through instructions and intermixing stories of his own boating adventures, John noticed the tall man with the strange, confused expression walking over to them. Right in the middle of Jerry's third big fish story, the man interrupted, "Excuse me folks."

Jerry stopped and they all looked up at the man standing above them on the dock. "I don't mean to butt in," he said. "I couldn't help but notice that the engine on this craft is quite a bit larger than the norm for a small boat like this."

"It handles just fine," Jerry defended.

"I'm sure it does, sir. I just wanted to offer the suggestion that you keep your family toward the front of the boat so that the boat will ride more level."

"I was just getting to that," Jerry said a little flustered at not getting to finish his fish story.

"And when you stop," the tall man continued, "don't stop suddenly, just slow down and make sure the wake of water created by the boat doesn't overtake the stern and flood in."

"Right," Jerry said looking at John. "Don't sink my boat!" Jerry turned back at the tall man. "Any more words of unsolicited wisdom?" Jerry hadn't meant to be rude. He was just disappointed that his story had been interrupted, and now he couldn't remember which story he had been telling in the first place.

"I didn't mean to overstep my boundaries, sir. I just had this strange feeling earlier, like I was supposed to give you this advice. Almost like someone really wanted me to talk to you." He paused and again had an odd expression, like he had when John had first noticed him across the dock. Then without even saying good-bye or waiting for a thank you, he walked back over to his boat.

"That was really weird," Sarah whispered to John.

"Yeah," John agreed and then looked at the kids who were just as confused by the man's behavior. "Good advice though! I'd hate to accidentally sink your boat, Jerry!"

Jerry was lost in his own thoughts.

"Well," John said to Jerry, giving him a light punch in the shoulder, "I think we're ready." He was glad the tall man had caused Jerry to forget his story. Not wanting to give the old man a chance to start again, John looked at the kids, "Life jackets on? Good. Let's head out."

Lexie and Tim sat up in the front of the boat on the deck like the man had suggested. Sarah followed them, sitting just in front of the driver's console.

"Thanks again, Jerry," John said. "We'll have her back this afternoon." He wanted to start the engine and go but didn't want to be completely rude. "Anything else?" They all hoped not!

Jerry thought for a moment, still hoping to finish his story but realized they were excited to head out. He smiled at them and simply said, "You folks have a great time!" He glanced back over toward the tall man who was finishing loading his equipment into his boat, then turned back to John. "I guess that was pretty good advice," he whispered to John. "The engine is a little too big, but I like the speed. I've almost sunk her myself by stopping too quickly and by having too much weight in the back. One time I . . ."

"We'll take good care of her, Jerry," John interrupted to halt the beginning of a new story. "I really appreciate this!"

A few moments later, they were off. John felt proud to be among the other boats as they slowly made their way out of the small bay, even if it wasn't his own boat. There's something special about the feeling of wind blowing past you that has been gliding along the surface of the water.

John and Tim took to the skis easily. John was impressed by the boy's ability to ski on his first try. Sarah and Lexie enjoyed the tube more. Lexie tried the skis but couldn't quite make them stay straight beneath her. All four enjoyed the wind blowing in their hair and the splash of water along the side of the boat.

Several times, John noted how easily the wake of water would come racing toward the back of the boat when he would stop. He would go forward again just in time to keep the water from pouring in over the stern that definitely seemed to ride low in the water due to the large engine. He thought about the tall man for a moment, wondering who he was. "I probably would have sunk this thing if he hadn't said something," he thought. Then, looking at the smiling faces of his family, he forgot about the tall man and enjoyed the rest of the day.

Late that afternoon, they thanked Jerry and kept any additional fish stories at bay by telling of their own adventures that day. By 9:00 p.m., they were all so worn out that they went to bed. Tim and Lexie talked for only a few moments together in the tent about his zone. Within less than five minutes after lying down, they were both asleep.

At 12:13 p.m., Tim woke. He was exhausted but couldn't go back to sleep until his eyes rewetted and stopped aching. In the dim light that was filtering into the tent from somewhere in the campground, he watched Lexie sleep. She was lying on her belly with her face toward him. Her sleeping bag was partially open so he could see her red pajama shirt down to her lower back.

He wondered if holding hands last night with Lexie meant they were "going out" now. Was she his girlfriend, or were they still just best friends? Either way, he was glad she knew his secret. He had hoped they could experiment with his zone more, but this was the last night of their trip. At least, he could talk to her about it from now on. Watching her back rise and fall from her gentle breathing, Tim peacefully went back to sleep.

Lexie woke up shortly after Tim drifted off. She looked at him for a moment, grabbed his hand, and fell asleep while thinking how nice it was to have a boyfriend.

Chapter 7

RULES

THE TWO FRIENDS spent the rest of the summer playing and talking together. Lexie said that Tim should figure out the "rules" of his zone.

"Ya know, everything has rules," she said.

"Whatcha mean?"

"Well, like gravity pulls stuff down," she said. "And the sky is blue, except when the sun is down and then it's black. Trees and plants grow up and they lose their leaves in the winter. Everything follows some kind of rules. So, you need to know the rules of your zone."

"I don't know if it has rules other than being every night and my eyes getting stuck open."

"I think there is more to it," said Lexie. "You never remember anything from when you're in the zone which means either you are just turned off like a robot, or it means you just can't remember." Lexie bit her lip in thought and continued, "I forget most of my dreams, but my mom says we dream all night. So maybe you just forget."

"Maybe. Or maybe I'm dead. You said yourself that my eyes looked dead."

"Well, I don't think you can die every night and come back to life. There's a rule about that too. If you die, then you're dead. At least until heaven."

When school started in September, Tim was off to the 8th grade at the Junior High. Lexie was in 5th grade at the elementary school. Their rural school district was a little slow to modernize and grouped the 1st through 7th grade together in elementary school. 8th and 9th were Junior High, and High School was for 10th through 12th grades. They would never be at the same school together again. Lexie was sad to see Tim get on the bigger kids' bus that passed by their house ahead of hers but still waved good-bye with a smile on her face.

The two friends still played together daily after school and on weekends. Lexie came straight over to Tim's house when she got off the bus, thirty-five minutes after Tim's bus dropped him off. Almost every afternoon, she would run by her house just long enough to drop off her school bag and tell her mom she was off to play with Tim.

Together, the two friends played in the woods, threw rocks into the pond, explored the new neighborhood being built by their homes, tried building forts with scrap wood and branches, and mostly just laughed together.

Sometimes, Tim would report back the results of experiments he tried at night. He taped his eyelids shut to see if it helped with the burning, but the tape never seemed to hold. He covered his head with aluminum foil to see if he could block any radio signals that were causing his zone. That too seemed to do nothing. Several times, he tried to force himself to stay awake by doing jumping jacks just before the zone would start. That only resulted in bruises when his body would go limp and fall to the ground at the start of the zone. He even tried consulting his Magic 8 Ball that Lexie had given to him on his tenth birthday, but its simple answers to his yes or no type questions failed to shed any light on the reason he zoned.

"Maybe your zone is like zoning out," Lexie suggested to Tim one afternoon. "My dad says all the time that he sometimes drives all the way home from work and doesn't remember anything he passed along the way. He says, 'Guess I zoned out again.' Sometimes he says it when he's trying to ignore my mom too."

The only real answer to any of their questions came when Tim set up a camcorder in his room at the urging of Lexie. The first few nights gave them no new information until he started placing his clock next to him in view of the camera. After several nights of tests, it was clear that his zone started at 11:35 p.m. each and every night.

Often, when they were just being kids and not trying to solve the mysteries of his zone, they enjoyed crawling through the unfinished frames of the new houses being built nearby. The workers were gone for the day by late afternoon leaving a massive playground of wood piles, cement slabs, and house-shaped jungle gyms.

Lexie and Tim enjoyed playing tag and hide-and-seek in the houses. Running and crawling through the studs and rafters was quite dangerous, but to them, it was like an obstacle course. Sometimes, a stray nail or splinter would stop the games momentarily, but they quickly got over it and would be back to playing.

One day in October, on a day just like so many others, the kids were crawling across the newly erected wooden beams in what would become an attic. Colorful leaves were blowing to and fro across the ground below. One caught an updraft against the unfinished house and flew into Lexie's hair. She squealed in delight, "Oh, I just love the fall!"

"You said you loved summer best just a few months ago," Tim reminded her as another leaf popped up from below in the vortex of spinning air created by the vertical studs.

"That was when it was summer. In the summer, I like it best. In the spring or winter, I like them best. Now it is fall, so that is my favorite right now." She smiled and happily twirled away across the rafters.

Tim couldn't argue against her optimist logic. She was always happy and would find something good in any situation. That was who she was, and it was one of the many reasons he loved being around her.

As she danced, using the beams as her stage, Lexie found a tool left behind by the workers.

"Hey Tim, look at what I found," she said, picking up the gray metal box with a string and metal weight hanging out of it. "What is it?"

"I think that's a plumb bob," he responded as he took a look. "They use it to make sure walls are completely vertical." Tim climbed down from the attic as Lexie uncoiled the string from the box and let the conical weight dangle down into the lower floor of the house.

"You should let me hypnotize you!" Lexie yelled down to Tim. He had jumped down onto the plywood floor below her and was now watching the silver weight swing back and fourth.

"Why?" he asked looking straight up at her through the rafters.

"So we can find out where you go in your zone," she answered. "Some people get hypnotized so they can remember something that happened to them a long time ago. We just want to know what happened last night, so that shouldn't be too hard. I've seen it done on TV."

"What should I do? Sit in front of your string thing?"

"Yep. Make sure you can watch it without moving your head. Just move your eyes," she instructed. Tim sat down and crossed his legs. Lexie was already swinging the plumb bob in a gentle slow arc in front of him.

"Don't hit me," he warned. She rolled her eyes at him.

Tim tried to focus on the weight. It was sweeping a little too far in his field of view, so he scooted back until he could watch it by moving only his eyes.

"Now," she continued confidently after he seemed to get settled, "let your mind relax. Think only about the object in front of you. It is moving slowly and making you sleepy. Imagine this object is attached to your eyes and is gently pulling them back and forth. Now, you are starting to get sleepy. You are getting very, very, very sleepy." She paused and looked closely at Tim from above. From her vantage point, she couldn't tell if he was looking sleepy or not yet. What had the guy on TV done now?

Tim did feel a little sleepy, but he wasn't sure if it was hypnosis or because it was starting to get a little late. He decided it was just that he was a little bored. "Time to have a little fun," he thought to himself and then closed his eyes.

"You are very, very, extremely sleepy," Lexie continued. She looked again and was now sure his eyes were closed. Tying the string around a truss so it could continue to swing, she crawled over to a wall and climbed down gently without disturbing her subject. Finally reaching Tim, she sat down in front of him.

"When I count to five, you will be hypnotized and in my power. You will answer all of my questions and have the ability to remember anything I ask. Ready? One . . . two . . . three," she scooted closer to him and then continued with excitement. "Four . . . ready? And . . . fi—ve!" She dragged out the five for emphasis and then waited. Tim didn't look any different.

"Are you hypnotized?" she asked.

"I am Tim Caston. I am now in the power of Alexis Gracen Michols," Tim said in his best robot voice. It sounded strange to use her full given name but he thought it added to the effect. "What is your bidding?"

Lexie smiled to herself. "Wow, it really worked!" she thought. What should she ask? Maybe she should ask him to kiss her! They hadn't even held hands again since those two nights while camping. They had never talked about it since both were unsure how the other felt about it. She had wanted to kiss him for a long time. Now would be her chance! He'd never know, right? "No," she thought. She wanted their first kiss to be special and memorable. How memorable could it be if Tim didn't even know about it? Besides, this was about understanding Tim's zone.

"Tim, you will answer me when I ask you some questions. What is your full name?" She decided to start small and build up to it.

"Timothy William Caston."

"When is your birthday?"

He thought about joking, "You know when my birthday is, you were at my party!" But instead, stayed in robot tone and answered, "May 10, 1972."

"How old are you, Timmy?"

"I am thirteen years, five months and," he had to stop and think for a moment, "seven days old."

"Who is your best friend?" she questioned, unable to help herself. Maybe she'd ask if he thought of her as his girlfriend next.

"My best friend in the whole world is . . ." he paused for emphasis. Lexie smiled anticipating her name.

"My best friend is . . . 'Tuttle,' my pet turtle." Tim's lips started to curl into a smile, but he quickly regained his composure. Lexie frowned. That definitely wasn't the answer she was expecting. Hurt but determined, she skipped the girlfriend question and got to the point of all this.

"Timmy, something happens to you every night. What do you see while you are in your zone."

Tim thought for a moment, then said, "I go to a land of fairy princesses where they all bring me chocolate cake all day. One of them looks a lot like my friend, Lexie." Lexie's face brightened. She was excited to be part of his zone!

"In fact," he continued, "she looks so much like her . . ." he paused again theatrically. "She looks so much like her . . . that all I can do . . . is . . ." he waited again. "All I can do is . . . tickle her!" He screamed as he jumped up and attacked Lexie. She rolled and giggled as he tickled her sides and then around her neck causing her to push her shoulders up as she tried to get away.

"You tricked me!" she yelled in laughter as she fought to escape.

"Pretty funny, huh?" he laughed.

"Not that funny." Lexie huffed and frowned as she remembered his refusal to name her as his best friend. He wondered if he had made her mad. She answered his unspoken question by turning her frown into a large grin and then jumped on him and attacked with her own barrage of tickles. They laughed and played until dusk and then headed home before their parents could start to wonder about their whereabouts.

Rarely did any of the four parents worry that Tim and Lexie spent too much unsupervised time together. They had learned to trust the two kids.

"Tim's a Boy Scout," Gracie had said about her daughter's friend when John raised the question of their friendship after the camping trip.

"What does that mean?"

"Boy Scouts are like saints, right?" she said, "They don't have hormones."

Chris and John both laughed, and Sarah smiled at her friend.

"I was a Boy Scout too," said John. "And believe me, scouts still have hormones!"

The four friends laughed again, but agreed that as long as the kids gave them no reason to worry, they wouldn't.

Lexie and Tim continued to talk about his zone occasionally after that October evening. But with no new information to discuss, their conversations slowly reverted back to normal talk of school, friends, bullies, etc . . . . Sometimes, they'd talk about Lexie's mom who had been acting more and more strangely each day.

"Yesterday she told me to put the old red bedspread onto my bed since it was fall," Lexie told Tim after school a few days later. They were expertly constructing a fort out of some boards they took from the new neighborhood up the hill. "I told her we had just washed my pink one, and I liked it better. But she said I had to. So I did."

Tim laughed to himself as he imagined Lexie angrily pulling off her favorite bedspread, throwing it on the floor, and then tossing the old ugly red one onto her bed. He guessed that she probably didn't try very hard to tuck it in straight or evenly.

"Then today when I went up to change out of my school clothes, I saw the red one on the floor and a really gross looking green one on my bed. It had stains on it and smelled bad."

"Sounds nice." Tim laughed. "Your mom put it there?"

"Yeah, she stopped me when I came down and she said, 'I know you hated that red one so I bought you one at a garage sale I went by today. It reminds me of spring and looks so much prettier'. I told her I thought it needed to be washed, and she started yelling at me! She said I was always ungrateful and never cared about how much she did for our family."

"Whad'ya say?"

"Nothing. She didn't give me a chance. She was already running up the stairs while she was yelling. She pulled the green thing off and tried stuffing it in my trash can. When it wouldn't fit, she pulled it back out and took it to her room and started putting it on her bed."

Tim didn't say anything. He thought Gracie was loony but didn't want to say that to Lexie, even though she probably already thought that too.

"That's when I left my house and came over to see you. Tonight she probably won't say anything about it. She'll just be mad about something else."

They worked on their fort until it started to get dark and knew it was time to go home. As Lexie expected, her mom did get angry about something else inconsequential that night, but it wasn't even worth the effort for Lexie to remember the reason. She wished her parents were more like Tim's. His mom was quiet, but she was gentle and intelligent. His dad worked hard but always put Tim and Sarah first. She wished her dad wasn't always working late and traveling for his job. It seemed like the more she needed him, the more he was gone. All she could hope for was that her mom would get better.

Chapter 8

GRACIE

AS FALL BECAME winter, Gracie didn't get any better. In fact, she seemed to worsen. By February, all of the Castons were aware of Gracie's outbursts and odd behavior. John and Chris had started talking often about whether she just needed love and acceptance or professional help. John encouraged Chris to try to talk to her about it. He believed that Gracie was sick. But any time Chris tried to bring it up with Gracie, she would explode at him verbally and change the subject.

"She would never hurt anyone," he reasoned to John one evening while they stood out by the garage. "She's never been physically abusive, so I can't justify forcing her to get help."

"How do you know it won't reach that point? What if it is too late to do something about it then?" John asked Chris.

"We just have to let her calm down. Her anger seems to come in waves. She'll be all right again soon. Maybe when I get back from my next trip, I'll try to talk to someone." Chris seemed to think to himself about something and had a faint smile on his face.

The smile didn't go unnoticed by John. "Chris, this is none of my business, but . . ." John sighed and tried to think of the words he needed to proceed. "Chris, are you having an affair?" he finally said bluntly, unable to think of a gentler way to phrase the question.

"What?" Chris retorted sharply. "No! I can't believe you'd even ask that." Chris had at first looked away from John as he spoke, but then looked him in the eye and said, "No, I am not having an affair."

John wasn't sure how to read his longtime friend. Something seemed wrong with Chris's answer, but maybe he had been off the mark with his accusation. "I'm sorry, Chris. I just thought . . . Well, you have been working late a lot recently. And your trips have been coming up more often."

"It's been busy at work. You know how it is," Chris answered quickly. Then he sighed again and shook his head as someone does when they feel defeated.

Chris looked at John and then looked around as if to double check that they were alone out by John's garage. "John," Chris finally said, "I am not having an affair. But I'd be lying if I told you I was happy with my marriage. And maybe part of me even wishes for an affair.

"There's a new girl at work. Amber. She's way too young for me," Chris continued, "but she listens to me. She actually seems to enjoy being around me. We talk a lot, that's all, but it feels really good to have someone who wants to be near me. I know this sounds dumb, but I miss having a woman to talk to. I can't talk to Gracie anymore. Not when she is like this.

"When I am home, she is yelling at me about things I can't even figure out. She screamed at me last night because I wasn't wearing socks. She said it was too cold outside for me not to be wearing socks to bed. I told her it didn't matter inside because we had the heat up and plenty of blankets. Then she started talking about someone she had known who had gotten sick from not wearing socks, and how she hoped I got sick too. She went on and on, just ranting. I'd say it was strange, but really, it's normal lately.

"I just have to get out sometimes. My business trips are legit. But the more often I'm gone, the more I want to stay away. Eventually, maybe I just won't come back. It would serve her right for acting like this."

"She's sick, Chris," John argued. "She needs help, not revenge. And what about Lexie? You have a daughter to think about too."

"I know, I know. She's a strong kid though. And Gracie hates me, not her."

"Chris, you should . . ."

"Just drop it okay!" he snapped, unwilling to continue the conversation. "Listen, I'm not having an affair, but it's my business. I'm sticking by my wife for now, but I don't know for how much longer. I love my daughter and I'll take care of her. So just leave it."

John stood with his mouth slightly open. Chris had never been so defensive. John watched him retreat back toward his house, but then Chris turned away from the house and went to his car instead. He drove off quickly, leaving a light trail of dust from the long gravel driveway.

A few days later, Chris was away on business again. He knew John was right, that it wasn't Gracie's fault. And he did still love her deeply, so he knew he should want to help her. He also wanted to be a good husband and father, but it was easier to simply volunteer for travel again and escape from it all. Besides, this time, Amber was going on the trip too. She would need guidance since this was her first marketing trip. They worked well together, so it made sense for him to go. Mostly, he was just relieved to get out of the house.

Lexie wasn't so lucky though. It was true that she had always been strong, but Chris hadn't realized that when he was away, Lexie became the focus of Gracie's irrational anger. Day after day, Gracie would launch into a tirade about something: Lexie's hair was too long; her shoe laces were too loose; her face was too pretty. Lexie had learned to ignore it and usually just left the house to play outside, but it wore on her. She felt abandoned by her dad.

On Chris's 8th night away, Lexie had been sound asleep until a loud smashing sound woke her up. "Crash," the sound rang out again. Her clock told her it was 11:40 p.m. She had only been asleep for a couple hours, but her body felt alert. She listened and heard it again. "Bang, Crash."

Lexie got up and opened her door. The light downstairs was on, and in the large glass window at the front of the house, she could see her mom's reflection in the kitchen. "Mom?" she asked without a sign of sleepiness.

Lexie walked down the stairs and turned toward the kitchen. "Mom?" she asked again as she took in the scene. The kitchen cabinet was smashed on one end where Gracie was standing. Most of the glass jars that had been stored in it were sitting on the counter except for two that were still in the back of the cabinet and two or three more broken on the floor. Gracie turned to her and smiled. Lexie didn't notice the smile at first because she was looking at the baseball bat in her mom's hand.

"Hi Honey," her mom sang sweetly. "I'm sorry I woke you up."

"Mom? What are you doing?"

"I've been thinking for a while that these cabinets are too old. So I'm taking them down tonight so that tomorrow when Chris gets home we can go to the store and get new ones.

"There's still stuff in them," Lexie remarked with a condescending tone typical of an intelligent eleven-year-old girl. Surprisingly, Gracie's smile never faded. She just turned back to the cabinets.

"I know," she agreed with an odd bubbly tone and then swung the bat at the cabinet again.

Lexie started to walk up the stairs, but then changed her mind and walked out the front door. The sky was clear and it was cold. She wasn't sure what she was going to do. She knew she couldn't sleep with the batting practice going on below her bedroom, but she also knew she'd freeze if she stood out here in her socks and lightweight flannel pj's.

Remembering that the time was a little after 11:40 p.m., she thought of Tim and then decided to walk over to his house. His room on the first floor was dark. She walked up to his window, pushing aside the crape myrtle branches that partially covered one side of the glass. She peered in and saw his shape lying under the covers.

Lexie had seen Tim get lectured several times by his mom about leaving the window unlocked. She closed her eyes and pushed up on the window, hoping he had forgotten again to lock it. It opened. She quietly pushed it the rest of the way up and pulled herself into his room.

Closing the window behind her Lexie welcomed the warmth that surrounded her from the central heat. She hadn't been outside for long, but she realized now how cold she had gotten. Tim's clock read 11:49. She knew he must be in his zone, so she didn't try to speak to him. She crossed the room silently and crawled into his bed. She was slightly relieved that he was facing away from her, so she didn't have to see his zoned eyes.

Lexie closed her own eyes and wondered what he would think when he woke up. She decided she was too tired now to care. Sleep came back to her as quickly as it had been driven away by her mother only fifteen minutes earlier.

When Tim woke up, he was surprised to feel a small arm wrapped over his side. He knew instinctively that it was Lexie, even before his vision cleared and he recognized the flannel sleeves of her nightshirt.

Lexie's face was buried against Tim's back. He held his body still as he wondered why she had snuck into his room. It wasn't too difficult for him to guess that it had something to do with her mom. He was glad she was there, and as soon as his eyes stopped burning, he fell back to sleep.

He awoke again at 7:00 a.m. to the voice of Cyndi Lauper singing out of his clock radio. "Lying, in my bed, I hear the clock tick and think of you," she sang. "Caught up in circles, confusion is nothing new."

Lexie was gone, but he could tell by the way one of his curtains was stuck under the window that she must have come and gone through it. Tim wondered what Lexie's mom had done last night to cause Lexie to sneak over.

Cyndi sang on. " . . . the second hand unwinds. If you're lost you can look and you will find me, time after time. If you fall I will catch you, I'll be waiting, time after time."

Tim was glad Lexie had come to him. She was his best friend, and he always wanted to be there for her. In a way that he could not yet understand, he loved her.

The next night, Tim intentionally unlocked his window before he went to sleep. His nighttime visitor returned. As much as he wondered about the details of her visit, he felt it would be better not to ask.

Almost every evening, they played as usual and talked about many things. But they never talked about her visits; visits that for the next few months became commonplace. Sometimes she would come and go without him knowing. Other times, she'd accidentally wake him up if he was just sleeping normally, but he never said anything. She always vanished before morning. The only evidence of her visits was the occasional wet tears on his shirt or pillow.

Chapter 9

TIMES CHANGE

AS 8TH GRADE rolled into 9th, Tim was growing fast. Most of his classmates were having growth spurts as well. Lexie, twelve now, seemed more like a little girl to Tim when compared with the girls at his school. Girls his age were really blossoming while she still looked like a kid.

Lexie felt very hurt the first time he ignored her and chose new friends over her. Several of the guys had come by to ride their bikes down to the river that ran through the valley below their town. He wanted to invite her to join them, but the guys had already made fun of him several times for hanging out with "the little girl." Of course, in reality, their taunts came mostly from jealousy. Even if she was younger, Tim was the only one of them who had anything close to a girlfriend. And at twelve, her potential as a future beauty was already evident.

Gracie, despite the distance that had grown between them, recognized her daughter's pain and tried to comfort her. She reminded Lexie that Tim was two-and-a-half years older and was just trying to fit in with kids his age. Time would heal, she had said.

The reassuring words from her mom were a surprise to Lexie but did little to help. Tim was her best friend. He had always chosen her first. She was crushed.

Her mom had been right, though. Time did heal, and as Tim and Lexie drifted apart, she found more friends her own age. By the end of that school year, Tim and Lexie no longer played together. Sometimes, they would wave at one another or even say hello if they saw the other outside. But their eternal friendship seemed to be lost forever.

The next year, Tim entered high school. His innocent classmate crushes developed into more serious feelings for girls. Unfortunately, despite spending almost every day with a girl as a child, he felt awkward and clumsy around them now. He didn't know what to say or how to approach them. Finally, one named Becka approached him. For about three weeks, they occasionally held hands in the hallway, but neither really knew what to do next. Being only fifteen made it difficult to see each other outside school since neither could drive, and within a few weeks, they shyly ignored each other having never officially "broken up."

He tried dating other girls as well. He went on two dates with Brandi from his history class. Then he flirted with Kari in his typing class so much that his A slipped down into the C range. He spent a semester wooing Christi, who was his lab partner, in physical science. He missed the entire lesson on "The Theory of Relativity and Its Implications for our Universe," as he and she passed notes back and forth.

Lexie was moving on as well. She was busy in her world at the new middle school which finally put 6th, 7th, and 8th grade together. Voted the prettiest girl at Savannah Middle, she was popular, funny, and incredibly smart. The unhappiness she felt due to her mom's antics and the loss of her best friend was easily covered up with her radiant smile. Joining the cheerleading squad seemed to cement her future status in place . . . that is, until her mom had an embarrassing public mental breakdown at the Middle School boys' last basketball game of the season.

No one knew for sure what set off Crazy Gracie, as she was infamously known from that day forward. It was speculated that the guy in front of her in the stands said a rude or crude comment about the girls as they cheered between first and second period.

Regardless of the actual catalyst to her action, it was the action itself that went down in history.

Crazy Gracie jumped onto the man from behind and used her highly manicured nails to claw at his hair and face while screaming like a banshee at the top of her lungs. Lexie didn't know what was happening until she saw the security guards run across the court and up into the stands where her own mother was now climbing up a support truss, still screaming. The man sat bleeding and holding his ear where she had bit him at some point during the struggle.

One security guard finally reached her and grabbed onto her leg, pulling her down onto the bleachers. The two other guards then dragged her out. Her screaming continued all the way out the door as the entire crowd watched in shocked silence. Lexie was mortified.

One of her co-cheerleaders was the first to recognize that Lexie's last name rhymed a little with the word "psycho." The weak rhyme may not have been very sophisticated, but it was good enough for 7th graders, and the name "Psycho Michols" stuck.

Within a few days, Lexie heard the name everywhere she went. Everybody knew what had happened, and they were cruel to her in a way that only middle school kids can be. Through siblings, parents, and other sources, it didn't take long for the news and the name to reach Tim at the high school. He felt sorry for Lexie and wanted to go talk to her. He had made up his mind to do just that after school the next day when he saw her get off her bus and head toward her house.

Tim called to her, "Lexie!" as he started to run over to her. Lexie turned to face Tim, surprised to see him approaching. Tim was surprised too. Still fifty feet away from her, he stopped and looked at his friend's face. He had never seen her so pale or so weak. Her shoulders were slouched forward, and he could see that she had been crying.

Lexie waited for Tim to speak again or to step closer. But as the bus drove off and Tim tried to think of what to say, the biker gang, as his mom referred to his friends, crossed the road and pulled up to him on their BMX's.

"Hey, Tim," Paul said loudly enough for Lexie to hear. "You weren't gonna talk to your crazy girlfriend, were you?"

Tim didn't say anything at first. Lexie was looking right at him, her eyes piercing his heart. She looked so sad and alone. His friends were watching him too. He wanted to yell at his friends and run to her. He wanted to protect her. He wanted her to know that he was still there for her.

But what if all his friends abandoned him or called him "psycho" too? It didn't occur to him that he could defend her without alienating his friends. At fifteen, it seemed like these types of conflicts had to be settled clearly in black or white.

"No way!" he finally responded. "I wasn't going to talk to Psycho Michols," he said with convincing cruelty. His friends laughed. Lexie cried and ran the rest of the way into her house, slamming the door so hard that one of her mom's decorative statues fell off the wall stand and shattered on the floor.

Tim and his friends didn't hear the porcelain break. They went on with their laughing and riding as they waited for Tim to get his own bike and join them. It wasn't that they were mean kids, they simply didn't understand the pain they had encouraged Tim to cause Lexie. Tim understood though. He was more ashamed than he thought was possible.

With Lexie's mom in the nut house and Lexie miserable at home and school, her father did what he thought best; he divorced Gracie and got remarried to a woman half his age. Chris had met his new bride at work, and John was not surprised to learn that her name was Amber.

Knowing that Lexie was the constant target of ridicule and wanting to have a fresh start himself, Chris spontaneously pulled Lexie out of school and moved the three to Nebraska. The house soon went up for rent, and Tim believed he would never see Lexie again. The guilt inside him would remain for years, having never gained the courage to apologize to her.

1988

By the time Tim turned sixteen, he had grown to almost six feet tall. He wasn't one of the popular kids but was well liked by most people. He and his friends hung out after school and on weekends. They would play basketball at the neighborhood park, work on each others' cars, and just hang out and do nothing. Tim never stayed with them past 11:00 p.m. He told them it was his curfew.

Something else was changing in Tim as well. He felt like he was growing up. It wasn't just the growth spurt or some other physical change. He felt like he was maturing, faster than other boys his age. He wasn't interested in the little petty fights and disagreements his friends would have. It seemed like he could sense a bigger purpose in his life. He didn't know what that purpose was or how he should change to be part of it, but he still felt it.

He also started to see people in random places that looked familiar to him. They never seemed to know him, but he was sure he knew them somehow. He wasn't sure if he had a memory of them or if it was just one of those odd feelings.

On a Tuesday just like many other Tuesdays, Tim and his friends met at the Dairy Queen after school. They were laughing about Brett's girlfriend cheating on him. Brett tried to act like he was glad she was out of his way. "Karine was always bossing me around, telling me how to brush my hair and what to wear," he reasoned.

"Yeah, I hate that," some of the other boys agreed.

Tim was only half listening. He was looking out the window next to their booth at a woman who was crossing the street. About twenty or so, she was absolutely gorgeous. She was tall and slender and looked like she should have been wearing a "Miss America" sash over a swimsuit instead of carrying a bag of groceries and a purse. But her good looks weren't what caught Tim's eye. It was something else. She seemed very familiar. Almost as if he had met her in a dream.

"Who is that?" he asked Terry who was sitting next to him. Terry grabbed another fry from his basket as he looked up at the woman and shrugged. "Wish I knew," he responded with a full mouth.

"But I'm sure I know her," continued Tim. Then as he looked around, he realized that everything seemed very familiar. Of course it was normal to be sitting at Dairy Queen with his friends. But everything seemed exactly like he remembered it from some previous moment. "Wow, déjà vu!" Tim exclaimed. The other boys were looking at the woman now too, forgetting about their amusement at Brett's humiliation. Just then, Tim remembered something else. "She is going to trip," he thought out loud.

"What? Who? That girl?" Terry asked with interest.

"On that pothole, she's gonna step in it, trip, and her purse is going to spill out." The other boys were listening now.

"Hey, Timmy thinks he can predict the future!" Larry laughed, and the others, even Tim, joined in.

Then it happened. The woman started looking into her purse for something. She slid the plastic grocery bag up her left wrist and used her right hand to dig into her open purse. She wasn't paying attention to the ground as she walked. When she stepped into the pothole, her heel caught against the broken edge of the pavement. She stumbled and fell right onto the curb. Her purse, which was already a little open from her digging, went flying ahead of her and spilled all of its contents as it struck the ground. Something in the plastic grocery bag looked like it was leaking out.

The boys were all silent. Then Larry spoke first. "Wow, how did you do that?" Tim realized he had just stepped over the line of normalcy. He sighed as casually as possible, "Dunno, just got lucky I guess." Terry suddenly smiled and stood up. "Maybe if I go over there and help her pick up her stuff, I could get lucky!" The rest of the boys laughed, and Tim was glad to have the focus off him.

That wasn't the first or last time Tim had such vivid memories of random events and people that seemed to predict the future. It seemed to him that the older he got, the more often it happened. He would see families at the grocery store that he could have sworn he knew, or men and women walking along the street that looked familiar.

One day after school, he saw a homeless man sitting next to a tree in the park. Feeling that sense of familiarity, he decided to walk over and talk to the man. As he approached and saw the leathery lines on the man's face and neck, he realized that the man not only looked familiar, but also he knew his name.

"Bill?" Tim asked cautiously.

The man looked up at Tim, then looked around. Finally looking back at Tim, the man asked with a raspy voice, "You know me?"

"I . . . I'm not sure. Your name is Bill though, right?"

"Yeah, that's me." Bill seemed nervous at Tim's questions. He picked up some of his things and quickly put them into a tattered backpack.

"I have a memory of you," Tim said, wondering how much he should reveal.

"What kind of memory?"

"I'm not sure. I feel like I'm supposed to tell you something. Something big or important."

"Well? What is it?"

"I don't know. That's the problem. I just have this weird feeling that I've met you before."

"Kid, I don't know what your problem is or why you are bothering me. Just leave me alone. I have my own issues to deal with." With that, Bill gathered up the rest of his belongings and walked away.

Tim stood there trying desperately to latch onto the tiny thread of a memory that seemed just beyond his reach. Bill was walking away; time was running out. He was supposed to tell him something.

Suddenly, Tim yelled out the first word he thought of—a name, "Jack!" Bill stopped and then turned around, slowly looking back toward Tim. Tim knew there was more but couldn't pull the memory from his mind.

"What about Jack?" Bill asked hesitantly, not bothering to walk back the twenty feet he had covered.

"Jack . . . ," Tim thought. "Jack needs you. He needs you to come back." Where was all this coming from? It seemed like he was remembering part of a dream. "If you don't go back, Jack will end up in prison for . . . for . . ." his mind was blanking again. It seemed as though he was reading a story written in watercolors, and the text had run, smearing parts beyond legibility.

"Sure, Jack's gonna end up in prison. Well I've been there too. It ain't so bad. At least there's food, water, and shelter. I got none of that now. Jack is with his mom and his new dad." Bill paused and turned his head away from Tim. "They're better off without me," he said softly but then yelled back toward Tim, "Now leave me alone!"

Bill hiked his bag up higher on his shoulder. Despite his stiff joints and serious limp, he walked off as quickly as he could. Tim watched him go, wishing he could have remembered more, but at the same time seriously freaked out about knowing as much as he did. Who was Bill? Who was Jack? How could he have dreamed about them, people he had never met?

There was a beer can on the ground left behind by Bill. Tim picked it up as he tried one last time to recover the memory. Then, in frustration, he yelled, "What is wrong with me?" as he threw down the can and walked back toward his car.

Most of the time he just tried to ignore the familiar strangers. His drive to be a normal teen won out, and he found he could just suppress those strange feelings he got when he saw certain people. He could ignore them and get on with his life. He couldn't avoid the nightly 12:13 event, but even that bothered him less as he busied himself with school, friends, and dating. It worked too; outwardly he had achieved "Mr. Normal," and hoped that it could stay that way forever. Inwardly, however, he couldn't help occasionally uttering those hated words, "What's wrong with me?"

Chapter 10

AMY ASHTON

Friday, March 9, 1990

"WHAT'S WRONG WITH you?" Amy Ashton asked Tim as he threw on his shirt. She glared at him with contempt. Tim glared back. "What's your problem, Tim? It's not a big deal!" Tim looked again at his watch. It was 11:23 p.m.! It would be almost impossible for him to get home before his zone began. How could she have done this to him?

Amy and Tim had been dating for about seven months. They were both seniors and met during the first week of school in their World History class. He was a little shy around her at first, but soon, had asked her out for their first date.

Tim had been taught by his dad to always treat women with respect, and Amy appreciated that about him. She let him open doors, pay for their dates, and pull out her chair at dinner. She loved the way he complimented her and showed her that he cared about her every chance he could. He was a great boyfriend, even if he never took her out to late parties or drive-in movies. Instead, Tim liked to have early dinners or spend the day together on weekends.

The first time they held hands was while watching the movie *Ghost* at the early showing on a Saturday afternoon. On screen,

Patrick Swayze kissed Demi Moore as her character molded clay with her hands on a spinning wheel. Tim glanced over at Amy, wondering if she would someday like him as much as Demi seemed to like Patrick. She was pretty like Demi Moore, but her hair was long like Lexie's had been. Unlike Lexie, though, her hair was dark brown and more wavy.

Tim shook his head and reminded himself that he needed to stop comparing every girl he met to Lexie. Amy was the one on a date with him. She was the one he wanted to be with. Lexie lived somewhere in Nebraska and probably hated him.

Amy looked over and caught him staring at her. She smiled. Tim dropped his gaze, a little embarrassed at being caught, but then noticed her turn her right hand over and lay it on her thigh. She left the hand facing up and opened her fingers slightly, as if inviting him to take hold of it. He did.

By their fourth month of dating, Tim drove Amy home after school almost every day. Her parents had made it clear to both of them that he was not to enter their home while no adult was there. But by their fifth month, that warning was forgotten, and they snuck inside to clumsily make out until the sound of the approaching school bus alerted them of her nine-year-old brother's arrival. The noisy pneumatic bus brakes gave Tim just enough time to slip out the back door and get to his bronze-colored 1975 Chevy Nova.

On February 14, Amy's eighteenth birthday, their seven-month anniversary, and of course, Valentine's Day, Tim bought Amy a gold pendant necklace. It had taken him months of work at the carwash to save up for the purchase. Amy thought it was very pretty and immediately put it on, even though she was a little disappointed that it wasn't larger. It seemed that young love was in full bloom, and only three weeks later, Amy decided that she was ready for them to take their relationship to the next level.

"My parents are staying away all weekend in Tulsa for their anniversary. I was thinking maybe you could come over Friday night. Brian goes to bed at nine."

Tim stopped playfully kissing Amy's arm and looked up at her with a mix of lust and confusion. "What? I'm not even allowed to be here right now." He glanced shamefully at the family photo on the table next to them by the couch. Her dad's frozen expression seemed to be glaring right at him.

"I know," she responded, putting her hand on Tim's chin and pulling his face toward her. "But I just thought it would be nice to have more time together. You know, by ourselves."

The innuendo in the way she spoke the words "by ourselves" was pretty clear to Tim. "How long would you want me to stay?" he asked.

"I don't know, a while. Actually, I guess I was hoping maybe you would stay all night. I mean, we can just talk, or snuggle, or . . ." She seemed a little nervous asking him but also excited. "We don't have to do anything, you know? I just thought that, well, we could spend time together. Just being together and . . . ," she stopped again and looked into Tim's eyes longingly, hoping he would agree.

Tim thought he loved Amy. The idea of spending the night with her was exciting, even if they just held each other all night long. Maybe they would do more. He liked that idea too, even though he had promised himself and her parents he wouldn't. The image of her father glaring at him flashed through his head as he thought of the possibilities.

"I realize that boys your age get thinking about things," Mr. Whitmore had said one evening, pulling Tim aside a few weeks ago after Amy had shown her parents the gold necklace. "And I know that you and Amy really like each other. But just remember that you still have a long time before certain things should be done. You and Amy are probably just temporary." He had lectured awkwardly for another ten minutes talking sporadically about birds, bees . . . and hunting. Tim never said anything until the end of the well-planned but poorly executed lecture. "Do you know what I'm getting at, Tim?"

"Yes, sir. We don't do that sort of thing."

But not "doing that sort of thing" and not "thinking about that sort of thing" were two completely different sorts of things. Now, Tim couldn't stop thinking about "those sorts of things." What would Amy wear to sleep in? What wouldn't she wear? Would they actually sleep together or "sleep" together? His mind swam with the possibilities.

Then Tim's thoughts finally caught up to the situation. He sat up suddenly and said, "Um, I can't." He couldn't let Amy see him zone. She'd freak out and break up with him on the spot! She was not open to something so out of the norm like Lexie had been. "I have to be home by eleven," he said.

Amy started to argue just as the sound of the school bus reached them.

"Sorry, I have to go," Tim said shortly as he quickly pecked her cheek and then slipped out and left through the back door as usual.

As Tim drove home, he thought about what Amy had offered. Her parents would be out of town, and she wanted them to sleep together! She had let him touch various parts of her body through her clothes before, but now she was offering everything! How could he pass that up? They could still be together for a couple of hours, and then he could leave at eleven. "That would be enough time," he reasoned to himself. He just needed to be home, in his bed, by the time his body collapsed into his zone.

Tim called Amy a few hours later to accept her invitation for the evening. She was frustrated by his refusal to extend his curfew or to just break it and accept the consequences. "Don't you love me enough to break one little rule?" she pleaded to no avail. He knew the rules of his zone. He remained firm and stated that leaving by eleven was important to him. But she had a plan.

"Bye Brian. Bye Amy. We love you!" Amy's mom yelled as she pushed through the storm door backward with an arm full of bathroom items and an evening dress.

Her dad was finished loading the car with his things and gave his kids one last hug good-bye. This wasn't the first time they had gone out leaving Amy in charge. But it was the first time they would be gone overnight. "Amy, you know the rules. No one comes in while we are gone." She couldn't tell if he suspected something, or was just reemphasizing his authority.

"I know, Dad." She huffed trying to cover up any hint of guilt in her voice. Her eyes shifted nervously, but fortunately, her dad had already turned to her brother.

"And Brian, you listen to Amy. She is in charge. Okay?"

"Yes, Dad . . ." Brian sighed. He didn't mind Amy being in charge. Usually she left him alone. He just didn't like to be reminded that she had authority over him.

Amy waved one last time as her parents drove off a minute later. She shut the door and turned toward Brian. "Brian, take your bath and get ready for bed." It was already 8:00 p.m., and Tim would be there in just over an hour. Brian whined something about wanting to stay up late. Amy cut him off.

"Do it now!" she ordered.

Brian stomped to the bathroom and did as he was told. He really was a good kid, she thought, but tonight, she just wanted him out of the way. When she heard the water running, she set out quickly to change the clocks around the house thirty minutes fast. Once done, she knocked on the bathroom door and ordered Brian to finish up and get to bed. She hated being so bossy and promised herself she would make it up to him tomorrow night with ice cream and his choice of movie. But this night was to be hers.

When Brian exited the bathroom, he was surprised to see how late it had become. He obediently dressed in his pajamas and went to bed. Amy listened at his door until she was convinced he was asleep. Then she set out again to set all the clocks back a full hour. As long as Tim didn't look at his watch, she'd have him for an extra hour whether he wanted it or not.

Amy slipped out of her T-shirt and jeans and redressed for the evening. She changed her clothes three times, then stood in front of the mirror and admired her reflection. She had debated for the last few days if she would wear something Tim was used to seeing her in, or something slinky and sexy. Finally, she had chosen a sexy and silky red slip given to her by her friends when she told them about the night she had planned. It would be perfect, she thought. She loved the way it mixed sheer and opaque fabrics to cover her but left little to the imagination.

She spun in front of the mirror and watched as the high slit along the side of her leg opened, revealing her thigh. Was the slit too high? Was it high enough? This was a very special date for the two of them. She wanted the night to be perfect.

However, she worried that Tim seeing her like this so suddenly at the door might cause him to run if he was already nervous. So instead, she put on a still flattering but less revealing nightgown.

At 9:10 p.m., Tim arrived just as planned. "Hey cutie," Amy purred when she opened the back door for him wearing a T-shirt and shorts. She had changed her mind again just a few minutes before his arrival and put her standard shorts and school T-shirt back on. It was a good decision, she decided. Tim looked terrified.

"Brian asleep?" Tim whispered nervously as he looked past Amy into the house. Now she wished she had worn the red slip to get his mind on her instead of worrying about her little brother.

"Of course he is," Amy reassured Tim, grabbing his hand and pulling him into the house. "He's a good kid and went to bed when I told him to." She didn't mention that she had tricked him into bed early by resetting the clocks. She realized suddenly that if Tim examined the clocks now, he would see that they were an hour behind. She changed the subject and led him to her room.

Tim was more nervous than he thought he'd be. He was glad Amy seemed relaxed and was taking charge. He let her guide him into her bedroom where it was clear she had an amazing evening planned. Candles were lit, the room lights were dim, and soft music was playing.

They whispered, cuddled, and petted each other for what seemed like both minutes and days at the same time. Amy slipped off Tim's watch claiming it was catching her hair. She put it out of reach and smiled to herself as she looked up at her own clock on the wall. With any luck, he'd completely forget about the time, and they would have all night. Together, they explored each other further and further as the minutes melted away.

Tim thought that it felt later than Amy's clock suggested when he snapped back to reality just long enough to glance at the time. She quickly brought his mind back onto her by grabbing his hand

and placing it on her breast. More minutes passed, and Tim looked up at her clock again. He could feel that something was wrong. He wasn't pulled back by Amy this time as she tried to regain his attention. His internal clock had always been strong, especially in the hour before his zone began. Regardless of where he was or what time zone he was in, he could sense that his Tim zone was approaching.

Tim jumped off the bed. "Where's my watch?" he huffed. Amy stared, then closed her eyes and shook her head as she pointed down next to her night stand. He groped in the semidarkness and found it. "11:22?" he exclaimed. He looked back up at her clock, "You tricked me!" he yelled even louder, forgetting her brother was asleep only two doors down the hall.

"I just wanted you to stay. I thought that if you were here with me long enough, you would forget about your silly curfew. For me!"

Tim finished dressing as Amy glared at him and told him it wasn't such a big deal. Then he stormed out of her room. "You don't know what you've done," he sighed as he headed for the front door. Amy followed him to the back door without redressing. She didn't know what to say. It just didn't make sense to her.

Tim was thinking the same thing as he started his car and threw the old transmission into drive. None of this made sense. He looked up at Amy who was hiding her nakedness only partially behind her door. She was so pretty, and he thought he loved her. Why couldn't he tell her the truth? Why did he have to hide his zone from her? Maybe she would accept him like Lexie had. No, she wasn't Lexie. She could never accept him like Lexie had. Tim looked away from Amy and drove off.

"Lexie . . ." he thought again. Lexie had been his only true friend. He had loved her, he realized. She was the girl he wished he had been with that night. But how could he be thinking of her after such an amazing evening with Amy. Amy was his girlfriend. Amy had just given herself to him, and he to her. Yet as he drove, the closer he got to home, the more he thought of Lexie.

A few minutes later, just a quarter mile from Tim's home, an oncoming car with blaring horn swerved to miss Tim's Nova as he veered across the center line. Tim didn't hear the horn. He didn't hear anything. Not even the sounds of crunching metal and cracking wood as the Nova slammed into the large oak tree at the entrance of his neighborhood.

Chapter 11

HOSPITAL CONFESSION

Early Saturday Morning, March 10, 1990

TIM AWOKE AT 12:13 a.m. Lights were on all around him, and his eyes felt surprisingly good. He started to sit up. "Whoa buddy . . . you stay put." Tim stopped and looked toward the voice just next to him. A man in scrubs was fiddling with a valve on an IV drip next to his bed.

"I'm in a hospital," Tim stated flatly.

"You sure are buddy. But don't worry. Not a broken bone in ya. I'm Clint. I'm Dr. Bruin's number one LPN."

"Dr. Bruin?"

"Yeah buddy, best head doc around. You came in unconscious twenty minutes ago. Looked like you were doped up on something, or had one heck of a concussion." Tim tried to remember what he had been doing and realized he must have gone into his zone while driving.

Clint finished adjusting the IV and then checked both of Tim's eyes. "You sure look better now. I'm gonna fetch the doc." As he hurried past the privacy curtain and out the door, Tim heard Clint muttering to himself, "Weird, so weird."

Tim sat up carefully despite Clint's earlier command to stay still. He pulled back a thin white sheet and looked over his body. He was wearing only a hospital gown so it was easy to see the scratches and bruises on his body. Overall, he felt pretty good. He saw some kind of medical eye gel sitting on the tray next to his bed. That explained why his eyes weren't as dry as usual.

At the sound of fast approaching steps, Tim looked up to see his dad running into the room with his mom close behind. "Tim!" John yelled. His mother sobbed intensely when she saw him sitting there. Looking over him quickly, John continued, "Are you okay? What happened? You look okay!"

"I'm fine, Dad. Mom . . . I'm fine." Tim assured his parents.

"But the . . . the police said . . ." Sarah stammered.

"Tim, your car was wrapped around a tree. We saw it on our way here. The police came to the house and said it was really bad. They wouldn't even answer us when we asked if you were okay. Then we heard a doctor say you might be brain dead!"

"Brain dead?" Tim repeated.

"No," a doctor interrupted as he strode into the room. He looked more like a scientist than a doctor. He was tall and lanky and had graying hair. Tim guessed he was in his early fifties or so. He had on a pair of reading glasses, but took them off when he spoke. "I said that Tim had a possible severe concussion and signs of brain death as well as persistent vegetative state. I was only listing possible scenarios as we have only completed a few tests."

"But he looks fine." Sarah sobbed again as she held his hand and protectively nuzzled his head.

"Mom, you're crying all over me!" whined Tim.

"Obviously, he is not a vegetable or brain dead!" laughed John at his son's reaction to his mom's gushing.

"We do need to run more tests," Dr. Bruin jumped back in. "It is wonderful to see Tim conscious and alert. Frankly, from the description of the accident, I am amazed at his apparent condition. But let's take things slowly, one step at a time. I am Dr. James Bruin. I am the head neurologist."

For the next several hours, various doctors and nurses came in to run tests and ask questions. It was clear to Tim that despite his miraculous delivery from what should have been a fatal crash, the doctors were still concerned about the unconscious state he had arrived in. It seemed that his body was so relaxed when the crash occurred that he was spared serious injury. This implied to the doctors, and the police, that drugs or alcohol were involved. However, breath and urine tests cleared Tim of any illegal substance suspicions.

"Fully dilated eyes and a fixed stare can be caused by a number of things," the doctor had stated factually. "Simple head trauma, drugs, even brain death had to be considered. We eliminated brain death quickly. In fact, looking at the scans, it seems that during your state of unconsciousness, your brain was highly active. The patterns look like REM sleep brainwaves, except much more intense. It's almost like you were completely awake and active."

Tim thought about the experiments he and Lexie had tried. But they had been just kids then, without any real knowledge of brain function or psychology. Having an actual brain scan both terrified and intrigued him at the same time. He still wanted to be a normal kid, but this might be a chance to learn more about his zone. He thought about Lexie again and wished his old friend was there with him. She would know what he should do.

"Tim? Are you listening?" Dr. Bruin asked.

"What? Yeah, just thinking." Tim responded.

"What are you thinking about, Tim? Is there something you can tell us?"

Tim thought again about Lexie and something she had said to him so long ago. "What if they study you and think you are an alien?" she had asked. "And they put you in a little cage underground and poke at you and dig into your brain?" She was so young then, and the question was mostly just her thinking out loud. But that fear of being identified as a freak stuck with him.

"No," Tim answered finally. "I'm just thinking about my car. I guess I'm glad to be alive."

"We're all glad you are alive!" John jumped in. "Dr. Bruin, don't you think Tim has been through enough? Can't we let him rest now?" The doctor agreed to let any additional questions and tests wait until morning.

"Tim, you get some rest. It has been a long night for us all," Bruin said as he picked up his charts and started to leave. "But please think about what happened. I need to know if something like this has ever happened before."

Tim watched Dr. Bruin leave. John followed him to the door and closed it. He flipped off the overhead lights, leaving only the light above the bed tray on. "Sarah, why don't you take the car and go home to sleep. I'll stay with Tim tonight." Sarah protested, but John insisted. "You can come back in the morning and trade places with me." Sarah reluctantly agreed. She had been sitting next to Tim for almost three hours. She was sore and very tired.

"Are you sure you'll be all right?" she pleaded one last time to Tim, hoping he would ask her to stay.

"Yeah, I'm fine. Dad will be here, and you need to sleep."

"Okay, honey," she conceded. "I love you! Get your rest!"

"Love you too, Mom!" Tim was surprised at how relieved he was when she finally left. He loved her deeply but just didn't feel like he could talk to her about what was going on. He wasn't sure yet if he could tell his dad either.

He watched John unfold sheets and blankets onto the portable cot that Clint had brought in for him when it was clear he would be staying the night. He thought about how it felt to have kept this hidden inside for so long. Since losing his close friendship with Lexie, he had no one to confide in. When his dad zipped up the bag that had held the linens, the sound reminded Tim of all their camping trips. He remembered the night Lexie had first discovered his secret and how quickly his dad had rushed in to save whoever needed saving. He made up his mind at that moment.

"Dad?"

"Yes, Tim?" John finished putting on a pillow case and then stopped to look at Tim. Tim didn't know how to begin.

"Do you remember that night in the tent when I scared Lexie?" John frowned and squinted his eyes as if trying really hard to think back.

"Yes, I remember. You scared her but then seemed to be even better friends than before by the next day. Your mom and I really worried about what had happened but decided to trust you. Why are you thinking about that right now?"

"I didn't scare her on purpose that night. I didn't even know I had scared her until I woke up." His dad looked confused, but Tim continued. "I just woke up and she was crying and you were coming into the tent." John didn't understand where this was leading so just waited for Tim to go on.

"I have a 'zone.'" Tim finally whispered after a long pause.

"A what?"

"Remember, Lexie said I looked like something from the *Twilight Zone*? Well, that's what we call it."

"I don't understand. Call what?"

"Every night, I go into some kind of trance. Lexie said my eyes become so dilated that they look completely black. It really freaked her out at first, but she got used to it. I don't blink the whole time I'm in my zone, so my eyes hurt really bad when I come out of it. I also go completely limp, like I'm dead." John still didn't know what to say, so Tim continued after another pause.

"I don't know why it happens to me. I just know that it does. Every night, my zone starts at 11:35 p.m. and ends at 12:13 a.m. Well, except for when we are in a different time zone or when we change the clocks back for the winter. But it is still thirty-eight minutes long every time."

"That doesn't make any sense, Tim." John shook his head. "Why would you fall asleep and wake up at the same time?"

"I told you, I don't know. I never remember anything while I'm zoned either. Lexie tried to wake me up a couple of times, but she couldn't. Not until 12:13. But then I just wake up on my own, with my eyes burning."

John was trying to listen but just couldn't get past the strangeness of the story. "What about tonight?" John asked, as he struggled to not doubt his son's story. "Are you saying that is why you crashed? Because you . . . zoned?"

"Yes. I always try to get home before it starts. Usually, I'm already asleep, but if I'm not, I just try to get into my room and in bed so no one will see me. I don't want anyone to know. They'll think I'm crazy or messed up!"

John didn't believe Tim but considered how careful Tim had always been about getting home and into his room by 11:30 p.m. He had never wanted to stay the night at any of his friend's houses and had never wanted to have a sleepover. Maybe even if this zone thing wasn't true, Tim believed it was true. Why else would he make up a story like this? "Are you just trying to cover up the real reason you wrecked the car?" John heard himself ask.

Tim heard the doubt in his father's words and stopped talking. Finally after what seemed like several minutes, John said, "Tim, I love you. I believe something happened tonight. And maybe that something has happened before. I just don't know what to think yet." Then he added, "But I know you are not crazy . . . or messed up in the head!" He got up off the cot next to Tim's bed and put his arm around him. "I'm just glad you are okay. And if this is real, then I am officially giving you an 11:30 p.m. lifetime curfew!" He smiled at his son reassuringly. Tim gratefully hugged his dad back. He and his dad hadn't hugged in years, but he was glad to do it now.

Tim told his dad more about all the experiments he and Lexie had tried. John listened intently. He was amazed at how strong Tim had been to keep this to himself for so long. He also felt guilty for never catching on himself. One thing was for certain, they couldn't tell Sarah, at least not yet. She would worry constantly or withdraw from them as she tried to understand it on her own.

Several times while Tim and John talked, nurses and doctors arrived to check on him. Tim and John would hush and wait for them to leave before continuing. John agreed with Tim that most people wouldn't try to understand his condition and might outcast him. But he also felt that Tim deserved to know what was happening to him.

Just before six in the morning, they both passed out from exhaustion. Tim slept peacefully, feeling relieved to have finally shared his secret with only the second person in his life. His dreams were calm and his body relaxed. It was a Saturday, and it was his last 'normal' day.

Chapter 12

NOTHING OUT OF THE ORDINARY

TIM AND JOHN only got a few hours of sleep before the doctors returned to run more tests. Most of the morning tests evaluated only his physical well-being; reflex, x-rays of the spine, whiplash evaluation, fluid tests, etc. Dr. Bruin arrived around ten. He must have only slept a few hours too, since he had been in Tim's room several times throughout the night.

It was interesting to Tim to see how the other doctors quickly reported their results to Dr. Bruin and then got out of his way. He seemed to carry much more authority in this hospital than Tim had first realized. Or maybe he was just very well respected. Either way, Tim felt comfortable with him.

"My associates tell me you seem to be in good shape," Dr. Bruin began. "It seems clear that from the neck down at least, you got very lucky. However, I'd like to repeat some of your brain scans as well as try some additional tests on your head."

Tim wasn't sure what they would find since he knew his zone only happened at night. But maybe that was the safest way to have these tests. Hopefully, they could uncover something without knowing about his zone. Maybe they would even discover some benign tumor that was putting pressure on part of his brain. And once removed, maybe he could finally have a normal life.

For the rest of the day Dr. Bruin, Clint, and the rest of the doctor's team put Tim through MRIs, DOIs, CAT scans, and just about every other brain imaging technology available. However, nothing seemed out of the ordinary. Test after test came back normal.

As the hours wore on, Tim was exhausted even though all he had done all day was sit in a wheelchair and lie down on various hard examination tables. Finally, Clint wheeled the chair back over to Tim and said, "Man, are you as bored as I am?"

"Just tired. How many more tests do you think Dr. Bruin . . ."

"Call him 'Doc.' It drives him crazy!" Clint grinned.

"How many more tests will *Doc* want to run?" Tim finished.

"Too many," Clint laughed. "Let's get you back to your room before he thinks of more!"

Tim smiled at Clint, who had been around through most of the tests, adding his version of humor to the otherwise sterile environment. "I think we used just about every piece of equipment we've got in this stinkin' hospital on your brain. And nada! Your head is just normal, boring, and gooey on the inside like everyone else's."

Tim was somewhat relieved by this news even if it meant he may still not know anything more about his zone. But hearing he was "normal" always made him feel better.

John and Sarah got up when Tim and Clint returned to his room. "So?" John said, looking right at Tim.

"Your boy's head looks as good as any to me." Clint laughed. "But I sure hope you guys have good insurance. Those tests are *ex-peen-seeeve!*"

"So he really is fine then!" Sarah cried.

"I ain't the doc, but I've seen a lot of head injury scans, and Timmy's looked fine to me. Doc's gonna be in here in a little while. He'll let you know officially. Till then,"—looking back at Tim—"you get some rest."

Clint left the room after making sure Tim got into his bed safely. "So you are fine then?" John half winked at Tim.

"Guess so. Clint said I was normal."

"That's great! I'm so proud of you!" Sarah hugged Tim again as if he had just won the spelling bee.

"What's next then?" John asked.

"Dunno. Guess we have to wait for Doc to let me go. Unless . . ." Tim stopped as Dr. Bruin walked into the room.

Without greeting anyone, Doc looked at Tim. "Large scale structural imaging tells me that you don't have any serious gross scale head trauma. Functional imaging, which I use to diagnose finer scale problems, also indicates that you are in good health."

Sarah sat back in her chair. She smiled with relief. "So he can go now, right?" she said.

Doc went on, ignoring Sarah and continuing to speak directly to Tim. "We reran the brain scan tests we had performed on you last night while you were unconscious and saw no hints of the abnormalities we had observed."

"Yepper . . . Boring!" Clint chimed in as he walked back into the room.

"Despite the lack of exciting test results that Clint hoped for," Doc said as he shot his usual "not appreciated" look at Clint, "and the apparent clean bill of health from the other doctors, I've recommended to the hospital that you stay one more night so we can monitor you while you sleep."

John could see the unease in Tim's face and spoke up, "I don't think that is necessary, Dr. Bruin. You said yourself that everything is normal."

"Mr. and Mrs. Caston," Doc finally directed his attention to Tim's parents, "Tim was completely unresponsive last night. Tim can't tell us why he crashed, so it is possible that he went unconscious while driving. Despite appearing to be healthy now, we need to be certain that this won't happen again. He may not be so lucky next time."

John shot Tim another look and then responded, "It's time for Tim to come home."

"No, Dad. I want to know, you know?" Tim looked into his Dad's eyes and tried to look confident.

Surprised, John asked quietly, "Are you sure, Tim? You have had a very long day. Maybe we should go home and think about this?" his dad guided. Doc looked back and forth and could see their unspoken communication.

"What's going on here? This is the second time I've gotten the feeling that something isn't being said."

"How secret are the tests?" Tim asked, looking away from his dad and back at the doctor.

"How secret? Well, all medical records are confidential . . ."

"Yeah, but if we do another test tonight, can it stay just between us and no one else?"

"I don't understand."

"I want to know what is going on with me, but I don't want people to think I'm weird or crazy."

Doc hesitated and then replied cautiously but curiously, "I think we can keep the tests tight. Right, Clint?"

Clint looked at Doc and then at Tim. "Yeah, sure, buddy. I have to help Doc with the equipment, so I'll be there, but we can keep stuff quiet."

"Ok," Sarah jumped in. "Now I'm really confused. What is going on, Tim? Why don't you just want to come home? Why should the tests be secret?"

"It's okay, Sarah." John put his hand onto her shoulder. "Let's let Tim and Dr. Bruin talk."

Everyone in the room looked back at Tim. He was looking down, trying to think of what to say. Doc seemed like a trustworthy person. He had explained all the previous tests to Tim in a way that was understandable and yet didn't treat Tim like a kid either. He had always talked directly to Tim while many of the other doctors that had been in and out of the room seemed to talk mostly past Tim to his parents or to the nurses.

Tim liked Clint too. He was blunt and honest, usually making other doctors mad. But it was clear that he worked most closely with Dr. Bruin, and Doc seemed to like him also. Tim had made a decision.

"I've blacked out before," Tim finally began.

"When? You never said anything," Sarah jumped in worriedly.

John stopped her again, "Sarah, let Tim talk."

"I've blacked out before," Tim said again. It happens at night . . . I mean, when it happens, it happens at night." He wasn't ready to admit to Doc or to his mom that it happened every night and always at 11:35 p.m.

"So if you want to run a test tonight, maybe it will happen then." He looked up and saw everyone staring at him. He decided he had said enough.

Doc was good at reading patients and recognized that Tim was holding something back. He waited another moment to see if Tim would add more to his revelation of past blackouts but saw that Tim wasn't ready to reveal more. After another minute of silence, Doc agreed to the private tests.

"Ok then," Doc said. He had hoped Tim would say more, but knew it wasn't necessary. Tim's anxious expression made it clear that new tests that night would have different results from those they had done earlier that day. He just hoped the tests would speak for themselves.

"We will passively monitor your brain this evening and run another suite of functional MRI scans if something changes. Clint, let's let these folks rest."

Clint and Doc left the room. Tim told his mom everything he had told John the previous night. An hour later, they were all asleep, knowing it would be a rough night.

Chapter 13

TESTS

JOHN AWOKE FIRST to the quiet sound of a wheelchair rolling into the room. Tim and Sarah were startled awake when that same chair accidentally ran into Tim's bed.

"You ready?" Clint asked quietly to Tim. It was 10:00 p.m.

"Yeah," Tim replied, nodding his head. He looked at his dad and then hopped into the wheelchair. "You know, this really is stupid that I have to sit in this. I can walk."

"I know. It's just all part of our five-star service. Plus, the hospital can charge your insurance a lot more money if we use this!" Clint laughed. "You folks stay here, and we'll have Tim back by morning."

Tim countered, "I'd like it if they came. Can't they just stay out of the way?"

"Well, Doc never lets family watch. So I say, let's bring 'em!" He smiled conspiratorially at Tim and then John and Sarah.

Clint rolled Tim to the elevator and pushed the button to take them to the twelfth floor. John and Sarah followed, pleased to be able to stay with Tim.

"We're not going to where we had the tests today?" Tim asked.

"Nope. Too many people around those rooms. You want secret, right? So we're using the teaching lab up on twelve where nobody will be around this time of night."

Clint wheeled Tim into the large room with several different imaging machines. Doc was waiting and frowned at Clint when Tim's parents stepped in. "You two need to go into the observation room if you are going to be here." He pointed to a small partition in the larger room with a glass wall.

John nodded at Doc, took Sarah's hand, and guided her into the room. Doc set up some more equipment as Clint rolled Tim over to the flat table in front of the large MRI machine. "Ok Tim, we are all set," Doc said casually. "Clint, help Tim onto the table."

Clint let Tim step up onto the padded table himself and then wheeled over the IV. Doc stepped over to them and put his hand on Tim's shoulder. "This will be just like earlier today," he said, "except we're going to try to combine some of the tests, so we can see more at once."

Clint inserted the IV needle into Tim's arm. "This is the Gadolinium that you liked so much last time," Clint commented sarcastically as he dabbed off a tiny bit of fluid at the insertion point and then taped the needle down. "It will help us see the contrasts in your brain."

"That stuff is cold!" Tim commented as the fluid began dripping into his vein.

"Yep, cold as the Rockies and refreshing as a mountain stream. Just like my favorite beer!" Clint had a way of calming patients that even Doc admired. Tim almost thought he saw Doc hold back a smile.

A few minutes later, Tim was dotted with multiple electrodes and wires for monitoring his body and brain. "We'll pull some of these off if we start the MRI," Doc assured Tim, seeing the concern on his face. Tim didn't know much about this stuff, but he knew that metal and MRIs didn't go well together.

It was 11:00 p.m.

Clint moved back and forth between Tim and the monitors, occasionally making small adjustments. "All patterns normal, Doc. Equipment functioning as usual."

"Good. How do you feel, Tim?"

"Fine. Tired, but fine."

"We are ready with just about any tests we need, so hopefully you won't have to do this again."

"Good." Tim sighed under his breath. He was still nervous. What would they find out? Would his mom freak? Maybe it was a bad idea to ask for them to stay. What if she saw his eyes? She might never see him the same way again. Not as her baby, not as her boy, just as a freako.

Tim looked over at them. His mom was looking down at something on the floor and was squeezing her hands together tightly. She seemed more nervous than he did. John was watching Clint and Doc but then noticed Tim looking over and gave him a reassuring nod.

11:30 p.m.

"You seeing something, Clint?" Doc asked noticing a slight frown on Clint's face.

"Not really, just . . . well, it looks like Tim is falling asleep." Doc and Clint looked at Tim. He was staring at the ceiling.

"I'm not asleep," he said hearing their conversation. "I do feel a little weird. This is how I always feel just a little while before it happens."

"Everything looked normal until just a moment ago," Clint said.

"His heart is speeding up, but his brain waves are slowing," Doc said over Clint's shoulder after stepping around the consol where Clint sat at the controls.

"I know; that's what I'm talking about."

"Keep monitoring," Doc commanded.

"Duh," Clint sighed.

11:34 p.m.

"Whoa! Did you see that, Doc?" Clint exclaimed.

"Yes. What is causing it?"

"Well, you're the doc, Doc."

Tim was still awake and could hear them. He was used to this feeling and knew it was about to happen. "This is it," he called out to them in a weak voice. John stood up in the observation room. Sarah looked up from the spot on the floor at which she had still been blankly staring. A moment later, she saw Tim's eyes close.

"There it is again," Clint reported. "Some kind of alpha wave spike."

"Look at the delta waves, he is in stage four sleep already."

"He was awake just a moment ago," Clint argued. "It's impossible to reach this level of delta so fast."

"Nothing is impossible, Clint. Keep reading me those del values. Normal is between two and four cycles. I'll watch the patient's vitals."

"At four cycles per second now, Doc."

"Heart rate slowing. Respiratory rate dropping. Temperature normal at 98.9."

"3.5 cycles per second, Doc. Rhythmic pattern with no dream signature. Whoa, 2.7 cycles now."

"Heart rate and respiratory dropping fast."

Clint looked up from his monitors to John and Sarah. Both were standing in the observation room. John was next to the door ready to come out.

"Doc, we need to stop this. Something is very wrong!" Clint said worriedly.

"What are the other patterns doing?" Doc asked while checking Tim's vitals again.

"Beta steady at fifteen and has been there since he fell asleep. Alpha and theta waves also normal for someone sleeping. But . . ."

"How about those deltas again?" Doc interrupted quickly.

"That's what I was about to say, We're down to 2.0 cycles, and they're still slowing."

Doc looked up at John as he came out of the ob room. "Please stand back, sir. We're going to wake Tim up now." Doc walked over to the monitors to see the readings himself. The delta wave reading had fallen to 1.8 cycles per second. Whispering to Clint, "Tell me if the dels move below one."

"I've never seen them less than two before. What happens below one?"

"He will be brain-dead," Doc whispered even quieter. He saw John was trying to listen. Speaking more loudly and looking back at John, "Everything will be fine. He has just gone into a deep sleep."

"You said his heart and breathing were dropping! What's happening?" John shot back. "Wake him up!"

"Ok," Doc agreed. He put his hand onto Tim's head. "Tim?" he called loudly. "We want you to wake up now, Tim."

"Doc, we're at 0.9 cycles now! And they're still slowing!"

"What does that mean?" demanded John. Doc ignored John and checked Tim again. "Heart rate still dropping. Clint, get the paddles over here. He is going into arrest."

"Doc, 0.3. No wait, 0.1!" Clint yelled to John, "Mr. Caston, see that red box next to you, grab it!" John picked up the red defibrillator box without hesitating and brought it over to Doc.

Doc took the box from John and threw it open. He pulled out the paddles and then saw Tim's eyes. Although he had seen Tim's eyes black and dilated the night before, the sight startled him. He stepped backwards, tripped over the deliberator box, and fell onto the floor.

John saw Tim's eyes too. He had heard Tim's description of his eyes but hadn't fully understood. They were wide open and completely black. Despite the sight, John leaned in close to Tim. "Tim," he started, "Dad's here. Can you hear me? Wake up, Tim." John checked Tim's pulse and tried to feel for breath even though his vitals were being prominently displayed next to him. "I can't find a pulse!"

"No, it's okay. Look," Doc said as he pulled himself back up and pointed to the graph. "His pulse is coming back now. Respiratory is returning to normal too. Clint, what is his delta now?"

"Still 0.1 Doc, but that's not what's weird. He has strong beta waves now and normal alpha and theta waves. He must be awake now."

"That doesn't make sense, Clint." Doc bumped Clint over and sat down at the monitors. "You keep an eye on his vitals now."

Clint followed the orders and switched places with the doctor. He looked back toward the observation room to see Sarah standing with one hand against the glass wall and the other cupping her mouth. "Ma'am," he said without betraying his own fright at what had just happened. "Ma'am, everything is going to be all right. Tim is doing fine now. I haven't got a freakin' clue as to what just happened, but he is doing fine now."

That, of course, wasn't completely true. Nothing was fine about the brainwaves Doc was seeing. He culled through the readouts of the past couple of minutes. None of it made any sense. He should have been brain-dead based on some of the readings. However, by other measurements, Tim seemed to be completely awake. All that was clear was that Tim was far from normal.

John still leaned over his son. He was relieved to see the regular pulsing heartbeat on the monitor with that reassuring beep . . . beep sound. Then standing up straight again, he asked, "Please tell me what is going on. Tell me what is happening with my son."

Doc peered over his glasses and past the monitors toward John. He started to speak, paused, looked back at the readouts, and finally said quietly, "I don't know. This is the strangest thing I've ever seen."

"Is he okay though?"

"Clint. Vitals?"

"Peachy, Doc. All normal."

Doc waved John over to the monitor. "Let me show you something." John watched Tim breathing for a moment. Feeling confident that he seemed okay now, aside from the wide, black eyes, John moved to Bruin's side.

"See these wavelets?" Doc waited for a nod from John who obliged even though he didn't really know what a wavelet was. He saw twenty or twenty-five separate lines clustered into groups of four. All seemed to be wiggling up and down in zigzag patterns. "The digital readout is monitoring the electrical impulses from Tim's brain. Each cluster is measuring a different part of his brain. Tim looks to be asleep, right?" Doc motioned back to Tim.

John looked at his son and replied, "Well, yes, except for his eyes."

"Right. His eyes indicate a complete loss of brain function. But we are reading a tremendous amount of brain activity just like we measured last night." His words trailed off as he looked at the oscillating patterns and then he mumbled back to himself, "Absolutely tremendous!"

"But why is this happening to him?" John insisted, waking the doctor up from his thoughts. "Will he be okay?"

Doc thought deeply for a few moments. He had never seen anything like this in all his twenty-two years as a neurologist. This was a phenomenon he wasn't prepared for. He would need to study medical journals and call some colleagues. But first, he needed more tests. Now wasn't the time to speculate or talk. He needed data.

"Mr. Caston," he said with authority, "I don't have the answers yet. Right now I need to continue the tests." Without waiting for John to respond, Bruin stood up from the monitors and moved back to Tim. "Clint, get some ocular gel to put over his eyes to keep them from drying out like we did last night." Clint nodded and left.

"Mr. Caston, since you are here, please stay at the monitors and tell me if the patterns change. I'm going to prep Tim for the fMRI." Doc removed the metal electrodes but left the rest.

John spoke up, "Some of the lines are flat now."

"Yes, a few of the electrodes can't be in the MRI machine. We'll still have the critical measurements from the others, and the fMRI will give us a picture of the brain activity."

Clint bustled back into the lab. "Here we go," he said as he put on gloves and opened the gel he had pulled out of medical storage. Cautiously, he put the gel onto Tim's eyes. "Bet his eyes hurt every time he wakes up from this thing."

John felt another tinge of guilt as he realized that he hadn't ever been aware of Tim's pain each night.

Clint helped Doc finish prepping for the MRI and reattached one of the plastic fiber optic wires that would be safe in the machine. Sarah continued to watch from the glass ob room and had sat back down.

"Ready," Clint called out a few minutes later. John was asked to stay at the monitors and report any changes. He still wasn't sure what he was looking at, but was glad to be able to help.

The board on which Tim lay moved slowly into the enclosed cylinder at the center of the large machine. Had he been awake, he may have felt claustrophobic.

"Imaging on. Everything checks." Clint stepped back and let Doc take over. It was midnight.

Doc captured images in all regions of Tim's brain. He was astounded at the levels of activity throughout the cranium; some of which were occurring in parts of Tim's mind that he had never seen active in any other patient.

12:10 p.m.

"Hey, Doc, his temperature and heart rate are rising. Breathing still normal."

Doc looked up from the images on his screens. "How much up?"

"Uh, 102 degrees and 110 beats per minute."

"Dr. Bruin?" John called out. "Something is changing here too."

Doc rolled his chair to the other monitors. "The active portions of his brain are settling down now," Doc said, "but the alpha is spiking again. It must be a loose connection in one of the leads. Those waves can't just spike like that."

"Doc, temp still 102 but he's up to 180 BPM now. Breathing still nominal. I'm going to check that lead." Clint followed the wires out of the back of the computer as far as he could until they entered the MRI machine with Tim. As he came back around the machine, he noticed one of the readouts that was usually ignored.

"Doc, look at this. Look at the background wattage on the machine." Clint pointed to the screen on the side of the MRI as Bruin hurried over.

"What? That's impossible. That should be reading less than ten watts."

"I know, but it is over two hundred now and still going up!" Clint said.

"We're reading a surplus voltage on the scalp sensors too," Doc added.

"Doc, we gotta shut this down!" Clint pressed.

"I agree. Start the shutdown procedure."

Clint ran to the control panel. "On it," he shouted.

"Clint, we're over three hundred watts now. Get it down."

"Doc, it ain't working!"

"What do you mean? Get if off. Now!"

"I'm telling ya, I'm trying! It ain't shutting down! Look at the beta waves. What does that mean?"

"I . . . I'm not sure. His brain is in both a disengaged theta state and active beta state at the same time. I've never seen this."

"Doc, over five hundred watts now, and this thing still won't shut down! It's gonna fry him!"

"Unplug it, Clint. Now!"

Clint looked over to the wall to locate the outlet and then kicked the large plug out of the wall with his foot. "Got it," he breathed. "No wait, we're still picking up the brain activity. There's a reverse flow on the field."

"That's impossible," Doc snapped. "The machine only creates a field in one direction."

"It's unplugged. I don't think the machine is doing it."

"You're right!" Doc gasped. "It's Tim! He's creating the field! Look at the voltage in the sensors. I've never seen it above fifty microvolts. He's producing over fifty thousand!"

"Doc, look! Do you see that?" Clint pointed at the center of the MRI machine where Tim lay.

"I see it! I think the field is ionizing! Get him out of there!" Doc yelled to Clint. Hearing that, John jumped up and ran around the monitors toward the MRI machine. He arrived at about the same moment as Clint, and both men grabbed for Tim's legs.

A bluish glow seemed to be emanating from Tim's body. As the two men reached into the field they felt a strong electric shock and were thrown back several feet from the machine. Sparks began shooting from the MRI control panel.

"Tim!" John yelled from the floor. Sarah came out slowly from behind the glass as the lights in the room began to flash.

"You're electrocuting him!" she screamed. Just then, one of the fluorescent bulbs in the ceiling directly above the machine exploded. Less than a second later another blew, sending glass and sparks down from the ceiling. The gentle hum that had been coming from the machine was now a terrible ear-splitting resonance.

Sarah ran toward Tim's legs and shielded her eyes as four more of the bulbs detonated around her. The blue glow enveloping Tim flashed brightly and then faded suddenly.

Sarah grabbed onto his feet but wasn't thrown back like Clint and John had been. She pulled Tim out of the tube and off table. He fell onto her limply. His eyes were closed, but he began to stir. It was 12:13 a.m.

"Mom, what happened?" Tim said seconds later. Sarah burst out crying. John grabbed onto the chair he had fallen against and pulled himself up off the floor. His tailbone and head hurt, but he barely noticed as he ran over to his family.

"My baby, my baby! Are you okay?" Sarah wailed. "I was so afraid."

Tim looked around. He could see better than usual, and his eyes felt all right. Rubbing them, he realized Doc or Clint must have coated his eyes again like they had the previous night. "I'm fine, Mom," he assured her as he noticed the mess in the room. He saw Clint sitting on the floor near the opposite wall, holding his elbow and looking pale. Doc Bruin seemed to be in shock but was at least still sitting in a chair. Broken glass, plastic, and wires seemed to be all over the floor and the MRI machine was smoking. "Did I do this?" he said, looking up at his mom.

Chapter 14

THE JOURNEY BEGINS

Sunday, March 11, 1990

"SLEEP IS DIVIDED into two main phases," Doc explained the next morning. He looked tired. He had spent the entire night studying the data. Now he stood in front of the Castons in Tim's recovery room with a thick binder of notes and printer readouts that made very little sense to him. "Non-REM sleep, which is considered a resting state for the brain, and REM sleep, when our dreams prevail. The brain imaging tests we did yesterday morning showed that when you are sleeping normally, you, like everybody else, cycle through periods of REM and non-REM sleep.

"However, at exactly 11:35 p.m. last night, just as it seemed you were entering a deep stage of sleep, your active brain patterns suddenly shot up. At the same time, your deep sleep delta waves slipped into what can only be described as a coma. But within a few seconds, most of your brain was more active than someone taking a calculus test while running a marathon!"

John and Sarah listened but didn't quite follow the doctor's explanation. Tim occasionally glanced toward his parents but listened to Doc's explanation attentively.

"We also ran functional magnetic resonance imaging, fMRI, and electroencephalography, known as an EEG," Doc continued.

"In all of these tests we saw the same strange response when your brain should have been slowing down."

"Interestingly, the most intense activity during this phenomena occurred in parts of your brain that usually interpret the senses while you are awake; sight, hearing, touch, taste, and smell. These parts of your brain should not be active while in non-REM sleep, and I've never seen activity as intense as yours, even in patients who are awake. In addition, while the phenomenon continued, you were completely unresponsive to external stimulus. Needle pricks, loud sounds, bright light, nothing affected those brain patterns. Your brain seemed to be reacting to stimulus that was not coming from anything around you."

Clint suddenly chimed in. "It was like you were having an out of body experience!" Doc shot Clint a disapproving side glance but Clint continued.

"Really! Doc's looking for scientific explanations, but let's be real. You looked asleep, your body was in a coma, and your brain should have been dead. But instead of being dead, your mind was off fighting some dreamy-time dragon that you could actually see, feel, and touch, ya know? Then somehow, as you returned to your body, you fried the MRI machine and used it to create some kind of field that made me think it's time for a career change. You know, someplace nice and quiet where my patients don't create force fields and blow up the room!"

"Enough, Clint!" Doc bellowed and frowned. "Look, the truth is folks, we just don't know what is going on. I've never seen anything like it. I'd like to run . . ."

"No!" John shot back, stopping Doc mid sentence. "No more tests. Tim has been through enough. He is healthy and ready to go home. Right, Tim?" Tim was grateful to his dad and smiled unconsciously.

"Yes. I'm ready to go home."

"But there is so much more we need to understand," Doc jumped back in. "Tim is offering us the chance to delve deeper into the human mind than ever before. We just . . ."

"I said no! Tim is ready to come home, and that is my final word."

Sarah stayed silent. She was surprised by how forceful John was acting toward the doctor but wanted her son home just as much as he did. It had been a difficult two days for all of them. Only once before had she ever felt so scared for her son's life. Watching helplessly from the observation room brought back memories from her past that she wasn't prepared to deal with yet; memories she had thought were forgotten but that would haunt her again now.

Doc, frustrated at John's apparent lack of understanding, tried to change their minds. Didn't they realize how incredible their son was? He appealed directly to Tim but with no success. Finally giving up, knowing he couldn't hold them without breaking his promise of secrecy, he stormed out the doorway, trying to slam it hard. The door's shock absorbing piston caught and arrested the force, furthering his frustration.

Clint followed him. "I'll get the release papers ready," he said with uncharacteristic solemnity in his voice as he walked out the door.

Two hours later, the three were finally on their way home. The hospital had no reason to keep Tim there. And true to his word, Dr. Bruin didn't say anything about the tests to his peers, though it was going to be difficult for him to explain the damaged equipment in the lab. As a final resort, Doc had given John his card and offered to run more tests at no charge if they did ever reconsider.

"Dad?" Tim asked from the back seat of their car.

"Yes?" John answered, looking into the rear view mirror at him.

"Why is this happening to me?"

John was silent. He looked at Sarah who seemed lost in thoughts of her own. He pulled the car over into a CVS parking lot. It was early afternoon on a Sunday. The after church rush had started, and men and women in suits and dresses came in and out of the store with their kids. Had it been a normal Sunday, the Castons could have been doing the same thing.

Yet for them, it was not a normal Sunday. Today felt so different to John. He felt like his whole world had changed in the blink of an eye. How could he have missed something so huge in his son's life? What kind of father was he to have never known what his son was going through?

Realizing how selfish he was being, he decided to stop thinking about how his world had changed and focus on Tim. He parked in one of the open spots away from the front doors. Then, John opened the door and stepped out leaving the keys in the ignition, which caused the warning bell to begin chiming as if to say, "Hey, stupid, you forgot your keys!"

John opened the back door and crawled into the seat next to Tim, putting one arm around his son while he thought about what he should say. These melodramatic actions served two purposes. First, he wanted to show Tim his support and concern. But second, he was stalling; he had no clue how to answer Tim's question.

Finally, John sighed and said, "A lot has changed in the last forty-eight hours for your mom and me, Tim. But you have been bravely dealing with this your whole life. I feel like I've failed. I haven't taken care of you or paid enough attention." He paused again. The bell continued annoyingly.

"Dad, you haven't failed. I just didn't want anyone to know I was a freak."

"You are not a freak," he spoke decisively. "I don't know what this thing really is or why it is happening, but I believe there must be a reason. We need to figure that reason out, but we'll do it at your pace, not at the pace of some doctor trying to earn another PhD." He paused again and looked toward Sarah. She still seemed lost in thought. John turned back to Tim. "I guess, the real question is, what do you want to do?"

"I've been trying to figure out the rules," Tim responded.

"Rules?"

"Yeah. A long time ago, Lexie told me to figure out the rules. She said everything has rules, and if I could figure them out, I'd know how to deal with this. She thought there must be a reason I have this."

"Lexie was pretty smart, I think," John thought out loud.

"She tried to hypnotize me one time, but it didn't work. I was thinking we could try that. With a professional."

"You mean a psychologist? Maybe that's not a bad idea. Dr. Bruin was convinced that you're brain is active while you are out, so maybe there would be something to remember."

"Ding, ding, ding . . ." continued the car.

"What do you think, Sarah?" John asked, suddenly bringing Sarah's thoughts back to the present.

"I think you should have taken out the keys if you were going to leave the door open," she huffed. "Can we please talk about this on the way home so you can shut your door and stop that noise?"

John agreed that the alarm was rather annoying. He wondered if Sarah was still a little put off that Tim told him about the zone first.

"Right. Let's get home, get some sleep, and we'll figure out what to do in the morning."

John gave Tim another quick hug, crawled out of the backseat and back into the front. Before closing the door, he looked at Sarah playfully as the chime continued, hoping she wasn't angry. As he let it ding a little longer, her glare changed to a smile. She never could stay mad at him. He closed the door. "About time you closed it," was all she said as she punched his shoulder playfully.

All three sat silently for the rest of the ten-minute drive, deep in thought. John's mind raced through the last couple of days. He was glad to be taking his family home. He was determined to help Tim figure out what was going on.

Tim thought about the playful hypnosis he and Lexie had tried as kids. He had not given it a chance that day; instead he just made a joke of it. But Lexie, as usual, had been on to something. And just because it failed when he and Lexie were kids didn't mean it wouldn't work with an actual hypnotist.

Sarah thought first about how annoying the car's chiming had been. She also thought about Tim. It was true that she was a little upset that he had never come to her in all those years. They had a good relationship, and she had been a good mom.

But her thoughts also drifted back to the past. Ever since last night, she couldn't stop thinking about what had happened the day Tim was born. She couldn't help feeling that maybe she was partly to blame for what was happening to Tim now. Should she tell him about the day he was born? Even John did not know the true details of that day. He didn't know how close he had been to losing both his wife and son that day.

"Morning, Dad." Tim yawned the next morning when he found John sitting at the kitchen table circling names on a list. "Mom still asleep?"

The kitchen chair squeaked as John leaned back from his list. "Yep. You still want to try hypnosis? I have a list of some doctors nearby."

John had spent the night compiling a list of psychologists who performed hypnosis. He had spent hours on the Usenet searching dial-up servers for lists of doctors in their area. Unlike the Internet, which was still in its infancy and not used publically yet, John had to manually and tediously sift through dial-up text sites that contained nondescriptive lists of doctors.

"Yes," Tim answered without hesitation.

"Good." John pointed to the printed list on the table. "According to my Commodore, there are six doctors close enough for us to go to." John was really proud of his new computer but didn't tell Tim that it had taken hours to compile his list for Tim. "I don't really know who is best, but this one is pretty close to us."

"That's fine," Tim said looking at the name at which John pointed. "Can we go today? I don't really feel like going to school."

"I've already called my boss. Mr. Cain was very understanding and wishes you a speedy recovery. I called your school too. The attendance warden at your school was less sympathetic. She gave me a long lecture about the value of consistent attendance and the legal issues of truancy. She didn't seem to care about the accident or hospital stay. But I promised to have you back tomorrow with a doctor's note."

"Thanks, Dad. Glad I didn't have to talk to her. Although, I am eighteen, so it isn't like they can arrest me for skipping school."

John laughed. "I'll make the appointment then. You get cleaned up, dressed, and have some breakfast."

Chapter 15

HYPNOSIS

Monday Afternoon, March 12, 1990

"HAVE YOU EVER been hypnotized before, Tim?" asked the stern-looking psychologist in a slow, grating voice. She had been the only doctor on John's list with an appointment available at such short notice but seemed to be professional, even if a bit scary.

Tim told her about his attempt with Lexie years before and laughed nervously as he described how he pretended to have been hypnotized. The doctor looked on sternly, not finding any humor in children's games.

Half an hour later, Tim's parents watched from stiff-backed chairs at the side of the room as their son descended into true hypnosis. With her thick-rimmed reading glasses slipped out low on her nose and her gray hair tightly pulled back into a bun, Dr. Minden skillfully completed the initial process. Their son's eyes were closed, and he lay comfortably on the brown leather sofa.

"When I clap my hands twice," Dr. Minden began, "you will remain relaxed, calm, and ready to follow all of my suggestions. Do you understand?"

Tim nodded yes.

"Good," she said. "Now . . ." She straightened her back and then clapped sternly two times. Tim's eyes remained closed, and he seemed to relax further. He let his right leg slide off the sofa and put his left arm casually back behind his head.

"What are you thinking about right now, Tim?" Minden asked.

Tim spoke calmly and quietly, "Oh, I was just thinking about my parents. And about getting hypnotized. And about girls. I like to think about girls."

John laughed out loud. Minden threw a disapproving glance at him at the same moment Sarah jabbed him in the ribs with her elbow. John apologized silently but continued to smile.

Minden continued, "Tim, do you feel comfortable that your parents are here now?"

"Yeah, I like girls," Tim responded as if not hearing the question. "Especially pretty girls."

John and Sarah were both smiling now. John jokingly whispered to Sarah, "That's my boy!"

Minden's stoic frown deepened, and she decided to get to the point. "Tim, you will answer my questions as I ask them."

Tim seemed to shrug his shoulders. "Ok," he said.

"What happens to you at night, Tim?"

"I sleep, then I wake up, then I sleep again."

"Why do you wake up?" she coaxed.

"Don't know. It's no big deal. Everybody wakes up sometimes in the middle of the night. My friend Lexie used to wake up. She used to hear her parents fighting or her mom acting all weird and stuff. So she would wake up and come over to my room."

Sarah looked at John concerned and started to stand up as if she was going to question Tim. John pulled gently on her shoulder and shook his head slowly as if to say, "That's not important right now. Let her keep going."

The doctor continued her questioning. "We are talking about you, Tim. Why do you wake up at night?"

Tim's casual smile faded. "I said I don't know." He pulled his arm out from behind his head and started feeling the buttons on the leather sofa nervously.

"Tim, I want you to think back to last night. Think back to the time shortly after you went to bed. What was the last thing you thought about?"

"I was thinking about if it was a good idea to be hypnotized. I was afraid of what the doctor might find."

"What exactly are you afraid of?" Minden asked, more sympathetically than usual.

"What if something is wrong with me? What if I'm a freak?"

"No one here thinks that, Tim. Now tell me, what is the first thing you remember after falling asleep?"

"I was scared."

"Scared of what people would think?"

"No." Tim paused and seemed to be remembering something. "I . . . was lost. I was falling."

Minden probed further. "Tell me more about what you experienced."

Tim sat up suddenly. His eyes opened, but he didn't appear to be awake. "I can't see anything." He put his hands out in front of him and felt at the air. "I . . . wait, what is that? I'm falling! I'm falling!" Tim stood and then fell toward the end table, knocking a lamp off the table with his probing hands. The lamp crashed onto the floor.

"Tim, listen," Minden called with calm authority. "Stop." Tim obeyed and held suddenly still. "Sit back down." He felt for the sofa and found his seat in the middle. "You are calm and relaxed. You will answer my questions. You will remember back to last night, but you will not move from your seat. Do you understand?"

Tim nodded and said, "I understand."

"Skip forward a few minutes in your memory of your night. What are you doing now?"

"A man. He needs help. The mountain! This is bad, very, very bad."

"Who is this man? Is it your father? Where are you?"

"I don't know him, but he needs my help!" Tim said agitated. "I need to get to him."

"Why do you want to help him if you don't know him?"

"'Cause, that's just the right thing to do! When someone needs help, you help them!" Tim struggled to stand up again. The memory he was experiencing was intense but the doctor's suggestion to stay seated held him.

"An angel?" Tim continued while the doctor, Sarah, and John struggled to understand what he was experiencing. "No, not an angel." He struggled again against the invisible glue on his seat. "I can't hold on!" Tim yelled. He was fidgeting and shifting but still unable to break free from the bond between the sofa and his denim jeans. "Help me!" he screamed out.

"Tim, I want you to calm down again. Skip ahead a few more minutes and . . ."

"You have to hold on! I can't! It's too hard! No, no, no, no, no!" Tim jumped up off the sofa and then began running madly through the small office, knocking a plaque off Dr. Minden's wall and falling over her desk.

"Tim, Tim . . ." Dr. Minden quickly recognized that she had lost control. She clapped her hands twice as loudly as she could.

"Who is that? Who is that boy? Not Human," Tim yelled just before her claps stopped him in his tracks. His eyes, though still open, seemed unfocused and lost in his subconscious.

"Tim. Tim? We're still here, Tim. Clear your mind. Listen only to my voice. When I clap again, you will wake up, refreshed and relaxed. You will have a full memory of your dream but will not be afraid of it. It was just a dream."

Dr. Minden clapped her hands. Tim looked around. His mom, dad, and the psychologist were all staring at him with curious looks. The hypnosis had worked!

"I remember," Tim stated to himself in amazement.

"Tim, what do you remember?" the stern-looking Dr. Minden asked.

"I . . . I'm not sure," Tim stammered. He needed time to put it all together. It seemed clear to him now that he had just experienced a true vision from his zone. He wasn't sure how he knew that, but he did. The visions from past nights were also coming to him now. It was as if the hypnosis had unlocked some kind of vault of memories in his brain.

The flood of thoughts was overwhelming, but the memories from last night's zone were the most clear. He felt as if he had completely relived those thirty-eight minutes while sitting on the psychologist's couch. It was just a dream, he told himself. But was it a dream? How could he explain what he experienced?

"Just start at the beginning," Dr. Minden pressed. Tim wasn't ready. It was just too much to describe to all these people staring at him. Too much detail to just repeat.

"I can't," he answered.

"You were under hypnosis. While under, you described a mountain. Do you remember that?"

Tim didn't say anything.

"You also described a man you wanted to help and an angel."

"I can't!" Tim argued loudly.

"You can't remember, or you don't want to talk about it?" Minden frowned.

"I don't want to talk about it!" Tim screamed. He grabbed his jacket and walked out. He hadn't meant to yell, he just needed to be left alone. The memories were so intense, how could it have been just a dream. All he knew was that he needed time to sort it all out. He had just seen so much. And dream or not, what had happened was a nightmare. Now that he could remember last night's zone, he wanted to forget. But he couldn't forget what had happened.

Chapter 16

THE ZONE

ONCE HOME, TIM excused himself to his room. He lay down on his bed and closed his eyes. The images, sounds, and experiences from his zone filled his mind as he easily recalled what he saw while under hypnosis.

He remembered Dr. Minden slowly counting backward. The next thing he knew, his mom, dad, and the doctor were gone. Instead, complete darkness and silence surrounded him. He couldn't see, smell, hear, touch, or taste anything. His senses seemed to be turned off or completely separated from his mind. Then a pinpoint of light shot into existence ahead of him, or what seemed to be ahead of him. He wasn't sure if he could see the light, or was just experiencing it from inside his mind. Either way, the light grew brighter and larger.

Bits of shooting embers seemed to leap away from the now blinding light still growing in front of him. He tried to blink but couldn't find eyelids with which to blink. He tried to look away but had no eyes to turn. He could only stare at the light. Sudden flashes of radiance surrounded him, and the world around him seemed to fill with dim colors. The random colors, and then shapes, grew out of the central light which now engulfed most of his view.

Unidentifiable sounds began to fill his mind. First soft sounds like the rustling of tree leaves in a light breeze, then louder. He thought he felt something now too; it was the sensation of falling.

He was falling toward the light! He tried to scream but nothing happened. The colors and light continued to brighten, and the shapes began to look like objects. The random spectrum of the colors seemed to converge toward peaceful greens and blues.

Then Tim saw something more solid as it took form ahead of him. It moved toward him with incredible speed. The new solid outline grew from the center of the brightness and seemed to reflect the light from all the radiant sources around it. As the sensation of falling intensified, he realized he would strike the growing form, which now looked more like a flat island.

Tim yelled again, and this time he heard the sound of his cry initiate from somewhere in the distance. The sound did not materialize from where he believed his mouth should exist but instead seemed to echo from the solid surface ahead. He decided that it must be the Earth he was falling toward. It continued to grow ahead of him. There was no wind, but he believed he was falling through atmosphere now, faster than any skydiver, faster than sound or light.

The surface was still a blur when he seemed to slam into the Earth like a falling meteorite. There was no pain, but something was different. His mind blinked his eyes, and this time he felt eyelids. He understood that his body was with him now. His skin, his limbs, and organs all had caught up to him. With regained senses, he could feel the grass on his hands when he tried to move his fingers. Until now, he thought he was dead. Maybe he still was. He wondered how he would know.

Finally, Tim sat up in the grass and looked around. The sounds and visions he saw were far from normal. The trees were twitching back and forth quickly and unnaturally. When he looked up, the clouds were zipping from one end of the sky to the other. He noticed a road about two hundred feet from where he sat. Cars seemed to blur as they passed by with odd high-pitched squeals. "Where am I?" he thought.

Tim tried to stand up, but the odd motion of his surroundings made it difficult to find his balance. However, as soon as he was up and on both feet, he felt as if he had connected himself to this place. Time seemed to slow down to a normal pace. Or maybe his perception had sped up to match the surroundings. The trees were gently swaying, and the clouds were moving in a slow crawl across the sky. Occasionally, a car would pass, but now the sound of their engine and rubber on road seemed normal.

Tim thought again about where he was. "Hello?" he called out. His voice still had a distant quality. It seemed as if the sound was being echoed back to him instead of coming out of his mouth. He tried again, focusing his mind on his breath and lips. "Hello! Can anyone hear me?" This time the sound realigned as he spoke and moved from a distant echo to his own mouth. "That's better," he said out loud to affirm the change.

Tim looked around again and decided he was in some kind of forest. Tall straight pine trees surrounded him. The light from the sun filtered down through the needles and fell warmly on his face. The air smelled clear and fresh.

Tim walked down toward the road and looked in the direction where he thought he could hear a car. The road curved down a steep hill and had an almost vertical rock face next to it. "I'm on a mountain!" he thought.

The car he heard got louder as it finally rounded the bend and chugged up the steep hill toward him. Tim waved for the car to stop, but the driver must not have seen him. Another car passed moments later and also failed to acknowledge him. Tim looked at his hands and arms, half expecting to be invisible. But he was there; he could see himself just fine.

Deciding not to continue standing there any longer, Tim began hiking down the hill along the road. A couple more passing drivers still did not acknowledge Tim in any way. "How can they not see me?" he wondered. As he rounded the next bend, he looked up, amazed at the height of the sheer cliff to his left that towered above the two lane highway. It occurred to Tim that this was a particularly dangerous section of road. The pavement curved left around the sheer rock face. On the outside of the curve, the downhill traffic would have to stay close to the middle line to avoid a second sheer cliff just below the roadway.

Tim stepped over to the edge of the road. Looking in both directions from where he stood, he saw a shoulder. But here, the shoulder was gone. He walked further down the road where the shoulder reappeared and looked back up to the narrow part of the roadway.

"It's collapsing!" Tim said out loud. He could see boulders and debris several hundred feet below the road where it was clear that the rock had fallen out from beneath the pavement. A guardrail also lay mangled at the bottom of the cliff. He crawled down onto an overhang for a clearer view. A large hole had opened up under almost half of the outside lane, but the pavement was still intact.

He heard another vehicle approaching and looked back. A white and yellow Department of Transportation truck was racing up the hill toward the curve. The truck approached the bend too quickly, despite the warning signs indicating a tight turn ahead. The trucks tires squealed a little as the driver crossed into the other lane to widen his turn.

Tim tried to wave and yell at the approaching truck. Again, he was ignored, and the man driving the truck passed him. However, a moment later, the truck pulled over a few hundred feet up the hill, then backed up slowly toward the tight bend and stopped.

The driver stepped from his truck and stared at the eroding shoulder from across the road. He wore denim coveralls that strained to hold in his round midsection and had a short white beard and bald head. It was unclear at first if the driver had seen Tim or had recognized the problem under the road and stopped. Tim crawled back onto the roadway from where he had been investigating the collapse and walked quickly toward the driver.

"Sir, the road is collapsing!" Tim warned as he reached the man.

The old driver again ignored Tim and seemed to step around him as if unconsciously avoiding a pothole. Stopping a few feet from the edge, the DOT worker quickly surveyed the roadway with his eyes as he scratched at his beard. "Hmm . . . Should be a rail here I think," he mumbled to himself.

"Don't you hear me?" Tim yelled. "It's not just a missing rail. Look down. The rock has collapsed out from beneath the concrete!"

There was still no response from the old DOT worker. It was obvious now that the man somehow couldn't hear or see Tim.

The old man turned to walk back to his truck. Tim ran to him and grabbed his arm. "Stop," he yelled. The worker paused for a moment, but then walked on with only a light brush to his arm as if he had felt a fly land on him. Tim watched, dumbfounded, as the old worker got into the truck, closed the door, and put the still running vehicle back into drive.

Tim tried one last time to get the DOT worker's attention. He ran up alongside of the truck as it started pulling back onto the road. He began pounding as hard as he could on the window and door. Still nothing. The driver sped off leaving Tim standing alone again.

"Why does no one see me?" Tim thought. "Where am I?"

The lettering on the truck door he had been pounding on read, ARDOT.

"A, R, DOT," Tim thought. "AR. This must be Arkansas," he concluded, finally learning a little more about where he was.

A few minutes later, as Tim sat next to the road contemplating his situation, a large logging truck rumbled down the mountain toward the collapse. Tim heard it coming and decided he had to find a way to warn the large truck. Scrambling up the hill next to the inside part of the road, he found some tree limbs and dragged them down. He worked fast to arrange them along the outside of the curve to try to force the driver of the logging truck to slow down and hug the turn in the inside lane.

The truck arrived at the turn as Tim finished pulling the last limb into place. He had created a twenty-five foot long line of tree debris to guide vehicles toward the inner lane. As the truck approached, the driver saw the limbs and slowed down. He began to follow their line toward the inner lane, and Tim breathed a sign of relief.

However, Tim's reprieve was short-lived. A small, white two-door Honda appeared around the corner. It was quickly approaching the dangerous curve from below in the inner lane.

"No! Stop!" Tim called out to both drivers. He hadn't heard the small car over the sound of the large truck. The logging truck slowed more as he realized he was about to collide head on with the car. He turned and drove over the limbs to clear the car, his wheels dangerously close to the broken edge of the concrete.

Tim heard a loud pop and saw immediately that the concrete had fractured. A large slab lifted up slightly as the front tires of the truck passed over it. As the rear tires of the cab hit the slab, it gave way and fell into the cavity beneath the pavement. The truck had enough momentum to force the rear tires to slam into the roadway and skip out of the new hole. The two tires on the right rear of the cab exploded forcefully on impact as the jagged concrete pressed through the tires and into the rims.

The driver acted quickly to keep the cab steered around the curve, but the heavy trailer loaded with logs caused even more of the roadway to collapse into the hole. The wheels at the rear of the trailer fell into the hole and then slid to the side toward the drop-off.

Tim watched helplessly as the trailer tipped and fell off the side of the road, dragging the cab with it. The tires skidded across the roadway while the driver applied the breaks. Metal creaked and popped, and the hitch began to break. Tim hoped the trailer would simply break free of the cab and fall on its own. But the hitch held, and the trailer came to rest against some small pine trees that grew out from a ledge twenty feet below.

For the moment, time seemed to stand still. The cab sat flat on the edge of the roadway with the rear tires dangerously close to slipping back. The trailer was hanging almost vertically down against the cliff and small trees. The lone female driver of the white Honda car had pulled over to the shoulder a little way up the hill, close to where the DOT worker had stopped just a few minutes before.

Then, Tim saw something appear at the edge of the road near where the car had stopped. It was a boy, standing just inside the woods near the car. He looked to be about twelve years old and stood stiffly, watching the action. Had he been in the white car? Why had it seemed like he had just appeared there? He had no expression of fear, concern, or even interest in the dire situation in front of him. He just stood there with his arms straight at his sides.

The Honda driver, a middle-aged, heavyset woman with tightly curled hair, stepped out of the car and started to walk toward the logging truck. She didn't seem to notice the boy as she walked quickly toward the precariously suspended vehicle. "Get out of the truck!" she yelled toward the man still sitting in the cab. He seemed to be in shock. His hands tightly gripped the steering wheel and both feet pushed hard against the brakes. "Get out!" the woman yelled again, recognizing the unstable position his truck was in. He heard her and nodded but still seemed dazed. He threw open the cab door and twisted to the side, but then nothing happened. Something was wrong. He couldn't get out of the seat.

"It's stuck!" he screamed. "My seatbelt!"

Suddenly, the straps holding the logs to the trailer snapped. Now free, the logs began sliding off the trailer and falling to the bottom of the cliff. One of the logs rotated and struck the strongest of the trees that had been bearing most of the trailer's weight.

The truck driver struggled with the belt for another few seconds but then grabbed instinctively at the steering wheel again when the truck lurched backward. The trees growing out of the side of the cliff had done their best to support the trailer, but they were now cracking under the load and allowing the trailer to slip further.

The woman and Tim both ran toward the truck simultaneously. She stopped at the gaping hole in the pavement, but Tim found a way around it and jumped up onto the cab.

"I'm going to get you out!" Tim yelled at the man, still half-expecting him to hear his voice. The man only gripped the wheel harder. His knuckles were white. Tim reached over the man and grabbed at the seat belt. He quickly realized the release was stuck.

Metal creaked again, and the trees gave way completely. The trailer pulled backward on the cab. Tim pushed the release with both hands and finally heard it click. The driver let go of the steering wheel and pulled on the seat belt again. He was surprised that this time it came free!

Tim grabbed onto the man and jumped from the cab just as the truck went over the edge. Both men landed side by side on part of the broken roadway with their legs dangling over the edge. Tim was able to pull himself up onto the gravel covered concrete, but the trucker was slipping backward. As the truck below them fell to the bottom of the cliff over two hundred feet below, the man slipped further off the concrete with only his arms on the roadway.

Tim reached back toward the driver and yelled, "Grab my hand!" The man still didn't react to Tim and scrambled for traction with his fingers. Tim lay down, grabbed onto the man's hand and tried to pull him up. Looking at his hand where Tim was pulling it, the man cried quietly, "Help me."

Tim struggled to pull the man up, but his weight was too much. Gravel, sand, and sweat covered both their hands making it difficult and painful to hang on. The woman finally reached them and lay down on the pavement next to Tim. "Help me pull!" Tim yelled to her. She grabbed the man's fingers above where Tim held on.

"What should I do?" she called down to the trucker.

"Help the angel," he replied breathlessly.

"The what?" she yelled back. Then she felt something against her. She had lain down next to Tim on the roadway and grabbed the man's fingers without noticing Tim. But now, she felt the side of his body pushing into her own, and his arms intertwined with hers as they pulled on the man. She panicked and let go. The sudden shift in weight caused Tim's hands to slip. One of the man's hands slipped completely out before Tim regained his grip. The man was hanging freely now, held up only by Tim's invisible hands. Smoke was rising from below, and the stench of burning plastic and rubber filled the air.

Tim's fingers were growing weak. Sweat made it even more difficult to hang on. He sensed that the man was giving up. "Hang on!" Tim shouted. "Don't let go!"

"I'm sorry," the man whispered. Tim didn't know if the man was talking to himself or to Tim. The woman looked over the edge again just as the man let go. Together, Tim and the woman watched in stunned silence as the man fell silently to the rock and debris below.

Tim's hands and fingers were bleeding from the gravel. He suddenly felt dizzy and couldn't see the body down below anymore. His vision started to blur, and he tried to sit up but couldn't. He looked to his side and saw the boy again, still standing at the edge of the woods. The boy stared back blankly at Tim.

The colors around Tim faded. The sounds blurred together and then were gone. Darkness engulfed him. The zone had come to an end just as quickly as it had begun.

The next thing Tim remembered was waking up in the psychologist's office. Dr. Minden and his parents were staring at him, almost frightened. Broken glass and pieces of paper littered the floor of her office. What had they seen him do? What had he said while hypnotized?

He had not wanted to think or talk about what he had just witnessed in his mind. But now at home, safe in his own room, he couldn't stop thinking about what happened on the edge of that Arkansas mountain.

Chapter 17

WHAT IS REAL?

TIM OPENED HIS eyes and tried to clear his head. He was amazed at how vivid the vision or memory remained. But what kind of vision was it? Was it just a hallucination caused by the hypnosis, or was it really what he saw in his last zone?

Dr. Minden had told his parents after he stormed out of the office that she thought he may be suffering from too many medications. Those medications were causing intense dreams. When Sarah told her that Tim wasn't on any medications, Dr. Minden said that maybe he should be.

Could it have been just a dramatic dream? A lot of what he had seen made no sense. That's how dreams are, right? Like falling to the ground and not feeling pain. And no one, except for the trucker could hear him. He had thought Tim was an angel.

Tim winced as the memory of the man struck him again. His heart pounded as he remembered the man falling to his death. The blood and smoke was too real. He remembered it as if he had actually been there. He must have been there! How else could he remember such detail? It couldn't have been just a dream. It had to be real.

"But what is real?" Tim thought to himself. He left his room and walked into the living room. His parents were in the kitchen cooking supper together. It was hard to believe that only three days ago he had been anticipating his evening with Amy, and only a few hours ago that he had taken his first look into his zone. So much had changed.

Tim listened from the living room to his parents in the kitchen. He could hear them talking quietly. Only some of their hushed words reached him, "Tim . . . doctor . . . dreams . . . sick." He could tell they were worried about him. What was real? Their worry was real.

Tim looked around the room and then sat down. He could feel the soft fabric on the seat of the couch. He could feel the weight of his body pushing into the padding in the seat and back. That was real. He could feel the air blowing from the floor vent. That was real too. He put his feet down onto the floor and stood up. The feeling of balance and the rush of blood from his head because he stood up too fast, that was real.

In his zone, everything looked real, but no one could hear him. When he yelled, his voice echoed but never left his mouth. He could see the people, but they couldn't see him. That couldn't be real.

Tim looked out the window and saw his new neighbor, Larry, pulling up and parking in Lexie's old driveway. He and Maxine, his wife, had been renting the house for a few months and lived there with their two daughters, who were in the first and second grade.

Larry honked the horn pleasantly, and Maxine stood up from her spring garden. She greeted him with a smile and a wave and said something to him that Tim couldn't quite hear through the window glass. Larry echoed back a greeting and then turned as his daughters ran over to him from their tire swing. They laughed and told him of their day as they all walked to the house together.

Tim thought about their muffled voices through the window. Maybe that was like his "zone." He could see out the window and into his zone, but no one could see in unless they knew where to look. Maxine and Larry didn't see him because they weren't looking for him. They saw only the world immediately around them and were unaware of him watching from behind the glass. Was the zone like that? Was he like a voyeur peeking in on the world through a window?

"No," he thought as he remembered that he could interact with that world. He had had no problem walking around or moving the tree limbs. He had even held the man up, all two hundred or so pounds of him. And the woman had felt Tim next to her. That was why she had panicked and let go of him.

"I let go," he thought out loud again. "I let that man die. Somehow I should have held on longer."

"What man?" Sarah asked unexpectedly. Tim hadn't heard her step up behind him.

"What? Uh nothing," Tim responded, realizing he had thought out loud. "Is supper ready?" he asked changing the subject.

Sarah reached out and put her hands on her son's face. She thought about saying something but, in the end, put her hands back down and nodded yes about the supper.

He followed his mom back into the kitchen. She had warmed up a mix of leftovers, none of which really went together, but tasted good. She hadn't felt like cooking tonight.

No one talked all through supper other than an occasional "Please pass the salt" or "Is there any more gravy?" John and Sarah were lost in their own thoughts about Tim and the weekend they had just spent with him. Tim was still recounting the vision, sifting through the details.

After supper, Tim excused himself and noisily slid the chair across the linoleum. "I'm going to bed," he announced.

"Do you need anything?" Sarah asked and stood up to push his chair back in.

"No," Tim started. "I just want to rest. I'll be fine." He tried to give a half smile. Sarah and John looked at each other but didn't say anything. Tim walked down the hall to his room and closed the door behind him. "What's wrong with me?" he thought. "Why am I a freak? Why couldn't I just sleepwalk or grit my teeth like a normal person?"

He thought again about his memory that had been revealed by the hypnosis. Remembering the terrible moment when the man had fallen from his hands, he recalled seeing his own bloody, gravel-scratched hands.

"My hands!" he whispered excitedly. His hands had been a mess, but now they were fine. No scratches or cuts. No dried blood. No scarring. It was obvious that he hadn't really been there, so it must have been a dream. Yet it was so clear in his mind. Dreams are usually distorted and details fade away quickly.

He spotted his Magic 8 Ball toy on his shelf and grabbed it. "Magic 8 Ball, was I really there?" He flipped it over as he asked and then looked into the little answer window.

The tetrahedron inside floated and settled up against the window: "Difficult to say, ask again later."

Looking out his window, he saw Lexie's old house. Several lights were on, but Lexie's old room was dark. He wished she was there. She always had such good ideas and could make him feel better. He felt like such an idiot for letting their friendship dissolve like it had before she moved away.

"I wonder where she is now?" he thought.

Suddenly, a memory popped into his head. He remembered some past conversation with Lexie, but she was older. Much older in fact. He remembered her saying something about having a child and a husband. But how was that possible?

Then as suddenly as the first memory popped into his head, he had another image flow through his mind. He was standing in the middle of a park. He remembered a little boy playing with a red ball. The boy seemed to be about his own age, so he wanted to play too. He looked around to ask his mom if he could play with the boy, but she wasn't there. He didn't recognize the park, and he remembered feeling afraid and lost. He started calling for her, but his voice sounded strange.

Tim saw a mother with a baby stroller walk by, so he went to ask her to help him find his mommy. But the mother didn't stop for him. She acted like he wasn't even there. He gave up and went to play with the boy and his ball. He too ignored Tim. Tim remembered sitting down in the grass and crying. He had been just a little boy, and he had been all alone.

Tim shivered as the memory of the emotion faded. He didn't think he had actually been lost in a park even though the memory seemed real. Getting up off his bed, Tim walked back out of his room and found his parents still in the kitchen.

"Mom, have I ever been lost?" Tim asked directly, startling Sarah who hadn't seen him walk in.

"Um, no. I don't think so," his mom finally said. Then she added, "There was one time that we were in the grocery store and you had walked over to the next aisle. I panicked for a moment but found you pretty fast. I think you were three."

"What about at a park when I was four or five?"

"No. You know me. I wouldn't have let you out of my sight."

"What's this all about, Tim?" John asked, unable to make the connection with all that had been going on.

"Don't know," Tim replied. "Just remembering a dream, I guess. I'm going to bed now. Good night."

"G'night," John and Sarah said in unison as they looked from Tim to each other, shaking their heads in confusion.

Chapter 18

MESSING WITH CHONG

AS TIM WASHED his face and brushed his teeth, more memories materialized in his head. All seemed vague and confused, and most blended together indistinctly. Only some stood out apart from the noise he now felt in his thoughts. He remembered places that he had never been and faces of people he didn't know.

Tim went back to his bed and closed his eyes. His mind continued to swim in the flowing river of memories. As he lay there trying unsuccessfully to go to sleep, he thought about what the hypnosis had done. These random memories were not from his life but from his zone. The hypnosis had not only helped him remember the zone from the previous night but opened him up to every night.

An excitement welled up through him that was mixed with fear. Would he remember tonight's zone after he woke up? What would happen? He knew he could learn much more if he could remember them, but did he want to remember? Watching a man fall to his death was not something he wanted to experience again.

Tim tossed and turned for almost two hours before finally falling asleep. When he did, it was 11:15 p.m.

Only twenty minutes later, Tim awoke in darkness. He tried to open his eyes and realized they were already open. At least his brain told him they were open. His mind instructed his arms to reach out in front of him, but he felt nothing. Not just an absence of something to touch but an absence of arms to move. There was nothing to touch and nothing to touch with. He felt completely separated from his body.

There were no smells or sounds either. "This is the zone!" he thought. He wondered how long this darkness and silence would last. Then a light appeared ahead of him as if it had been waiting for him. The fearful excitement he had wrestled with before falling asleep returned to him. What if he turned away from the light? He tried turning in another direction but nothing happened. He didn't know if that meant the light moved to stay ahead of him, or if it was just impossible to move when no body seemed to exist.

The center light grew toward him quickly, and he saw tiny sparks shooting in all directions from the source, just like he remembered from the hypnosis. What he hadn't noticed before was that each of those tiny sparks floated away from the original source and then exploded into more light all around him. Flashes of color began flowing from each discharge of energy, and a picture of his surroundings began to form. The source light had grown to cover his full forward view, and the sparks were quickly filling in the peripheral views; up, down, and to the sides. Somehow, he could even see the light and color filling in behind him.

As his mind began to interpret the perception of sound again, he heard a soft hissing, like wind through a tunnel. Next the awareness of falling overwhelmed his other senses, and he tried to brace himself for the impact that he remembered from his previous zone. However, just as before, there was no sensation to the impact.

The blurred colors and shapes all around him had made it seem as if he was moving toward the ground with tremendous speed and force. But the abrupt termination of that fall not only failed to kill him, but also was a welcome end to the descent as his body smashed softly into the ground.

The lackluster crash also seemed to serve the purpose of letting his body catch up to him. An infinitesimal moment after stopping, he felt his arms, legs, and body again. He seemed to be lying on his back and could feel rock beneath him. The sounds around him were loud and distorted, and he wasn't sure what he was looking at.

Dark colors and shapes zipped past him, and thick or humid air was pushed around him by those blurred objects. He looked up and saw huge skyscrapers towering over him. They seemed to jitter like they were vibrating from some unseen mallet striking them. Looking past the buildings, he saw clouds racing through a bluish-gray sky.

Then, Tim remembered that he needed to stand up for the world to slow down around him. He got to his feet, and he felt himself connect with the ground and the city around him. He realized that the rock he had thought he was lying on was actually a sidewalk. The blurs slowed down and became crowds of people hurrying all around him.

At first, Tim thought the people could see him. They seemed to be shifting their course as they walked to avoid running into him. However, due to the massive crowds, some of the people couldn't move completely out of the way. They would lightly brush up against him or occasionally bump into him. Still, they gave no indication that they noticed his presence.

Another observation that Tim made was that everyone who passed him appeared to be of Asian descent. He also observed that there were very few women in this flowing stream of professional Asian men. Large signs and billboards marked the front of buildings, advertising various goods and services. Most of the writing was impossible for him to read, but occasionally, he would see smaller English print or a familiar logo. Where was he? Was this some large Chinese metropolis?

Tim also wondered why he was there. In his previous zone, he had just wandered toward the road. Had he somehow been guided to walk along the mountain road just before that terrible accident? Was he about to watch someone in this crowd die too?

He felt no force of direction acting upon him. Nothing to push him in one direction or another. So he waited and continued to observe as the river of men flowed smoothly around him. It was clear that they did not see him, so why did they not smash into him? How did they so automatically move to avoid him like he was a lamp post or other obstacle in their path?

It occurred to him that all these people must be able to sense him somehow. They couldn't see, hear, or feel him, but they still adjusted their course around him? He remembered the highway worker on the mountain. Tim had grabbed his arm tightly to try to keep him from leaving. The man had noticed Tim's touch, but then brushed his arm off as if some small bug had landed there. So that meant he had been wrong. They could in fact feel him, at least slightly. Maybe in this thick crowd, they just ignored his presence like that of a tiny inconspicuous bug.

Maybe people had a sixth sense. He had heard scientists speculate on such things but never thought there was proof. Maybe that sixth sense here allowed these people to somehow perceive his position but not enough to care.

Tim decided he was tired of just standing there. Moving in the same direction as the crown passing him, he began walking. As he moved along with them, they continued to avoid the space he occupied.

Feeling a little braver after a minute or so, Tim took a large step sideways instead of moving with the crowd direction. A man stopped in his tracks to avoid running into Tim causing the man behind him to run into his back with a briefcase. Forgetting why he had stopped in the first place, the man in front shoved the man in back for hitting him with the case and then continued on his way around Tim.

Tim tried it again several times. Each time the result was the same. To an observer above, Tim's presence would have looked like a person-sized hole in the thick crowd that held its shape as it darted left and right, forward, and backward through the people. Those pedestrians closest to the hole had looks of confusion as they struggled to avoid running into something that wasn't there.

Losing interest in the game, Tim stepped out of the crowded streets and into the entrance of a small restaurant with a red sign above the door that he couldn't read. He grabbed at the door handle and easily pulled the door open. How could he be barely detectable to the people of this place, yet still have a presence that was physical enough to interact with inanimate objects?

It suddenly occurred to him that the door must have appeared to magically open by itself to the patrons eating their lunch inside. However, as he looked around, no one seemed to notice the magic door. Conversations continued casually in a language he couldn't understand as waitresses busily brought food to tables.

Tim let the door close behind him with a slight tap as the metal latch linked back up with the metal frame. Unable to resist testing the situation further, Tim pushed the door open again. This time, instead of letting it close slowly, he pulled it hard, causing it to slam. Still nothing from the hungry patrons. Grabbing the door, Tim forced it to repeatedly slam.

"Bam, bam, bam, bam."

An older man, probably in his late fifties, was eating alone at the table nearest the door. He paused as he brought the chopsticks up to his mouth and turned his head to look at the door. Giving a slight expression of wonder, he turned his head back toward his plate and finished delivering a long noodle to his mouth.

"So weird!" thought Tim. No one could see him, yet they moved to avoid him. He could move physical objects, but no one seemed to care. The door slam had been loud enough for anyone in the room to hear, but they all ignored it—except for the man nearest the door. Why had he reacted? His reaction was only slight, but it was a reaction nonetheless.

Tim pulled out the chair across from the man. The chair slid smoothly on the tile floor, but the man didn't seem to notice.

"Hey, Chong!" Tim shouted, thinking of the first stereotypical Chinese name he could think of. "I am here! Do you hear me?" There was no answer as Chong continued to eat. "Hello! Did you see the door move? That was me," Tim shouted again.

He found it strangely amusing to be yelling at some strange man he was calling Chong while in a strange foreign country. For all he knew, Chong probably couldn't understand English even if he could hear Tim. "You saw the door slam, right? Did you wonder what was going on?" Chong still ignored him completely and continued slowly eating his food.

Giving up, Tim started to look around. None of this made sense. Why was he here? How long had he been here? Would he just evaporate back into his bed in a few more minutes?

Less amused and now more frustrated at his inability to get any reaction from old Chong, Tim got up. As he did, he let his fist pound the table once. Chong stopped eating and put his hands onto the table on either side of the large bowl. "You felt it!" Tim exclaimed. He hit the table again, this time harder. The man reacted again. His eyes opened wider, and he held his arms stiff against the table.

Tim leaned over the man and took his chop sticks gently from his hand. Strangely, Chong didn't seem to notice this and continued to focus on the table. Tim dangled the sticks in front of Chong. No response.

"You felt the table vibrate, but now you can't see chopsticks that you yourself were using just a little while ago? This is crazy!" Tim said to Chong only a few inches from his ear. "I give up," he said exasperated and dropped the sticks onto the table.

Chong did notice this time! He muttered something Tim didn't understand and stared at the chopsticks. "You see them now!" Tim grabbed the sticks and held them up in front of Chong. Chong recoiled back in his chair, falling against a decorated wooden support post behind him. The post kept the chair from falling all the way back, but Chong slid out of it to the side anyway, keeping his eyes glued to the sticks as he did. Tim watched Chong stand up and take a large step back from the floating sticks.

The other patrons were now staring at the man who had just jumped up from the table while almost dumping the chair onto the floor. Tim looked around and then waved the sticks high in the air. Chong continued to watch the possessed sticks, but no one else saw them. Their eyes were on Chong.

Seeing the humor again in the situation, Tim threw the sticks at Chong, who began screaming as he shielded his face even though the sticks hit him in the chest. Screaming Chong ran to the door and crashed into it causing him to recoil backward. Still screaming, he pushed on the nonhinged side of the door and ran out of the restaurant.

Realizing that he had probably just sent Chong to a therapist, Tim felt a little bad. He followed Chong out the door but quickly lost him in the crowd. Having no idea of what to do next, he walked slowly back toward the restaurant.

As he neared the door again, the crowd suddenly pushed toward him and then broke apart like a bubble expanding and then bursting. Tim started to step into the opening but stopped when he saw a man struggling on the ground as three boys pulled at him viciously. The man wasn't Asian. Then Tim saw the man's face more clearly. "Dad?" Tim asked.

No, the man was too old to be his dad. But the resemblance was amazing. Tim watched for only a moment as the boys pinned him down. He saw that the man was in trouble and, without further hesitation, ran into the gap in the crowd.

He yelled at the boys, "Get off him!"

All three boys stopped pulling on the man and looked up. Tim saw that the three were identical. The same hair, face, body, and even clothes. He had seen them before! It was the boy—the same boy he remembered from his zone in the mountains. The boy that had watched from the woods as he desperately tried to save the logging truck driver.

As the boy closest to Tim looked up and saw him, his little mouth instantly shot open. The movement was unlike anything Tim had ever seen. The mouth stretched farther than humanly possible as if its jaw was completely separate from the skull. Then in the same instant, it let out a terrifying screech that caused Tim to reflexively cover his ears. The other two boys let go of the man and started toward Tim.

Tim turned in fear and was ready to run, but he looked back one more time, trying to understand what was happening. The man was trying to get up but was forced back down by the remaining boy. He fought one last time out of the boy's grip and turned toward Tim. "Remember this place!" he yelled. "Find yourself here when you return! Nothing is impossible!"

The screeching boy forced the man down against the concrete without touching him. From the ground, the man managed to yell one more word. "Run!"

Tim obeyed and ran into the crowd just as the two boys reached him. He pushed through as fast and hard as he could. He was moving too fast for the crowd around him to subconsciously clear a path. Instead, he had to bump and push through them. Many stopped and turned in reaction to Tim's forceful pushes creating turbulence in the usual flow of the crowd.

Tim looked back. Would the confusion slow down his pursuers? He hadn't actually seen them run after him, he just knew they had moved toward him somehow. But now as he looked, he saw nothing but the crowd behind him.

The people in front of Tim seemed to be slowing down, and he had to work harder to get through them. He looked forward and saw that he was getting close to an intersection where the crowd ahead waited patiently for the light to change. Tim continued to push and force his way through the people, just as the man had told him.

Turning to look back over his shoulder again, Tim misjudged the distance to the intersection. He stumbled off the curb and fell hard onto the ground. A car seemed to fly over him or through him—he wasn't sure. Then another car, followed by a truck. He didn't feel any pain but noticed the sound of the people and traffic dimming. Then the colors began dissolving around him, and just as blackness fell over his eyes, he saw the boys again, standing motionless over him.

Moments later, Tim awoke in his bed. His eyes hurt, but he didn't notice. He used his hands to feel all over his body. He wasn't injured. Those boys had caught up to him but hadn't touched him. Had they kept the cars from hitting him? Or were they just about to capture him like they had the other man? He wasn't sure. What would have happened if he had stayed long enough for them to get to him? Would they have killed him? Was it possible for him to die there in the zone?

Tim had so many unanswered questions. He still wondered if it was real or not. He knew what a dream felt like, and this hadn't felt like a dream. It seemed so real. It just didn't seem possible. How could a person travel to the opposite side of the earth, be invisible like a ghost, be chased by alien boys who looked like triplets, and then return to good ol' Oklahoma, all in thirty-eight minutes.

"Rules!" he blurted out loud to himself as he jumped off the bed and scrambled through his desk for paper and a pencil. For the next forty-five minutes, he wrote down everything he could think of that described what he saw, felt, and experienced. He also listed the things he could do and could not do. It was a very disorganized list but filled almost ten notebook pages.

Some of the most interesting scribbles included:

> *No one can hear me, see me, or touch me, but somehow they try to avoid bumping into me.*
>
> *I can make them feel me if I really push hard, but they don't seem to know what it is.*
>
> *People ignore things I've moved unless that thing already has their attention. If they are looking right at something, then they do notice if I do stuff.*
>
> *I have to stand up after I arrive to attach myself to that place and time. Otherwise, I don't think I'm really there yet.*
>
> *When I see people I know here, maybe it is because I saw them in my zone. That must mean that I travel to nearby places too and not just far away.*
>
> *There are scary boys in the zone. They are either triplets or the same boy several times. I don't know how that could be, but I don't think he, or it, is human.*
>
> *The boys can see me.*
>
> *They don't seem to want me there. That one screamed like nothing I've ever heard. Maybe he didn't want me to interfere. I think I'll call them 'screamers.'*
>
> *I saw one of the screamers in the Arkansas mountain zone, too. Why was he there?*
>
> *There was a man who could see me too. He seemed to recognize me and told me to 'remember that place and find myself when I come back.' That must mean I will return there. Not sure what he meant by 'find myself.'*
>
> *The screamers didn't want him to talk to me.*

Tim wasn't sure how many of these notes were really unchangeable rules. Maybe the rules changed each time. Maybe the things he wrote down were observations specific to that night's zone. Still, it was a start. He decided that each night, he would take more notes. Observations that were consistent night after night, he would use to better define his zone state.

He wondered if the screamers would always be there. They had been in both zones of the last two nights. In the mountains, that screamer seemed harmless. It just stood there watching. But the ones he had just seen terrified him! He wondered how often he had run from them before. Maybe he had run every night of his life. He couldn't remember. Surely he would remember something as terrifying as that scream! He hoped to never see them again!

The rest of the zone hadn't been too bad. It had even been a little fun. He could mess with people with no ramifications! Although if it was real, then maybe there *would* be ramifications. He needed to figure that out. If it was just a mental state, then he could ignore the screamers and have fun. If they caught him, so what? He'd just wake up safe and sound in his bed, right? But if it was real, could they hurt him? So many questions. So few answers.

Chapter 19

QUEST FOR NORMALCY

THAT NEXT MORNING, Tim woke up to the sound of the school bus. It was the elementary bus—the same bus in fact that he and Lexie had ridden when they were young. The brakes squeaked loudly and then hissed as the pneumatic air forced the brake pads closed to stop the heavy, yellow machine.

Tim watched through his window as Larry and Maxine's daughters happily ran up the long driveway toward the bus, just in time to meet it. He continued to watch as the bus slowly released the brakes and then continued on its route. A minute later, he saw Larry blow a kiss to his wife as he hopped down the porch stairs toward his car. Their family always looked happy and so full of life.

The look of his own parents when he saw them a few minutes later was the complete opposite. It was clear that they had been up most of the night, unable to sleep. Lines of worry and stress marred their features. Had they sat there in the living room all night? He wasn't sure. All he knew was that he was the cause of their worry. All his life, he had sheltered them from his zone. They had been a normal, happy family.

Now, without warning, he had messed that up. He knew his parents and knew how this new component of his life would affect them if he didn't somehow stop it. His mom would be constantly lost in her own thoughts. Maybe she would even blame herself somehow. John would launch himself at full speed toward a mental breakdown until he solved Tim's problem. He would consult books and medical journals, and when not reading, he would be pacing back and forth, all in a futile effort to solve Tim's mystery. But Tim could feel that this mystery was his to solve, not his parents. He needed to set things right again.

"Morning Mom, Dad," Tim said as cheerfully as possible as he entered the living room. Both seemed a little startled and sat up straighter on the couch.

"Hey, son," John replied. "How'd you sleep?"

"Better than you, I think. Actually, I slept really well. I think the hypnosis helped me a lot."

His mom and dad gaped at him. Then John said, "Really? What do you mean?"

"You know, I just feel better. I slept really well. I woke up after midnight when I usually do, but who cares. It's not that big of a deal. I'm used to it."

John started to speak, but Tim continued. "Guess I forgot to set my alarm though. I'm late for school. I'd better get ready." Without giving them a chance to respond, he walked back to his room.

Days went by. Tim successfully convinced his parents that there was nothing to worry about. Sarah was happy to drop the subject of Tim's zone. John tried to bring it up for a few days, but in the end, he could see that Tim wanted to let it go. Life went on, and their happy family returned to normal.

For Tim, normal meant his zones continued each night. Only now, he remembered them all. He was relieved not to have seen the screamers since they had chased him in Chinaland. Each night at 12:13 a.m., he would take out his notebook and add to his notes and rules. He got into the habit of naming the zone and giving a short summary so he could go back through them quickly.

Zone 3: March 14, 1990: "Kansas Field." Grassland. Didn't see any people but found an old car with Kansas plates. Nothing interesting. No screamer.

Day 4: March 15, 1990: "Camel Fun." Maybe I was in the Middle East. It was very hot and dry. A camel spit on me. No people. No screamer.

Day 5: March 16, 1990: "Raining in Oklahoma." Sign said, 132 miles to Oklahoma City. A few cars and trucks passed by, but I couldn't make anyone stop. Sky was green, good tornado weather but didn't see one. No screamer.

By day thirteen, life had returned to normal. Tim's mom and dad acted like nothing had even happened a couple weeks earlier. He was still car-less for the time being, but Jimmy, one of his friends and coworkers at the carwash, was picking him up for school in the morning and bringing him home after their shift at work was over.

The manager at the carwash, Steve, was only two years older than Tim. He was a college flunk-out with a pimply face and lopsided hair. When Tim requested that his shifts match up with Jimmy's so he would have transportation to and from work, Pimply Steve gave Tim a hard time and at first refused. In the end, he gave in to Tim's request after the owner, Mr. Suddo, reminded him that Tim was one of their most hardworking staff.

Tim hadn't yet spoken with Amy about their last evening together or what happened to him on his way home. He saw her a few times in the hallways, but she was always surrounded by her gaggle of girlfriends. When their eyes met, she'd give him a confused look filled with both anger and doubt.

Tim wondered if the awkwardness between them was due to his guilt for yelling at her, her guilt for tricking him, or just their mutual, uneasy reflection on what happened between them that night. He didn't know what to say to her, so for the time being, he just wouldn't say anything.

Despite the uncertainty in his and Amy's relationship status, Tim felt great. He found himself able to concentrate better than he had in months. This new part of his mind that had opened up to his zones seemed to also help him focus and observe. Just like his new habit of taking notes each night after his zone, he also took mental notes of his surroundings during the day, and reflected on all he had heard and seen. Unlike most eighteen-year-old seniors, he wasn't focused on impressing others and showing off. He simply wanted to understand all that was happening to himself and to those around him.

For example, why did Susan let Brad, her on again, off again jerk boyfriend, push her against her locker when he got angry with her? Why didn't she break up with him? He saw her crying several times in History. She would lie to the teacher and act like nothing was wrong.

Why did Mr. Jamison and Miss Connors try to hide their secret romance? Tim thought it was obvious that they were in love, although no other student at school had figured it out yet. He could read it in the way they looked at each other across the senior hallway from their separate classrooms.

Why did so many of his fellow seniors seem satisfied with staying near Tulsa the rest of their lives? They had no desire to see more of the world. Didn't they know there was a huge variety of sights and experiences to be had outside of Oklahoma?

Being able to remember his nightly trips around the world was an adventure to Tim. Each night, he got to explore part of a new state or country. He couldn't tell anyone about his experiences, but he was gaining a new hunger to see more of that world.

So far, there really wasn't much to tell of his nightly escapades. Except for the nightmare on the Arkansas mountain and then the screamers chasing him in China, most of his zones were relatively calm. Mostly, he simply explored quiet places and landscapes on his own. He enjoyed seeing parts of the world he knew he may never have seen otherwise.

One interesting observation he made was regarding his zone attire; or lack thereof. Tim found that his clothing in the zone was limited to what he wore to bed. If he slept only in his underwear, as had been his usual practice, he would arrive in his zone clad only in those same briefs.

As an experiment, on the sixth day after his hypnosis, Tim wore his best church pants and sport coat to bed. Sure enough, he was dressed in that same outfit upon his arrival at a swine ranch in Wyoming. He felt a little over-dressed compared with the pigs.

He worried when one of the pigs passed by him too closely and smeared foul-smelling mud onto his pants. His shoes too were covered in the waste-filled muck. However, when he awoke a few minutes later in his bed, his shoes and pants were as clean as a teenaged boy's clothes could be expected.

From then on, he went to bed wearing comfortable clothes and sometimes even shoes. No one could see him in his zones, but it still seemed wrong to be wondering around the world dressed only in underwear.

The fact that he and his clothes returned at 12:13 each morning, unmarred from his journeys, confirmed to Tim that his trips to faraway places were just dreams, despite the realism of them all. Or if they were real, then he and his clothes weren't really arriving in a new place physically. He was just there in spirit or some other less complete way. Regardless, he was enjoying the adventure.

Chapter 20

ALAINA'S KISS

ON DAYS HE wasn't working, Tim would walk the two miles to the library and dig through travel books. He wanted to figure out if the places he had been were real places. He wanted to believe that he was seeing real people and events, but the impossibility of it all made that difficult to accept.

He continued his nightly entries into his zone notebook.

Zone 7: *March 18, 1990: "Australia!" Didn't see any koala bears, but did see a kangaroo and lots of sheep.*

Zone 8: *March 19, 1990: "Subway Boy in NY." Saw toddler boy fall onto tracks in subway station. Parents didn't see him fall and were looking for him in wrong direction. I lifted him back up onto the platform before a train came. No one seemed to notice.*

Zone 9: *March 20, 1990: "Deserted town in California." No people at all in this town. Need to research intersection of Pine and Hillsdale to see if it was a real town.*

Zone 10: *March 21, 1990: "Stop, Thief!" Jumped in front of a purse thief. He was confused when I kept moving in front of him. This caused him to hesitate long enough for a witness to grab him. Seemed like a big city but I didn't recognize the language. Maybe Russian?*

Zone 11: March 22, 1990: "African Mountain." Not sure if it was really Africa. No people, but heard the sounds of a lot of animals; monkeys, elephants, other weird sounds! Found the most beautiful waterfall I've ever seen!

Zone 12: March 23, 1990: "Miss Daisy." Small looking Northern US or maybe a Canadian town, judging by the accents. Found a diamond on the ground near where an old lady was upset. It looked like the diamond had fallen out of her wedding ring. She couldn't see the diamond when I held it up in front of her, but when I set it next to her as she looked around, she found it.

Zone 13: March 24, 1990: "Alaina." Scotty's Pub. In Scotland I think. Tried some new things on some people. Same results. They couldn't see me and didn't know I was there—except for Alaina.

Zone 13 was the first time since China that Tim tried hard to interact directly with people to see if they'd notice him. He hadn't had a chance to try to talk to the boy on the tracks in Zone 8. After he had lifted him back onto the platform, his parents had whisked him off too quickly as they were entering the same train that would have run him over.

In the case of the purse thief, and the old lady's diamond, he simply hadn't tried to make his presence known since he was more focused on observation. Tim felt good when he was helping people, even if they didn't recognize that he was there, and even though he wasn't sure if it was real or just a vivid dream.

Dream or not, in zone 13, Tim stood up after his arrival into the zone to find himself at a pub in what he assumed to be Scotland, judging by the occasional kilts and thick Nordic accents. He was excited to see people. He felt somehow that the zones were more real if people were around. Standing next to the waterfall in Africa in zone 11 was beautiful, but that seemed more dreamlike than when he could try to interact with others.

Tim watched as men and woman of all ages poured into the pub in celebration. It was clear that they were excited about some great Rugby victory between the Warriors and Scarlets. This Scarlet-bashing crowd was so excited, he found he couldn't get anyone's attention, even when he stomped on one man's foot and pulled on a woman's long hair. Nothing. They were too wrapped up in their celebration to notice a curious ghost who didn't know why he was there.

Tim looked around to see if there was anyone who needed help from an invisible man. Groups of men and woman excitedly recounted the events of the game with waving arms and animated expressions. Two waitresses busily steered through the crowd trying to deliver food and drinks to the patrons who were not crowding up to the bar.

Tim wandered around through the crowd like he had in China and found the same effect as before. The people would subconsciously move out of his way like they were avoiding an unseen obstacle. If he stood still, and they were approaching him, they almost always moved around him without touching him at all. However, if he were the one moving and they were sitting or standing still, he would have to push them a little to get them to move out of his way.

It reminded him of the way magnets can repel each other with their invisible force. At slow speeds, their repulsion is enough to keep them apart, but force them together quickly and they will bump.

Tim wondered what other kinds of influence he had in this world. Since he saw no opportunities for heroics in the festive crowd, he decided to experiment. Could he make them hear him? Could he make them see him? Did he want them to see him?

The shorter of the two waitresses quickly and carefully edged past three young men dressed in Warriors' blue and gray. She turned toward a table, just past where Tim was standing, with a tray of beer mugs and a large pitcher. Feeling a little mischievous, Tim stuck his foot out in front of her just as she subconsciously moved to avoid him.

The short waitress must have felt something as her ankle connected with Tim's foot, because she looked down suddenly and tried to step over the invisible appendage. Her reaction wasn't fast enough, however, and her foot caught right under Tim's calf. Although she righted herself quickly, the pitcher tipped onto its side, and two of the large frozen mugs fell from the tray. Both mugs broke as they struck the wooden floor, and the pitcher poured all of its contents out, into the lap of a man named Carl. Tim learned Carl's name as soon as the spilling ceased and the waitress, apparently named Kelley, yelled at him for tripping her.

"Hey, Carl, you blubbering idiot. Whad'ya playing at, tripping me?" she yelled.

"I wouldn't a trip ye lassie? And why ya yell'n at me Kelley, I'm the one with a lapful of Ale!" Carl argued back through an amused grin.

Tim suddenly felt guilty about what he had done but was glad to see Carl's jovial smirk. It appeared that the man was a regular at the pub and although surprised by the downpour of liquids onto his chest and pants, he seemed to retain his cheery mood.

As Kelley wiped up some of the mess with a towel, Tim pushed back out into the crowd. Noticing a very attractive girl standing among a group of young men, he decided to try an even bolder experiment. The young woman stood at the apex of the semicircle formed by the attentive men.

Tim approached the group and wedged himself into a small space next to the girl. They were discussing the game, just like everyone else in the pub, and did not notice Tim's intrusion.

Tim learned that the girl's name was Alaina from the man on her right when he said, "Alaina completely missed that goal! She was too busy messing with her hair!" The group laughed and Alaina smiled, taking it as a compliment anytime someone mentioned her hair.

She looked to be about twenty-two, Tim thought. A little older than him and at the prime of her life. The men in her fan club standing around her were probably similar in age. Maybe they were college students from some nearby university.

Six men in all had formed the half circle around Alaina. Two were short and round; three were tall, lean and good looking; and one looked like he had been on steroids since birth.

Alaina had long straight blonde hair that fell over her shoulders. Her eyes were a stunning blue and at just the right distance apart. Her light complexion was flawless. She wore a short jean skirt and tight Warriors jersey, which accented her long narrow legs and firm, high bust. There was no doubt that she both encouraged and relished the attention that was being bestowed upon her.

Tim listened to her speak. Her words were delivered with an almost stereotypical Scottish accent. He realized as he listened and watched that he was just as drawn to her voice and beauty as these other men, but he also knew that in real life, this girl wouldn't give him a second look.

"She wouldn't even know I was alive," Tim laughed to himself. "Let's see if she notices me as a ghost."

Tim stepped in closer to Alaina. So close, that it almost seemed like the men were looking and talking to him. He ignored them and ignored the conversation. He could smell the subtle scent of her body and wanted to touch her soft skin.

Tim whispered into Alaina's left ear. "Alaina," he said softly. "My name is Tim. Do you hear me?" No response. He put his hand onto her smooth cheek to see if she would notice his touch. Nothing. Then he waved his hand in front of her face. Still nothing.

Tim moved over and stood directly in front of Alaina and looked into her eyes. She went on laughing and talking. Because of his proximity to her, it looked at times like she was talking to him, but then she'd turn her head a little and talk in a different direction making it clear that she was just looking through him.

He looked at the features of her face; her small nose, long eyelashes, her perfect mouth with a hint of red lipstick. He was only six or so inches from her face and could see the clean pores and tiny wisps of hair of her skin. It felt strange standing so close to a girl he didn't know and to be able to examine her with such scrutiny. He felt a sense of complete freedom. He could do whatever he wanted.

The autonomy of this situation gave Tim a sudden feeling of power that led him to touch her again. He ran his hand gently down her face from temple to chin across her cheek. He lightly felt her lips as they opened and closed when she spoke. He could feel her breathing on his hand and moved his face closer to feel her breath on his own cheek. There was a slight smell of liquor, although she wasn't drinking now and seemed completely sober. That couldn't be said for the crew around her.

"I'm still here, Alaina," Tim spoke three inches from her lips. "You can't see me, but I am standing right in front of you. Do you hear me?" She gave no sign that she could. He was completely unperceivable to her. His touch on her skin, although real to him, was nothing to her. She continued laughing and talking to all those around her.

"Every one of these guys is hitting on you. They all want you, Alaina. But you already know that don't you." As expected, she still gave no hint of sensing his presence. "I'm not going to hit on you, Alaina. I don't need to." He felt her arm and then her hand. Her skin was perfectly soft and smooth.

Tim wondered what Amy would think of him if she could see him now. He decided he didn't really care. He was still upset that she had tricked him, even though he had to admit that it was a pretty cool evening with her until that moment. But her action had led to his crash and now he was without a car. In fact, now that he thought about it, it wasn't just he who wasn't trying to talk to her. She hadn't tried to talk to him either these past two weeks. She had barely even looked at him. Was it because he couldn't drive her around?

Tim knew the idea that Amy wasn't talking to him simply because he had no car was ridiculous. Yet it gave him the justification he was looking for in that moment. He stepped even closer to Alaina and spoke up toward the cobweb-covered rafters of the pub, "Amy, watch this!" Then looking back into Alaina's blue eyes and then at her lips, he leaned in and kissed her.

Their lips met right as Alaina started to say, "I think I'm ready to leave." But the only words she got out were, "I think I . . ." She stopped mid sentence and closed her eyes for a moment. Tim felt her lips moving as she spoke, and then felt them stop. She wasn't kissing back, but he realized she did feel something as her mouth opened slightly to welcome the touch.

Tim finished his gentle kiss and then backed off and watched. Alaina seemed slightly stunned. She brought her hand up and touched her fingers to her lips. The men were waiting for her to finish her sentence and stood patiently watching her, wondering why she had stopped so suddenly. The rest of the pub remained obnoxiously loud, but this little corner had gone silent.

Alaina pulled her fingers back from her lips and stared at them peculiarly. Then she felt her cheek where Tim's hand had been. The men watched with a confused hush. "You all right, Laina?" one of the two shorter men asked with genuine concern, breaking Alaina out of her silent contemplation.

"I think I . . ." Alaina started again. "I think that I . . . want a drink," she finally finished. Her neck was flushed slightly red. At first she only looked at her fingers but then looked around at her attentive men.

Tim continued to observe her for a few more minutes until his zone ended. Four of the men raced off to buy her a drink. The short considerate man stayed long enough to ask her what kind of drink she would like. The tallest man stole a chair out from under a less attractive woman and swooped in to offer it to Alaina. Tim wondered if all women this striking received such service. Probably, he thought as Alaina faded away from view and the dark nothingness of the zone transfer engulfed his consciousness.

Chapter 21

POWER AND ILLUSION

TWO DAYS LATER, Tim was back at school and still thinking about the kiss while Mr. Falstaff, Tim's English Literature teacher, droned on and on about Hamlet's inner demons. The kiss hadn't been anything special as far as kisses go, but the fact that Alaina had felt it, was exciting. Plus, she was the best looking girl he had ever kissed! Amy was very pretty, but Alaina could have been a supermodel. Her silky blonde hair, perfect skin, and bright clear blue eyes all echoed vividly in his mind.

As he played over the images in his head, they started changing. The coloring of her skin, hair, and eyes remained the same, but her facial features began to morph into an even more beautiful and pure form. They changed so much in his mind that it was no longer Alaina's face he was imagining when he thought of the kiss. He suddenly realized who the new face belonged to. It was Lexie.

Feeling a new sense of guilt, both for kissing Alaina to spite Amy and renewed remorse for his treatment of Lexie years before, Tim decided to seek out Amy. He wanted to apologize to her. Apologize for ignoring her and running out so abruptly that night they were together. He didn't want to feel the same remorse that he felt for Lexie again with Amy.

Yet he also knew that his treatment of Lexie had been far worse. She had been his best friend, and he had turned on her. She had never been anything but the most wonderful and faithful friend he had ever had. Apologizing to Amy wouldn't make up for his treatment of Lexie, but he knew it was still the right thing to do.

Falstaff concluded his Hamlet discourse as the bell rang. Tim found Amy a couple of minutes later next to her locker in the science hallway. As usual, she was surrounded by her throng of ever-present girlfriends. She shot him a look of disgust when she noticed his approach. Her look caused him to consider turning away to avoid the confrontation. But he knew he needed to say something. Somehow he felt like he was doing this for Lexie.

The gaggle of girls around her seemed to stand guard over Amy at first. It was clear that they all reflected the anger that Amy must have expressed against him. But then, as if on cue, the girls separated enough for Tim to pass through. Oddly, it reminded Tim of the way crowds instinctively separated to allow his invisible zone presence to pass.

"Amy, can we talk?" he asked hesitantly, wondering how she would react. Her face flickered with uncertainty for an instant but was quickly replaced with indifference. It was noisy in the hallway around the group of girls that surrounded Tim and Amy, but the horde of girls was silent and seemed more interested in what Tim would say than Amy did.

The listening ears made Tim more nervous as he waited for a response. "Maybe," he said, not waiting more than a few seconds, "if you want, we could to go somewhere after school, find someplace quiet to talk. I don't have to work today."

To his surprise, Amy smiled at him, and he thought she was going to say yes. To his surprise again, the smile changed and she quietly, but sarcastically, said, "Oh, so you finally want to see me? A quiet place, huh?"

Tim was taken aback by the tone and didn't respond, so she spoke again, loudly this time. "How about we go to my house where you can get me naked and then run off all mad at me just 'cause I'm trying to show you how to loosen up and enjoy having a girlfriend!"

Some of the boys in the hallway stopped and turned at the sound of the word, 'naked.' Amy didn't seem to mind this public spectacle and continued, "Or maybe you want to go and wreck your car again so you don't have to see me anymore! Was I really so bad that you even told the hospital staff to keep me out?"

Tim had expected anger but not like this. He stood flabbergasted next to her locker, unable to respond. He knew he hadn't explained anything to her about what had happened. He supposed he hadn't tried hard enough to talk with her after the wreck. Actually, he realized, he hadn't really tried at all. He just didn't know what to say. Maybe he should have tried to explain why he left so suddenly. Even a lie might have been better than just ignoring the issue.

Tim realized now how badly he had handled everything. He had been angry at her for deceiving him but hadn't realized that he had hurt her too. He had been so wrapped up in what was going on in his head that he hadn't thought about her feelings. Instead, he blamed her for something that really wasn't even her fault.

She had prepared for a great evening and had probably rehearsed it in her mind for days. He showed up, had a great time, but as soon as they got to the point she had dreamed of, he got angry and stormed out of there. At the hospital, he hadn't wanted anyone to visit him. It hadn't occurred to him what others may feel bad if they were turned away. She must have tried to see him and felt rejected by him yet again when the nurses told her he wasn't seeing anyone, not even his girlfriend.

"I'm so sorry, Amy. I guess I've acted like a jerk. I . . ."

"Yeah, you have!" Amy interrupted as she slammed her locker door closed, not giving him a chance to go on. Tim paused to see if she was going to say more. He wanted to fix this. He loved her. Right?

Maybe not. He hadn't tried to talk with her since that night. What kind of boyfriend ignores his girlfriend for two weeks if he loves her? He had plenty of excuses. He had been too confused and lost in his own thoughts. He was afraid. Afraid of what she would think of him and afraid she would force him to tell her what had happened.

"Yeah, a real jerk," he repeated quietly. "I guess I was just really confused."

"Look. Just save it," she said with false sweetness in her voice. "You've been done with me since that night. It took me a little longer to get over you, but I'm over you now."

"I . . . I am sor . . ."

"Just leave me alone. It's been over." With that, she hiked one strap of her backpack over her shoulder, spun around, and walked away.

Tim stood alone, puzzled, as the activity of students in the hallway faded until the next class bell rang. He hadn't expected that response from Amy. He wasn't sure what he expected. Maybe that she would be a little angry but would still forgive him? That she would want to pick up where they left off, like nothing had happened? It seemed silly now to have thought that was possible. So much was different.

She was right though, he decided. He had really made a mess of things. He ruined their relationship because he wasn't willing to talk to her and trust her. It was a good lesson in life, but a lesson he would be doomed to repeat.

Tim walked to the public library after his last class. He had his notes and wanted to search for the pub. However, he discovered that it was a fruitless search. The local library didn't have business directories outside of the US. The Usenet that his dad had used to find a psychologist was tedious to use, and although he did find some pubs mentioned in the endless directory lists, there was no simple way to find out where they were.

He thought about what he had seen that night. He should have left the pub to see what the town was called. He should have kissed Alaina more too, since he no longer had a girlfriend! Would he get more chances like that? Was it ethical to kiss girls who didn't know he was there? Alaina seemed to like it though, hadn't she? Or had he just assumed that.

What did it matter? He shut down the Usenet and gave up. It was probably just a dream anyway. They were all just dreams. That answer made the most sense. A friend had talked about controlling dreams once to him. What was it called when a person could control their dreams? Maybe that was what he was doing. He was just acting out his fantasies in dreams. Controlling them and traveling to strange places to kiss pretty girls!

Tim found some books on dreams and started paging through them. They talked about the stages of sleep that Dr. Bruin had mentioned. Stage Four was the deep one. According to the books, no dreams should be occurring there. But wasn't that the stage Doc said he was in during his zone?

He read on. There it was! "Lucid Dreaming," he read, "a dream in which the person sleeping is aware that they are dreaming. A person in a lucid dream can actively participate in and manipulate their experiences within the dream. The dreams can seem completely real and vivid, especially if the participant achieves a high level of self-awareness during the dream."

That was it. It had to be. Maybe that was why Doc said his mind was active during his zone. He was controlling his dreams instead of just passively having them.

As he continued to read, Tim was surprised to see that it took people years to master their dreams. He had apparently been doing it all his life. Maybe he was just born with the ability. Most people ignored their dreams. They were too busy being asleep. But he had always been fascinated by them.

He checked out two of the most interesting dream books and then walked home. Lucid dreaming made sense. Why hadn't he ever thought of that before. He was able to make decisions in his zone and do whatever he wanted!

Tim thought again of the power and freedom he felt kissing Alaina. Since it was just a dream it was sort of like his own personal fantasy world in which he was the ultimate ruler. No consequences. No pain. No limits!

If he hadn't just broken up with Amy, this new sense of control would have left him feeling on top of the world. As it was, he still felt pretty good. He was surprised how well he was taking their breakup. Maybe that proved he didn't love her after all. Maybe it had only been lust, just like her dad had warned him during that awkward lecture of his. Or maybe it was like she had said in her public tirade, he was just over her.

Tim put the books down on his dresser when he reached his room and picked up his Magic 8 Ball. "Did I love Amy?" he asked while shaking the black plastic ball and then turning it over to let the answer float to the small transparent window at the top.

"Very doubtful," the words came, confirming his suspicions.

"Just lust?" Tim asked thoughtfully and waited for the new answer to appear after turning the ball over and back up again.

"Signs point to yes," the wise ball answered silently.

After dinner, Tim finished his homework and then sat down to watch the news with his Dad. "What's going on in the world, Dad?"

John looked up. Tim had seemed to be in a better mood the last couple of weeks, but today at dinner he had seemed a little distracted. Before John could answer Tim's question regarding the state of the world, Tim spoke quietly, "Amy and I broke up."

"Oh?" John picked up the remote and turned the volume down as the clean cut male news anchor concluded a description of a fire at a New York nightclub. "You and Amy? What happened? Are you okay?"

"Sure, Dad. I'm fine. I guess I haven't treated her very well since the accident. I've ignored her and she moved on. But I think . . ." Tim broke off his words as he noticed a new picture on the television screen next to the news anchor.

Tim stepped closer to the screen. "Dad, turn it back up!" he said.

" . . . declared dead when rescue crews reached him. The man, Arthur 'Art' Sumpter, had worked for Arkansas Logging for twenty years. He had safely driven that stretch of mountain highway for the last eight years."

The picture up on the left hand corner of the screen had changed from truck wreckage at the bottom of the ravine to the photo of a man, the same man that Tim had tried to hang onto during that first zone that he remembered through hypnosis.

Phil, the anchor, continued his report, "The only witness to the tragic accident was traveling Northbound up the pass as Mr.

Sumpter passed her in the opposite direction. His wheels fell into an opening in the roadway causing the truck to slide off with the man still inside."

"What?" Tim said aloud. "That wasn't how it had happened." John looked at Tim, wondering what he was talking about. However, it was clear that Tim was talking at the TV and not to him.

"Authorities say a collapse of the underlying rock below the pavement is to blame for the accident," Phil went on unsympathetically. "An Arkansas Department of Transportation employee had reported the problem only a few minutes before the accident occurred. An investigation is underway to determine if proper procedures were . . ."

Tim stopped listening. He had recognized the ravine and the wreckage. The man in the photo, Art, was definitely the same man he had tried to save. "His name was Art," Tim mumbled to himself.

So it was true. He really was traveling somewhere. He now had absolute proof! But why was the report wrong? Why did the woman tell reporters that he never left the truck? She had been there next to him, hanging onto Art until she panicked.

"Are you okay, Tim?" John asked. "You look like you've seen a ghost."

Tim's face was white. "I sort of knew him," Tim said. "The man in the accident. But that's impossible isn't it," Tim stated more as a fact than as a question.

Without looking back at John, Tim stood up and walked back to his room. He moved the trash can in the corner of his room and then pulled back the edge of the carpet. Finding his zone notebook hidden safely in its place, he opened it and began to write:

Rules: Continued.

My zone is NOT lucid dreaming. It is real.
I can travel to the future in my zone.
But changes I make to the future do not seem to take root.
The future just occurs as if I was never there.

Tim stopped writing and thought about Art and his interaction with him. He had really been there. He had released the man's seat belt. He had changed the way Art died by pulling him out of the truck and trying to pull him to safety onto the road. Art had spoken to him. That had been in the future.

Yet despite all that, when time caught up with the actual event, his actions were erased. Nothing he had done made any difference at all.

"Art died," Tim whispered to himself, staring at the notebook. "That was real life, not a dream. A man really died. And even if I had pulled him up, he still would have died."

Tim sighed, feeling the hope he had found in his power deflating out of him. "I never had any ability to change anything."

Tim put the pen back to the page and added:

> *My actions are useless.*
> *I am useless.*
> *I have no purpose.*
> *My zone just means I am a freak!*

Tim threw the notebook across the room. He felt nauseous at the thought of Art's terrible death, the man who had called him an angel. He was no angel. He had wanted to use the zone as a playground. He had been thinking all day about kissing Alaina and wondering what else he could do while invisibly controlling his environment. What kind of angel does that?

The Good Samaritan in him had tried to help some people. That old lady whose purse was almost stolen, the little boy on the tracks. And Art. But if nothing changed when he tried to help Art, then that boy on the tracks died too.

Tim felt completely useless. "What good is it?" he yelled at the notebook that was now lying half open and upside down on the floor. The people, the places, and the screamers were all real, not a dream or an illusion. He knew that now. But the power to make a difference, the power to help people, that was the illusion. Nothing he did mattered at all.

Tim didn't add any notes after his new zone later that night. Instead, he threw the notebook into the metal trash can that had, up until then, been hiding the book's location under the carpet. That night's zone seemed like a waste of time anyway—Just a crowd of men and women at a stock trading floor. How could people spend day in and day out yelling across a packed trade floor watching a bunch of stock prices go up and down? Tim thought that must be the worst job in the world.

He decided to just wait out the thirty-eight minutes by lying down in the middle of the floor and closing his eyes. The people were busy rushing around him, trying to avoid stepping on the invisible shape. But he didn't care about them. None of this made any difference anyway. The young hero in Tim was suddenly gone.

After that, Tim refused to reflect on his zones at all. He would think of other things after he woke up at 12:13 a.m., until he could fall back to sleep. Sometimes he would see a person in danger, but reminded himself that it made no difference what he did. He had given up.

At school, he had given up as well. Tim failed every one of his last semester finals. His shocked teachers asked for the principal and guidance counselors to step in, but Tim blew them all off. There wasn't much the school could do. Even with the failed finals, he had already accumulated enough course credits and good overall grades to graduate.

When his mom and dad tried to talk to him, they too met with failure as he refused to discuss his sudden change. He simply didn't care anymore, and he believed it wasn't anybody else's place to try to change his mind.

Most observers assumed it was the breakup with Amy that set Tim into a tailspin. They had no way of understanding the depth or source of Tim's depression. As high on life as he had felt with the notion of being special and having the ability to help people, his depression fed on the elimination of that belief and the certainty that he was only a freak.

Chapter 22

FINDING PURPOSE ON A PATH OF DESTRUCTION

Monday, July 23, 1990: Three Months Later

"YOU CAN'T BE serious," Tim scoffed at his pimply young boss on an extremely hot July afternoon at the carwash.

"He is serious, Tim." Mr. Suddo frowned as he stood next to Pimply Steve. "You used to be one of my most valued employees, but now I hardly recognize you. What happened? Nothing you do seems to add any value. In fact, it's the opposite! You damage customers' cars, you show up late, your work is sloppy. I need someone who is dependable. I've been making excuses for you for the last two months. I'm done defending you. You need to leave."

"How am I supposed to pay my rent?" Tim moaned back to Mr. Suddo.

Pimply Steve snickered, "That's something you have to figure out, smart boy. Now leave, like Mr. Suddo said."

Tim shouldn't have been so surprised. He knew he was skating on thin ice ever since he scratched a red BMW two weeks earlier. The clean brush he was using had dropped onto the ground by accident. Then, without making any effort to thoroughly clean out the grit that had been picked up by the bristles, he continued to scrub the car. All summer long he found himself doing a careless job just to get by.

But now, the sudden realization that his only source of income was gone hit him like a pile of bricks. He had moved out of his parents' house and into an apartment shortly after graduation. His job had never paid much, and he found himself constantly broke, but he was glad to be away from the questions and troubled looks. He was tired of his mom's silent disapproval and his dad's endless lectures on self-respect and responsibility.

All summer, he knew he needed to find a way to make more money, but even the effort needed to look for a new job seemed to escape him. He found it easier and more enjoyable to just sit around and watch TV.

The same escape was used again as soon as Tim got home from his now ex-job. He turned on Jerry Springer and found himself disgusted by the petty fights and scuzziness of the guests. But he watched anyway, to see which man really was the father of the kid no one wanted.

At the first commercial, Tim started to flip channels. He had a lot of channels, thanks to the cable splitter he used outside his neighbor's window to "borrow" his cable signal. Flipping to WGN, he saw that one of the *Back to the Future* movies was on. He had seen this one before and recognized it immediately as the second movie of the trilogy. This time, Marty McFly, a slightly lazy dreamer and Dr. Emmitt Brown, a crazy but brilliant wild-haired scientist, were in the future. Marty was being chased on a hoverboard by Griff, his nemesis Biff's grandson.

Marty raced along the streets on the pink wheel-less hoverboard that he had stolen from a little girl to escape the bully of the future. Floating off the road and into a city fountain, the board stopped, and Griff closed in. Tim didn't care and flipped the channels again.

There were commercials for spandex shorts, Tickle Me Elmo, and an old lady who couldn't get up. MTV was playing "The Humpty Dance" by Digital Underground. Two different stations were showing reruns of "I Love Lucy." A few minutes and clicks of the remote later, Tim was back to Marty and Dr. Brown.

Marty had escaped Griff and then wandered into an eighties memorabilia shop in the future town of Hill Valley. There, he discovered a sports almanac describing many of the past decades' sporting outcomes. An idea struck Tim as Dr. Brown caught Marty with the sports almanac.

"What's this?" the scientist asked Marty.

"Uh, it's a souvenir," Marty replied with an expression of childlike guilt.

Dr. Brown read the cover, "Fifty years of Sports Statistics. Hardly recreational reading material, Marty."

"Hey, Doc, what's the harm of bringing back a little info on the future? Thought maybe we could place a couple bets."

"Marty," the scientist lectured, "I didn't invent the time machine for financial gain."

Tim watched and listened intently. He had seen this movie before but never connected the storyline to his own ability.

Doc continued his lecture, "Marty, I didn't invent the time machine to win at gambling. I invented the time machine to travel through time!"

Tim couldn't believe he had not thought of this sooner. "That's it!" he thought aloud. "That's the purpose of my zone! I will be rich!"

Ever since seeing the news story about Art, the truck driver, he had known that his zone was not just a three-dimensional phenomenon. It not only took him to random places all around the world, up, down, left, and right, but his zone also moved him four-dimensionally. Time was the fourth dimension. However, until now, it had never occurred to him that predicting the future could be a profitable talent.

That night, Tim found himself in downtown Chicago. There were people all around him. Some happy, some sad, some just walking aimlessly through their routine, up and down the streets of midafternoon downtown. For Tim, he had but one goal and ignored the happenings around him until he saw what he was looking for.

A coin-operated newspaper dispenser sat at the corner of Adams and Michigan Avenue. Tim spotted it and ran up to a man who at that moment was retrieving a copy of the Tribune from the blue rectangular metal box. It occurred to Tim that he had no money with him, so his only chance was to steal the paper from the overweight, red-haired business man who had just opened the box.

Tim grabbed at the newly purchased paper in the man's hands and felt the man tighten his grip. Realizing his mistake, Tim let go and waited. He had learned that people would notice him moving an object if their attention was already on it. As long as the man's focus was on the paper, he would notice Tim's attempt to steal it.

Tim hoped that the man would put the paper under his arm and then turn his attention away. But instead, he turned around and plopped himself down heavily onto the bench next to the stand. The bench creaked under the weight as he slowly began unfolding the paper.

"I should have just taken it from you, Red," Tim spoke at the unhearing red-haired man. "I'll make you a deal," he continued as he walked around behind the bench to look at the paper over Red's shoulders. "I won't steal your paper if you turn to the sports section. Okay?"

There was no magical compliance by Red, but he did slowly begin flipping through the first few pages. As he did this, Tim read headlines.

"Legal brief links Souter to antiabortion stance." "Bush aims 'kinder, gentler' policy at the executive suite." "Bomb kills British lawmaker . . ."

"Come on, get to the sports!" Tim coaxed impatiently. Then, almost on cue, Red flipped quickly to the sports section and stopped. Tim wondered if it was just chance, or if he had actually influenced Red. Pushing that thought aside for the moment, he read, "Cubs pull out 2-1 victory last night to win three of four games against the Expos." Tim skimmed down to see the stats. "July 26: Expos over Cubs 3-2; July 27: Cubs beat Expos 2-0; July 28: Cubs beat Expos 10-7; July 29: Cubs beat Expos 2-1."

"July 26-29," Tim memorized. "Expos, Cubs, Cubs, Cubs. 3-2, 2-0, 10-7, 2-1. Okay. Got it!" He wondered if he should try to read more info on the page but decided to just focus on remembering these four games for now. There was no way to take notes back with him, so he would have to completely rely on his memory.

A bus approached the corner, and Tim realized that Red had been there waiting for it. Red quickly folded his paper under his arm and stood up. As the bus pulled to a stop and Red stepped up onto the stairs leading past the driver, Tim recognized that he had forgotten to look for some critical information.

"Hey," Tim shouted, "what year is it? What is the year?" The man didn't turn back and the driver closed the door.

Tim felt stupid. "How could I have forgotten to check the year?" he whined to no one.

Tim tried to open the metal newspaper boxes, but as expected, they were all locked. He ran along the sidewalk, hoping to find someone else with a paper but found no one else reading one at this time of day. He knew his time was running out, and in frustration, he kicked the side of a trash can at the next corner. The can was bolted to the concrete and sent a reverberating pain through his bare foot.

"Idiot!" he thought as he bent over and massaged his throbbing toes. Why hadn't he worn shoes to bed that night?

As Tim stooped, he peered absently at the trash in the receptacle. A partially wet newspaper lay half buried by some Styrofoam cups and fast-food wrappers. On the top right edge of the paper was the date, "July 30, 1990."

Tim woke up in his bed a few minutes later. "1990, July 30. That is in just a few days I think." He checked his digital watch and saw that today was in fact July 24, 1990.

"I have two days before the first game," he thought excitedly as he wrote down from memory the dates and scores he had read in the paper. He then spent the rest of the night awake, making plans, and figuring out how to place his first bets.

A week later, Tim had enough money to pay his rent and plenty of extra for more bets. But his future fortune wasn't found in sports bets alone. He discovered that in his zones, he could use all sorts of information to unlock the future potential of sports teams, public stocks, lotteries, and even insurance. The possibilities were endless. He stole a paper spiral notebook from a gas station near his apartment and was once again paying attention to his zones.

Finance

— *Tech stocks will boom in 1998 but then crash in 2000*
— *Overall market will have huge gains in 2006-2008 but crash in Fall of '08 and Spring 2014. Buy in early '09 and 2016.*
— *Oil companies will have huge profits in early 2008 but then plummet.*
— *Need to find out what Yahoo! means and invest now.*
— *Microsoft—Some kind of computer system monopoly?*
— *World Wide Web—Invest in this after 1991 but sell before 2000.*

Sports

Superbowl winners:
-2000—St. Louis Rams
-2006—Pittsburgh Steelers
-2010—New Orleans Saints
-2018—Nashville Hicks

World Series:
-1990—Oakland loses all four games to Cincinnati
-1993—Toronto over Philadelphia in six games
-2005—Chicago sweeps Houston Astros
-2023—Billings Capitalists over LA

History:

— *Middle East uprising in 2015 will lead to shift in world economy. New Arab Democratic Union will challenge the US economy by 2028.*

By October, Tim had made over $50,000; a lot of money for an eighteen year-old. By the next summer, he had his first million. Not all of his zones led to profit, but it only took a few stock market tips or sports outcomes to make a lot of money!

The sense of power he had felt briefly when he first learned to remember his zones had returned. Only this time, instead of studying it and trying to understand the zone, he only concerned himself with becoming richer and enjoying the nightly visits around the world.

He tried to find a way to control where and when his zone would take him, but it seemed to be completely random. Sometimes, he'd be alone in the middle of nowhere. Other times, he arrived in crowded cities.

Twice so far, he stood up, after the dizzying voyage into his zone, to find himself in a gym locker room. The first time in the men's locker room wasn't nearly as memorable as the second incident when he found himself in a shower room full of attractive women at a gym in California.

The Tim his parents had raised would have respected the women enough to vigilantly exit the room. However, he wasn't that Tim anymore, and he savored the experience that his power provided him. His only regret was that it could last only thirty-eight minutes.

In many of the zones, he would see the boy, one of the screamers. It never seemed to acknowledge him. Sometimes it did look at him, but only if he was trying to interact with another person. Even then, the screamer usually didn't seem to care.

Tim discovered that in many of his zones he would find someone in need if he walked around and explored his surroundings long enough. Often the need was physical, but at other times it was an emotional need, or he would find a person at a critical decision point in their life.

Those critical moments, especially the ones where the outcome seemed unclear, would often coincide with the appearance of a screamer. To Tim, that was a sign that he should turn and walk the other direction.

A part of Tim, a part that he had buried deeply, still felt compelled to help. But believing that his actions had no positive impact, it was easier to just ignore the pain and suffering of the world, both in and out of his zone. He didn't want to see the sadness and grief if he could do nothing about it.

Art Sumpter had died right in front of him. Trying to guide the truck safely around the broken roadway and freeing Art from the truck had not only failed to save him, but also, in the end, didn't seem to make any difference at all. Since the news reported that he fell with the truck, having never escaped it, Tim held to his belief that his presence was meaningless.

The years passed, and Tim accepted his zone as it seemed. He had concluded that the future there was like a previously published book. It had already been written and was unchangeable. He would allow the zone to take him to random pages in that book, but he refused to take responsibility for a future that he could not change. His mission would only be to gather information that suited him—information that would make him rich. He would simply exploit his zone and have fun in a world of no consequences.

PART II

Time for Change

The winds of change for some,
Arrive swiftly in the night.
Do not ask from where they come,
But let them take you to the light.
—Unknown

For time and the world do not stand still. Change is the law of life. And those who look only to the past or the present are certain to miss the future.
—John F. Kennedy

Chapter 23

A CHANGE ON THE HORIZON

Tuesday, May 9, 1995

ON THE NIGHT before Tim's twenty-third birthday, he came across a girl who was crying on the steps of her home as she talked to someone on the phone. The suburban neighborhood into which he had just zoned reminded him of the clean-cut, well-manicured lawns and homes he saw on reruns of *Leave it to Beaver*. He knew, however, that he wouldn't be running into the 1950s Cleavers from the show. The cars here looked to be about the same 1990s styles and makes that he would find in his own neighborhood when he woke up from this zone. The air was humid, and the trees and landscaping signaled that it was midsummer.

The girl on the porch, with auburn hair pulled back, wore glasses and sat next to a pile of mail. Tim guessed she was about eighteen years old. She seemed like someone who was intelligent, but also a little intense and bookwormish. He watched her as she spoke to her friend through controlled sobs.

"I worked so hard," she cried into the cordless phone. "I was in all the right college-prep classes, got my A's that I worked for, was in all the honor societies—everything they said I needed to get accepted. And now they don't even have the decency to send me a rejection letter."

The girl swatted at the stack of mail next to her and then pushed it to the side. Several other stacks lay just inside the house on the floor. It was clear that she had been checking and rechecking several days of mail for the letter.

Tim wondered which school she was so upset about not getting into. He too had considered going to college one day. Maybe he would go after he finished making his fortune. Yet who needs college when you can jump back and forth through time and make money on sure bets?

"It should have been here a week ago!" the girl sobbed angrily, pulling Tim's attention back onto her as her friend tried to calm her down. More quietly, she then admitted to her friend, "It was the only school I applied to. I was sure I would get in. It's too late to apply somewhere else decent."

Tim had been walking the neighborhood hoping to find a newspaper in a driveway or a TV that was turned on when he had stumbled upon this crying girl. He had learned that nightly news was a great source of quick info, especially if someone was watching financial news. He didn't expect this sobber would be turning on the TV anytime soon, so he turned his back on her and walked toward the street.

That familiar pang of guilt crept stealthy back into his mind. But what could he do? He didn't know what school she had applied for. He couldn't march into the enrollment office and demand her acceptance. And even if he did, the future was written. He couldn't change anything. She just needed to accept her situation and move on. That's what he had done when he realized he was a freak of nature. He moved on, and now at age twenty-two, he was rich and had a gorgeous girlfriend!

Tim reached the edge of her short driveway and paused next to her mailbox. Despite his self-reassurance that she would be okay after she got on with her life, he still felt as though he could and should help. He hated this feeling. This contradictory battle inside him that seemed to demand a response made no sense.

"There is nothing I can do!" he yelled to no one, looking up toward the warm blue sky.

Despite the futility of his desire to help the girl, he remained paused at the end of her driveway, unable to just walk away. Then, looking to his side toward her mailbox, he noticed something white in the bushes along her sidewalk. It was only a few feet from the mailbox post but was hidden by the vegetation to anyone who wasn't looking at just the right angle.

Bending down, he realized it was a large white envelope. He pulled it out and looked at the rain-soaked paper with a Northwestern University insignia on the front. Looking up at the crying girl, still sitting on her porch step, he realized that the envelope had somehow been dropped there.

If he hadn't come along, would anyone have found it? If he took it to her now, she could open it and have her answer. It looked like an acceptance to him, judging by the weight. Of course, if he left it alone, eventually she would just call up the school. She'd ask why they hadn't written to her, and they'd say that it was sent out weeks ago, and she was accepted. All would work out fine, right?

There wasn't anything he could do about it anyway. Whether he gently handed her the missing envelope or threw it back into the bush, this future was unchangeable. Somewhere back in the world where his body was sleeping in his bed, this girl would still end up crying to her friend.

Frustrated with the new but still pointless dilemma, Tim threw the envelope toward the girl. Just as his hand released the envelope into flight, he saw something in the grass near her porch. It was the screamer! It was standing only a few feet from the girl, just off to the side of the porch. Its body was turned toward her, but its head and eyes were turned directly at Tim in a very unnatural posture.

Tim hadn't thought the envelope would fly very far, even though he had thrown it as hard as he could. Usually, paper catches the air and falls gently to the ground. However, this heavy, wet envelope sliced through the air from the force of his throw and hit the girl's phone, knocking it from her hand. The screamer turned its attention back to the girl as she let out a squeal and then looked for her fallen phone. She found it behind her, right next to the envelope. Her eyes widened when she recognized the emblem on the front.

"Tonya!" she screamed toward the phone as it still lay on the porch. "It came!" She picked up the envelope with both hands and held it high in front of her face.

The screamer seemed to turn and walk away from the porch. However, Tim realized that it didn't really walk; it just sort of turned and then faded out like a dissipating mist.

"I can't believe it finally came!" the girl shouted again as she picked up the phone and started tearing into the soft wet fibers of paper. He had to admit that it felt good to have been able to help the girl, even if this was just a farcical future.

Tim watched as she opened the letter inside and delivered the news to her friend that she had been accepted to Northwestern University after all. She never questioned how the envelope arrived or even why it was soaking wet. There seemed to be an unexplainable barrier that kept people from recognizing his involvement. If he had still been keeping up his original notebook, he would have written:

> *My actions toward others in the zone are usually missed or misinterpreted. It seems that their minds cannot accept my presence and therefore cannot accept the reality of my actions.*
>
> *The Screamers still appear to mostly observe. Maybe they are making sure some larger plan is carried out through the decisions and actions of people.*

Tim thought again about the screamer. Had it been there all along? He was sure he would have seen it. Had it just appeared suddenly or walked up while he was looking at the envelope? He didn't know.

Tim also wondered if the screamer was glad that he had given her the letter. Apparently it accepted his action since it hadn't tried to stop Tim's delivery. What if he hadn't thrown it? Would the screamer have delivered it to her? Did the screamer cause Tim to notice the envelope in the bushes? Did it cause the guilt in Tim's head that forced him to stop near the mailbox in the first place?

Maybe the screamer didn't care at all what he did. It didn't act very interested. Maybe it just observed and reported back to some higher power.

The obscure purpose of the screamers would remain a mystery for now. Tim had bets to place, lotteries to enter, stocks to buy, and money to make. He also had a girlfriend to get back to. He knew that he would open his eyes in just a few moments and find himself back in bed next to her. She would be asleep and oblivious to the fact that he had been running around some suburban neighborhood a thousand miles away in some near future or past time.

What Tim didn't know yet was that while his body seemed comatose and his mind was in "Cleaverville" suburbia, Natalie, his girlfriend, hadn't been asleep. She was dragging his limp body out of the house and into the woods where her tiki torches were already set up. About the time he first saw the crying girl on the porch, Natalie was reading from an odd spiritual book and chanting demon-removal curses at his body. By the time he threw the envelope at the girl, Natalie had given up, wandered back into the house, undressed, and fallen asleep on the bed.

Her ritual coincided with Tim's birthday—by coincidence only. She would forget the day, just as she had forgotten it the year before and the year before that.

The house that they shared belonged to Tim. He bought his new home for himself on his 21st birthday, two years earlier, at the urging of Natalie, even though he hadn't really felt he needed a house, especially not one this large. But since money wasn't an issue, he let her pick one she liked.

Tim and Natalie had met at the Bank of America, where she worked as a teller. He brought in his winnings, sometimes in cash, for deposit. The pair were a perfect match from the day they met. She had been attracted to him the first time she laid eyes on him, and his bank statement. He was immediately attracted to her many non bank-related assets. Their relationship bloomed quickly into a perfect symbiotic companionship of money, sex, and misery. He gave her money, she gave him sex, and they both swam in lonely misery.

Tim crawled into bed next to Natalie after coming in from the woods where she had left him surrounded by the flaming tiki torches. He admired her beautiful body that always seemed to give her power over him. Her slender arms and legs seemed delicate and fragile. "How in the world did you drag me out into the woods again tonight?" he thought. He knew she worked out and knew she was stronger than she looked. Still, he was a little over six feet tall, and though fit, he did weigh almost two hundred lbs.

Tim tried to imagine her straining to pull him down the stairs and out the back door. Maybe she just pushed him down the stairs and rolled him down the hill. He wondered if she had the tiki torches already set up, or if she had to drag them out there too after he went into his zone. Why did she feel she had to cure him? Did it really matter if he was cursed? She still got to use his credit cards to buy all her junk. "Why can't you just accept me for who I am?" he asked her in a whisper.

"Accept me for who I am," his mind wandered sleepily. "Who . . . I . . . am? Who am I?" He didn't know anymore, so he closed his eyes and went to sleep.

When Tim woke again, the sun was up. Natalie was still sleeping peacefully next to him. She had gotten cold and pulled the sheets off Tim and onto herself sometime in the night. He quietly got up, dressed, and headed back into the woods for a walk.

He passed the burned out tiki torches and walked down toward the bayou trail. This trail had been part of the reason he let Natalie talk him into the house. He didn't really care where he lived, but having this scenic trail so near to his home was appealing. He used it often on his bike for exercise, but he also enjoyed just walking on it when he needed to clear his head and escape.

Natalie was gone when Tim returned home two hours later. He thought she was probably at the gym. That's where she went most mornings now that she had quit her job. According to Natalie, she had quit so that she could pursue a new career. He wasn't sure what that new career was going to be, since she hadn't tried to find another job or apply at any schools.

"Don't worry, baby," she had purred sweetly when he tried to bring it up last month. "I'm just carefully planning my next move."

Tim had been unable to resist smiling at her assurance even though he was pretty sure she hadn't started planning anything. He supposed it didn't really matter. He had more money than the two of them knew what to do with.

"So what do you do all day?" Tim had asked, genuinely interested to know how someone could spend an entire day at the gym and shopping.

"Well, I get up, shower, and change for the gym," she started.

"Why do you shower before the gym?"

"To look good, of course."

"For who?" Tim asked, wondering if there was someone specific she was trying to impress. It was normal for her to flirt with waiters and store clerks. Even the surgeon who lived next door seemed to be the recipient of extra smiles and waves. Was it possible she was being unfaithful to him with the neighbor?

"I like to look good for everyone!" she said truthfully. "Plus, I go in wearing the same outfit that I will wear for the day, so I need to be clean from the start."

He supposed that made sense. It just seemed excessive. "Why don't you just put on your workout clothes here at home?" he reasoned.

"Because then I can't show off all my cute outfits that you buy me as I walk past the front desk staff." She gave him a falsely innocent smile and wink. He melted easily, as usual. She had won that argument.

"So, usually I bike first, just to get warmed up," she went on. "Then I run. Then, depending on the day, I either lift weights or swim. Did you know swimming burns more calories than any other sport?"

"I think I have heard that somewhere," Tim agreed. She had repeated that fact to him several times before. "But I didn't realize you lifted weights." Tim looked at Natalie's bare arms extending from the tank top she was wearing. They weren't bulging, but they were definitely toned.

"Of course!" she had answered with an attitude that implied superiority over all lesser women. "How else do you think I got such a perfectly shaped body?" He couldn't argue.

"See," she said pointing to her triceps, "no flab at all! And look at this," She lifted her top up to just below her breasts to show off her stomach. "See any excess fat here?" She flexed her abdominal muscles revealing several toned but feminine ripples. She had made her point, but he was happy to let her continue.

"And check this out," Natalie said enthusiastically like a little kid about to show off a new Christmas gift. She turned around with her back to Tim, bent slightly at her waist, and dropped her pants and underwear to reveal her rounded posterior. "What do you think of that?" she purred as she moved into several flattering poses. "Perfect, right?"

Again, he couldn't argue. "Perfect," he grinned as he stepped forward and put his arms around her waist and pulled her backward against himself. He nuzzled her neck with his nose and mouth.

"There, you see?" she said turning around in his arms and pulling her pants back up to signal that she was still in control of their love life. "That is why I work out and why I use weights," she smiled knowing he would do anything she wanted.

Tim smiled and asked, "So, what do you do with all my money after you're finished at the gym?" It really didn't bother him much that she spent thousands of dollars each week. He didn't have a plan for the money, and deep down, he felt a little guilty when he spent it on things for himself.

He thought that if he let Natalie spend it however she wanted, then he wasn't the one being greedy and cheating the world. Besides, it made sense to share the wealth with someone he loved. Of course, he knew that was a lie. He didn't love Natalie. Never had loved her, he supposed. Sure, he liked her. And they did have fun sometimes. But even when she was right next to him, he felt lonely.

"I spend it, of course!" Natalie teased, bringing Tim back out of his thoughts. "A girl like me needs to stay up-to-date with fashions and experiences. And someone has to decorate this place. You sure don't have a flare for making this crib fabulous!"

Tim laughed. "Fabulous, huh?" He walked over to a four-foot-tall statue of a middle-aged, overweight nude woman carved out of dark driftwood. "Like this voodoo momma here?" he laughed again as he patted it on the head. It was the most hideous statue he had ever seen.

"Yeah, fabulous! And don't make fun of 'Nagy Anya.' She is a beautiful representation of motherhood. Not that I ever want to be a mother." Natalie laughed. "Especially if being a mother makes me look like that!" Both of them laughed now, although his laughter wasn't because he didn't want to have kids. In fact, the truth was that he had always hoped to someday be a father. His laughter grew from his mental image of Natalie as a mother and knowing that she would probably be the worst mother in all of human history!

Chapter 24

UNEXPECTED ENCOUNTER

Wednesday Night, May 10, 1995

TIM STOOD UP and found himself in complete darkness. There were no sounds and no light. He wondered if something had gone wrong this time. Was he lost somewhere in between the random pages of his zone? He attempted a step with his right leg and heard a crunching sound beneath his foot. It was snow! A wave of cold caused him to shiver as he felt a gentle breeze move over his skin.

He and Natalie had gone out for a late dinner a few hours earlier. Their conversation was shallow and boring, and once again, Natalie completely forgot it was his birthday. But the food was good. After dinner, they stopped for coffee and then came home to do the only thing they were really very good at together. It was while lying naked in bed afterwards that Tim slipped into his zone.

Until Natalie moved in with him, Tim had worn a shirt, pants, and sometimes even shoes to bed. He only took them off after he returned from his zone. But Natalie had complained that it was weird to wear clothes to bed . . . especially a full ensemble, complete with shoes. Like so many of their arguments, she won him over with her body and convinced him that sleeping au naturel was best.

However, now he stood in the snow, in a place he had probably never been, and he was completely unclothed. It wasn't the nakedness that bothered him, as he knew he was invisible to anyone he might find in this darkness. It was the cold.

Some things like water, fire, heat, and smoke, he felt only passively when he stayed in one place too long. Cold, however, seemed to penetrate into his zoned existence more quickly. He knew he would need to find shelter fast before the true temperature of this place settled in.

In the silent, snowy darkness, Tim began shuffling his feet carefully forward. After a few minutes, the thick clouds above seemed to thin just enough for some starlight to create a soft glow on the winter landscape.

He could faintly see a barbed wire fence near him that marked the edge of the field he had wandered through. A road lay just beyond the fence and was also covered by the winter blanket that muffled all the normal outdoor sounds. The complete silence around him was only broken by the crunching his feet made on the snow and an occasional light wind. Ahead of him, he saw a single set of tire tracks marring the fresh snow on the road. "It must be the middle of the night," he thought out loud. "Otherwise, there would be more tire tracks."

Tim began to shiver as the surrounding chill penetrated him. He wanted to find a warm place to rest, even though he knew his zone would only last another twenty minutes or so.

Zones like this one annoyed him. There was no apparent way to pick up information. No one to watch or mess with. He was just cold and tired.

Tim looked in both directions along the road. Something inside him caused him to turn right and start walking up hill. That same something, maybe a subconscious instinct, tugged at him. He kept walking even though after a few minutes he was convinced that he was walking in the wrong direction if he was going to find any civilization and warmth.

But after cresting the next hill, he was rewarded with the sight of several lights, and he quickly marched up to the first house he saw. Not surprisingly, it was locked. The second and third small homes in this rundown neighborhood on the edge of town were also locked.

It had not occurred to him until this moment that he had never tried to walk through walls or doors. Maybe physical laws didn't apply to him anymore. He had just assumed that the same physical limitations that existed at home would apply here as well.

Looking straight at the door of the third locked house, Tim closed his eyes and took a large step of faith forward.

"Ow!" Tim yelled. The wooden door responded exactly as a door should, causing Tim to slam into it hard, first with his head, then with his chest.

Rubbing his forehead where he had struck hardest, Tim looked around sheepishly to see if anyone had seen his failed attempt. As he looked, he caught sight of the lone tire tracks that he had first seen out past the fields where he had arrived. He followed the tracks with his eyes and saw that they led to the fourth house along the road.

The tracks started near a small pile of snow where someone had hastily brushed off their windshield. They led out of the driveway and then fishtailed back and forth across the road before the driver seemed to gain control and headed away in the direction from which he had just walked.

The house was small and old. Duct tape patched a broken window, a partially fallen gutter lay against the porch, and the front yard looked more like a sleazy used-car lot. "Maybe the person who left those wild tracks was in such a hurry that they forgot to lock the door!" he hoped.

After cutting across the yard and weaving around two rusted out Buicks and one wheel-less Chevy, Tim jumped over a broken step and landed on the front porch. His wish was granted as he reached the door and saw that not only was it unlocked, but it wasn't even completely closed. Warm air and light trickled out through the open crack between the door and frame. A larger rush of warm air greeted him as he gently opened the heavy wooden door and slipped inside.

Not surprisingly, the inside of the house was just as dirty and worn-out as the outside. But the warmth felt fantastic as it slowly penetrated his invisible skin.

Peering down the short hallway, it was clear that there were only one or two bedrooms, a small bathroom, kitchen, and living room. Tim started to turn left toward the kitchen of this tiny abode, but then suddenly spun to the right when he heard the voice of a woman. It wasn't the voice that startled him, it was the fact that the voice called out his name.

"Tim!" the woman had almost screamed at him in what sounded like delight. Tim, shocked, turned to face the tall, slightly overweight woman. She was standing with her face in the shadows of the room. She seemed to be looking right where he stood, but not quite into his eyes. She had the same kind of expression a blind person has after they've forgotten the natural custom of looking at another's eyes when talking.

The woman didn't move like she was blind, however. She swiftly walked toward him with her arms out as if ready to give him a hug. He moved to avoid her, and she stopped her approach.

"Timmy, what's wrong?" Her voice was familiar as if from a long ago dream. Where was this voice from? Could it be . . . No, he thought. This woman must have been over fifty years old.

"It is you Tim, isn't it?" she asked with less certainty than she had when she first used his name. He had thought he recognized her face when she first called his name, but he had refused to believe it was her. This woman was bruised and looked like she had been crying for a week, maybe longer.

He looked away and surveyed the room again. Many things seemed familiar like any normal living room, but there were definitely differences that could only be explained by many years of technological changes and advances. Maybe it *could* be her if this was far into the future.

The shattered looking woman raised her hand and reached up to his face, startling Tim. Could she see him? She was still looking a little too low to meet his gaze but found his shoulder with her hand. Then she moved her hand up along his neck and found his face. Using her touch as a guide, she lifted her eyes a bit more and looked into his own. In the dim lamplight, he saw blue. It *was* her! Those deep blue eyes could only belong to her. They were swollen and red around the sides but still just as beautiful as he remembered.

"Lexie?" he said hesitantly. At the sound of his voice, she broke down crying and threw her arms around him. She hugged him closer than anyone had ever hugged him before. It was a hug of extreme emotional grief and of joy mixed together.

"You came. I knew you would again," she sobbed. "I've been waiting so long." She practically pulled herself onto him with her embrace, and he stumbled back a little.

"Lexie? How? I . . . I don't understand," Tim whispered into her graying hair.

"You don't understand what?" she laughed slightly as the tears subsided. "Oh," she said with new realization of something Tim couldn't comprehend. She still hung on tight as if she was afraid he'd float away toward the ceiling if she let go. "This must be the first time. You told me this would happen, but I had forgotten."

"The first time?" he considered, "I don't . . ."

"Yeah, the first time you find me while in your zone. Well, the first time you remember finding me at least." She laughed and released him a little. "You are in your zone, right?"

"Yes, but . . ."

"And you turned twenty-three years old today?" she continued, looking directly into his eyes.

"How did . . ." he sputtered again, unable to complete any thoughts.

Lexie turned her gaze away from his face and toward the floor. "Wow, I must seem so old to you. And I look terrible . . ." she worried aloud.

"Lexie," Tim said interrupting her unease. "No one has ever seen me or known I was here."

"Well, I'm very special!" she said with a smile, looking back into his eyes with ease. "I've seen you, sort of, and felt you many times."

"But I've never been here before," Tim reasoned.

"Not yet, but you will." She continued smiling, knowing she was confusing him. Then suddenly, her face fell slack, and she sighed deeply letting all the breath leave her chest.

"What's wrong?" It looked to Tim like she had just witnessed the death of a loved one. Lexie grabbed Tim's hands and put them around her waist.

"Hold me again, Tim." She raised her arms around his neck and clutched onto him even tighter than the first time. "You have told me a lot about your zones. I have cherished every moment I have had with you. But you also told me about this moment. I don't have much time with you. You took too long to get here. Next time, find me here as fast as you can. I love you Ti . . ." Her voice faded out even though her mouth had finished saying his name. The room around them faded. The last thing he saw was her eyes. Her beautiful blue eyes.

Chapter 25

NEW RULES

Thursday Morning, May 11, 1995

"WHO IS LESSY?" Natalie asked sleepily the next morning. She was still in bed. The sheets were playing a show-and-tell game across her body as she woke up and stretched. Tim had woken up a few minutes earlier and was now brushing his teeth in the open bathroom doorway. He was oblivious to her display as his mind raced with questions to which he had no answers.

"What?" Tim asked, surprised by the question that had startled him from his thoughts. "Who is who?"

"Lessy. You were whispering her name in your sleep. Well, actually, I think you were still in your weird zone thing. That really freaks me out you know."

"I know, you've told me," Tim said between brushstrokes with annoyance in his tone. He was tired. He hadn't slept much after returning from Lexie's embrace. What did it mean that he would find her, of all people in this world? That he would find her in the middle of nowhere far off in the future? He had contemplated that question for several hours next to another woman whose presence he couldn't care less about.

As Tim brushed, he continued to think of his visit to Lexie. It probably didn't mean anything. Nothing in his zone really meant anything. Then he thought about what Natalie had just said. He paused brushing and looked into the bedroom. "I don't talk during my zone."

"That's what I thought too. But I looked at the clock and it wasn't 12:10 yet."

"12:13," he corrected automatically.

"Whatever. I looked over and your eyes were all buggy and gross."

"Why do you have to say things like that? I can't help what my eyes do. It is just part of me. It's not a freaky thing or a weird thing. It's just a thing."

"Hey, what crawled up your butt and laid eggs?" Natalie said as she sat up with the slick sea-green sheet held across her chest. Tim walked back into the bathroom, spit, and rinsed the toothpaste from his mouth. Then he walked back into the room to find some clothes.

As he pulled on blue sweatpants, he mumbled quietly, "Her name is Lexie."

"What?" Natalie responded as she watched him tie the sweatpants and then grab a T-shirt.

"I said, my friend's name is Lexie. That's the name I must have been saying."

"Is that the little girl you lived by in Ohio?"

"Oklahoma. And yes. She was my best friend growing up until I screwed it all up."

"Screwed what up?" she asked.

"My friendship with someone who understood me. Screwed up my whole life. Nothing has been good since then."

"Ahh, don't go feeling sorry for yourself. Dreams are like that. Everything is going fine, then you have a dream that makes you think of the past, then you feel sad, like maybe you could have done something different. Just think, all your choices led you here right now. If you had done things differently, I may never have met you, and that really would have been sad."

Tim listened while he finished dressing and put on his shoes. Sad for who, he thought. Sad because she couldn't live like a spoiled rich girl playing house? He needed some air.

Natalie saw the upset look in his eyes and realized the danger of what she had just said. The last thing she wanted was to lose her sugar daddy. She spoke again quickly and made sure her tone was as supportive and appealing as possible.

"Tim, you have a great life! You are successful. You have a beautiful house and a very beautiful girlfriend. Don't you think?" She playfully let her right leg edge out from under the silky top sheet.

"You're just trying to distract me."

"So?" she agreed. "What's wrong with being distracted when you're feeling down? Let's not argue with each other. Life is what you make it. Let's make it fun! Don't think about things you may or may not have screwed up in the past. Think about the present. And if you really want to screw something . . ." she paused, letting the meaning of her double entendre soak into his mind.

He looked over at her exposed leg and thigh, then up to her face. Natalie smiled seductively as she let the sheet slip off her chest. She had won again and he was still hers; at least for one more day.

Tim redressed an hour later and went for a long run along the bayou. Despite Natalie's demonstration of extraordinary talents, now that he was away from her, he thought only about Lexie.

Lexie had been right—he had thought she looked old. She was a little overweight and had lines on her face and neck. Her features were swollen and bruised, and her clothes seemed dirty. Actually, her whole house was dirty. Natalie would have called it "skanky." It looked like someone had just taken everything that wasn't nailed down and thrown it against the walls. Why would she live like that?

He thought about the bruises again and the tire tracks leaving the house. Maybe someone had attacked her and left. Or maybe it was her husband. Was she married? He felt stupid for not looking at her hand to check.

Then an old memory resurfaced in his mind. After the hypnosis, other memories of past zones had slowly filtered in too. Since those zones were not fresh, they had seemed only like faded dreams. At the time, he didn't trust any of those memories, since he was not convinced that any of it was real. But in one of those vague recollections from a long ago zone, he thought he remembered Lexie saying that she was married and had a child. That Lexie from that old memory was very much like the one he had just met; old, sad, and broken.

How was it possible that she was able to know he was there? Had she heard the door open? She had said she could see him "sort of." But what did that mean? Was his invisibility less complete than he had always assumed? She had not said anything about his lack of clothing. Maybe she really couldn't see him. Maybe he was more like a spirit to her, or a shadow that she was aware of through some kind of sixth sense.

If only she could have told him more. Why hadn't they had more time together? But she knew the time was to be short, didn't she? She said *he* had told her about that visit. That must mean he would see her again, in his future, but her past.

What about Natalie saying he had talked during his zone? Had his limp, wide-eyed body really said her name? He never had spoken aloud before while in a zone.

"New rules!" Tim laughed to himself as he thought of going back to Lexie and telling her of all the zone rules he had discovered over the years. Of course, the Lexie he had just met must already know those rules. If he had been there before, he would have talked to her and told her all he'd learned.

Tim stopped running and looked around. He was much farther from his house than he usually ran, so he turned around and started walking back. He had been this far by bike many times and knew it would take over two hours to walk back. He was in no hurry though. Somehow, seeing Lexie again had changed him.

He longed to return to her in the distant future place. He didn't care that she was old and overweight. Actually, maybe she wasn't even as old as he thought. It may have just been the bruises and her crying that made her seem older. "I need to get back to her," he said out loud. There must be a way to guide the zone. He could find her and rescue her from the abusive husband. She would forgive him for abandoning her so long ago if he saved her from that life.

Maybe enough time had passed that she already forgave him. She had said that she loved him, right? Yes, she had, he remembered. Right before he zapped back to his body next to Natalie.

"Oh Natalie," he sighed. What would Natalie think of all this. "Hey Nat," he imagined to himself as he walked. "Remember that little girlfriend of mine? Well, I've decided I still love her. Except, she is old now. No, not my age. She is really old. And she isn't even pretty anymore. Well, she is pretty to me though. So, could you please leave now so I can try to learn to control my 'curse' well enough that I can get back to her? Thanks! Bye-bye."

Ok, so maybe he could think of a better way to let Natalie go. He laughed. "I'd probably have to pay her to leave," he said to himself. "Probably have to give her everything I own." Of course, even that would be worth it to find Lexie, he thought. With time, he was sure he could get back into her future and rescue her from that abusive man.

Then his thoughts skipped back to the Arkansas mountain road. Tim had tried to change the future before. He had tried to rescue the truck driver. First he tried to divert the traffic away from the collapsed roadway. Then, because of the timing of the other car, the trucker couldn't avoid the hole.

On the news, however, there was no mention of any tree branches in the road that would have guided traffic. And the woman from the white Honda had said Art had fallen with his truck. It just didn't make sense. Tim had held onto his hands, trying to save him. Art had looked right up at him and known he was there.

Lexie had seen him too, and apparently she had seen him before. That had to mean something. Maybe he could find her earlier, before she was abused, before she was living in poverty, before she was married.

"That's it! You're an idiot!" he yelled. An older couple that sat on a park bench along the trail jumped, startled by the man who had just yelled at them.

"Sorry," Tim said to them as he walked past, "I'm sorry. You are not an idiot. I was just talking to myself."

Silently this time, Tim completed his thought. Lexie wasn't old right now. She was only two-and-a-half years younger than himself somewhere here in the same time in which he lived.

There was no need to skip through zone after zone just to find a version of Lexie that could only see his shadow. He could find her in Nebraska, or wherever she lived now, here in this time. "I will find you, Lexie!" he whispered to himself. "I will save you."

Chapter 26

RETURNING HOME

Friday, May 12, 1995

NATALIE DIDN'T COME home until early the next morning. She had been out shopping and partying with a group of friends until almost 4:00 a.m. Tim had been up after his zone for a few minutes, but then had fallen back to sleep. He had been disappointed but not surprised that the zone had not taken him back to Lexie this time. He was startled awake again as Natalie bumped first into the bedroom door while trying to quietly pass through and then into the dresser next to the bed.

"Natalie," Tim said with a slight crack in his voice as he forced himself to sit up. "We need to talk."

"I'm tired, let's talk tomorrow," she slurred slightly.

"It is tomorrow already. I have to do something. Find someone. It is important."

"What? Why is it so important that I can't go to sleep? I'm tired."

"I know. You're drunk too."

"Not drunk, just . . . tipsy," she tried to say "tipsy" in a cute voice but it was no longer cute to Tim. Nothing she said or did now would deter him. He felt changed and confident. He knew who he wanted to be and what he wanted to do.

"In my zone last night, I . . ."

"Ohhhhhh!" she moaned loudly. "I hate it when you talk about your stupid zone thing. You have a great life! Don't let your curse mess it up. Just pretend it doesn't exist and let's sleep!"

Until now, he had had no idea what he would say to Natalie. But as she stumbled to take off her $600 heels that looked just like so many others in her closet, he realized that she represented everything bad about himself. He was no better than her in the way he was using his zone.

"I know you don't understand this, but I have this thing. You call it a curse, and I think the way I've been using it, it has been a curse. For too long, I have been selfish and thought only of myself, money, and fun."

"Good!"

"No, not good," he continued. "I have to choose to use it for either myself or for others. Well, I've chosen. From now on, I choose to use it for others."

"Fine," she moaned again, dropping herself onto the bed. "I'm going to sleep."

Tim didn't go back to sleep. He watched Natalie roll away from him, still in her clothes she had been out in. She smelled of alcohol and tobacco smoke. For the first time, he saw how ugly she truly was. He had been blind and selfish. But now, looking at her in the dim light, he felt encouraged that he was finally about to do the right thing. He wished he had his Magic 8 Ball with him. It still sat in his old bedroom at his parents' house. Would it agree with his decision now?

He waited as Natalie's breathing slowed down and she either fell asleep or passed out. Either way, he was glad he wouldn't have to talk to her again. It was easier this way. He got up, tore off part of a paper shopping bag, and wrote a simple note:

Natalie,

I have to move on now. Take care.

Tim

When morning came, Tim hired a real estate lawyer, went to the bank, and signed the house title over to the United Way charity. He left explicit instructions that Natalie could live there as long as she chose to, but the house, contents, and all profit from an eventual sale would be given to the charity. All of his assets would also be donated to several charities, including one to help abused women. The wealth and material possessions that had taken him five years to attain took only five hours to set free.

Nothing at the house meant anything to him. All he kept were the jeans and T-shirt he had worn as he had walked out of his house for the last time and his rusted Ford Ranger that Natalie had detested. He had bought that truck while working at the carwash, before he started using his zone for profit, so he felt it was his to keep. But the rest of it was now gone.

Tim took a deep breath as he drove north, away from Natalie, and away from the life he had manufactured so carefully. As he breathed in the warm, late afternoon air, he felt something heavy lift from his chest. It was as if a chain that had been tugging on him had finally been removed. It was a chain that had grown heavier one link at a time for the last five years.

Tim spent his first night at a rest stop off I-35 in northern Texas. He slept only a few hours and was glad no one bothered him or his truck while he zoned. The zone had been a simple one, and it left him feeling good about his decision to leave Natalie.

He had watched an elderly couple, a husband and wife, sitting quietly together, holding hands on their front porch. As Tim watched them invisibly from his seat against a large shady oak tree, he imagined himself sitting just that way with Lexie; hand in hand at the end of their lives.

The couple only spoke occasionally to each other. Mostly they sat in satisfied, harmonious silence that can only be understood by a pair of lovers at peace with each other and content in their lives.

As he drove on the next morning, Tim knew that the route that would lead him to Lexie was still unclear. Where would he find her? How would he convince her to forgive him? He didn't know the answer, but he knew where he was going first. He just hoped they too would forgive him.

His parents' house looked just like it had when he had left five years ago. It felt bizarre standing there, almost as if he had stepped back in time. The shrubs looked a little taller and less groomed, and the paint seemed faded. But his dad's truck was parked in the usual place next to the house, and his mom's car was sitting in the open garage. It was very comforting to see the familiar sight and know how close they were.

He didn't go to his house though. He parked his truck off the road behind Lexie's old house. It was in bad shape. Several windows had been smashed in, and part of the garage wall had graffiti on it. "What happened," Tim thought aloud.

A voice startled Tim from behind. "Vandals hit it last year. It had been vacant a while," the voice said behind Tim. He turned his head, surprised by the sound, and saw his father standing nearby.

"Dad?" Tim said uneasily. He felt so bad for walking out and never telling his parents where he had gone or if he was okay.

"I was out back, feeding Nugget, and heard your truck," his dad said. "Son, are you okay?"

Tim turned around and walked slowly toward his dad along the stone walkway. "I'm sorry, Dad," he said with his head low. John didn't respond. He lifted up his arms, stepped the remaining distance to Tim, and pulled him into a warm fatherly hug.

"Everything's all right, son. Come inside." They embraced for a few more seconds and then Tim obeyed his father and followed him into the house.

"Sarah?" John called to his wife as he and his son stepped into the back door by the kitchen. "Come here, hon. Someone has come to see us."

They heard her chair in the family room squeak as she hastily stood up and rushed toward the kitchen. Something in John's voice instinctively told her that their prodigal son was home. Sarah gasped as she reached the doorway and saw John standing with one arm draped around their boy. "Tim!" she cried out as she crossed the floor to him. She hugged on him for several minutes and let tears of joy wet his chest.

The reunited family enjoyed a frozen pizza dinner together as Tim told them about his life over the last five years. He told them the details factually and humbly and felt an odd relief come to him through his verbal confession. John and Sarah listened without judgment as Tim described his selfish use of his zone, lifestyle, and even Natalie. His parents were not surprised that his zone had continued but were amazed at how he had been able to use it to his advantage.

They continued to listen but appeared confused as Tim described his visit to the future Lexie. "She was so sad and needed help," Tim said as he described the older Lexie. He explained how he was changed because of seeing her again. "So that is why I left Natalie and all that money. I feel different now, better than I have in a long time. It's like I was asleep but am now finally awake."

"Son," his father tried to interrupt but Tim continued.

"She didn't have a chance to tell me anything, not much about my zone or anything . . ."

"Son," John tried again.

" . . . but I believe she wants me to do good things with my zone. And while I'm doing good, I'll be looking for her."

"Tim," his father interrupted gently but firmly enough this time that Tim stopped and looked at him. "Tim, I'm not sure how to say this, but . . ." he paused and looked at Sarah for encouragement.

"Go on," she whispered. "Tell him."

"Tell me what?" Tim asked.

"Tim. We got a letter in the mail a couple months ago. It was from Chris, Lexie's dad." John looked at Sarah again, then to Tim. "We're not sure of the details, but . . ." John stopped again. His face was pale and grim.

"Dad, no. That's impossible! I saw her just a few days ago in my zone. She was alive. She was old and beaten up, but alive!"

"Tim, she died. Over three months ago. Her boyfriend was detained and questioned but then released. Like I said, we don't know many details. I am so sorry."

Tim was in shock and said nothing.

"In the letter," John continued, "Chris told us that Lexie had left Nebraska when she was seventeen. She called him occasionally to tell him she was okay, but she moved around a lot with different boyfriends. He didn't say why she left.

"We think she might have come by here one night about three months ago. It must have been right before she died. A sound woke us up in the middle of the night, and so we went into your room to see what it was. We found your bedroom window unlocked and slightly open. The curtain was tucked under the closed window to the outside."

"I thought we had had a burglar," Sarah added. "When I looked out of the window, I saw a young woman running off, but it was dark, so I couldn't tell who it was. Nothing was taken as far as I could tell."

"We're not sure why she came to your room or if that was even her," John continued the story. "We would have let her in if she'd asked. Heck, we would have let her stay as long as she wanted. If only we had known she was in there. Maybe we could have talked to her. Found out what she needed. Maybe she just needed a friend?"

John had been looking down while he talked until he said the word friend. He looked up and saw the guilt welling up in Tim's eyes. "I'm sorry, Tim. I know how bad you felt about what happened between you two." Tim looked away from his father's gaze. "But you can't blame yourself for this, Tim. She had a hard time after leaving here, and it isn't your fault."

"But it is my fault," Tim argued. He felt broken, devastated, and confused. He thought of the last time he had seen her before she moved away so long ago. He hadn't even waved good-bye. Then, three nights ago, she had held him and had forgiven him.

"Dad, I saw her. I talked to her," he wept. "How could I have seen her if she was dead? How could she be alive many years from now if she died?" It made no sense.

"Could it be a dream," asked Sarah. "When you are in your . . . your zone?"

John spoke up again. "Dreams don't fry MRI machines and cause the dreamer's mind to leave his body."

Tim didn't want to discuss his zone. He had come, hoping to discover a way to find Lexie. Instead, he found out it was a hopeless search.

He ran outside into the cool clear Oklahoma night. "What am I supposed to do?" he yelled at the starry sky. "God, please tell me! Why did you make me a freak? Where is Lexie?" He saw no answer from the stars. He heard no answer from God. There was only silence. No barking dogs. No cars. Not even the sound of wind in the trees on this silent night.

Lexie's house was dark and vacant. It looked dead too. But when he closed his eyes, he could see her jumping off the porch and running over to him, her ponytail flopping behind. Then he could see her crying and running into her house the day he chose his friends over her. He saw her sitting on her porch by herself after her mom had been taken away. Lastly, he saw the empty porch after she had moved to Nebraska. Empty like it was now.

Could she really be dead? Slowly, the truth of it sank in, like rain into concrete. Lexie was dead. His zone had once again failed him and shown him a lie.

He wondered why she had come back to his house before she died. Had she been hoping to find him? What would he have said if he had been here? Asked for forgiveness? What if he had been here with Natalie? Would he have broken up with Nat on the spot and taken Lexie into his arms?

He stood there in the winter air for many minutes, contemplating the questions that couldn't be answered. He thought about the word "dead." What did that even mean? People like Lexie didn't die. Old people died. Grandparents died. Not someone young. Not Lexie. He sobbed again, quietly but deeply. He had lost her forever, again. She existed only as a lie within a zone and somewhere as a marble headstone with her name and date of death.

"Tim, it's cold. Come inside," his mom called from the front door.

He didn't respond but slowly turned away from Lexie's dead house and walked toward his own. His mom was waiting. "Come sit down, please," she beckoned as she led him to the kitchen table. He minded his mom and sat down. "Tim?" she asked and waited for a response.

"Yes, Mom?" He was a little surprised at the seriousness her voice portrayed. Usually, she avoided deep or serious conversations. But something in her manner told him this was different. He could tell that she wanted to say something, but didn't know how to say it.

Finally she spoke. "Tim. There is something I should have told you a long time ago. I guess at first I didn't think it was important. Then, I thought it wouldn't matter. But I think now, it may answer some of your questions."

Tim looked up at his mom and waited. She had her eyes closed and took a deep breath before going on.

"There is a reason I never had another child after you. My doctors said it wasn't safe. They never could explain what was wrong with me but just that they were concerned that another baby could kill me."

Tim listened.

"While I was pregnant, I had severe headaches. Not everyday, but very often. One evening, when I was about eight months along, the pain was so severe that I drove myself to the hospital."

"Where was Dad?"

"I was in Utah," John answered from the doorway. He had heard them talking and looked in. Thinking it unusual that Sarah had initiated such a deep conversation, he leaned back against the wall, just inside the room, but stayed out of the way. "I was at a business conference. I didn't even know anything was wrong until the next day when Sarah called me from the hospital."

"I just didn't want anyone to worry. So I went in on my own and asked them to find out what was wrong. They said that my body was trying to reject the baby. They said my hormones were reacting to the early stages of miscarriage. But they couldn't explain the rejection or why it had appeared to have been going on for a long time. There didn't seem to be any explanation.

"I told the doctors that sometimes it felt like I wasn't pregnant anymore. My stomach would loosen up, and I couldn't feel you kicking or pushing. This same feeling happened that night while I was in the hospital. I called a nurse in to check on you, and she couldn't find your heartbeat. She called in the doctors immediately. They tried to find the beat and pushed around on my abdomen, the whole time saying everything would be fine. But I could see the looks on their faces. They didn't think everything was going to be fine. I knew that something very serious was wrong.

"The endocrinologist was called in. When he started to explain that he thought I'd lost you, I must have gone hysterical. My heart stopped and they called for more help. He started CPR while other doctors ran in with one of those defibrillator things. They used it on my chest and got my heart started again but yours still wasn't beating well enough for them to hear.

"They rolled me into the operating room and did an emergency C-section. You weren't breathing when you were born. I woke up screaming for you, but the doctors wouldn't let me see you. The surgeon kept saying, everything will be okay, but he seemed nervous or upset. I asked what was wrong with my baby, but he just kept repeating, 'Relax, let's take care of you right now.'

"Finally, after what seemed like forever, they brought you to my room. When I saw you, I was so happy to see that you were fine that I never asked what had been wrong. Maybe I just didn't want to know.

"Tim, until five years ago, I never thought about what had happened that night. But after seeing what happened during Dr. Bruin's tests, I remembered I had hidden this away all those years ago." She pulled a manila folder out of her sewing bag and handed it to Tim.

Tim opened it carefully. At the top of several yellowed pages, Tim read in fancy script, "Tulsa Memorial Hospital."

"Is this your hospital chart?" Tim asked. "From the night I was born?"

"You never told me any of this." John said as he came over from the doorway and leaned in to see the chart. "You said the C-section was done as a precaution. I thought they had trouble finding a consistent heartbeat so decided to deliver."

"I hadn't intended to keep anything from you. But I think I just wanted to forget how scared I was that night. It was easier to just tell you about our son, our beautiful baby boy, and forget about the details. I didn't want to think about how different things could have gone."

"Mom, this has everything from that night, your headache, heart failure, c-section," Tim said, not really listening anymore. He was digging through the documents and records, looking at all those details that his mom had wanted to forget. Would this explain his zone? Was there anything in this file that could unlock secrets of his past?

"It has your chart too, Tim," she said reaching over and turning to the back. "Right here. A lot of it, especially the medical terms and descriptions, doesn't mean anything to me. But look here," she pointed.

Tim read some of the lines next to her finger. "Initial diagnoses: still birth; Retinal Vein Occlusion and Complete Pupil Dilation of the eyes. Resuscitation Successful."

"Look at the times, right there," Sarah suggested. "Over at the right."

John and Tim both read through the list and matched it with the time stamps.

"Tim!" John shouted, pointing at the resuscitation time. Next to the resuscitation description read the time, "12:13 a.m."

Quickly Tim skipped back a few pages. There it was. Next to the scribbled words on his mother's chart, "electric defib started," was the time, "11:35."

"That's the time range of my zone," Tim yelled excitedly to both his parents. John leaned in over Tim's shoulders and continued scanning the pages with him. As John read, he scratched his head in the back where his hair was thinning.

Sarah sat down in an uncomfortable straight-backed wooden chair sitting near her men. They continued flipping back and forth through the records. She felt guilty having waited so long to share this history but also felt relieved to finally provide it for Tim.

"So," John spoke up again after several minutes, "the electric shock, the energy from the paddles must have caused the zone to start."

"And then," Tim added, "after the C-section, something the doctors did to resuscitate me brought me back out of my zone. And ever since, I've been locked into that pattern."

"So that explains it," John said thoughtfully. "I've read that our brain functions on electrical impulses. Somehow, part of your brain was stimulated, a part that allowed you to do something . . . something amazing."

Tim looked over at his dad incredulously. "What? That explains nothing. No offense, Mom. It's interesting and maybe explains the timing of it, but what am I supposed to do with it? I still know nothing."

John sighed, admitting his blunder. "No, you are right, Tim," John responded softly to his son's protest. "At least, you are right about this folder not containing all the answers. I think we may have to assume that we will never really understand what your zone is," he continued, shaking his head slowly. "But this is another step. You never know, maybe you will find out more."

Tim looked up at Sarah and saw the hurt in her eyes. He knew that she was blaming herself for this and was probably even more confused by all of it than he was. "Mom," he said, softening his voice, "I don't blame you. I'm not sure what I was hoping to see in these records. I guess I hoped it would help me understand my curse?"

His mom looked up. A soft motherly smile replaced the hurt. "Tim, I know you don't blame me. I just wish I had helped you more as you struggled with all this on your own." She sighed, looked at John and then back to Tim. "I know Natalie told you that you were cursed, and I'm sure it must feel like that often. But I disagree. Your zone is not a curse. It is a gift."

"A gift of lies," Tim scoffed. "I see things and experience things in the future but in ways that can't be true," Tim spoke as he pulled the folder back from his dad and continued scanning the pages. "What good is it if I can't trust what I see?"

"A lot of it made sense though, right?" Sarah asked. She had hoped that the hospital records would provide more relief to Tim, but now she realized that it wasn't information he needed. He needed direction. "The things you saw while there in the other places? Isn't that how you said you got all that money? Your gambling bets and actions were accurate, so you do have a gift of seeing the future."

"Yes, I guess so," Tim responded absently as he read the description of his resuscitation. "Except for Lexie and Art," he thought out loud as he looked back up from the pages to his mom. "He was the guy I told you about in the truck. And I suppose there have been a lot of other things that I never checked. Oh, and I've noticed that every once in a while, something minor is different. Like a baseball team winning by four points instead of three. Or a person wouldn't show up at the same time they did in a zone. I usually just thought that maybe I'd remembered it wrong in the zone."

Tim paused and looked out the window toward Lexie's dark house. "None of it matters though. I wanted to help Lexie. I wanted to make up for what I did when we were young. I wanted to do what was right for a change, for someone else." He paused again and he thought about how he had lived for the last five years. "Dad, Mom, I am a bad person. I cheated people out of money, I played with peoples' lives, I left you guys and never called to tell you I was okay, I . . ."

"Tim, stop. Come here." John motioned and then opened his arms to pull Tim into a hug. Sarah stood up from the chair but then hesitated. She had never been as comfortable with affection as John was, but she too put her arm around her son.

"I'm so sorry. I am ashamed of my life," Tim wept.

"Tim, I don't know all the details of what you've done, but it's okay to be ashamed of part of your life," his mom spoke. "That means you know how to do what is right. Now is your chance to change your path and be proud of the rest of your life."

"So what do I do?"

"Use your gift." Sarah said matter-of-factly.

"I told you." Tim shook his head. "I want to change. I don't want to cheat through life anymore."

"You're not listening, Tim. You need to listen to me now." Sarah said again with conviction. Tim and John looked at her, surprised by the show of strength from this woman who had always seemed to stand at the side.

"Tim, you have a gift. A real gift. You don't know why you have it and maybe never will. But you do have it. The things you witness in the future are accurate enough for you to get rich and take advantage of people. The parts that seem inaccurate or completely wrong, well, they are telling you something too. You may just have to look deeper.

"But this gift is real, and I think it is a God-given gift for you to use. Any power can corrupt. We are all capable of acting badly. Now is the time to use your power well. Use it for doing good. You said you wanted to help others. So do that! Look for people who need help. Learn how to help them in your zone and then come back here and do it.

"Do you remember what Lexie used to say when we'd see a homeless person under the bridge, or a baby crying, or even a bug caught in a spider's web?" Sarah didn't wait for a response. "Lexie would say, 'Let's fix it. I don't want him to be sad.' Remember that, Tim? She had a heart for others, no matter the situation.

"Lexie may be gone, but think of how proud she'd be of you if you helped others now."

"But who do I help? The people in my zone or people here?"

Sarah didn't hesitate, "Both, Tim. Everyone!"

Chapter 27

FLIGHT 4612

AT 11:35 THAT night, Tim stood up and found himself inside an airport terminal. It was dark outside due to a storm, and it was unclear whether it was day or night. Heavy rain was tapping against the large glass windows that lined the walls and part of the ceiling. He looked around to find a clock.

Instead of a clock, Tim was amazed to see a large display showing the gate number and time: 5:50 p.m. It wasn't the size of the display that caught Tim's attention, or the time that struck him as interesting, but it was the fact that unlike any television screen he had ever seen, this one was completely flat like a paper-thin pane of glass. The opaque and brightly colored images and text seemed to float in front of the transparent glass. "I wonder what airport this is." Tim thought out loud knowing no one would hear him anyway.

The oddly flat pane and the images displayed on it reconfirmed his understanding that his zone moved him four-dimensionally. Instead of displaying the gate number and flight status on a chalk board or with stationary text on flipping plastic letter cards, this amazing futuristic panel presented information with colorful, animated motion and bright, easy to read 3D text. On the left hand side of the screen floated the gate number and time that he had noticed before, but now he also read the date. September 22, 2026. Tim had traveled thirty-six years into the future! He had journeyed further before, including the night he met the older Lexie, but this was the first time he had seen the future in a place surrounding him with modern technology and a specific date and time.

The future was always strange to Tim. This place in 2026 was no exception. At first glance, it was often difficult to recognize his place in time. So much of this world looked just like what he would expect to find in his own world, thirty-six years in the past. The funny connected airport seats, a bank of outdated pay phones along one unused wall, the buildings outside the windows, even the planes looked pretty much the same as from his time.

A little boy around eight years old sat next to his mom waiting for their flight. He wore jeans and a dark blue T-shirt with a truck on the front. His shoes were Nike. Nothing odd there. His mom, however, was a different story. Her clothes seemed fairly normal, but a blue light next to her ear was slowly pulsing on and off. She spoke and laughed as if someone familiar stood directly in front of her. Then she waved "good-bye" and the blue light faded off. It must have been a type of cell phone, Tim thought, like others he had seen in different future zones. Though, he had never seen one like that.

As he looked around more, many of the people waiting had those small lights next to their ears, though not all were blue. Tim saw red and green lights too, but those users weren't speaking to anyone. Instead, they seemed fixated on visions that only they could see. He guessed those devices must directly interact with the user's brains.

There were a few older people holding physical cell phones like those he had seen in zones not so far into his future. But even those handheld devices seemed to require that the owner gaze hypnotically onto the small screens.

Tim wanted to see one closer, but knew that if he grabbed it from someone's hand, they would notice. Then he spotted a young girl, probably around five years old, with an unused pink phone sitting on the seat next to her. She wore a matching pink butterfly shirt and was busy scribbling on a pad of paper. Since her attention was away from the phone, he knew she wouldn't notice his inspection.

Tim picked up the pink device and examined it. This one was fatter than some but had no buttons. He couldn't figure out how it worked. One side was black and smooth, and the other sides were all pink. Suddenly, as he turned it around in his fingers, the black side lit up! A picture of a puppy dog adorned the screen, and number and letter keys seemed to rise and float above the surface just like the large airport display.

Without warning, the entire phone began to glow bright pink and it buzzed in his hand while playing an odd electronic tune. The buzz startled Tim causing him to drop the phone onto the girl's foot. She noticed it now, due to the simultaneous impact on her foot and youthful ditty emanating from its speaker.

The girl picked it up and squealed, "Hi, Daddy!" after placing the phone up to her head. "What? Oh," she said and then turned the phone the opposite way, putting the top toward her ear instead of her mouth.

"Hear me now, Daddy? Okay. Mommy and I are still waiting . . ."

Tim smiled and walked away. His inspection of the device was over. He walked to the other end of the seating, remembering his mom's words from earlier that evening.

"Help everyone," she had said. Tim looked around. No one here seemed to be in any danger.

An old wrinkled man was having a conversation at one of the antiquated pay phones. He seemed to be the only person in the large terminal to even notice the twenty or so phones lined up along the wall.

Gate workers chatted casually with each other while an occasional automated announcement blared from hidden speakers in the ceiling, "Please keep carry-on bags with you at all times. Never leave baggage unattended . . ."

Tim tuned out the message and sat down close enough to listen to the old man at the pay phones. He seemed to be talking to a son or daughter.

"I know, I know," the man said emphatically. "I just have a weird feeling." The man paused while something was said on the other end, then he continued. "I've been around much longer than you. I've learned to trust my feelings." Pause. "Yes. Yes." Pause again. "No."

The conversation went on. Tim looked around again at the waiting population. There seemed to be a sea of people deep in conversations, yet no one spoke to one another. This future was a world of virtual communication, Tim thought, as the automated message droned on. "Report any unattended packages, baggage, or vectorlites anywhere in the airport to security or airline personnel . . ." the message said. Tim wasn't sure what a vectorlite was, but apparently it was important here in the future.

Tim looked back toward the old man and his heart leapt a beat. A screamer was standing next to the man, motionless. It was the same boy he had always seen before and as usual, it didn't seem to notice Tim. Its attention was on the wrinkled man.

Tim was ready to bolt out of the terminal, away from the boy, if it came after him. This was the closest he'd seen one since being chased in China. But for now, it didn't seem to care about any one other than the man. It watched the man with a steady gaze; its arms at its side as the man continued to argue over the phone.

A gate supervisor came over the loud speaker. "Attention passengers. Flight 4612 to Bangor, Maine will be delayed due to weather."

"You hear that?" the old man shouted to the receiver. "They've postponed my flight. Didn't I tell you I had a feeling! Good. I told you I didn't want to leave Boston."

Tim noticed a child standing behind the gate attendants' podium next to the red-vested man who had just made the announcement. Some kid must have wandered off from his parents and was waiting to be found, Tim thought.

Then the male attendant grabbed the intercom again. "Attention passengers," he said with the same monotonous voice he had used moments earlier, "Flight 4612 to Bangor, Maine will leave on time. Please prepare to board."

"They're telling us to board now," the old man repeated into the phone. "I don't think they know what's going on."

Tim also thought it strange that the flight's status would flip like that. He looked outside and saw more lightning. Why would they decide to fly? Then he saw the kid by the gate more clearly, and he realized that it was not a kid. It was a screamer! The old man's screamer remained next to him, so there were two. No, three. He saw another next to a woman looking fearful at the lightning outside.

A moment later, ten or so more screamers appeared from nowhere. As they appeared, the people seemed to begin obeying the gate attendant and started lining up at the entrance to the gate. The screamers still ignored Tim and stayed focused on the passengers. As their "assigned" passenger entered the plane at the end of the ramp past the gate, each screamer seemed to turn and walk away. Tim never saw where they went, however. It seemed as though they disappeared shortly after turning.

The old man's screamer remained stoic and focused intently on him next to the phone. "Okay," the man said to the phone. "Yes, okay. I'll get on the plane. At my age, what do I have to lose? But if something happens, you are out of my will!" With that, the man slammed the phone down onto the hook, grabbed his small bag, and marched toward the gate.

The screamer stayed put but watched the man enter the gate and slowly start down the ramp toward the plane. As soon as the man entered the plane, the screamer was gone.

It was apparent to Tim that the screamers had arrived to insure the passengers got on the plane. But why? He decided to try something he hadn't done yet in a zone; he would fly. Something was supposed to happen. He could feel it.

As he walked down the ramp, he saw rain leaking onto the floor from the seams in the movable walkway that led to the plane. Lightning continued to flash outside, and the quick thunder response confirmed that the storm was near. He was surprised all the passengers entered the plane so quickly. If he hadn't felt somewhat invincible, he never would have entered this plane. However, he knew his real body was still lying at home in his bed, safe and sound.

He had always wondered what would happen to his body as it slept, if his mind died here in the zone. If the plane crashed, maybe he would find out. He thought of Lexie and of the news of her death. "I'm just like that old man," Tim thought. "What have I got to lose?"

The plane was medium-sized, Tim guessed a 737, and had about one hundred and thirty seats. As Tim scanned the plane, he saw that there were only three open seats remaining after all the passengers had boarded. He decided to take the one next to the same old man he had watched by the phones. The plane's intercom erupted with static as a flight attendant in the front of the plane gave the same safety intro that he had seen every time he flew in his own time. It was funny how some things changed so little.

"Look at the emergency pamphlet in the pocket on the seat in front of you . . ." and "Note the emergency exits . . ."

Only a few of the passengers seemed to be listening to the instructions. Most were turning off their electronic devices, reading, or already sleeping. How someone could sleep with the storm raging outside the plane was beyond Tim's understanding.

The old man muttered to the stranger in the seat across the aisle, "I haven't flown since 1974. Never needed to, really. Now my kids are forcing me to move. Think I shouldn't be living on my own anymore. But Old Herman Johnston here was doing just fine on his own, I tell you." Tim laughed as the old man referred to himself in the third person. "Yes, sir," his discourse continued, "ever since Bess passed, I've . . ."

Tim felt the plane back out of the gate and begin taxiing toward the runways. "Welcome to flight 4612 to Bangor, Maine," a voice erupted from the overhead speakers. "We are first in line for the runway and will be in the air momentarily. Flight assistants, prepare cabin for takeoff," the strong male voice called over the speaker.

Tim wondered why the pilot had called the flight attendants, 'assistants.' Would politically correct terminology advances outlaw the term attendant?

Old Johnston was unconcerned with being politically correct, and he continued his rant to the unknown and uninterested passenger. "Judging by the weather, I won't have to live much longer anywhere. Maybe my blood's just thin in my old age. They say that's why I'm cold in the winter. But I'm hot in the summer. But my thin old blood is telling me right now that this flight is a mistake."

The plane was speeding down the runway now. The roaring engines seemed almost deafening, and Tim felt himself being pushed back into the seat from the rapid acceleration. Tim looked at the runway and could see the wheels splashing through puddles on the tarmac. The rain poured down faster than the water could drain away. The strength of the turbine engines pulled the plane up to liftoff speed. Tim felt the wheels separate from the concrete and then retract into the body of the plane.

He wondered if instead of getting on the plane, he should have used his time to inspect it. Maybe he would have found a hydraulic leak or crack in the wing. Deciding that he would not have known what to look for, and that it was too late now anyway, he settled back into his seat nervously.

Another bolt of lightning struck ahead of the jet. Johnston rambled on, almost shouting to speak over the engine noise and thunder, "What kind of moron flies a plane in this? I ain't the smartest rock on the ground, but I think any rock on the ground is smarter than any of us rocks up here in this."

Another bolt of lightning ignited so close to the plane that several passengers screamed from the sudden explosion of light and thunder. Tim was scared too.

He reflexively turned his gaze to the window on his left as another bright flash lit up the sky. However, he was even more terrified when he looked away from the window and discovered dozens of screamers were packed into the aisle. He tried to count them. Well over one hundred screamers! Probably one for each passenger, he thought. He could only assume that another pair of screamers stood in the cockpit with the pilot and copilot. There was no way to run from them this time. No where to hide.

Without thought, Tim yelled, "Why are you here?" at the screamers closest to him. One was staring at Johnston, and the rest each stared toward the other passengers. Each one's attention seemed to be locked onto a specific passenger just like Tim had observed in the terminal. They stood completely still as each gazed directly at their target.

Even the flight attendants had a screamer assigned. However, since the attendants were on the move, the screamers seemed to glide in and out of view around obstacles and other screamers, staying only a few feet from each attendant. The screamers assigned to the stationary passengers were equally adept at fading in and out to avoid interfering with the workers as they moved through the aisles. None of them acknowledged Tim or his question.

"Answer me! Why are you here? Who are you?" There was still no response. Lightning struck again, and the plane bounced on the turbulent air. This time, no passengers screamed. Even Johnston was silent. Tim looked at him and saw that he was just sitting, facing forward now. He seemed calm. All the passengers looked calm. It was as if the screamers were somehow tranquilizing them.

The plane shook hard again in the turbulent air. "You are the reason this plane took off in this storm, aren't you?" Tim yelled. "You want this plane to crash and for all these people to die!"

The pilot spoke through the intercom again. "Passengers, we are experiencing extreme weather conditions. Thank you for staying calm. We are beginning a course change and will try to get above this storm."

The screamers remained stoic and silent. One middle-aged man with a beard and glasses picked up a magazine and smiled dreamily.

"What is going on here?" Tim thought aloud. Without thinking, he unbuckled his seatbelt and stood up. He forgot how short the ceiling was over his seat and hit his head on the overhead compartment. "Oww!" he yelled. No one noticed. The plane suddenly seemed to drop, and Tim felt his whole body being tossed up into the air. After hitting his back on the overhead compartment, the plane found flight again, and he was thrown downward into the seat in front of Johnston's row. Tim's elbow and shoulder impacted a business man's stomach and crotch. His feet narrowly missed slamming into a second man seated next to the man in the suit.

The suited man yelled, "What the heck?" as he pushed Tim off his lap and seemed confused, unable to identify the source of his sudden pain. Tim landed on the floor in the narrow space between rows on the feet of the two male passengers. When he looked up, he saw that the screamer that had been watching the suited man was now looking down at him instead.

The plane shook violently again, and the suit yelled to the man seated next to him. "This is the worst turbulence I've ever seen. Hey, you hear me, Larry? Where you at, man? What's wrong with you?"

"Huh?" Larry responded absently without turning to his business partner. Tim pulled himself up off their feet and tried to stand.

"I said . . ." the suit started again, but then stopped suddenly. The screamer's expression had remained unchanged but was now turned back to the business man, somehow suppressing his awareness.

Tim felt angry. He felt powerless. It was the same anger he had experienced when he learned that Art had really died. And the same sense of helplessness when he heard of Lexie's death.

"Leave him alone!" Tim yelled at the screamer. Again, he was ignored. "Why do I have the ability to be here if I can't do anything about it? What are you doing to these people?"

The plane hit more turbulence. Tim held on as hard as he could but was still thrown back up into the air. This time he landed half on a woman's head and half on the back of the seat in front of her. "Ow!" she called out. Then, aware suddenly of her surroundings, she yelled, "What's happening? This is suicide!" She seemed to have been woken up from the unnatural calm that all the passengers were exhibiting. "Why are we trying to fly in this? We need to . . ." She trailed off just as the suit had.

Tim thought about what he was witnessing. The screamers only seemed to care about his presence when he interacted with others.

When his body had been tossed by the plane, causing him to slam into the man and then the woman, the screamers' attention was turned toward him and thus, their mind control was interrupted, and the passenger became aware of the situation. Maybe their tranquilization of the passengers was only to calm them. But why?

Tim assumed that the pilots were also being calmed in a similar way, but did that mean they were making good decisions about flying the plane, or were they so drugged up on mind-numbing screamer juice that they'd fly this bird right into the heart of the storm?

Tim tested his theory. He punched the business man hard in the face. Sure enough, the screamer's gaze turned to Tim, and the man yelled out in pain. "My nose! My freakin' nose is broken!" Blood was pouring from his nostrils. Tim hadn't meant to hurt him, just sever the effect of the screamers so he could see if he was right.

The plane bounced again and then began to dive. Tim felt he knew what to do. Somehow, he needed to get to the pilots and wake them up. He jumped into the aisle and put his arms straight out, expecting to have to push the screamers out of the way. But instead, his arms met only a liquid-like resistance, and he fell to the floor in the aisle. The screamers were not solid like he anticipated. There was something physical to them, but it was more like thin warm syrup.

Shaking off his surprise, he crawled through their legs toward the flight attendant and cockpit door. One of the screamers behind him let out the same ear-splitting cry Tim had heard years before when he tried to help that old man in China.

Tim looked back and saw it gazing at him with a wide open mouth. The mouth opened so large that it seemed to be detached from the skull. Any lingering belief that these boys could be human was erased in Tim's mind.

The screamer's finger was pointed directly at Tim. Other screamers turned their attention to him as well and began to howl just as the first had. As they did, the passengers seemed to awaken from their trance and became aware of the diving plane. They too began to scream.

Tim reached the door to the cockpit but found it locked. He started to pound on the door but was suddenly grabbed from behind by the screamer that had been next to the flight attendant. As he was pulled backward, the attendant, now alert, grabbed the intercom mic and heroically instructed the passengers to assume their crash positions.

Two of the screamers were able to pin Tim down. The passengers were in various stages of panic and terror. Some had removed their seatbelts and were standing up. Others obeyed the flight attendant's order to put their heads down and brace for impact. All were terrified.

A moment later, however, the panicked wails and crying hushed as all but two of the screamers had returned attention to the passengers and crew. Tim saw that each passenger now looked eerily calm again. Their eyes seemed blank. Some even had an odd dreamlike smile. Only the two flight attendants remained alert to the final moments of the plane. Their screamers remained with Tim, holding him down against the cockpit door.

Tim watched in horror as the left side of the plane was torn off by the rigid timber in the northern Massachusetts deciduous forest. Old man Johnston flew forward, fatally slamming into the cockpit door, his limp body falling next to Tim. Heat and flames erupted from the tail section, engulfing the remaining, oblivious passengers. A sudden darkness filled Tim's consciousness. The zone had ended.

Tim jumped from his bed as soon as his consciousness returned to his body. His leap to the floor of the small room knocked the bedside table hard against the wall. He passed his hands over his body and quickly reassured himself that he was completely unscathed by the violent crash.

"All those people," he thought. "I couldn't save them. Why can't I ever help them? Over and over again, I see these things and can't do anything about it. Why? Why let me get rich off my zone but not let me help people?"

Then he cried out toward the ceiling, "What do you want from me?"

The door to his room burst open. "Tim!" his dad and mom both yelled as his dad flipped on the light.

"What? What am I supposed to do?" he yelled angrily at them. "You said I could help others. You said that Lexie would be proud," he shouted, looking at his mom. "But I can't! I tried and I couldn't save them." The anger in his voice dissolved into hopelessness.

Somehow understanding his son's despair, John pulled Tim and Sarah into a strong embrace. It had occurred to John that Tim may be too old for these animated displays of fatherly affection, but he didn't care. He didn't want Tim to ever run away again, even if he was an adult now.

"I don't want this 'gift!'" Tim scoffed. "You said it was a God-given gift. Well, I wish God would take my zone away!"

John sighed but then smiled. "Tim," he said, "I remember one time when you had fallen out of a tree and badly scraped your arm. You were in terrible pain even after the bleeding had stopped. You asked me to hold you until the pain went away."

"What has that got to do with anything," Tim argued.

"You asked me to hold you, but you didn't ask me to take away the pain. You didn't ask me to keep you from falling out of the tree either, just to comfort you until the pain was gone."

John paused, trying to pick his words well. "I suppose what I am saying is that, maybe you shouldn't ask for your ability to go away. Instead, pray that you learn how to use it."

"But Dad, so many people died. I had to watch it happen, but there wasn't anything I could do about it."

Tim explained where his zone had taken him and all that he had witnessed. While Tim's story was told, neither Sarah nor John said anything. They only listened. When he was through, they all sat silently.

Then, Sarah broke the silence with words Tim hadn't expected to hear from her. "Tim, it is all about the rules," she whispered calmly.

"What?" Tim asked, confused.

"The rules. Lexie was right. You figure out the rules and then use them to change things." She turned away from them and started to walk out of the room. "Wait here," she commanded.

Sarah returned moments later with a notebook in her hand. Tim recognized the tattered binder as soon as the book came into view.

"My zone notebook!" Tim exclaimed. "But I threw it away. I thought it was gone."

"I found it in the trash one day when I was picking up," she said as she handed him the lost book. "I didn't know what it was, so I opened it. I wasn't trying to snoop, but I was curious. When I realized it described the things you saw in your zone, I had to read it.

"Tim, I think you are a lot like me sometimes. You hold so much inside that when it comes out, it wants to explode from you. I thought reading this notebook may be the only way to understand what you were going through.

"Your zones are amazing, Tim. The things you see and can do are incredible. I read the rules you had put together too. I wasn't surprised when you told us about using your zone to take advantage of people and steal their money. Well, I was a little surprised you would do that, but I wasn't surprised that you could. Your rules told me that seeing the future is possible for you.

"But Tim, you have still missed something very important. The people of the future you see, the ones who have been hurt or have a need, you can change things for them here. Instead of finding out their account number, find out what they need for a better life or to make better decisions. Save them from tragedy before it happens. If you can make a difference for them in your zone, do it. If not, figure out how to make that difference here. You know what flight number is going to crash, right? You even know when. You can still help them!"

Tim couldn't believe he had missed such an obvious interpretation of his own rules. He had first been too focused on the zone itself and his own gain. Then, his narrow focus shifted to saving the future Lexie. He was good at memorizing details of the future and using them financially. But he had missed the simple connection that he could do the same for people.

"Use your zone like you know you should," Sarah finished.

Tim looked at his mom. She had often seemed so distant and unhelpful. He saw her differently now. Both of his parents would support him and give him strength. He could rely on his dad's emotional uplift and his mom's quiet introspective wisdom.

"I will, Mom. I couldn't save Lexie, but it's not too late for those people on the plane."

The Castons sat together on Tim's bed, reading through some of his early zone notes. His early interpretations and experiments had seemed so long ago, but the memories flooded back to him now. Some of the observations and details were sad, some happy, a few very scary, and some funny.

The family discussed possibilities and new interpretations for Tim's rules. In light of his recent observations and under the guidance of his parents, Tim formed a new outlook for his life. Even in these old notes, it was clear that some of these people could be helped if he just paid more attention to their needs and details. He would need to know how to find them in his own time and space.

A little after three o'clock in the morning, Tim's parents left to get some sleep. However, Tim continued to add as many new notes and zone recollections to his notebook as he could before he fell asleep an hour later. He started a new list of people, places, and situations that he would seek out to make a difference. Top of that list was Flight 4612 to Bangor, Maine. He knew the day, year, time, and location. All he had to do was wait, and someday, somehow, he would stop that flight from taking off. He would save each and every passenger on that flight. He would act like a man that Lexie would have been proud of.

Chapter 28

A HERO IS BORN

DURING THAT FIRST summer back at home, Tim became more than just a good man. He was a hero. Headlines from the Tulsa Times and local TV news reported:

> "Anonymous bystander caught baby in his arms after the toddler tumbled out of her third story apartment window. Witnesses say the man was in the right place at exactly the right time."
>
> "Mysterious man led police to drug cartel hideout behind Tenth Avenue pool hall."
>
> "Three missing children found safely after kidnapper turned himself in to police. Jacob Smite, came to the police after an unknown man knocked on his door and simply asked him to confess. 'The man seemed to know everything about me,' Smite reported. 'He said he knew my future and that I still had a chance to change.' No information on the negotiator is known at this time."
>
> "Anonymous hero at it again, this time rescuing baby from family washing machine. Who is this man and how does he do it?"

Many other acts of courage, kindness, and heroism were attributed to the unknown man Tim had become. His uncanny timing, foresight, and generosity earned him the nickname, "The Heroic Stranger" around Tulsa. Witnesses described the man as a young twenty to twenty-five year-old white male usually wearing a baseball cap, T-shirt, and jeans.

When Tim wasn't fighting crime, saving lives, or simply helping someone, he worked for his dad at Newton Drilling Co. John had worked his way up to drilling manager at the small consulting firm. He was proud of what his son was doing and so gave Tim the freedom he needed at work to help others. A few of the other employees grumbled about the independence given to the boss's son, but John accepted that struggle as his contribution to the difference Tim was making.

In the same year of Tim's return to Oklahoma, Chris also returned to his abandoned house. His young wife in Nebraska, Amber, had run off with a man closer to her own age, leaving him unsure of his next step in life.

Chris had come back, sad and lonely, hoping there may be comfort found in the home he had shared with Gracie and Lexie so long ago. He hadn't realized how dilapidated his old house had become. The front door was partially ripped from the frame, and a leaking roof had caused considerable damage to the upstairs bedrooms and hallway. Much of the siding needed to be replaced, as well as windows and some wiring.

He spent a full day trying to get the front door to fit back into the frame. Once in, he couldn't get it open again.

Tim saw Chris's frustration and spent the next day helping him tear out the whole wooden door frame. They rebuilt it together as they talked about the past. Mostly, Tim just listened as Chris recounted his life. It seemed to Tim that Chris was as broken down and in need of repair as the old house.

Chris spoke of Lexie and the mistakes he had made raising her. He wondered aloud what he could have done for Gracie instead of just abandoning her for the young and vivacious Amber. He also recalled the many good times they had had together so long ago as a family of three.

When the door was finished, Chris surprised Tim with an offer to sell him his house for practically nothing.

"Sir," Tim had responded humbly, "Your home is worth more than that. I can help you fix it up and get it on the market."

"That's why I'm offering it to you, Tim. You are willing to work on it. It needs someone who will put their sweat into it. I think I just want a fresh start. I thought I could do that here, but now that I am here, I want out; too many memories here, good and bad."

Tim thought about how Chris's last fresh start had taken Lexie away and ultimately ended with her running away and then . . .

"Tim," Chris said rescuing him from his thoughts, "I can't think of someone I'd rather have building a life here. I had planned to give this house to Lexie, but . . ." Now Chris's thoughts overwhelmed him. He shook them off.

"Anyway, you were a great friend to my daughter. You were her best friend. I know you feel like you let her down, but she still talked about you even after we moved. She hoped the two of you would someday become friends again. I think the more her life got tangled up in webs of bad influences and manipulative boyfriends, the more she thought of you. At first when she talked about you, I thought she wanted you to help her. Maybe she thought that you could somehow release her from the pain she was experiencing. But then I realized it was you that she wanted to help. For some reason, she thought you still needed her."

Tim looked up and met Chris's eye.

"Funny, huh?" Chris laughed uneasily as he went on. "She didn't want to deal with her own life, so she wanted to help you with yours." Chris's smile faded a little, and he said seriously, "She loved you, you know? She always did. I know you were just children, but I think it was genuine. At least as genuine as it could be for a young girl."

Tim wondered why Chris had to say such things. Knowing she loved him only made the loss even more painful to Tim. Didn't Chris know that his words were like a dagger into an already wounded heart?

"One time," Chris continued, "I remember her crying in her room when she was fifteen. She was mumbling something about you. 'It was Tim, I'm not crazy.' she kept repeating over and over. 'That was his voice. I'm sure of it. I'm not crazy!'

"I went into her room and she wouldn't tell me what had happened, but she wanted to call you. I told her to go ahead. Why not, I said. So she called your parents' house, and they informed her that you had moved out and hadn't told them where you were. They said they had tried to find you but had not been successful.

"Lexie was devastated. I guess that's about when she really got messed up with boys and drugs. She started coming home beaten up, her clothing was often ripped and dirty, she smarted off to me constantly. Basically, there was nothing left of the Lexie we knew."

Tim looked white. It *was* his fault after all. First, he rejected her as a friend before she moved away, then when she had tried to find him, he hadn't been there for her. He was off trying to get rich and selfishly indulging in all his zone had to offer him.

Chris saw Tim's expression. "I know what you are thinking, Tim. But it isn't your fault. You can't blame yourself for the things that happened. No one knows the future, Tim."

Tim remained pale. It was true, even he didn't really know the future. The future he knew of didn't fit reality. In that future, Lexie was still getting beaten and abused just like her father had described. But at least she was alive.

A thought popped into Tim's head. "Chris, are you sure she's gone? I mean, isn't there a chance that . . . that she's alive?"

"What?" Chris was surprised by the question. He straightened up in the dirty chair on the porch where they had sat down to rest after finishing the door. His face flashed a mixture of confusion and pain.

"Couldn't it be possible?" Tim asked again. "Maybe they just thought it was her but is was really someone else?"

"Tim, no." Chris's face was pale. "I drove all night from Omaha to the morgue in Oklahoma City. I had to identify her," he said while seeming to shiver slightly. Not a shiver of fear but of painful memories. Tim watched him for a moment. He seemed to be recalling what he had been forced to see.

"But it might have been a mistake," Tim urged. "Maybe you made a mistake, and she really is still alive."

Chris looked up at Tim. There was a moment that Tim thought he looked angry. Then Chris's face slackened and he sighed. He didn't cry, but Tim saw tears moistening his eyes.

"No," he said softly. "No. It was her. I had hoped the same thing as I drove to her. Kept wishing and praying that it was a mistake. When I arrived and they pulled back the sheet, I prayed that it was someone else's daughter in that room. Can you believe that? I actually prayed that some other father would have to suffer instead of me." Chris shook his head, ashamed. Tim listened silently.

"I looked at her, Tim. Even as I stared at her beautiful face, I hoped that it wasn't really her. Maybe just a girl who looked like her, but it was her. I couldn't deny it. The girl in that room . . . on that gurney . . . she was my daughter. My only daughter." Chris wept visibly now. "She had already been gone for about a day when I saw her. Her death was ruled a suicide."

Chris couldn't continue any more. Tim waited and considered what Chris had said. He had to accept that she really was gone. Something was wrong with his understanding of his zone. The future could not have a living Lexie if she was dead now. There must be a rule he did not comprehend.

Chris wiped his eyes and cheeks with his left sleeve. He regained his composure and spoke again to Tim.

"Anyway," his voice cracked slightly, "my point is that through it all, she loved you. So, please, take our house, her house. You were always a great friend to my daughter," Chris said, looking at the boy that she had missed so much. "I know she loved you and missed you. So, I'm happy that you will give the old place life again. Maybe in a small way, having this house fixed up will be like giving her life again too."

A few weeks later, Chris said good-bye to his old neighbors once again. They exchanged hugs and well wishes, and the Castons hoped that their old friend would find whatever he seemed to still be looking for. Chris and Tim hugged also. They hugged with the kind of emotion that can only be expressed by men who share a common sorrow.

Chapter 29

JEFFREY

AS THE MONTHS flew by, Tim continued to successfully balance his mission to the world, to his job, and to Lexie's house; his house. He worked hard for his dad and soon was rewarded with more responsibility and pay. The extra pay, his dad knew, wouldn't be wasted on selfish materialism. Tim used the money to increase his area of influence. His zone showed him suffering all over the world, not just Tulsa. So his money was spent on plane tickets, cabs, trains, and even occasional nontraditional transportation like mules or camels. Wherever there was need, Tim did what he could to get there and help.

Tim's notebooks became volumes of handwritten instructions. Each page contained all the information necessary to change someone's life forever. Tim was truly a hero to all the people he helped. He hoped that his life now somehow made up for his failure to Lexie.

Early in the morning on September 19, 1995, Tim loaded up his old truck and started the nine-hour drive toward Brenham, TX. Thirty-five days earlier, he had witnessed a man saving sixteen boys from a burning home in the small Texas town. The man, he realized, was a future version of himself!

As he drove, he recalled his notes from that future world, a world that in a few hours would become the present.

Zone Date: August 15, 1995:
Event Date: September 19, 1995:

Brenham, TX—At Trail . . . something . . . Group home for foster kids.

Arrived too late to stop boiler explosion. Wasted too much time looking for ice cream factory that was nearby. Arrived at the home after hearing explosion. Another man had already rescued sixteen kids from the home and then had tried to get back into the house for the adult caregivers. It was dark, so I couldn't tell at first, but then I realized, I knew the man. He was me! I tried to get closer but the screamers appeared and blocked my way. He wasn't able to rescue the adults, and before the police and fire trucks arrived, he ran. I wanted to chase after him, but the screamers wouldn't allow it.

When it was clear that he was gone, I spent the rest of the time trying to figure out how I could change this event when it happened for me. I, he, wasn't able to save the two adults, but maybe I could change that.

The sixteen kids will be in the four dorm rooms on the backside of the building. Boiler is on the side closer to the adult room. If I can get to the adults first, maybe they can help get themselves and all the kids out.

Date found in newspaper on neighbors' driveway. Group home on corner of Bastin and Bluebonnet Drive. Time of explosion 10:32 according to officer I overheard interviewing a witness.

On the next page of the notes, Tim had drawn a diagram showing the locations of the kids' and adults' rooms. He had even planned a route through the house to reach all eighteen in time.

The diagram was based on his exploration of the home while it was burning. The screamers hadn't let him approach while his other self was there. But once the other Tim was gone, they seemed unconcerned about his entry into the house.

It was not Tim's first experience with burning buildings while zoned, though it was always a strange feeling. He had learned that he could walk through the flames without too much discomfort as long as he moved quickly. Oddly, standing too long in the flames created a feeling of nausea as opposed to the pain of burning flesh. It was yet another intriguing rule he had added to his notebook.

As he explored the partially collapsed building, he saw where it looked like the other Tim had used a door to cross over burning beams in the hallway. He also took note of the fallen ceiling on most of the now burning beds. It was clear that had the other Tim not acted, all of the children would have perished.

He found the bodies of the two adults, still in their bed. It must have been a husband and wife, judging by the way their charred limbs embraced each other. The window near their bed seemed to have been broken open from the outside by the firemen, who had then apparently retreated from the flames.

It seemed odd to Tim that the two hadn't tried to escape. Surely the blast would have awoken them. The passageway between them and the children would have been leaping with flames, but their room was probably still fine for awhile. There should have been plenty of time to grab a lamp or nightstand to break the large window and get out.

After getting themselves out, they could have come back into the other side of the home to help the children escape. The details didn't add up, but Tim hoped he would be able to make sense of it in time to save all eighteen.

Now, thirty-five days later, he was heading back to that home, hopeful of doing even more than the previous Tim had been able to accomplish. While driving, he considered the confusion of time travel. Would an earlier version of himself be observing his actions from the hill above the house? And since he was trying to change the future differently this time around and save the adults too, would the observing Tim see something new? How would that observation change the way Tim responded to the circumstances? Could it affect his own actions now?

Maybe it didn't work like that. Maybe the Tim he had seen was doing exactly what *he* would do today even if he tried to do it differently. Maybe time was locked in place, and he could only do what he had seen the other Tim do. Sometimes, it drove Tim mad trying to rationalize it all.

By that afternoon, Tim entered the small town of Brenham, Texas. Signs advertising the town name abounded. These were a proud people, proud of their history, schools, and apparently their ice cream.

"I wouldn't mind some ice cream," Tim thought as he looked at the sign pointing to the Blue Bell Creamery. "Stay focused!" he chastised himself, remembering that looking for ice cream had delayed him the first time he was here in the zone. "I need to find the group home."

Tim drove south, remembering his course from his first visit.

"Hey, Bluebonnet Drive!" he thought out loud and quickly turned left onto the road. Only a few blocks later, he found Bastin St. and saw the home. It was looking much better than the last time he had seen it after the explosion. A large sign, the same one he had partially recalled from his zone, identified the corner lot as "Trail Hills Recovery Group Home."

He parked in front and got out of the truck. The lawn was green and thick with slightly overgrown Saint Augustine grass. Mature hedges lined the walks up to the front door of the extra long ranch style home. His own research since being here in his zone had told him that this place was for children taken permanently from their families but who were not ready for individual foster homes or for adoption.

Tim could hear the distinctive sounds of boys playing in the backyard. He had often observed that boys were usually louder than girls in their play. This was something he had noted when he was a child as well. When he played with Lexie, he and she were much better behaved than when he and a group of boys got together.

"Get the ball!" one of the children in the backyard yelled.

"Billy threw it!" responded another.

"But you're closer, and you should have caught it," the first voice responded.

Tim crossed the yard and knocked on the door. He had decided weeks ago that he would simply warn the couple about their boiler and avoid having to fight the flames at all.

As he waited, a new voice from the backyard called out, "I don't care who gets the stupid ball! Just someone get it! It's my turn to bat."

"Why don't you just get it then!"

"'Cause it's my turn to bat!"

"You don't even know how."

"Do to!"

"Do not!"

"Do to!"

The arguing went on another minute as Tim waited at the front door. Finally, Tim heard the sound of the lock being worked on from the inside.

"You're stupid!" Tim heard from the backyard again.

"Am not!"

"Are to!"

"Am not!"

The latch clicked, and a small boy, about four or five years old, opened the door. His face was covered in chocolate, and he had a half licked cake beater from a mixer in his right hand. In his left hand he held a model airplane with a broken wing.

Tim looked down at the scrawny kid and smiled. "Uh, hi. I like your airplane."

The boy smiled and pushed the plane through a high circular loop while making an engine sound with his pursed lips.

"May I please speak with your guardian?" Tim asked politely when the boy looked back up at him after completing a second loop.

The boy didn't respond verbally but gently put the beater down onto the tile floor and then stuck out his right hand in front of him. Tim looked at the hand, covered in almost as much chocolate as his face.

"Shake. Hands," the boy finally said with short blocky sounds.

"Oh. Uh . . ." Tim looked at the boy's hand again causing the boy to look at his own hand. Seeing the chocolate smeared on his fingers, he pulled his hand back and started licking the darkest spots first.

From the backyard, a new voice sang out, "Mikey is a stupid, Mikey is a stupid." Then there was the sound of a bat falling onto the ground and someone started crying.

The little airplane boy finished licking the fingers as clean as he could and then stuck the now "washed" hand back out to shake.

Tim gave in with a smile and took hold of the little boy's slimy hand. The boy gently shook it and then turned around and walked into the house leaving Tim standing with a wet hand at the door.

"Aaaaaaeeee," wailed the crying boy in the backyard.

Tim started to turn around, not sure how to proceed, when the loud voice of a woman screamed from somewhere inside the house, "What do you want, Jeffery? I already gave you batter to lick. Now get out of here. Go find one of your stupid planes you leave all over the place and play with it outside with the other boys!" There was a pause and then she yelled again, "Go! You're five now, old enough to get OUT OF MY WAY!" She shrieked the last four words causing Jeffrey to quickly back out of the kitchen.

The little boy, Jeffery, appeared again in the hallway. He stood there for a moment, looking at Tim. Tim thought the kid would start to cry, but instead he took a deep breath and calmed himself down. He walked over to the front door where Tim stood silently.

"Play. Planes?" Jeffery asked Tim in the same soft voice he had used earlier. He didn't seem five. Tim supposed he was a bit stunted by first having a rough enough life to be brought to this home and now to live with that beast of a woman in the kitchen.

Tim needed to speak to that beast. He needed to warn an adult. And it sounded like the only adult around at the moment wasn't looking for company. He knew his mission though.

"Jeffrey, I need to talk to her," he said tilting his head toward the kitchen. "Can you take me to her?"

Jeffery looked down and seemed both worried about interrupting her and disappointed that Tim wasn't going to play.

"Maybe we can play planes later," Tim added, seeing Jeffrey's response. This resulted in an immediate improvement in the boy's mood. The boy reached up and pulled Tim's hand to lead him in. Tim followed him down the hallway, and he remembered the layout of the house from his diagrams and from his first visit here.

Before he reached the kitchen, Tim looked into the common area that connected the two parts of the house. This was the section that had collapsed immediately after the explosion. Suddenly, a man's voice yelled out, "What? He was safe!" Tim looked over to where the voice had come from. He thought the room had been empty but now realized the man was simply slumped deep into the cushion. "Where do they get these freakin' umps?" the man yelled again, accenting every word in a way that almost made Tim laugh.

Tim dropped Jeffrey's hand and let him stand back as Tim walked around the couch. He looked at the man sitting on the couch in his undershorts and dingy white undershirt. He was thin in the chest and soft in the belly. Next to him were five open, and probably empty, beer cans. A sixth was in his hand. The man's whole body seemed to sink into the couch like he was part of the cushioning himself.

"Stupid!" the man yelled again with a strong Texas accent. "Y'all are all freakin' stupid!"

Tim cleared his throat to let the man know he was there. Jeffrey slipped out of the common room toward the bedrooms and hid.

"What . . ." The man jerked his head around and spilled some of his beer. "Who the . . ." Then he sat up a little. "Hey," he said changing his tone suddenly, "it's just been a rough week and I was trying to relax. I never have beer in here. This is just one of those weeks, you know? I mean, Johnny and Tyler were both sick, and Billie keeps fighting with Avery. And well, we didn't know you were coming today."

Tim wondered what the man was talking about.

"Sir," Tim began. "I just need to tell you . . ."

"Hank, those kids are driving me crazy!" the woman yelled as she started walking out of the kitchen. "The money the state gives us for keeping them here isn't worth this."

Hank quickly tried to hush her up. "Brandy!" he said through clenched teeth. But she continued anyway without looking up as she kicked several toys out of her way.

"You said we could get money for every brat we took in if we opened this place back up. But you failed to mention how stupid they all are! I'm just about to strangle . . ."

"Brandy!" Henry yelled authoritatively this time. "We have a visitor." He nodded his head toward Tim.

"Oh, Mr . . . Mr?" She paused expecting him to say his name. Since he was trying to remain an anonymous hero, he avoided the question.

"You need to listen to me," Tim urged. "Your heater, the old boiler out back, is going to explode."

"What? Explode?" Hank questioned, his accent somehow turning the word "explode" into four syllables. "How do you know that? Who are you?"

"It doesn't matter. What matters is that you get yourselves and all the boys out of here until someone can come out and fix it."

"Fix the heater? It's July. It's 100 degrees outside. Why would we even be using the heater?" The change in Hank's tone made it obvious that he realized Tim was not a social worker for the state sent for a surprise inspection.

"Look," Tim said feeling frustrated, "you just have to believe me. If you do nothing, something will cause the gas line at the boiler to explode. I don't know why it happens, I just know it will."

It was normal for people not to believe Tim at first. Sometimes, he wondered if he should just wear a badge that said, "I'm the guy who keeps helping people, rescuing animals, telling the future, and saving people's lives—TRUST ME!" But he knew that it was just difficult for people to accept that a stranger would show up and know the future.

Still, he was extra frustrated with these losers. It was apparent that they operated this group home only as a means of income.

How did they get approved to care for all these boys? Maybe they just inherited the home. Maybe they weren't the primary caregivers. In any case, he was wondering how he was going to get them to listen to him.

"Sir, Ma'am, please listen to me. I have an ability to help people. I am trying to help you."

"We don't need your help Mr. We are just fine. We may be a little rough around the edges, but we give these kids food, water, and beds. You want me to take them out of here. Where? There are sixteen of them. You got a suggestion?"

"I'm not here to judge anything about how you are raising those kids. I don't know where you should take them. I'm just here to warn you to get out and to have the gas line repaired before you come home."

Now Brandy spoke up, having come out of her surprised shock. "How did you get in here anyway? Did that idiot Jeffrey open the door again? Where is that kid?" she fumed.

Tim couldn't believe these two. A normal reaction would be to distrust Tim, even to be angry at him for trying to force them to change their plans. But to be yelling at a timid five-year-old boy?

"I'll pay for the repair," Tim offered. "Just call a repairman out right now." Brandy frowned and Hank's eyebrows lowered. "At least let me turn off the gas!" Tim shouted at them. He hadn't meant to shout, but his frustration at these two oafs had taken over.

"You, sir, can get off my property," Hank hissed as he extracted himself from the couch and stood up. He towered over Tim, who looked in amazement at the couch. The squashed indention of Hank's body in the cushions remained. Didn't this behemoth ever leave that seat?

"I said," Hank hissed again causing Tim to look up from the suffering couch, "get off my property. If you don't get out of here on your own, I'll get you out!"

Recognizing the threat, Tim backed up. "Please, just turn off the gas!"

"I said get out. Now GET!" Hank roared as he looked around, found a baseball bat lying next to the couch, and started waving it at Tim.

Tim was dumbfounded. "You people are crazy! Don't you get it? I'm trying to help you!" Tim held his arms up to protect himself from the bat that was being waved in front of him. "Please listen!"

Henry swung the bat hard this time. Tim jumped back, but the bat still slammed into his wrist and hand, breaking the face of his watch and bruising his hand. As Henry cocked the bat back to swing again, Tim ran. The front door was still open, so he ran out.

Hank followed Tim to the door but stopped at the opening. He may have been drunk, but he was still smart enough to know that he didn't want neighbors to see him running outside in his underwear, viciously swinging a bat at someone. In actuality, the neighbors had known for years that Hank and Brandy Titus were an imbalanced couple. They watched in disbelief as the pair who couldn't keep jobs and couldn't have kids of their own started fostering kids at the home. They, like Tim, were amazed that the state would entrust children to them. But the Tituses weren't dumb. They had the ability to lie and mislead the social workers who came for scheduled visits.

The home's previous owners, Brandy's Grandparents, had done a great job with the kids until they got too old to continue. After they passed away, the neighbors watched with dismay as the Tituses pulled up in their old fender-less Datsun truck. The radio was blaring '80s rock, the muffler was missing, and the bed was filled with three large dogs.

A couple of years later, the dogs disappeared, and Hank finally mowed the lawn and trimmed back all the hedges. The cleaned-up yard only lasted until they were reapproved as a group home. The neighbors suspected that the home's previous reputation had helped them start their humanitarian endeavor, despite obvious concerns.

The Titus duo took the monthly checks intended for the children and used the money as an alternative to having normal eight-to-five jobs. They found babysitting the kids in front of a TV and sending them outside most of the day was easier than working for a boss.

Despite the response, Tim had just received as Hank beat him out the door, he was determined to help. He spent the next couple hours consulting with a local repairman and then found a boiler specialist.

"I can't go out there unless they call me," the old specialist stated in a slow Texas accent.

"But I think something bad is going to happen," Tim argued again to Chuck, a kind-looking, white-haired man, who looked like he should have retired years ago.

"Did you smell gas?" Chuck asked.

"Well, no, but . . ." Tim answered too fast, realizing he should have just lied and said yes.

"Then there is nothing I can do."

Chuck looked at Tim and saw his desperation. He believed Tim, even though he wasn't sure why he believed his story of impeding danger. Something urged him to help Tim out, but he didn't know why the young man was snooping around the old Listerman place. He had known the Listermans, and he agreed with most of the older folk in the town that their passing had been a blow to the community. Their granddaughter and that giant husband of hers were quietly disliked by all who had met them.

"Look," Chuck finally said, "lemme find something. Hang on." Chuck pulled open a long drawer in the filing cabinet that stood near the back counter. He flipped through several dividers, then closed the drawer and moved to a lower one. Tim heard him grunt a little as he bent down and started digging through more files.

"Ah ha. Here it is," Chuck said pulling out a folder. He opened the contents and lay out several papers and an old manual with printed text and diagrams inside. "See here," he said pointing at one of the pictures that diagramed all the inner workings of a boiler system. "That system they got is an old gas package boiler system. A pretty good one from the looks of it when I was out there, oh fifteen years or so ago, for Brandy's granddad. They owned the group home back then and kept the place up real nice.

"Anyway, usually these systems are pretty safe even if outdated. Ya got the pumps here and fuel cutoffs here. This is your relief valve, so if something goes wrong and the gas doesn't stop heating up the water, it will let out the steam gradually. But it's summer, so I don't think the thing should be running anyway. And if you think there is gonna be a fire, then my bet is that this gas line here is the problem." Chuck continued pointing out the sections of pipe leading from the natural gas lines to down under the boiler.

"If you really want to help those fizzlehead slackers, check the line for leaks. See if anything is blocking the valves on the side. If there is a leak, shut the system off, here or here."

Tim wasn't sure what the term fizzlehead meant, but it was now clear that Chuck knew Hank and Brandy. Maybe that was why he had not wanted to go over there himself.

Tim thanked Chuck and then sneaked back to the house to attempt the gas shutoff. The system was housed in an attached boiler room at the back of the house. What he found when he slunk around to the back was that the old "safe" heating system had been fixed and patched up many times. So many times, in fact, by someone who didn't really know what they were doing, that the shutoff valve had been completely removed. He assumed the "handyman" was Hank. Maybe this was why he had gotten so upset when Tim suggested getting a qualified repairman out to look at it.

"What. Doing?" a gentle voice said that startled Tim, even though he recognized it from his earlier visit.

"Hi, Jeffrey," he responded softly. "I was hoping to help you all by turning this heater off. But I'm not sure I can do anything."

"Plode? It. Will. Plode?"

Tim assumed Jeffrey had been listening when he had tried to warn Hank and Brandy.

"Go, boom, boom!" the boy laughed with no fear at all.

"Well, yes. I think it will. I was going to try to stop it, but I don't want to touch it. It is in such bad shape that I think if I did try anything, it would just be worse."

"Play. Plane. Now. Please?" Jeffrey asked cutely. Tim thought for a moment. It was already getting dark. His watched displayed exactly 9:00 p.m. The explosion would occur in about ninety-two minutes.

Jeffrey waited patiently for Tim's answer. The other kids seemed to be inside now. Did Jeffrey always stay away from the others.

"Okay, Jeffrey. Let's play. But just for a little while. I need to think." Tim picked Jeffrey up and held him out from his chest, laying him flat across his arms. Jeffrey put out his arms like wings and let Tim fly him around the backyard quietly. They flew together for several minutes as Tim thought about what to do next. Suddenly, the scratchy voice of Brandy bellowed out the back door.

"Jeffrey! Get in here!" Tim wondered if she had seen him, but guessed she hadn't since she immediately turned back into the house. Jeffrey gave Tim an endearing hug and then ran to the door grinning. Tim hoped Jeffrey didn't get in trouble for being too happy.

It was too dark for Tim to do anything about the boiler. He decided it was time to turn his attention to the rescue. He had come up with several plans over the previous month but all depended on having reasonable adults living there to help him. He tossed those plans out of his mind and ran back up the street to his car.

Chapter 30

THE RESCUE

AN HOUR LATER, Tim's car was reparked a quarter mile from the house on the opposite side of a narrow wood. This seemed like the best place for him to leave quickly once the fire trucks and police had arrived at the house. Ten minutes earlier, Tim had called in a bomb threat from a pay phone. "The house is going to explode!" he had said in a low voice after giving the address.

Tim hiked the short distance through the woods back to the house and waited in the shadows for the police to arrive and evacuate the house. 10:20 p.m. No police. 10:25 p.m. came and still no police or fire trucks had arrived. Had they not believed him? Why wouldn't they send out a squad car to check things out?

Then a memory from this event's zone struck him. The officer who had stated the time of the explosion had also said something like, "I thought it was another crank call. Those kids have made calls like that before."

At the time, that comment hadn't made any sense to him. But apparently, his other Tim counterpart had tried the same thing. It was too late to do anything different now. It was 10:27. The explosion would happen in less than five minutes.

Tim rushed up to the side of the house farthest away from the boiler. Grabbing a rock from an overgrown flower bed, he smashed the window leading into the adult's room. He wasn't sure why he still went to them first. Something had just led him to that subconscious decision. He expected a yell from Hank or a scream from Brandy but heard nothing. Tim looked in. A small lamp light with no shade was turned on next to the bed. As he crawled through the jagged opening, he saw the two together on their bed, asleep.

"Hey, wake up!" Tim shouted as he crawled over the broken glass into the room. He ran to the door and flipped on the ceiling light. They were lying in an embrace, asleep. "Wake up! Hank! You have to get out of here! I need your help to get the kids out!"

He shook their legs and then slapped Hank in the face. Nothing. They were out cold. He tried to lift Brandy up to carry her out, but Hank's grip around her was too tight. "What's wrong with you people!" He assumed they were stoned or passed out from alcohol, but he didn't see any evidence of drugs or beer as he rushed around them trying to pull them apart. They were frozen in place in an unnatural slumber that he could not understand.

Tim checked his watch: 10:31. He could not waste any more time on these two. He had only a minute left before the explosion. He started to crawl back out the window to avoid the main common room where the explosion would be most intense. However, halfway through the window, the same subconscious guide that had pushed him to Hank and Brandy first now seemed to encourage him to cut straight through the house to reach the boys more quickly.

Without delay, Tim rushed past Hank and Brandy and out of the room, slamming the door closed behind him. He raced into the hallway and into the common room between the halves of the house. He knew this was the room that would suffer the most damage when the boiler exploded, so he sprinted as fast as he could through the room and down into the boys' hallway.

Throwing open the doors to each room, he screamed, "Get up! We have to get out of here!" He got to the last room and opened that door. "Wake up kids! We have to get out!" As if his voice was drawing them in, the boys from all the rooms shuffled into the last room where Tim was hurrying over to the window.

As calmly as possible, Tim hushed the confused and sleepy boys and then said, "Boys, there is going to be an explosion. We have to get out fast. I know you don't know me, but you must trust me." As he spoke, he led them to the window and pulled up on the wooden frame. It was locked. He looked at the top and realized that Hank had bolted the frame shut.

Tim didn't hesitate. He grabbed a small desk chair and threw it at the window. The glass shattered outward at the exact moment a much larger explosion was occurring sixty feet away on the other side of the house.

At first, the boys thought the loud boom and shake of the house came from the window break. Then the oldest looking boy called out from near the doorway. "There's a fire!" he yelled. "Just past the hallway!"

The bigger boys helped corral the smaller ones toward Tim at the window. He lifted the small boys up and out through the opening and then rechecked the other bedrooms as the older boys crawled out.

"Is that everyone?" Tim called out to the oldest boy when he had verified the rooms were clear.

"Yeah, I think so!" the boy yelled back over the roar of flames coming from the hallway. Tim followed him through the opening and then ushered them all up toward the street. "How many are here? Tim shouted as he began counting."

"Sixteen!" responded a smaller boy.

The oldest shook his head, "No, I only count fifteen. We're missing someone, and the wardens aren't here!"

Tim counted too and only saw fifteen. "Who is missing?" Then, without waiting for an answer, he knew. "Jeffrey!" he yelled. "Where is Jeffrey?"

"Oh no!" a different boy who looked a little younger exclaimed. "Hank locked him in the bathroom!"

"Yeah, for wetting the bed," another added.

"Which bathroom?" Tim called back as he started running toward the house.

"Hallway! Past the bedrooms!" he heard one yell as he reached the house again.

One side wall of the hallway was already engulfed in flames when he made his way back in. One of the bedrooms was burning and part of the ceiling had collapsed. Tim could see a closed door just past the bedrooms at the end of the hallway. "Please God," he prayed, hoping that it was the bathroom door where Jeffrey remained. He crawled quickly below the flames and smoke to reach it. The heat was already intense.

The door was locked. "Jeffrey, are you in there?" he yelled as he pounded on the door. He heard nothing. There was one other door in the hallway, but it looked like a closet. The demolished common room beyond the hallway was impassable, so he prayed again that this was the right door. Moving back as far as he could into a section of the opposite wall that wasn't burning yet, Tim jumped and threw himself at the door.

"Ohhh!" he grunted as his shoulder met the door forcibly. He had struck the door more toward the middle than he had intended. The latch side stayed in place but one of the hinges had broken free from a rotten place in the wood frame.

"I'm coming, Jeffrey!" he yelled again as he backed up to ram the door a second time. A loud screech of metal caused Tim to look up just as several beams came crashing down into the hallway in a fiery arc.

Tim dove safely out of the way as they fell, but they landed across the floor. He and Jeffrey were now barricaded between the flaming beams and the collapsed burning common room past the hallway. Tim lay for a moment on the floor, catching his breath beneath the smoke and trying to decide what to do next. Then he heard a cough from inside the bathroom. It was weak but definitely the cough of a child.

Tim jumped to his feet and gathered his strength against the opposite hallway wall. He hurled himself forward and rammed the door even harder than the first time. His full force landed perfectly on the weak hinge side causing the final two hinges to break free.

The door fell into the bathroom, first opening the wrong direction and then falling completely free onto the old linoleum floor.

Jeffrey was curled up in the bathtub, still sleeping. He had wrapped his arms and legs in toilet paper for padding against the hard surface. "Jeffrey!" Tim said as he reached in and put his arms under the small boy. His shoulder and arm screamed at him painfully as he lifted the child out of the tub. "Jeffrey, are you okay?"

Jeffrey appeared to awake suddenly from a deep sleep. "Jeffrey, okay," the child repeated. Tim carried him to the door, saw the flames surrounding them and stopped. He put Jeffrey down.

"Take off the toilet paper, Jeffrey. We don't want it to catch fire!" Tim tore off some of the paper to demonstrate to the boy what was needed. Catching on, Jeffrey obeyed as Tim turned his attention to their escape.

Looking out the doorway, Tim saw that the common room continued burning and collapsing against the end of the hallway. To his right, away from the common room, the fallen beams in the middle of the hallway smoldered on the ground. New material, insulation, and ceiling tiles also burned now around the beams. It would be impossible to walk around them or jump over the jumbled pile of debris without sustaining severe burns to his feet and legs. Tim also feared that they would trip on the rubble and fall directly into the flames.

Tim looked back at Jeffrey as the boy finished tearing off the paper and threw it onto the fallen door at his feet.

"Jeffrey, step off the door. I have an idea!" Tim reported. It was more of a memory than an idea. That door had been in the middle of the hallway burning when he had walked through the house during his zone.

Tim guided Jeffrey off the fallen door and tore off a couple more small pieces of paper that Jeffrey had missed. Then he picked up the door and guided it through the opening. At first, Tim used the door as a shield from the heat as he and Jeffrey stepped out into the hall. Carefully, he placed the door over the flaming debris and then picked Jeffrey back up.

"You ready, kiddo?" Tim asked. Jeffrey nodded his head bravely. Tim pulled Jeffrey close to his chest and jumped up onto the door. He lost his balance slightly as the door shifted below his feet but he was able to adjust. Then, shielding Jeffrey as much as he could with his arms and chest, he leaped across the door and down the hallway back to the open window in the back bedroom.

"Aaron!" Jeffrey squealed happily as they met the oldest boy at the window.

"I wasn't sure if you were going to make it," Aaron said, looking relieved.

"I wasn't sure either," gasped Tim as he passed Jeffrey through the window. Another rumble was felt and heard as more of the hallway suddenly fell in. Tim followed through the window and breathed heavily as he tried to clear his lungs of the smoke.

"The wardens are still in there!" Aaron reported. "I tried to get them out, but they wouldn't move. The window was already broken, but they just lay there."

"I know . . . I tried too," Tim panted, trying to catch his breath. "Take him up to the other kids!" Tim ordered as he dropped to his knees and took more fresh air into his lungs. "Tell them to stay there. But you come back with that other tall kid. Maybe we can still get them out." His chest heaved heavily. Somehow, he found the strength needed to force himself back onto his feet, though what he wanted to do was drop completely to the ground.

Tim staggered toward the other end of the house. He hoped that with Aaron and the other tall boy's help, they could pull Hank and Stacy out.

Smoke was pouring out through the broken glass when Tim reached the window. He started to crawl in but realized the flames had already entered the room and engulfed the bed. It was too late.

He backed out of the hole and looked up to the boys. Jeffrey was safely sitting with most of the other boys. Aaron and the tall boy seemed to be arguing. Then Aaron threw up his arms and turned to run back toward Tim.

When Aaron arrived, alone, Tim stopped him from getting nearer to the window. "Pete won't come," Aaron said with his head down. "No one else wanted to help them either." Tim sensed that Aaron too was conflicted about helping his former caregivers.

"It's okay, Aaron," Tim said reassuringly. "It's too late for them. You did great. You tried to help them, and you helped get all those boys up there out safely. I think you are a hero."

Aaron seemed to shake his head slightly, unwilling to accept the praise. Tim wondered if this boy had been forced to stand up and be a hero for the younger boys before. Maybe he had stood up against Hank and then was torn down for it by those selfish, depraved . . . He couldn't think of a name to describe them. "Fizzleheads!" he thought finally. Tim could almost imagine Hank punishing Aaron for trying to do what was right.

"I should have pulled them out," Aaron said with his gaze down at the ground but nodding toward the window. "I got in there, but they wouldn't wake up. So I got mad at them. I was so mad. Mad at them for everything, but right then, mad that they wouldn't wake up. So I yelled at them and told them that I hated them. I told them that I was glad they were going to die."

Tim wasn't sure what to say to the young man. He knew that the boy would remember this night, and that it may haunt him for the rest of his life. He would always wonder if he could have done more to help his foster parents.

"I couldn't get them to wake up either," Tim finally said as he started to hear sirens in the distance. "We both did our best. When you think back to this night, remember that you did your best, despite your anger toward them. That took incredible courage! Aaron, listen to me. You are a hero. What you have done tonight, all of it, you should be proud of!"

Aaron seemed to consider this thoughtfully. Tim hoped he had said the right thing. He hoped that Aaron would be a hero again.

Tim heard the sirens again, close now. "Those boys need you now. Take care of them and help them find good places to live. They need a hero like you!"

Aaron finally let a half smile form on his face. He was going to be okay, Tim thought. Tim saw a police car and fire truck round the corner. Then, there was a commotion from the boys. "Jeffrey, get back here!" yelled Pete.

Jeffrey was running across the lawn to Tim. He leaped up onto Tim as soon as he got close. Tim thought he was going to drop him but was able to hold on despite the renewed jolt of pain he was feeling in his left arm and shoulder.

"Thank. You. Fireman," Jeffrey sputtered out through a massive smile. Tim laughed to himself at being called a fireman. Kids he saved, whether from falling, car wrecks, or actual fire, always seemed to assume he was a fireman. He was okay with that. They were heroes too, he thought.

Jeffrey spoke again as Tim gently lowered him back to the ground, "Fly. Planes. Again. Later. Okay?"

Tim smiled down at Jeffrey and put his right hand onto the top of his head. "You bet, little pilot!" Then Tim ruffed up his hair. "I have to go. Please keep the kids back, Aaron. Keep them safe."

Aaron smiled and nodded, putting his arm around Jeffrey's shoulders. Tim nodded back and then turned away. He ran around the house and into the woods. As he ran, he realized he had completely forgotten to look up to see if his zoned self was there. Was that other version of himself watching from up the hill where the screamers had stopped him? Would he have been able to see that other Tim if he had looked up there?

He realized then that the events he had just lived were a little different than what he had watched during his zone. The other Tim hadn't had the farewell moment with Aaron and Jeffrey like he had just had. The kids had been up at the road just like they were now, but the first Tim had been on his own. After getting the kids out, he ran to the adult bedroom but Aaron didn't meet him there. Then when he heard the sirens in the distance, he ran into the woods.

Tim continued to think through the events as he started his drive home to Oklahoma. It was already after 11:00 p.m., so he got as far out of town as he could before finding a hidden spot along the road where his mind could zone.

As he waited for 11:35, Tim compared tonight's events again to what he had witnessed in his zone a month before. The circumstances and results were the same. But some of his actions had been different. Had he changed the future? He had obviously made a connection with the boys this time that the previous Tim had not. "More new rules," he thought.

He also wondered why he had never seen himself before. He had witnessed a lot of events through his zone and then gone to change them. Shouldn't he have seen himself at some point? There was still so much to learn about his zone. So much he didn't understand.

There seemed to be a disconnect between the future he was creating here and the future he witnessed in his zone. He needed help. Over and over again, he wished he had Lexie to help guide him. "She would have been able to figure this out!" he sighed to himself.

He thought about the Lexie he had found far into the future. She was battered and bruised, and he remembered what Chris had told him that day they had worked on the old front door together. Lexie had had a string of bad boyfriends. She had been happy to be at a new school where people didn't associate her with her mom. And within a few days, she had her first boyfriend. Then another. The relationships didn't seem to last long, and she never seemed happy.

It had seemed to Chris that at first, they would just use her and want to show her off as their pretty girlfriend. Then she had started dating guys who verbally abused her. Once that got too boring for them, they had physically abused her. She had been stuck in that cycle for several years until her suicide. That abusive pattern still seemed to exist for the old Lexie he had met.

Tim had often reread his notes about that night, looking for a clue to her existence. But no matter how hard he tried, there was no explanation for how she could exist in the future if she was dead now.

As he felt his zone rapidly approaching yet again, he lay down across the bench seat in his truck. His arm was still in pain, and it was difficult to find a way to comfortably lie on the long but narrow flat seat. He had no idea where this next zone would take him and no idea what time, place, event, or situation. All he knew for sure about the future was that he needed a doctor for his arm.

Seeing a doctor would have to wait until morning. 11:35 p.m. had arrived, and all he could do now was pray. Pray that no one discovered his limp, lifeless body lying in his truck along the side of the road. And pray as hard as he knew how for answers to the multitude of questions that filled his life.

As the zone came, releasing his mind from the confines of his injured body, he was soon granted with some of those answers that he most desperately sought.

Chapter 31

A NEW UNDERSTANDING

Date: September 19, 1995
Zone Year: 2006

TIM LOOKED AROUND the small but tidy kitchen into which he had zoned. Something about the room looked familiar, but he couldn't place it. The sound of running water nearby seemed to emanate from the open bathroom door near where he stood. Without looking in, the sporadic noise of the water splashing against the wall and shower curtain confirmed that someone was bathing.

This of course wasn't the first time he had arrived in someone's home. He had watched families gather around the dinner table, witnessed the random conversations of friends, and laughed at the interactions between siblings that he had never experienced as an only child.

Sometimes he felt like he was intruding when arriving in someone else's home. Other times, he pretended he was part of the family during his short visit. He'd find himself unconsciously laughing along with them and wanting to jump into their conversations. They of course knew nothing of his presence, but it was still an enjoyable experience.

Often, Tim found little ways to help them out. Simple things, like guiding someone to their missing keys, or major things like pulling a baby out from beneath a kitchen sink where he was about to drink drain cleaner. Once back in his bed, he would pull out his notebooks and determine how he would find such a child again in his own time at the right moment to save him.

Several times, like tonight, Tim found himself in a moral predicament. Should he do the right thing and respect this person's privacy? Or should he take advantage of the unusual situation? He was an invisible entity in a private place. Why not indulge? No one would know!

"That's the old Tim talking!" he chastised himself.

Still, he wondered what the woman behind this curtain looked like. She might be beautiful. Then again, for all he knew, it could be a large hairy man in there! That had been the case several times before when he was hoping to catch a glimpse of someone far less revolting.

This time, though, he believed he could tell it was a woman. Maybe it was the way her movements gently affected the falling water. Or the smell of the scented soaps that percolated from the room. Yes, he was sure there was a woman behind this curtain. And somehow, he was instinctively sure that the woman was beautiful.

"Leave her alone," he rebuked himself again. "You are supposed to be a hero now, just leave her alone."

Tim forced himself to turn away. He walked down the short hallway into the living room and that sense of familiarity struck him again. The room was small, and there wasn't much furniture. There was an old couch with a clean sheet covering the cushions and an uncomfortable looking chair. Both sat facing an empty bookshelf and large consol TV. Baby toys were piled into a basket next to a folded blanket.

A 5x7 picture frame hung crookedly on the wall. In it, a picture of a man stood next to a baby boy. The man didn't seem happy to be in the picture, but he had posed anyway. Tim looked around for other pictures. There were plenty more of the baby but none of the mystery woman in the shower.

Refocusing on his task, Tim wondered why he had arrived here. Would one of these three people need saving. Maybe the baby would choke on something. Maybe there would be a break-in, and he would get to rescue the naked damsel in distress from the bad guys.

The shower turned off, and Tim heard the curtain slide back. He wanted to resist, but the temptation was too great. His mind struggled for excuses. It wasn't like he was opening the door to peep in. The door was already open, right? Maybe it would just be an ugly guy again. Then who would care. The joke would be on Tim.

Tim walked the short distance back to the bathroom door and looked in. He saw the curtain was only partially pulled back. As he had hoped, an attractive woman stood inside, drying herself off with the green towel that had been slung over the curtain rod earlier. Her back was turned to him, and he could only see her left leg, buttocks, and back. He admired the shape of her partially hidden form but then closed his eyes, searching for the strength again to turn away and give her the privacy she deserved. The possibility to find that strength dissipated completely when the sound of the curtain sliding further open reached his ears.

His eyes were wide now, taking in the vision of beauty that stood before him. She was magnificent. The green towel still covered most of her face as she worked it through her long honey-colored hair. He dropped his gaze to her slender legs as she stepped out of the tub and onto the worn cloth floor mat. Then, in a single flowing motion, she spun gracefully on her toes as she finished wrapping the towel into a tight twist on the top of her head. Her fluid movements reminded him of a ballerina, warming up before a performance.

Tim wanted to see her face, but she had her back to him again, her arms working on pulling the shower curtain closed. He noticed that one arm seemed to have a faint dark spot. He thought at first that it was a faded tattoo on her upper arm. Then he thought maybe she had just missed cleaning the five-inch spot of skin.

The young woman finished straightening the curtain and continued her dance with another quick spin over to the mirror. Except for the mark on her arm, which Tim couldn't even see now, her skin was flawless and smooth. Unconsciously, he whispered out loud, "Beautiful."

Her fluid motion stopped suddenly when he spoke. Had she heard him? "Who's there?" she called out as she pulled the towel from her head and clutched it tightly against her torso.

Tim gasped when he saw her face. Despite the impossibility of it, he knew instantaneously that it was her. He had once again found Lexie!

Her left eye was slightly swollen and the corresponding cheek was bruised. But otherwise, she looked like a grown-up version of the beauty he knew as a child. She must have been about his age or maybe slightly older. He was in shock. Lexie was alive! He didn't know what to do. He backed out of the room without taking his eyes off her.

Lexie looked confused. "Jack? Are you home?" She quickly reset the towel to wrap around her body and then peeked out the doorway. "Jack?" she called out again toward the kitchen. Hearing no response, she walked the other way toward the bedrooms and opened one of the doors. Tim saw a child sleeping in a brown crib before she quietly reclosed the door.

It seemed clear by her reaction that she had heard Tim's whisper. But now she didn't seem to know he was there. The older Lexie had known he was there before he had said anything. Maybe this younger Lexie had never met Tim in a zone, and so didn't recognize his presence. "Who cares!" he thought, she is alive!

Lexie walked into the only other bedroom of the small bungalow. It was now obvious to Tim that this was the same house he met Lexie in thirty years into the future, though it was cleaner than the last time he had been there.

Lexie opened a drawer and pulled out a nightgown. She started to loosen the towel but then stopped. "Is someone there?" she said as she looked around the room, her eyes never falling on Tim where he stood outside the room in the hallway. He wasn't sure what to do. If he spoke, it would frighten her, especially if she had never met him in a zone yet. But if he didn't say anything, he was just as bad as, well, as bad as he had been just two years ago when he treated his zone as an adult playground. He suddenly felt extremely guilty for giving in to the temptation of peering into the bathroom at her.

Tim did the only thing he could do. He ran. He would leave the house and run. She would never have to know that he had spied on her.

When he got to the front door, however, he stopped. Before tonight, he had convinced himself that he would never see her again. He thought maybe his sight of her in the far future was just a mistake. Maybe it hadn't even really been her.

But now, he had found her again. Maybe it wasn't a mistake after all. Maybe he was meant to find her. Yet he was running? Why? Because of his remorse for rejecting her when they were young? Because he was guilty now of watching her? He would ask for forgiveness. He had to. He couldn't just leave.

Lexie slowly came toward the front door where he stood. She was wearing the nightgown he had seen her pull out of her drawer. He saw the mark on her arm again and understood that it was a bruise, like the one on her cheek. The bruise was faded and had healed some, but it was clearly the shape of four long fingers that had harshly gripped her thin arm.

She paused, facing slightly sideways to him, when she was only a few feet from where he stood. Closing her eyes, she took a deep breath through her nose and mouth at the same time and then exhaled. Then she turned toward Tim with her eyes still closed and raised her right hand with her fingers slightly curled. She took another small step toward him, closing the gap to just a foot between them.

"Who . . . Who are you?" she whispered with her hand just eight inches from Tim's chest. "What do you want?" Lexie seemed scared and curious at the same time. Tim couldn't believe that she was standing here so close to him. He assumed the situation must seem as unreal and dreamlike for her as it did for him. He needed to say something. But what?

Lexie continued to stand there, waiting for what seemed like an eternity to Tim; waiting for an answer to her question of what this entity was that stood before her. Maybe, Tim thought, she was waiting for the feeling of his presence to go away. It didn't seem like she wanted him to go away, though. She crept inches closer, her hand still out toward him.

Tim reached up and grabbed her hand to pull it onto his chest. He wasn't sure why he did it; he just knew he needed to feel her touch, to prove to himself that she was real. To prove that this wasn't just a wishful dream. Maybe it was to prove to her the same thing about him.

"Lexie, it's me," he spoke softly. His heart was racing.

She inhaled sharply and then seemed to hold her breath. She didn't try to pull her hand away. Her eyes were still closed. He felt her hand move across his chest. Then she spoke. "T . . . Timmy? Timmy, is that you?"

"It's me, Lexie. I'm here."

"How are . . . What? I don't understand. What is happening?"

"I'm in a zone. My consciousness is here."

"A zone? Your zone! This is impossible."

Tim was thinking the same thing but for a different reason. How was it that Lexie was alive here in this place. Could something even more amazing than four-dimensional travel be taking place? The answer came to him suddenly as if the touch of her hand on him delivered a new power of intellect.

He was in an entirely different timeline or maybe a parallel universe. He had considered that possibility when he realized that his actions at the group home had not been the same as those actions from the other Tim he had observed. Maybe this new realization explained all the minor differences he saw from zone to real life.

If this timeline was parallel to his own but not identical, changes he made here wouldn't affect the reality of his own world. That would explain why the news report of Art Sumpter's death didn't match his own observations. But the lines were apparently similar enough that most events were the same, or at least close enough for him to react from within his own world.

Later, Tim would ponder the possibility of many parallel timelines or universes, all running side by side but with minute differences. However, right now, all he could think about was the one big difference between his timeline and this one. Here, Lexie was alive.

"This is where I go in my zone," Tim said, returning his thoughts to the moment from his unexpected contemplation of timelines. "I remember them now when I wake up. But what I don't understand is how you can hear me. No one else here can do that."

"I don't know," Lexie responded, still touching his chest and taking in the amazing new situation. "Actually, I don't exactly hear you. Or, I do, but not with my ears. It's like your voice is far away but, at the same time, right here in my head."

She pushed a little harder on his chest to test her own senses. "Are you really here in front of me? I think I feel you." She moved her hand up his chest to shoulder, then neck and up to his face, tracing his outline. She felt his chin, nose, and then mouth. "I do feel you," she whispered in childlike wonder, "I can really feel you. You have the same face." Then she smiled and let out a tiny laugh, "But you have hair on your face!"

"Yeah, I haven't shaved since morning. It's late at night for me."

"Oh, 11:35?" she asked, remembering the start time of his zone from when they were kids.

"Well, no, it's probably almost midnight now. I've been here for . . ." He stopped himself, realizing what he had just admitted.

"You were in my bathroom!" she exclaimed, tilting her head and smiling. She put her hands on her hips for added effect, and he realized she wasn't mad. She had a sly smile on her face, and her eyes sparkled. He had been prepared for her to hit him or yell at him to get out. Instead, her cute expression surprised him.

"I knew someone was there," she laughed as if catching someone playing a childish trick on her. "I just thought it was one of those weird feelings."

"Uh, yeah. I didn't mean to . . . Well . . ." he stammered, still embarrassed. But Lexie was already thinking about something else now and didn't seem bothered at all by his presence or his peeping. "I could feel you then too," she said looking down absently as she thought aloud. "I knew I wasn't crazy! I felt you. Not like I can feel you now, but you were there. It was the same feeling I got the other times."

"Other times?" he asked curiously, "I've only been here once before, and it was far into the future. You were, well, you were old, like fifty or something. And that time you could see me. At least, I think you could."

"Maybe I just have to learn how. Are you still in front of me now?" Lexie put her hand up again and gently touched his face without waiting for his answer. She looked up toward his eyes and seemed to be trying to focus.

"What can you see?" he asked.

"It's weird, actually. I can't see you at all, but I know where you are. Put your right hand up to the side."

Tim did as she asked. She could have asked him to stand on one leg and quack like a duck, and he would have obeyed willingly. He would do anything she asked as long as he could keep looking into her living blue eyes.

Lexie looked over at where his hand was and then reached out with her own. She easily lined her hand up with his, putting her palm against his palm. Then she curled her fingers, interlocking them with his as she looked up into his eyes. Eyes she couldn't see.

Holding her hand shot waves of emotion and electricity through Tim. He wondered if she felt it too. This simple act of innocent intimacy was so much more powerful with Lexie than he had experienced with any other woman. It was odd how instantly connected he felt to her after so much time.

Tim stared into her eyes. The blue seemed to get bigger with excitement, and then he saw her lips curl into a smile as she started to speak. "Oh Tim," she grinned with a look of wonder and curiosity. "I could tell where your hand was," she said, "I'm just not sure how. I couldn't see it, but I think I imagined the movement. When I put mine up, yours was exactly where I thought it would be. It's like . . . magic!"

She grabbed his other arm and led him to the couch, almost skipping in her excitement. He marveled at how easily she was accepting this. Lexie always had been brilliant. She had the ability to read situations quickly and then make decisions. Only Lexie would so easily welcome an invisible man into her home.

After sitting down, she flipped her hair just like he remembered her doing as a kid. "So," she interrupted his thoughts, "you can travel in time during your zone? That is so cool!"

He laughed. "Yeah, I have been forward and backward. Usually not too far from my own time but sometimes farther. I think I've been as far back at the early 1900s and as far forward as . . ." Then Tim remembered something Lexie had said earlier. "Did you say I had been here before? When you were younger? Why don't I remember?"

Lexie thought for a moment and then smiled knowingly. "I'm talking about when I was fifteen and then again when I was twenty. It wasn't here. That visit here to this house that you remember must be in my future, so it hasn't happened for me yet. And apparently, the visits I remember are in your future. They haven't happened for you yet. But they will!

"The first time, at least the first that I remember, I thought I was going crazy like my mom. I was terrified. I think you knew how frightened I was because you left after whispering, 'It is okay. You are not crazy. I am your guardian angel and will watch over you.' I didn't say anything about it to Dad or anyone else. I seriously thought I was losing it. I didn't want to be crazy, but I couldn't explain it any other way. Then the second time, you saved my life."

"When you were twenty?"

"Yeah, I was stuck in a terrible relationship. One of many I have had. Let's face it, I haven't been very good at picking men." She casually motioned to her face, acknowledging the faded bruises on her cheek. "Anyway, Zach, my boyfriend, and I were driving home from a wedding in Oklahoma. And as usual, he was drunk. I said something about him flirting with the bride's younger cousin, and he went ballistic. He started screaming at me and threatening to run the car into a tree to shut me up. I wasn't sure how serious he was, but I did know that I was fed up with it. I was fed up with everything. So when he stopped suddenly in the middle of an intersection, almost completely running the light, I jumped out of the car and told him to leave me alone until he was ready to grow up. Guess he didn't want to grow up, so he sped off, almost running over me.

"I wasn't sure what I was going to do since it was cold that night, and I was only wearing a sleeveless dress and heels. I realized I was just a couple of hours drive from my old house. I hoped it was still vacant like it had been the last time I talked to my dad, so I hitched a ride with the next car that came along and found myself standing in front of my old place about four hours later."

"Four hours?" Tim asked.

"Yeah, the creep who had picked me up stopped the car several times, hoping to get something. I had to keep pushing him off me and telling him to please just drive. When we finally arrived, he wanted to come in with me. I guess he thought he deserved a ride for the ride.

"I finally got rid of him and walked up to the old house, but I didn't go in. It just looked so dark and sad. Plus, I was afraid that guy would come back and rape me in there since he knew I was alone.

"I saw your house next door, looking just like it had when we were kids. It seemed more like home to me. So I walked over and tested your window. It was unlocked, so I crawled in. Right then, I felt you! I assumed I was just remembering what it had been like when I'd sneak in there as a kid. But it felt like you were there. I might have even said your name, half expecting you to answer. Or maybe I just thought your name. Either way, you didn't say anything. Did you know I used to sneak into your room at night whenever my mom was freaking out?"

"I knew," Tim whispered to the top of her head.

She had leaned back against him while she had been speaking. He couldn't see her eyes now since she faced outward away from him, but the feeling of her soft weight leaning on his chest with her long hair lightly tickling his nose was exhilarating. He was astonished at how comfortable she was with him.

"I felt so safe when I was with you," Lexie continued. "Sometimes you were in your zone. Other times, I just tried to be really quiet and not wake you up."

"I heard you come in sometimes, but I never knew what to say, so I didn't say anything."

"You didn't have to say anything. Just having you there next to me was all I needed." He wondered if that was why she could so easily lie against him now. It was something natural for her since she had allowed him to comfort her in this way back then. But he also remembered how she had stopped coming over when he began choosing his other friends over her. And he remembered what he had said in front of her when out of his own lips came the condemning insult, "Psycho Michols."

"Lexie, I was so terrible to you." All the guilt of the way he had shunned her came flooding into his memory. "I should have stood up for you. I . . ."

"Timmy, we all make mistakes." She sat up and turned to look at him, just like she could really see him. "We were kids. I don't hold that against you. I never did. And especially not after saving my life."

"It's so weird to hear you talk about something that hasn't happened yet. How did I . . ."

"How did you save me? You made me stay. I had only planned on warming up a little and then leaving. I was going to . . . Well, I felt so hopeless that night. My boyfriend was a jerk and a drunk. And it wasn't just him. Men used me, and I let them use me. They walked all over me. I used to think I was smart, and maybe I am about some things, but for some reason I am stupid when it comes to men.

"After I had looked around your room for a moment, I crawled into your old bed and curled up with your pillow. Then, all of a sudden, the feeling of your presence returned as I lay there. I felt calmer. I started to think about all the good things I had experienced. As I lay there thinking, I realized it wasn't just your presence I felt. I could feel your arms around me. I was so sure you were there that I rolled over to see you. But you weren't there. Still,

I felt your embrace. I felt just as safe and secure as I had when you'd hold me when we were young."

"I ended up falling asleep with your arms around me. When I woke up, it was already late in the morning. I hadn't slept that well in years. As I was about to sneak back out of your window, your mom walked into the room. She saw me and asked me to stay. Your mom and dad were always so wonderful to me. They let me stay for almost three weeks while I got my head together.

"Tim, I still do stupid things," Lexie continued after pausing and looking toward the hallway. "There is a wonderful little miracle in that bedroom, but he's a result of doing a stupid thing with a man that doesn't love me. But if you hadn't changed my direction that night, I never would have gotten a chance to experience being a mother. I'm alive. I was going to kill myself that night, Tim. But you, and then your parents, are the reason I'm still here. You saved my life, Timmy! Just by being there with me."

Tim was captivated by her story. Would he really experience this story himself in his own future? Would he find out when he opened his eyes in his world that Lexie was alive now?

No, he thought. This was a parallel universe. Somehow, he would change the future for this Lexie, but in his own, she was still gone. What happened here in this timeline, stayed here.

"What are you thinking about, Tim?" Lexie picked up and held his hand naturally as she leaned back against his shoulder on the couch in her living room. Her hair tickled his face again. It felt so good to be next to her, but he still felt saddened by the reality that she would be gone as soon as he woke up.

"I'm just trying to understand all of this," he responded. "Lexie, in my time, you are . . ." He didn't want to say it. "I mean, well, we don't see each other."

It was obvious to Lexie that he had changed what he was going to say. She sat up and looked directly into his eyes, which was impressive since she still couldn't see him. "This is complicated, isn't it?" she sighed. "I don't suppose you know when you'll come back to visit me again?"

"I know I'll see you in thirty or so years. But I don't know when I'll see you before that."

"Wow, thirty years?" she said softly. "That's a long time. Can't you do better than that?" she pouted.

Tim thought. "When I saw you before, well, when I saw you later, I mean, when you were older . . . Anyway, you said you had seen me many times. I guess you said you had 'sort of' seen me many times. You also said I told you a lot about my zone. So maybe I will find out more about it and then see you again several times."

"Huh," she thought out loud. "Maybe you come to me at regular intervals. Let me think, you found me when I was fifteen and twenty. That's five years apart. No, there doesn't seem to be a simple pattern. Unless I missed you somehow when I was twenty-five. But that still doesn't explain why you are here now when I'm thirty-one."

"Thirty-one! I was guessing you were in your early twenties like me!" Unconsciously, he looked down across her thin nightgown and reminded himself of how beautiful she had looked fresh out of the shower."

She laughed as if somehow she knew where his gaze and thoughts had gone. "Guess that is really a compliment since you've seen all I've got!"

Tim laughed shyly and blushed bright invisible red.

"Not that it really matters, but what did I look like when you saw me in the future?"

He thought about how bruised she had been. Much worse than the old faded bruises she displayed today. Apparently, her trouble with men had never resolved, even with his occasional visits.

"You looked beautiful," he said as he thought. Why had he said that? Hadn't she been beaten up, swollen, bruised, overweight, run-down?

"Ah, you are sweet, but I'm sure I wasn't beautiful."

Tim thought more and realized the answer had been honest. "You *were* beautiful. I still saw you as my long lost friend who I always thought was beautiful. As sappy as this sounds, I think that in my eyes, I will always see you that way, even if you change on the outside."

Lexie's heart melted and a tear formed at the corner of her left eye. When she raised her hand to wipe the tear, she felt her bruise. "I'm surprised you haven't asked about this shiner on my face," she said more seriously.

"I guess I was just so surprised to be here with you that I forgot about it. Can I ask now?"

"My husband, Jack. We got married after I got pregnant with my son."

"He hit you?"

"Yeah. He is a good guy really. At least compared with most of my past relationships. His step dad hit him and his real dad was out of the picture. He had it pretty rough, and he just gets upset sometimes."

"I can't think of any reason a guy would hit his wife, even if he is upset."

"That's because you are wonderful!" she smiled. "Actually," she continued after thinking back for a moment, "he hit me because of you."

"What? How could I . . ." he started and then broke off, not understanding.

She smiled again and he noticed a red blush flash across her face and neck. "I called out your name. And it wasn't a good moment to be calling out another man's name." Her blush brightened beautifully. "I have thought about you a lot over the years, Tim. Always wondered where you were and what you were doing. And at that moment, when I should have felt like one with my husband, I called out your name. I was wishing it was you that I was with." Lexie smiled again, slightly embarrassed by her confession.

Tim beamed, as if hearing the most beautiful music that had ever been written. "Lexie, do you really forgive me?" he asked thirty-eight minutes after arriving in her house. For Tim, time had been standing still, so the next moment came as a complete surprise.

Before she could respond, everything around him faded away and she was gone from his life again. He awoke, staring up at the newly painted ceiling of her old house. His house. In his world where Lexie was gone.

Rules: updated 9-19-95.

Lexie is alive! But only on a separate timeline.
My zone takes me along a timeline that is very similar but doesn't match my own.
Changes I cause in the zone change that timeline
Changes I cause in my world do not affect the zone's timeline.
I have only found two people who could sense me directly; the old man in china that was being attacked by the screamers, and Lexie.
Are there others who can sense me, or is there some connection between them?

Tim thought hard about the last note. Why was Lexie able to hear and feel him? She felt not only his touch but his general presence. Apparently, she had been able to do so since she was fifteen years old. Was that the earliest time he would find her, or is it just the first time she was able to know he was there? She had moved away when she was thirteen. What had given her such an ability in the two years since she had moved?

He felt a renewed energy to use his zone for helping others. He wanted Lexie to be proud of him, even if she was in an alternate timeline. He knew with confidence now that he would see her again, and when he did, he wanted to be able to tell her of all the good he was doing for the world. Would he have to tell her about her death in his world? Would that matter to her? What if he learned of her future death in her own timeline? Then maybe he'd tell her and find a way to protect her.

Tim also decided that he would continue doing good deeds in her world as an invisible force. He would have to be cautious, since it was apparent that the screamers were playing their own role in that world. But they had allowed him to save Lexie, so maybe he could do more.

Chapter 32

THE PRISONER

DOING MORE WAS exactly what Tim did. Though he still refused to use his zone for his own personal gain, he decided that the occasional financial benefits that came from knowing the future could be used for good. If financial opportunities came along, he would accept them as a gift or blessing to use for others.

Typically, Tim used the funds to travel quickly to places all around the world so he could reach those in most need. Occasionally, however, he found himself benefiting so significantly from his zone that he promptly donated all of those funds to charities. For instance, the children of Crossnore, North Carolina celebrated when according to police, a "mystery man left a $2 million winning lottery ticket in a sealed envelope addressed to Crossnore Orphanage" at the post office.

As he waited for his next visit to Lexie, Tim saved countless lives, delivered sixteen babies, stopped seven children from being attacked by dogs, rescued stranded motorist with flat tires and dead batteries, and found at least one person daily to whom he could make a difference, both in his world and in Lexie's.

Each night Tim drifted into a new time and place. As soon as he stood up, the world around him caught up to him, or maybe he was catching up to the world. Either way, he would always look to see if he was in a place where Lexie may be. It was hard not to get discouraged each time he found himself in a new location without her, but he persevered.

Date: May 2, 1999
Zone Year: Unknown

On one such night, in May of 1999, Tim awoke with his head against hard brown dirt. It never hurt when he arrived in a zone, despite the sensation of falling against the earth with great force. But now as he took in the odd scene moving around him, the hardness of the packed earth seemed to press against him uncomfortably.

His first thought was that he was lying in a desert again, where finding people was difficult, if not impossible during his thirty-eight minutes. But this was different. Blurs of orange whizzed around him. They were people, he realized. Hundreds of people, all wearing the color orange, were pouring past him, around him, and through him. The sense of another human passing through his body often left him feeling nauseous, so Tim stood up to attach himself to this reality as quickly as possible.

As soon as he reached his feet, the motion around him slowed and the rapid waves of orange melted into a scene to which he was unaccustomed. He was in prison. He stood in the middle of the outdoor recreation area surrounded by walls, fence, and guards.

Tim wondered why providence would bring him here. Men wandered all around him in the prison yard. Some talked in small groups. Others played basketball. A few just stood and stared blankly at the ground or across the yard as they kicked dirt and passed time. Fifteen or so guards meandered through the prisoners. Some visited briefly with the men, others stood stiffly, watching distantly from behind dark sunglasses.

Then Tim spotted someone. A man, dressed in orange just like the other prisoners, sat on a metal bench, alone, in the middle of the yard. He looked familiar. Tim walked up to the solitary man, who leaned forward with his head down toward the ground. Where had he seen the man's face before? Tim closed his eyes and thought backward through his zones. He was sure this man had been in another zone.

"Who are you?" Tim whispered to himself. Then it struck him as if his mind had known the answer the entire time but had waited for his tongue to ask. Tim *had* seen this man in a zone before. He had watched him in a dim basement apartment. This was a man who had been building a bomb! Tim remembered how the man had struggled emotionally that night. In one moment, he seemed to hate the world and believed he was doing what was right. Then in other moments, he had fought fiercely against his own emotions and seemed afraid. Tim had wondered if the man was being forced or coerced somehow to build the bomb.

Still, this man had planned to kill hundreds of innocent people. Whether he was forced or not, he must have succeeded. For now he was here in this prison.

"How could you have done it?" Tim asked in disgust at the unhearing prisoner. He felt hatred well up within him for this man. "What kind of evil monster plots and kills innocent people? Who are you to think anyone deserves to be blown up?" The man's face turned slightly toward Tim and then away again. It seemed as if he was shaking his head. The prisoner's eyes closed. There was remorse on his face.

Tim realized the face wasn't just familiar from that day in the apartment. There was something more. Another memory of the man? No, not of the man but of the face. Despite the guilt that shown on it now, verifying the truth of his actions, Tim felt like he had seen those features at a different time, a previous time, when the look of the face was that of innocence.

Something didn't add up. The man sat silently on the long bench in the sun. His face was sad but thoughtful. There must be a reason Tim had returned again to this person. Somehow, Tim felt that this man was not meant to be a murderer.

A whistle blew, startling Tim and breaking his thoughts. The men began filing up into lines leading back into the prison. At first one line formed and then the guards started splitting them into two lines for separate doors. The sad man remained on the bench.

One of the guards, an older man with a tight and weathered face that comes from working long days in the sun, looked up from the hushed lines of prisoners. He was not happy to see a prisoner disobeying his order to line up. He yelled, "Mitchell, get it in gear!" The name, "Mitchell," meant nothing to Tim. He didn't know any Mitchells.

The other men filed smoothly through the two separate doors, but Mitchell continued to sit. The old leathery guard looked back at Mitchell and then scanned the line of inmates. He stepped up to a large man in orange and yanked him out of the line. Tim saw the guard nod to Mitchell and then push the muscled inmate toward him.

"Hey, J!" yelled Muscles. "Yo yo, J!" he yelled again as he approached the much smaller Mitchell. "Boss says to get you in line."

Mitchell, or J, still sat there. "Hey, man," Muscles said more quietly as he reached the bench and stood behind Mitchell, "I have to bring you in. Boss says to get you in one way or another."

Still no movement from Mitchell. Leather yelled again. "Get him moving, Smith!"

Muscles Smith stepped up close and whispered sincerely, "Come on, J. Don't make me have to drop you again. This is just how it is. This is your life now. Do what they tell us to do, and it ain't so bad." Still no reaction from Mitchell. He was staring outwardly into the yard toward the outer wall. "It isn't like your life was better out there," Smith reasoned. "I've heard you at discussion. You and me, we're the same; messed-up childhood, no family, bad friends, bad choices, and now, here we are. We're both gonna be here for a long time so let's just do what we gotta do."

It was clear to Tim that Smith was genuinely trying to help Mitchell. He seemed like one of those men you see in the movies who has come to terms with his sin and wants to start again. Mitchell on the other hand, was still battling his sins from the inside, still staring outwardly toward the wall.

A plane flew by overhead, its distant rumble echoing in the yard. Mitchell looked up at it, and Tim saw tears in his eyes. Leather turned back toward Mitchell and Smith as the last inmates marched through the doors. "Do I need to take care of this myself, Smith?" he shouted with authority.

"No, sir," Smith called back. Smith put his hand on Mitchell's shoulder from behind. "Come on, man, let's go."

Mitchell turned suddenly on Smith, grabbing Smith's hand off his right shoulder with his left hand. Surprised, Smith lurched backward but not before Mitchell swung his right arm up above his head and then brought his elbow down forcefully across Smith's forearm.

Then several things happened almost at once. Tim heard the sound of bone cracking as Smith let out a roar. Whistles from the remaining guards in the yard blew, and Leather and another guard sprinted toward Smith and Mitchell, raising their black metal clubs as they ran. Smith, still roaring, brought his huge left arm around Mitchell's head and squeezed with lethal force. Mitchell's eyes grew large as the air in his esophagus was crushed from him. The guards, unsure of a proper response attacked both men with a barrage of metal blows.

Tim leapt into the middle of the fight, taking the blows from the guards as he squeezed between the prisoners. The sensation felt by the two men was later described by Smith as a "wriggling fish" trying to swim between them. For Tim the smell of sweat, blood, and dirt was overpowering as he "wriggled" his body in to separate them. His action worked though, and Smith released Mitchell as he tried to figure out what had pushed between their bodies.

"Smith! Mitchell" Leather yelled as Smith backed up in surprise and then looked at his arm which limply fell in the wrong direction. "You boys done here?" he said sarcastically.

Mitchell had dropped to the ground when Smith released his neck. He was clutching his throat and gasping for breath.

"Get Smith to medical," ordered Leather to one of the guards just arriving at the scene. "His arm needs a Band-Aid." Leather spoke with a grin, his adrenaline still pumping. Then his smile turned to a scowl, and he leered at Mitchell.

"You don't seem to appreciate rule and order in our little resort. You think you can just live your own life? Make your own decisions? Do what you want? Well that's what got you thrown in here, Mitchell. Obviously you can't make your own decisions, so we're here to make them for you. You will obey me. You will obey me like I'm your king." Then Leather grinned sadistically. He stepped up close to the wounded man fighting for breath on his knees. "The next time I see you," Leather fumed and then pushed Mitchells head down onto the ground with his boot, "you better bow down to me just like you are right now."

Leather lifted his foot back up and then turned. "Take him down to the pen," he called out to the guards behind him as he walked away. "Don't get a medic unless he collapses. He wants to live his own life, eh? Fine, Jeffrey Mitchell can be the leader of himself in solitary."

Tim's mouth fell open. "Jeffrey?" he thought. That was why he looked familiar. This man who had killed so many, and who now was being dragged off to solitary confinement, was once the little boy he had carried out of the burning foster home. The innocent child was not innocent any more.

Chapter 33

KNOWING THE FUTURE

THE NEXT MORNING, Tim went back through his notes. He had been unable to discover the year and date of the prison yard brawl, but he felt that maybe his purpose in this case was different. Maybe breaking up a fight in the prison yard wasn't what he was meant to do for Jeffrey.

Tim grabbed the Magic 8 Ball that he had moved from his old room in his parents' house to his new one here in the home he was making of Lexie's old place. He shook it and then turned it over. "Will I be able to figure out when the prison fight occurs and help Jeffrey?"

The ball's answer was slow in rising to the surface. Then as the fluid inside was dispersed by the floating answer inside, Tim read, "My Sources Say No."

Tim flipped back through the pages until he found the flagged page with the description of the bomb maker. That man was the same. He knew it for sure now. He had been brought to the foster home to rescue Jeffrey and the other boys. Then he witnessed Jeffrey building the bomb. Now he had seen Jeffrey's fate. Whatever or whoever was in control of his zone seemed to be giving Tim a few random pieces of a complex puzzle. "I could stop the bombing if you just let me know when and where!" he solicited aloud toward the ceiling. It seemed that the story of Jeffrey was much more complicated than he knew.

The story of Lexie also remained complicated. He had seen her when she was in her fifties, then when she was thirty-one. From those two encounters, he knew he would see her again when she was fifteen, twenty, and then at least several, if not many times, while she was in her thirties and forties. But when would those zones occur for him? Lexie hadn't said if he was young or old when he had arrived. He hoped it would be soon and had been counting the days.

Tim's count reached 1,318 days. Or, three years, seven months, and thirteen days since his last visit with her. Then it finally happened, and he found himself in that familiar rundown neighborhood of the living Lexie. He remembered what she had told him the first night he found her there. "Next time," she had said, "find me as fast as you can."

Date: May 3, 1999
Zone Year: 2040

Tim dashed down the street to where the dilapidated house should have stood. When he saw it, he was confused. It was the same house, but it looked new. It was freshly painted and clean. The piles of scattered trash were gone and the lawn was clean, green, and freshly mowed.

As Tim ran to the door, he subconsciously brushed his hair with his fingers. "I must be early in her past, before the house fell apart," he thought, looking at the clean porch and fresh paint. "Maybe she isn't married yet."

Tim's heart raced as he stood at the door. He didn't see the white-haired woman sitting quietly in a rocking chair on the front porch. But she saw him.

"Welcome back, Tim," Lexie's voice called to him from that rocking chair on the end of the porch. Tim spun on his heels to see Lexie, grinning through wrinkled and baggy flesh. Her face was worn but clean. No bruises, no wounds. Her hair was shiny white, and her eyes sparkled as blue and bright as ever.

"Lexie!" He ran to her and embraced her. She lifted her arms to him but could only hug back weakly. "I have waited so long!" he continued. "I have so much to tell you."

"I already know," she said through her wise smile. "You are twenty-seven and as handsome as ever."

"Can you see me? How . . ." Tim started to ask.

Lexie continued smiling calmly as she looked directly into Tim's eyes. "A little," she nodded. "I can see the sunlight bending around you. I see something like the opposite of a shadow where you stand. I watched as you ran up the road toward the house. I would have liked to have run out to meet you, but I don't have the energy anymore. Besides, can you imagine what the neighbors would think of this old widow running into the street to meet an invisible man? They'd call the authorities and have me put away!" She laughed a joyful but quiet laugh.

For the first time, Tim noticed how old she seemed. "What year is this Lexie?" He looked out at the driveway at an unusual silver car, unlike any he had ever seen. He realized now that he had been foolish to think this could have been close to his own time.

"You have reached out and found September 17, 2040. And this is the last time that I will see you." Tim frowned but Lexie continued, speaking slowly and with an air of wisdom that comes with many years of life. "Let me see. You have finished remodeling my old house in Tulsa now, right? And the last time you saw me, I was in the shower!" She laughed again and enjoyed imagining him flush with embarrassment.

"You got lucky that it was a young me you found in the shower and not this wrinkled me now. You never would have come back!" She laughed again, and the sound of her laugh brought many memories of their childhood back to Tim. He couldn't help but laugh too.

"Of course I would have come back," he said still laughing. Then more seriously, "I have counted the days that I've been away from you."

"Always the gentleman," Lexie smiled. "I'd say 'don't ever change,' but I already know you won't. Would you like to sit down with me?"

"Okay." Tim pulled over a freshly painted white wicker chair. "Your house looks great. It wasn't like this the last time I saw the outside."

"Ever since Jack passed away ten years ago, people have been showing up at my door, offering to paint, clean, repair, and basically take care of me. They usually say something like, 'You don't know me, but I had this weird feeling that I needed to come here and help you.' Any idea, Tim, who is causing random people to have those 'weird feelings'?" She smiled accusationally.

"I can honestly say that I have no idea what you are talking about. But I imagine that someday I will," Tim agreed. Then after a short pause he asked, "How do you know so much about my life right now? My age, what I'm doing in my world, all that? And why did you say this is the last time?" She thought for a moment but when she spoke, it seemed to Tim that she already knew he would ask the question.

"Tim, you and I have spent a lot of time together over the years, not nearly enough, but a lot. You are just beginning your journey, but the oldest version of you that I have met has told me that this encounter is my last. I don't know if that means I will die soon or if it just means that our paths don't cross again. It has been a moment I've longed for, to see you again, and a moment I have dreaded, knowing it would be my last.

"I was thirty-four years younger the last time you saw me. And the next time, well, I'll let you be surprised." She smiled again but more distantly this time.

Tim looked into her eyes and felt confused. He sensed great sadness in her. Somehow he had expected a much different meeting. And if he had visited so much, why was she still so sad?

Then, something else struck Tim as odd. This fragile, old Lexie looked at least seventy-five. He worked out the math in his head, adding thirty-four years to the last time he had seen her when she was thirty-one. "Thirty-four years? That means you are sixty-five?" he questioned. It didn't bother him that she was old, just that she seemed so much older than she should.

"I look older, don't I?" she asked, as if reading his mind and feeling the doubt and confusion from Tim. "I suppose my life has taken a lot out of me. I am content right now with my life, but I do feel that I've had to live only for these moments. In some ways, I suppose I've wasted away waiting, always waiting. Jack gave me company, but I never loved him. We married out of necessity when I got pregnant with Andrew. Then I suppose I stayed with him because I was afraid to be alone. He never loved me either. He stayed with me out of convenience and out of need to rule over someone weak."

"Weak? You have never been weak," Tim argued.

"Oh, I wish that were true. My life has been a weak life, Tim. But I accept that. It is my place I think. You are the strong one. You are the hero in both my timeline and in yours."

"So this really is a different timeline? Some kind of parallel universe?" Tim asked.

Lexie smiled and then pushed herself up slowly, letting the chair rock forward, and she stepped out of it. "Come inside, I want to show you some things."

Tim followed her slowly into the house. The house was silent, and he felt the need for small talk. Not the uncomfortable talk between strangers, more the casual chatter of old friends.

"What town is this, Lexie? I realize that I have been here three times now but have never figured out where I am."

"You've been here more than that. This is Brenham, Texas," Lexie answered.

"Texas? But the first time I met you here, the town was covered in snow."

"It does snow in Texas." She laughed. "Just not as often as other places. Andrew loved it on those rare occasions that it would snow, usually just one half inch or less, but he would run outside with the look of wonderment covering his face." Her own face changed now and appeared solemn.

"How is Andrew doing?" Tim asked. "Does he live nearby?"

Lexie stopped and turned to Tim. "Andrew died a long time ago, Tim." Her expression was somber but not sad. "He was killed by a stray bullet while we were at the park."

"Oh . . . I . . . Lexie. I am so sorry," Tim stammered, not sure what to say.

She only nodded, accepting his feeble condolence and then walked again toward the small bedroom at the end of the hall. Tim followed her as she stepped into Andrew's room. The entire house was clean, but Andrew's room was more cluttered. "It was difficult to convince Jack to let me keep our son's room like it was. Jack wanted to turn it into a workshop or TV room. But I needed this room to stay just like this. So I wouldn't forget him. And so I had a place away from Jack sometimes."

She sat down on the short child-sized bed across from a standard-sized mattress that lay on the floor. Tim watched her look around. "You know, Tim, it is strange how things happen just as you say they will. I knew you would be arriving today. I vowed to myself that I wouldn't get emotional. But you told me a long time ago that it would be this way."

"We can talk about something else," Tim offered.

"No, it's okay. It is what it is. I am glad that you will still have many wonderful visits with me. It makes me happy to think that the next time you see me, I will be younger and still beautiful."

"You are still beautiful to me!"

"You always say that. I guess it's about time I try to believe it." She smiled lightly.

Tim thought about her son again and suddenly burst out excitedly, "Wait, tell me when Andrew was shot. I can warn you the next time I see you. The next time I find you before it happens!"

"Tim, you already tried that. When I said that he was shot while *we* were at the park, I meant the three of us—Andrew, me, and you. You tried as hard as you could. You even tried to cover Andrew and take the bullet. You insisted that you could change his fate. But when the day came, I went to the park. I knew it was the day but for some reason, I couldn't stop myself from going.

"When you arrived, you said the guides had made me come but that you would still stop it from happening. But it still happened. I watched it all."

"The guides?" Tim asked.

"The time guides," Lexie answered quickly, then continued. "Andrew had been playing. A pickup truck drove by and lowered the window," she continued, not able to see the confusion on Tim's face. "They were aiming for a teen that was sitting with some friends at a picnic table far from us. Police said a young dealer was the target. A father was taking revenge on the teen for his own son's suicide. Funny how someone thinks it's okay to kill a son for a son.

"In the end, the driver of the truck swerved to miss a basketball that was rolling out into the street from another group of kids. The father in the passenger seat shot just as the truck veered. You leapt out in front of Andrew and then were pulled backward through the air. I never saw them, but the guides had you. They held you back as you tried to get to Andrew while he lay on the ground. There was nothing you could do. It had to be that way."

Tim didn't know what to say. Was it true that he couldn't save Andrew? Couldn't he think of a different way when the time came? Would he still try, even though Lexie said there was nothing he could do? Of course, he would try. Despite this information, how could he not try to save her son? "I can't accept that there is no way to help. I will find a way!"

"Timmy, some things just happen. And some things *must* happen. You have taught me that. My son was meant to die. I was meant to play an insignificant role in the world. In your timeline, I died. In this one, you were allowed to save my life, but my decisions have always resulted in a life of nothing and of tragedy.

"Some things you try to change meet with more resistance because they *must* be as they are. You can't save everyone. You have to let it go sometimes and accept it"

"But why? Why can't I use my gift freely? Shouldn't I try to save everyone?"

"Of course you should try, but don't be surprised or frustrated when the time guides stop you."

"Wait, who are the time guides?"

Lexie sighed. "The screamers are the time guides." Then she closed her eyes and shook her head. "Sometimes, I forget what you already know or don't know. You are still young. There is so much you will learn."

She opened her eyes and smiled patiently at Tim. "The last time I saw you, you were as old as I am now and explaining things to me." She sighed again. "You and Dr. Bruin came up with some amazing research on alternate universes a few years ago. I've got the book he published over here." Lexie stood up slowly again and pulled open a plastic bin with old baby clothes and children's books. "I convinced Jack that these clothes and books had a lot of sentimental value only. He would have tried to sell them or throw them out otherwise. He had no interest in this stuff, so I've used it to hide my notes, pictures, and memories that he wouldn't approve of. Like this." She was smiling again now as she pulled out a yellowed photograph from a binder at the bottom of the bin and showed it to him.

"That's us!" Tim stated in amazement. "I remember that picture!" He recognized the background as one of the state parks they had camped in as children. "Was that the summer you learned about my zone?"

"That's it. In fact, that is the day after we first held hands. See the way I'm looking at you?" The small pretty girl in the picture wasn't looking at the camera. She had a contented smile as she looked at her friend sitting next to her on a log bench. "I had always liked you Tim. But that was the day I decided I wanted to marry you."

Tim was again lost for words. He just stared at the picture, wishing he could do it all over again. If he could, he would protect Lexie when the school kids started making fun of her. He would have stopped her dad from moving them away. Maybe his parents could have taken her in. Or if she still moved away, he would have kept in touch and gotten back together as soon as they finished high school. Then, she never would have been abused and beaten. Andrew could be their son, and he wouldn't have to die. Everything could have been better.

But changing the past was something he could not do in his world. He could only change the course of the future. And in Lexie's world, he had no control of when and where he would arrive.

"I really messed everything up," he finally said softly, still staring at the picture.

"No, it was supposed to be this way." She pulled out the book that she had gone to the bin to retrieve and handed it to Tim.

It was a thick, heavy book. Tim read the cover aloud. *The Principles and Theories of Alternate Realities—A Universe in Repair* by Dr. James Bruin.

"You helped him write this," Lexie said when he looked up, "but you wanted to keep your name off it. Guess it's easier to be a hero if nobody thinks you are some kind of alien creature from another dimension. Doc actually did most of the writing and research. You were mostly just the willing lab rat." She grinned.

"Here, look at the acknowledgments page," Lexie said as she took the book back and flipped a few pages. Finding it, she read, "Dedicated to my lifelong friend, whose trust and cooperation allowed this book to become part of this alternate reality."

"So my other self from your world worked with Dr. Bruin? That is great! I always wondered if I should have let Doc continue to run tests on me."

"Not your other self, YOU. Tim . . . Wow, there is so much to tell you." Lexie reached back into the bin and pulled out stacks of newspaper clippings.

She handed him the clippings and then sat down on the small bed. Tim sat down next to her.

"Boy Survives Fall from Water Tower. Mother claims an angel caught him in midair!"

"Purse snatcher apprehended after he tripped and became strangely tied up in his own clothing."

"The Angel Saves Again: Twelve witnesses recall being pushed out of harm's way by an invisible force just before a sheet of glass plummeted from a walkway above."

"All of these are about *you*, Tim." Lexie took the bottom paper from Tim's hands and held it out to him. "This one is about you too, but the other you."

"Local Hero Shot and Killed by Scorned Lover." Tim took the paper from her hand and read below the headline. "Local man, Timothy Caston, was found shot to death in his apartment Tuesday morning. Witnesses report a woman entered the apartment at 2:00 a.m. and left after an argument. The woman, identified by police as Natalie Stassen of Houston, TX, has been apprehended and is undergoing questioning. Caston was made locally famous after it was discovered that he was the daring rescuer of sixteen children. Caston acted heroically when a fire erupted at the Trail Hills Recovery Group Home. He rescued the children as the house collapsed around them. All sixteen were unharmed but the two caregivers on-site perished in the explosion."

Tim looked to see if the article was continued somewhere else in the paper. Finding nothing else, he reread it several times and then looked for the date of the paper. He read it aloud, "September 7, 1995."

Tim was in shock. He felt like the pit of his stomach had just gone empty. It was his own death, and yet not his own. He had wondered if he would see his other self again in this reality but assumed that the lack of sightings was just verification that their paths were different. He thought of the children and of what it had felt like to watch the other Tim save them from the burning home. That home was just outside Houston, in Brenham. The same town where he now knew Lexie lived. Was there a connection?

"It said he was a local resident. But I never lived in Brenham. I just went there to get the kids out of the house. Then I left."

"The Tim that was killed was living in Brenham," Lexie said. "After I saw this article, I researched him. Your lives were very similar until about four months before your, I mean *his,* death. After *you* saved the children, you went back to Tulsa and continued fixing up my old house. I am gone in your reality, so you had no reason to stay in Texas. But *he* learned from my father that I was living here, in Brenham. So after coming here to save the kids, *he*, the other you, stayed. That is where your paths diverge. *You* stayed safely in Oklahoma, but *he* moved here, close enough for Natalie to find him."

How does one react to the news of one's death, Tim thought, especially when it isn't his own death? The Tim of Lexie's world had been a completely different person. He had had most of the same experiences but was still another person. Yet he had also been much closer to being with Lexie. If Natalie hadn't shot him, they could have been together.

"He had been trying to find me, Tim," Lexie said, confirming his thoughts. "I so wish he had found me. Maybe he could have given me a very different life." A hint of a tear seemed to fill one of Lexie's eyes. She looked at him, wondering what he was thinking.

Tim still felt strange. "I am not sure what to say about any of it. I think I feel like I have just heard the news of a brother dying. But it is of a brother I never met and, until a few years ago, didn't even know existed. I also feel a little jealous. Is it weird that I am jealous of the way you talk about that Tim?" he probed.

Lexie understood. "It is a strange situation," she agreed. "If he had not died and he and I had been together, I still would have loved you both, only he could have really been here with me. You will rescue me too but in a different way. You add joy to my life whenever you are here." She affectionately stroked his face and hair as she spoke. "Still, I can't help but wish life had turned out differently."

Lexie looked so old and worn-down, Tim thought. He could tell that she had been abused for many years. She had had a life of pain. He had no right to feel jealous. Her life could have been so much better had that other Tim been with her.

Lexie went on with the story, "The police reports that I was able to find indicated that Natalie was upset when he left her. She learned about his search for me and tracked him down here in Brenham. He had left her with thousands of dollars in clothes and possessions as well as a place to live, but she still sought him out, feeling rejected and cheated. She claimed to police that she loved him, but I was never convinced. Maybe I was jealous.

"When she found him, she tried to convince him to come back to her. But he refused, telling her that he had found his true love.

So she killed him." She stated it matter-of-factly, but Tim read in her expressions the conflicted pain that she felt inside.

Tim tried to digest it all. So much information, so hard to understand. How could Natalie have killed him? She wasn't Mother Teresa, but was she really capable of murdering him? Something else must have happened after he left. Something that made her more desperate or crazy.

Sensing Tim's doubt, Lexie added, "Natalie was not a good person. You know that. The police tried to tie her to the murder of your old next door neighbor too—shortly after you left her—but they couldn't prove it. However, she confessed to your murder and was sentenced to life in prison."

Tim trusted Lexie, even if it didn't yet make sense. The implications of it all would have to sink in later. "Ok, so the *me* here is dead. How then is *he* a lifelong friend with Dr. Bruin?

"YOU! *You* are his lifelong friend. He studied the tests that the Tim from this reality allowed him to run back when he was eighteen after the crash. They are the same tests that Dr. Bruin ran in your reality. He studied them for years even though you had never gone back to him. He figured out that . . ." She stopped and seemed to have just realized something.

"What is it?" Tim asked.

"Oh, I'm just thinking about a paradox?" she frowned.

"A what?"

Lexie sighed, but then laughed, "Tim, you sure are smarter later in your life!" Her smile reassured him that she wasn't laughing at him, even if she was making a little fun of him. "A paradox," she repeated after a time. "If you change something in the past that affects something in the future, will that future self be able to make that same change in the past? For instance, if you traveled to an earlier time and killed your dad before you were conceived, you would never be born and therefore never be able to go back and kill your dad, but then you *would* be born. Get it? That is a paradox. There are many variations on that example, but do you understand?"

"Yeah, that makes sense I think," he answered while shaking his head no.

Lexie laughed again. "I'm just wondering, if I tell you all of Dr. Bruin's theories, the same theories that you will help produce far into your future, will those theories be influenced by what I'm telling you? It's a circular loop. I tell you what I've learned from your future self and this book, then you go back and write this book with Doc in my past so that I can tell you what I've learned from your future self and this book. I wonder if I could break the loop by just making up something right now and change the book. What if none of this," she shook the book in her hand, "is correct because I incorrectly influence it. That's the paradox."

"I think I'm really lost now," Tim laughed at Lexie this time. "Let's just assume the paradox will work itself out and that this is all correct. Just tell me how I become friends with Dr. Bruin."

"After he studied your tests for years, he figured out a pattern in the brainwaves. I don't fully understand it, but he figured out that your consciousness was leaping to a parallel universe that was created by a split in the fabric of time. He used your terminology and called them alternate timelines. Because he understood it and accepted it, one day when your consciousness showed up at his office, he was able to hear you and communicate with you."

She bit her lip as she started thinking out loud again. "You told me once that you knew he'd be able to hear you. Now I understand why. You knew because I just told you! Isn't that remarkable!" she exclaimed with exuberance.

Tim laughed. This broken down, sixty-five-year-old Lexie was just as cute and funny as the younger versions he had met.

"That is why I have always felt you and heard you," she continued. "I accepted your zone when I was a child, so feeling your presence here has always been easy for me. And as the years go by, I am accepting it more and more. At first, I couldn't see you at all, I just sensed you. Then you were more like a shadow or a blur. Now, when you are close, I can almost make out the features of your young face." Lexie put her hand on Tim's cheek again. "Oh, how I wish I could live young with you again."

She sighed. "But the whole point of what I'm trying to tell you, Tim, is that you can't change everything. It isn't possible, and it was never meant to be possible. The guides won't allow it."

Tim shook his head in frustration. "So those weird boys, the screamers, are some kind of guides? Guides of what?"

"You call them screamers because of the way they communicate to each other. But inside that terrible scream are frequencies you can't hear. They all work together as timeline guides keeping track of the critical points in peoples' lives. They adjust the timeline based on the decisions and actions people take. But some of the things that happen are too important to the timeline for chance. The screamers influence people and actions when they have to push the timeline."

"Push the timeline? For what reason? Whose purpose would be achieved by the death of people or the misery of others?" He thought of Andrew and Lexie. Why would anyone or anything want their lives to be like this?

"You and Doc will theorize that the timeline was never meant to be split. Maybe there are just two alternate timelines. Maybe twenty. Or maybe even twenty trillion separate realities. He doesn't know. But he thinks the number is always changing and is caused whenever someone like you messes with things in the timelines.

"The Tim from my timeline was doing the same thing as you, but zoning into another reality. Maybe he was working in your reality. Remember that day we were camping and your dad borrowed the boat from that old guy? That really tall guy came over to us and told us how to avoid sinking our boat. He said that something in his mind had made him come over to us, like he was guided by someone."

"Yeah!" Tim could remember that day well, and he could still see the strange look on the man's face as he spoke to them. "That guy had the same confused gaze that people get when I'm trying to cause them to do something during a zone."

"Exactly! I think Tim from this reality or maybe some other Tim made that guy come over. That other Tim somehow knew we would sink without that advice."

"Did I tell you all this sometime in your past too?" Tim asked.

"No, this part of the theory I came up with. Remember, I'm smarter than you!" She grinned, showing the wrinkles and lines on her face.

Tim thought back to the screamers and the multiple timeline theory. "So, why would they try to change the timeline?"

"The guides?" Lexie asked and Tim nodded. "You and Dr. Bruin thought that the universe or God or something doesn't want multiple timelines. Maybe it's just an unnatural state. So the guides are not only observing and adjusting the timeline based on the natural course of decisions and actions, but they are also trying to reconnect and merge the realities. If they can align two or more alternate realities, then they can be merged."

"And all of that comes from my tests and his research?"

"Yep. You tried to find another person out there with your abilities. Doc tried too. But as far as you could both determine, no one else alive can observe or move between the parallel realities."

Learning that he and Doc would never find another like him was difficult to hear. He was disappointed. It would have been reassuring to have known that there were others like him out there.

Lexie continued speaking. "So he first relied on the original tests that *your* other *you* gave him. Then, when *you* found him again, you let him monitor *you* for years. He had developed new ways to follow you from your zone back to your reality. And because you were undergoing tests while here in my reality, he could study your zoned consciousness directly. At the same time, the Dr. Bruin in your reality was using the information you were passing to him from this world. They got so good at collaborating that they began communicating with each other through patterns they could introduce into your brain from one side to the other."

"I don't think I will ever understand all of this. I can't see myself doing all that research and coming up with theories. I'm not that special. I've always just wanted to be normal."

"Tim, you are anything but normal. But that is okay. All the greatest people are far from normal. And you are one of those great people! In the newspapers and media all across your world, you are referred to as "The Heroic Stranger" or "The Unknown Hero." But here, you have made an even bigger difference as the "Silent Angel." I've watched international news lights and info chirps for many years describing the amazing activities of the Angel."

Tim wasn't sure what a news light or info chirp was but decided not to interrupt as Lexie continued, "Many people close to death can see you even better than I can. They describe you as a radiant guardian, sent from God to rescue them. The ones you've saved often change their lives and use their second chance for good. I have been so proud to know you. Even though I can't tell any one."

Tim felt overwhelmed. He was just a man, not an angel. Yet if God was in control of his zone, maybe he had a greater purpose than he could comprehend. Still, how would he do so much? How could he possibly have such an influence on so large a world? Lexie read his emotions clearly.

"I know it seems like a lot, Tim. But this is forty years into your future. You would be sixty-eight years old in this timeline. You have time.

"Look here." Lexie pulled out another notebook from Andrew's bin, "This is the list of dates, places, times, and circumstances that we have met. I have put this notebook together slowly over the years. The listings are out of order for you since you jump around somewhat randomly. For me, though, they are a chronological record of my life. I have done all my living in these moments."

Tim flipped through the pages. It was clear that he would be seeing Lexie often. He found her description of their day in the park. "2009?" he read.

"Yes, Andrew was only four." A tear welled up in her eye as she lifted a picture of Andrew that was paper-clipped to the page. "He loved you too, you know," Lexie went on after wiping the tear from her cheek. "He accepted you and could see you better than I can. You would have been a great dad." She smiled. "Jack always thought I was having an affair with someone because Andrew would talk about the funny blurry man that came to visit. I, of course, denied it and reminded Jack that Andrew was only four and had a great imagination."

"Did Jack believe you?"

"No, he used you as an excuse to take out his anger on me. He always said I deserved it."

"Why did you really stay with him? Neither of you loved each other. Why not leave and start a new life?"

Lexie sighed. "Several reasons, I suppose. Jack is a freight driver so he wasn't here that often, so sometimes I just figured I could put up with him for a few days and then I'd be on my own again. A few times I really did try to leave. But whenever I thought about leaving, and those few times I actually tried, something would hold me back. Something convinced me to stay."

"The screamers?" Tim asked.

"I think so. I haven't ever seen them like you can. But from the way you have described their ability to push people into decisions or guide them at critical moments, I have to believe that they have influenced me too."

Then Lexie smiled toward Tim. "The last reason," she said, "is much simpler, and maybe the most important. I stayed because of you. This was where you found me the first time. I knew that as long as I stayed here, you would be able to find me again." Her smile broke, and Lexie wept. "Listen, we don't have much time left, Tim. If I really will never see you again, I want to make the most of this. I've told you everything I think I'm supposed to tell you. You will find out more along the way. Much of it we will learn together. But right now, just hold me. Just hold me one last time."

Tim pulled her into his arms and then slowly laid her down on the bed, their embrace unbroken. It didn't matter to him that this Lexie was weak and old. She was Lexie. To him, she was ageless.

"This is how you held me that night I almost ended it all," Lexie whispered.

"I'll have to remember that."

"You will," she responded. Then she rolled over to face him and looked into his eyes. Her eyes got bigger with surprise. "I can see your eyes, Tim. They look just like I remember." She lifted her head and kissed him.

The kiss was familiar as if she had done it many times and it caused Tim to wonder. "Lexie, have we ever . . ."

She stopped him with another kiss and then said, "That's for you to find out," and she grinned a youthful grin. Tim saw the colors and lines on her face begin to fade.

"It's happening," he said quietly.

"Good-bye, my Timothy, I love you," she spoke softly as their embraced tightened. He watched as the details and wrinkles faded from her face. In the moments before he left, the years seem to peel away, and her beautiful youthful glow was the last thing he saw before the darkness swept over his consciousness. The light returned, and he was home.

Tim didn't go back to sleep that night after he awoke in the familiar surroundings that he had made into a home. This house that had first been his best friend's, then a rental property to several families, then vacant, was now clean and remodeled with many of his own improvements. This was his house now. It made him feel proud to know that Lexie already knew of his work to fix the place up. She had known, because he had already told her. He would enjoy those many visits to see her.

It felt strange to be thinking of his future, knowing many of the details forty years in advance. How great it will be, he thought, to see Lexie as a young woman again.

Sadly, he also thought of the Lexie he had just left. She had said that it was their last time together. Had he even said good-bye? He couldn't remember now. He had meant to say many things—that he loved her, that he was sorry for the years of pain she had experienced, that he wished it wasn't the last time to see each other.

He picked up the Magic 8 Ball and asked, "Does she know I love her?" He turned it over and then flipped it back up so the little plastic window would reveal its answer.

It wasn't the assurance he hoped for, but it would have to do. "Most Likely," was the answer that floated to the surface.

Chapter 34

JEFFREY'S PATH

THE NEXT FEW years went by quickly for Tim. They continued to be full of adventure and heroism. And just as Lexie had foretold, Tim contacted Dr. Bruin, both in his world and in hers. Tim knew that the research they began in Doc's labs would eventually unlock many of the mysteries that the old Lexie had already understood. Doc seemed unconcerned with paradoxes and wanted to know everything the old and wise Lexie had told Tim.

February 28, 2001
Zone Year: 2003

Tim also encountered Jeffrey again. Tim recognized him immediately after standing up and finding himself just outside a suburban mall in Texas. Jeffrey and some punk friends were sharing a cigarette as they watched out for security. All looked to be around twelve years old. This Jeffrey was somewhere between the innocent little boy Tim had rescued and the radical pseudo terrorist he would someday become. His hair was like a dirty mop, and he and the kids around him seemed to like wearing their pants so loose that it was unclear how they didn't simply fall down.

Nonchalantly, Tim stepped invisibly past the punks just as Jeffrey was accepting the smoke again from the preteen boy next to him. Before the cigarette could be passed, Tim flicked it out of the fingers of the punk, causing it to fly out into the parking lot.

"Whad'ya do that for, Spaz?" Jeffrey laughed as the boy looked at his fingers. The other boys hadn't seen what had happened since their attention had not been on the cigarette. They were just upset that their last smoke was wasted.

A car pulled up past the boys and stopped just long enough to let three girls file out. "Be good," the adult driver yelled in a fatherly tone. Two of the three girls looked older than Jeffrey and his five friends, but they were apparently still young enough to need their dad as a chauffer. The third girl was younger and appeared to be a tagalong little sister, maybe nine or ten years old.

The lost cigarette was forgotten by Jeffrey and his friends, and the six boys made no effort to hide their interest in the older two girls. All twelve male eyeballs became glued to the leggy young females as they stepped out of the car and walked toward the mall entrance.

"Hey, ladies," Spaz sang to the girls after their dad drove off. The first two put their noses up and looked away to signal complete disinterest as they quickly made their way toward the doors. But the third smiled shyly at the boys as she lagged slightly behind her older sisters.

"Hey, I think the little one likes you," Jeffrey laughed at Spaz as the other boys joined in making fun. Spaz didn't think it so funny. "Shut up, you guys," he sulked.

"If you're gonna be a baby about it, why don't you go crying home to momma," Jeffrey mocked.

"At least I have a momma," Spaz retorted angrily.

"Shut the fu . . . oww!" Jeffrey yelled as Tim popped him in the head with the back of his unseen hand. "What the f—oww!" he yelled again as Tim swiftly punished him a second time.

Tim wasn't sure what he was trying to accomplish. He would only be able to flick cigarettes from Jeffrey's hand and stop his foul mouth for another thirty-two minutes. Then Jeffrey would be on his own again. And since he had already seen the future of this Jeffrey, could that be changed? He supposed that would create a paradox too.

It surprised Tim how well Jeffrey had felt his invisible slaps. Usually, people didn't respond to his touch at all or seemed to perceive only a slight annoyance, like a bug or an itch. The boys' laughter had turned from Spaz to Jeffrey as he put his hand onto his head where Tim had bopped him. "That was weird," Jeffrey said mostly to himself. Then to the group he asked, "Did someone hit me?"

"Maybe you do have a momma. And she come back from the grave to slap you around!" laughed the little fat boy of the group. Spaz snapped a look at the boy as if to say, "Watch out, Jeff's in a bad mood!"

The sudden reprimand Jeffrey had received from Tim had surprised him but had also pulled him from his bad temper. He suddenly saw the humor in the fat boy's words as his friends waited for his reaction. "That would suck!" Jeffrey finally said, laughing back. "Last thing I need is an invisible chaperone!"

Tim chuckled to himself at the irony of that statement.

"Ghost mom's gonna get you, Jeff!" Spaz said, happy that Jeffrey was in a better mood suddenly.

Fat boy defended him, "A ghost mom's better than a crack whore like yours!"

"Yeah," Jeffrey jumped in laughing, thinking of a South Park rerun he had just seen on TV last night and quoted the character 'Cartman'. "Your mom is such a crack whore that she is on the cover of *Crack Whore Magazine*!" All the boys laughed now.

Soon, Tim followed the laughing boys into the mall and watched as they flirted with more uninterested girls, picked on other kids younger than them, and then walked into the arcade. They weren't necessarily bad kids, not yet, but Tim realized that they were on a bad path.

Jeffrey wouldn't just wake up one day in the future and decide he was going to build a homemade bomb and kill as many people as possible. It would happen gradually. On this path, one day at a time, each little choice and event would lead him there.

He started to follow Jeffrey into the arcade but heard a scream back the way they had just come. Tim desperately wanted to stay with Jeffrey to try as best he could to keep the boy out of trouble, but the commotion was intensifying down the concourse next to the Orange Julius.

Tim sprinted over to where a small crowd had gathered next to one of the long silver escalators. A small boy, maybe two years old, was hanging on the outside of the moving stairway. It appeared that he had grabbed onto the progressing black rubber handrail at the bottom and then held on to it as it lifted him toward the second floor. The child appeared more confused than scared as the rail lifted him higher and higher. His mother screamed again for someone to help as she tried in vain to reach him from the floor below. The dozen or so witnesses just stood back in shock, unable to move.

Tim looked around to see if screamers were nearby, causing the bystanders' inability to act, but he saw none. "Why don't people do something?" he thought as he took in the situation. He had observed on many occasions that onlookers often stare in disbelief, doing nothing to help. Sometimes, the screamers held them back, to allow an event to take place. But usually, it seemed that their inaction was of their own choosing or was due to their assumption that somebody else would act.

In this case, that somebody else was Tim. He quickly ran up the escalator stairs as a woman near the mother uselessly yelled, "Somebody should do something!" Nobody moved. The child was dangling precariously over twenty feet above the hard tiled floor.

The boy's fingers slipped a little. Then, just as his tiny grip failed completely, Tim reached over the railing and grabbed onto his wrists, quickly but gently pulling him over the railing onto the moving stairs. The child, silent until now, suddenly began to cry.

"Oh, now you are scared?" Tim laughed as he carefully guided the boy over the seam at the top of the escalator where the grooved stairs and unmoving second floor met.

The boy was greeted at the top by a kind-looking middle-aged woman with frizzy brown hair. She picked up the boy and brought him back to his shocked mother below. "Looked like he just pulled himself up!" Tim overheard one of the ineffective spectators say to another. "That was amazing!" another one said. Tim gently grabbed that man's left forearm and lifted it up so he could read the watch. It was 2:18 p.m. on Saturday, April 5, 2003. He would record that into his notes. The man shook his arm out of Tim's hand and brushed it off, unaware of Tim's intrusion but obviously uncomfortable having his wrist up for no particular reason.

Meanwhile, Jeffrey and one of his friends had left the arcade and slipped quietly into the 'Game Stop' next door. Not quite as quietly, they tried to slip out, each with a stack of Xbox games under their jackets.

With alarms blaring, Tim arrived in time to see Jeffrey being hauled off by security guards. He looked more defiant than frightened. He swore at the guards angrily. Tim couldn't believe that this was the same sweet five-year-old boy that had hugged him tightly after he rescued him from the burning home.

Once back in his own time, Tim faithfully recorded the date, time, location, and events into his notebook, cataloged it by year, and flagged as a "must do" event. It was 2001 for him, so it would be another two years before he'd need to appear and save the little escalator boy. Maybe afterwards, he could bail out Jeffrey and find a way to mentor him. He flagged that as a "consider path forward" event.

In the meantime, life marched on and time passed quickly. Though the years were eventful, seeing Lexie was what Tim longed for most. He wondered how it worked. Was her timeline running along at exactly the same speed as his own? Was she out there in some parallel universe just a couple years younger than him like she would be if she was still alive here? Or had the events of her timeline occurred long ago and the two universes completely unrelated in time? What was she doing right at that moment? Why hadn't he zoned back into her life again? When would it happen? Was she thinking of him?

Before Tim knew it, two more years had lapsed, and he still had not seen Lexie again. He drove to the mall and parked his truck near the entrance where Jeffrey and the boys would be smoking cigarettes. Tim knew that Jeffrey had to be a secondary priority this time. He was there to save the child.

Turning off the truck, Tim looked up and saw the boys coming out of the mall and congregating near the entrance just as he had witnessed before. They still looked like punks with their baggy clothes and long hair, but fashion had caught up with his previous peek into this time and place. He understood now that many kids dressed like this.

Tim walked toward the boys as Spaz passed Jeffrey the cigarette. "Should you be smoking?" Tim asked as he walked past, not really intending to stop them but not able to resist.

Jeffrey looked up and saw Tim. A flash of recognition appeared for half a second. Did Jeffrey remember the man who had saved him from the burning home over seven years earlier?

This moment of distraction caused Jeffrey to reach out too far for the cigarette that Spaz was handing him. The lit end met the back of Jeffrey's hand and briefly burned his flesh.

"Ow!" Jeffrey cried. Realizing he had just burned his friend's hand, Spaz dropped the cigarette.

Jeffrey yelled, "Whad'ya do that for, Spaz?" after seeing their last cigarette fall to the ground,

Tim stopped and looked back. His actions here were different than the encounter during the zone. Yet the outcome now was almost exactly the same. The cigarette still ended up on the ground, and Spaz was being blamed for the loss. Tim knew he would need to ponder the event some more later.

The attention of the boys was diverted quickly from the dropped smoke to the car of girls that had just pulled up and started unloading. Tim hurried into the mall ahead of them and looked for the escalator. He spotted it and made his way over to the young mother who would soon be calling for help. He knew he must wait just a little longer since people usually wouldn't listen to him if he just marched up and announced what would happen.

Tim looked back toward the entrance and saw Jeffrey and the boys rolling in. A thought struck Tim. Instead of bailing Jeffrey out of jail later today, he just needed to distract him long enough to keep him from shoplifting in a few minutes.

Tim looked at the baby, still standing next to his mother away from the escalator. There was time. Tim ran up to Jeffrey just as he was about to enter the arcade. "Jeffrey," he called and reached for his arm.

Jeffrey turned and pulled his arm back fast enough for Tim's grip to slip. A slight hesitation or recognition flashed again across Jeffrey's face.

"Jeffrey, please come with me. I don't have time to explain," Tim said quickly. Jeffrey stared at Tim while his friends called to him from inside the arcade.

"I know you," he said with uncertainty. "You are . . ." he started to say but was interrupted by a scream back toward the Orange Julius.

"Please come with me, I have to help the boy and then we can talk," Tim urged. Jeffrey stood, his feet planted as he looked from Tim to the commotion down the mall concourse.

Tim couldn't wait any longer so turned and ran. He sprinted to the end of the silver escalator. The boy was already hanging high up on the outside of the moving rail. Would he be able to make it in time? As before, no one seemed to know what to do. They all just stood in shock as the boy was lifted higher.

Tim ran as fast as he could up the moving stairs but realized he was already behind. He had spent too much time trying to convince Jeffrey to come with him. That time wasted might be the difference of life and death for the small boy that neared the top of the lift.

"Do something!" a woman yelled from below. Tim remembered that the boy's grip had failed only a moment after that same voice had yelled out the last time. The boy dangled twenty feet above the tile below and Tim was still ten feet away.

Tim leaped up the final few stairs and closed the gap just as the tiny fingers began to slip. He jumped toward the fingers with his own and felt them slip against his palms. His grip tightened to catch the boy, but the tiny fingers were already out of his hand.

"No!" Tim bellowed as he slammed hard against the side of the rail. Screams echoed out below, as Tim bounced off the rail and landed on the grooved metal stairs. The boy had fallen. He had not made it in time.

The stairs brought Tim's crumpled form to the top, and he slid onto the upper floor as if the escalator was rejecting him and his failure. He heard the mother below wailing. Then the middle-aged woman with frizzy hair met him at the top. She offered him her hand. "You were almost a hero," she said with a kind smile. How could she be smiling?

Tim listened again as he let the woman help him up. The mother's wailing did not sound right. He heard someone say, "Looked like he showed up just in time."

"What?" Tim said.

Then another voice said, "Yeah, that was amazing!"

What was going on? Tim looked down over the railing at the mother. Her hands were outstretched toward her boy who was being handed to her by a kid in baggy clothes. It was Jeffrey!

"What happened?" Tim asked the frizzy-haired woman watching over the railing next to him.

"That wonderful boy caught him! He ran up behind you but instead of going up the stairs, he ran to get under him and caught him just in time."

"He saved him?" Tim asked, still trying to grasp what had just happened.

"He did. He caught him. That boy is a hero!"

A crowd led by the mother swarmed Jeffrey and heaped praise and hugs on him. Jeffrey stood shocked at first as if he too was unsure what had just happened. He looked at the adoring crowd and then looked up at Tim. Tim smiled at him and then Jeffrey smiled back. The recognition was unmistakable now.

Tim decided to let Jeffrey bask in the rewards of his deed. He agreed with the frizzy-haired woman that the boy was indeed a hero. Then he excused himself and walked away. This moment would be Jeffrey's. He would try to find him again and make sure he was doing okay. But somehow, Tim felt certain that Jeffrey was already on a new path now. His future was changed.

Once back at home, Tim made new notes as he compared the events in the mall with those he had witnessed in his zone. So much was the same and yet, for Jeffrey, so much was different. He wondered what had made Jeffrey follow him after all. Why had Jeffrey chosen to stay down below and get in place to catch the child? As usual, there were always more questions than answers. And as usual, his thoughts turned toward Lexie.

When would he see her again? Day after day he wished and prayed for his next zone to take him to her. Every night, he begged for this night to be the one. And finally, on his thirty-second birthday, it happened. Four-and-a-half years had passed since he saw her so many years into her future. This time would be her past.

Chapter 35

LEXIE'S PAST

May 10, 2004
Zone Year: 1990

"WELCOME TO LINCOLN, Nebraska," read a sign along a small road. Tim looked at the sign from a sprawled position on the shoulder of the road, having just jumped there to avoid an oncoming bus. The bus probably wouldn't have hurt him, but the driver may have unconsciously tried to swerve to miss his invisible form. A bus swerving at high speed could be disastrous, and Tim saw enough bad events occur without causing them himself!

Inside the bus was a cheering woman's softball team. A large banner tied to the side of the bus read, "Go 1990 Huskers!"

"1990!" Tim said to the Nebraska sign. He had been to the past before and usually found it to be an enjoyable break. There was nothing he could do about events that occurred here in a time already gone. What happened here had already occurred in his world.

He looked around as he sat up again, brushing gravel from his hands. The sun was shining and the sky, a brilliant blue. Wildflowers were blooming, and the air seemed comfortably warm. He assumed it was late spring or early summer.

Doing some quick math in his head, Tim realized that back in Oklahoma, he was an eighteen-year-old senior at Catoosa High.

Lexie must be fifteen, he thought. Then he put it together. "Lexie is fifteen! She lives in Nebraska!" he yelled.

Not sure where she lived, but somehow sure of the outcome, Tim ran along the road in the direction the bus and most of the passing cars were going. He scanned each car as it passed, wondering if she would be in one of them. He looked up at houses, trying to decide how he'd know if one was hers. And then, almost too easily, he saw her.

Lexie was jogging up ahead of him on a cross street. Her golden blonde hair swayed back and forth from the pink scrunchy ponytail tied at the back of her head. She wore white sweats and pink shoes that stood out brightly from the dark asphalt road. On the back of her sweatshirt were the bold letters of her school below the name, "Alexis."

Lexie reached the intersection ahead of Tim and turned onto the road he was on, but she was still jogging away from him. Before turning, she had quickly looked up toward him. He wasn't sure if she had sensed him, or if she was just checking for traffic. Probably the latter, he thought. Her face was still young, but she had grown taller since moving from Oklahoma.

Tim sprinted faster and caught up to her from behind. As he did, his footsteps fell heavy onto the ground. Lexie turned her head back over her right shoulder with a searching glance. Seeing nothing, she continued to jog on.

Wanting to see her face again, Tim tried to pass her on the left. As he did, she looked over to her side with a concerned expression. Her pace quickened, leaving Tim behind her again.

Tim was afraid she'd lose him. He had already been running for a few minutes before seeing her, and she was obviously in better shape than he. Then, as if answering his wish, she stopped suddenly.

Spinning on her heels, Lexie looked all around her. Tim stopped too, just a few feet back. He marveled at the youthfulness of her face. She hadn't been abused yet, and her whole life lay ahead of her. If only he could talk to her now, tell her to avoid those guys. Tell her to find the Tim in this world. He would be good to her.

"Who's there?" she yelled turning in the wrong direction away from Tim. "What do you want?"

Instinctively, Tim responded to her from behind. "Don't be afraid." Lexie jumped back, running into Tim. It was apparent that she had heard him but couldn't tell from where the sound was coming. It was also apparent that she was terrified.

Why had he said anything? The thirty-one year-old version of herself had warned him eight years earlier that his voice would scare her.

Her back was pushing against his chest. She didn't seem to feel his body, but for him, the touch was electric. He wanted to wrap his arms around her but realized that would only frighten her more. For a moment, she closed her eyes and seemed to press back against him more.

"Lexie, you are not going crazy. I am really here. Just think of me as your guardian angel," he whispered calmly and soothingly into her ear. She didn't react immediately. Had she not heard him that time? Maybe his words had calmed her down.

Then her eyes opened widely, and she leaped away from him as if the words had just taken longer to reach her. She sprinted from him, yelling to the sky, "I am not going to be my mom! I am not going to become like her! Leave me alone!"

Tim stood there, distressed. How could he have done that? He knew she would be frightened if he spoke. This fifteen-year-old Lexie was struggling to deal with her mother's mental illness. She was terrified that she was going crazy too.

With great effort, Tim let her run off on her own. He didn't try to follow her. "Good-bye, Lexie. I'm sorry."

Tim watched as she ran quickly along the road, hurdled a short hedge, and cut through several freshly mowed lawns. He lost sight of her behind the houses and wondered which house was hers. He imagined her curling up in her bed, trying to convince herself that she wasn't crazy. Why had he spoken to her? Why had he done exactly what he knew he shouldn't have done?

Tim wished for the moment back. He had waited so long to see her and had blown it only moments after finding her. When would he see her again? How long would he have to wait this time? Would he be able to talk to her then?

All he knew was that the next time Lexie would experience his presence, she would be twenty years old and considering suicide. What he didn't know, yet, was that the next time for her, five years into her future, would be the very next day for him.

May 11, 2004
Zone Year: 1995

Tim's room looked just like it had when he moved out of his parents' house. He wondered what year it was. Would he see a young version of the other Tim come bouncing into the room?

The clock radio next to his bed displayed 1:27 a.m. in large, orange, digital numerals, and he supposed that if his other self had been living here, *that* Tim would be in bed sleeping. This must be sometime after he moved out, Tim thought.

The room was spotless, much tidier than he had ever kept it himself. In the semidarkness, he wiped his hand across his old desk. There was no dust. His mom must clean everyday, hoping for his return.

His Magic 8 Ball lay on the nightstand next to his bed. Tim picked it up and shook it gently out of habit. He thought about putting it down in a new location to see if his mom would notice. What would she think if the ball had been moved? Maybe he should leave a note that told them their son was doing fine and living in Houston. But what if he wasn't in Houston any longer. Maybe he was in Brenham now. Maybe he had already been murdered by the vengeful femme fatale, Natalie. No, somehow he could sense that the other Tim was still alive, somewhere in this time and place.

Tim flipped the ball over and asked a question, "Should I leave a note for my parents? Should I tell them how to find the Tim of this world and warn him about Natalie?" How great it would be to save his own alternate self with a warning not to go to Brenham and be spared Natalie's wrath!

He turned the ball back up and looked into the ball's dim window. It had no answer. The little float inside had risen up, but instead of landing with one of the answer sides against the window, it balanced with just a corner up against the clear plastic viewer. He wobbled the ball, but the answer still wouldn't appear.

"That's weird," Tim said thoughtfully. Saving his alternate self seemed like the best reason God would have brought him back to his parents' house. "Unless," he whispered to himself, "it would cause a paradox." Would changing the lifeline of this Tim cause other ramifications? What if the other Tim avoided Brenham, TX in order to avoid Natalie finding him? Then all those kids would die.

"Would I create a paradox," Tim asked out loud, "if I try to change the path of this world's Tim?" He turned the ball over and back up again. The window was still blank. The dye inside seemed to refuse to level out and report an answer. Instead, it remained oddly balanced in place.

Giving up, Tim looked from the ball's window up to the room window. A face was peering in! Tim jumped slightly and dropped the black ball onto the bed. He knew immediately, it was Lexie!

Had he reached this night so suddenly, the one she spoke of so long ago? He tried to remember. What had the older Lexie told him? Comfort her. Hold her. Keep her here until morning so that his mom can find her and ask her to stay. What if he did something wrong and scared her away like he had just done when she was fifteen?

Tim stood back from the window so he could watch without alarming her to his presence. Was the window unlocked? He wished he had checked. Lexie pushed up, and it opened slowly and quietly. Tim couldn't believe his mom had left it unlocked after getting onto him so many times as a kid for doing the same thing. Maybe she thought Tim would someday return. Maybe the screamers had caused her to forget to lock it, allowing this moment to happen.

Lexie paused, looking in again. She had been as surprised as Tim that the window opened so easily. Then, her previous experience of sneaking into his room took over. She swiftly pulled up on the trim above the window and acrobatically sprung herself in, legs first.

As Lexie straightened herself up, she peered over at the bed. Then, walking over, she sat down on the edge and looked around. Her dress was damp from the soft rain outside. She made a quiet sigh and then sniffed. She was crying. Tim expected her to lie down, but instead, she stood up and walked back toward the window.

"No," thought Tim, "you can't leave." He moved slightly closer to her, still not wanting to scare her. As she started to climb out the window, Tim pleaded loudly in his own mind, "Please, please Lexie. Stay!" She stopped and turned back. He knew he hadn't said it out loud, but somehow, she heard him.

"Timmy?" she whispered, looking around the room again. "I miss you, Timmy," she said with her eyes closed. Then she turned toward the window again. Tim feared he had lost her, but instead of crawling through, she closed the window and then walked to the bed. She put her hand on the bed and felt along the covers.

Lexie scanned the room again, and it was clear that she did sense him. Tim didn't want to do anything that might scare her, so he remained as still as possible. Seconds or hours, he wasn't sure, seemed to pass as Tim held his breath and waited silently.

Finally, she walked back over to the side of the bed and sat down again, her small frame pressing gently into the mattress. The Magic 8 Ball that Tim had haphazardly tossed onto the bed started to roll across the covers. It seemed to seek her out as it picked up speed and then tapped into her thigh.

"Tim's magic ball," Lexie whispered.

She picked it up and thought about how often Tim had used the ball to make decisions when they were kids. She turned it over and over in her hands for a few moments, then she closed her eyes, rotated it again, and finally looked at the window. There was a slight change in her expression that Tim couldn't identify.

Twice more, she repeated her action of turning the ball carefully over, closing her eyes and then opening them again as the answer smoothly floated up to greet her gaze. When she received her third answer, she sniffed to hold back more tears but smiled slightly. The ball had worked for her! Tim did not know what her questions had been or what answers had appeared, but they had comforted her somehow. It was like magic, Tim thought.

Lexie pulled the covers back and felt the cool, clean sheets. "I'm here, Lexie!" Tim thought powerfully in his mind. "I'm here!"

She looked up again into the dark room as her hand felt the familiarity of his bed. Then she stood up and took a step backward. Tim held his breath, wondering again if she was going to leave.

Lexie reached behind her and unzipped her dress. She kicked off her shoes and let the cold, damp dress fall to the floor. Tim looked away instinctively, knowing that the last thing he wanted to do was take advantage of this situation. He heard her crawl onto the bed and pull the blankets over her. Her crying began again, but it was different now. It was a quiet, comforted crying.

Tim couldn't wait any longer. He moved over to the bed and crawled in gently behind her. She didn't seem to notice the movement of the blankets and sheets. As he brought his arms around her, her crying faded completely, and she seemed to settle back into his embrace. Her breathing slowed and matched his own as their bodies seemed to melt together as one.

Suddenly, Lexie stiffened noticeably and seemed to hold her breath. It was as if the impossibility of the moment finally sunk into the logical portion of her brain. The magic was broken, and Tim feared again that she might leave. He loosened his arms, and her breathing returned.

Lexie lifted herself up onto her elbows and turned around to face him. Her teary eyes scanned the bed where he lay motionless. Tim caught himself holding his own breath now as she continued questioning what she was experiencing. Finally, she lay back down, still facing him. Somehow she had convinced herself that the overwhelming and unexplainable feeling of comfort was okay.

She snuggled back into Tim's open arms and buried her head under his chin. Her hair tickled his nose slightly and he wondered if she could feel his returning breath. The rise and fall of their chests synchronized again, and after only a few minutes, he felt her drift into a peaceful sleep that would last until his mom found her in the morning. He knew that this moment was the one that changed the course of Lexie's life forever. It was the greatest moment of his life too.

Chapter 36

MERGING TIME

AS TIME WENT forward, Tim found Lexie more and more often. Weeks, months, and years passed, and what had started as a few random visits separated by years became once or twice a month and eventually several times a week. The frustration of not knowing when he would see her again dissolved entirely upon entering a zone and finding her. He could sense from the moment he stood up and inserted himself into those zones that he was in the right place and at the right time to locate her.

At first, their meetings continued to connect them randomly in time. Sometimes, she was older than him. Other times, she was younger. He even saw her a few times as a child and teenager, both in Oklahoma and Nebraska.

Strangely, in all of those zones where he found her before she was thirty-one, she could not, or did not recognize his presence like she had when she was fifteen and twenty. Either she was too young to perceive him, or there were simply too many other people around distracting her. His undetectable existence, somewhere halfway between ghost and human, could not be distinguished from the physical presence of those around her.

Other times, he just couldn't get close to her. He would spot her and start to approach her, but then suddenly there would be a crash or a scream nearby. Despite his desire to go to Lexie, he knew helping others had to come first. When he would return, searching for Lexie, she would be gone.

A few of those times, he saw the screamers near the incident that pulled him away. Were they deliberately keeping him from talking to her? Or was her timeline rigid, the events predetermined?

Lexie had been thirty-one years old the day he found her taking a shower at her home. She told him herself that she had never spoken to him before that day. Maybe there was simply no possibility of changing that moment. Enforcing such details might be how the screamers ensure that another split in reality doesn't occur? Tim felt like he had great power and freedom to move and act in the zone world, but he had to admit that the screamers had power beyond his own. Power to guide the timeline, control people's thoughts and actions, and thus control their destinies.

As Tim watched the interaction between people and the screamers, he realized how large a role they played, from seemingly insignificant decisions people made to matters of life and death. Tim didn't know who was guiding them, but they acted in concert.

For instance, Stacy and Hank, the foster parents from hell, were gently allowed to return there through the flames of their burning home. They weren't drunk or stoned when the fire erupted. They were peacefully numb to the world, incapable of saving themselves but were humanely allowed to perish for the good of the universe.

There was certainly a greater power at work. Tim was starting to feel it. He began to recognize it as he fought to make changes in Lexie's timeline and in his own. Changes that occurred identically in both lines could be accomplished with ease. But when he tried to act against the grain, he was forced to back down and to change his approach.

The same was true now as he sought to be with Lexie. It was frustrating for Tim when he would spot Lexie and then realize it was before she would be able to interact with him. No matter what he tried, he had to accept that in this timeline, she would not be able to interact with him again until she was thirty-one.

However, as he watched her in those younger times of her life, he realized he was being given the chance to know her more. He was enjoying parts of her life that he had missed the first time in his world. As she aged randomly in front of him, morphing from a cute three-year-old toddler to a stunning twenty-five-year-old woman and back to a precocious six-year-old, he found a much greater understanding of who she was. To him, she was not only the most beautiful woman in the world, young or old, but he also saw her kindness, intelligence, and beauty as a person.

January 2005
Zone Year: 2018

The randomness of time allowed Tim to report back to Lexie whenever he found her after her thirty-first year. He reminded her of good times and experiences she had had before her life turned mostly to misery and uselessness.

"Last week, I got to see you lose your first tooth!" Tim laughed as he visited a forty-three-year-old Lexie. "You were so excited. I think you had been trying to lose it for weeks."

"Months actually," she laughed back, suddenly remembering her struggle to force her first tooth out. "I kept saying to Dad, 'I think my tooth is going to fall out today!' He would laugh and just say, 'We'll see.' I even tried putting a string on it and pulling. But the string broke and then I just had a piece of string stuck up in my gums for several weeks!"

She smiled big and poked at her gums. Tim laughed again. After their laughter abated, he told her, "I saw you yesterday too. It was your thirtieth birthday."

Lexie tilted her head to the side and seemed to try and think back. "I can't remember my thirtieth. Wait, I was pregnant with Andrew that year."

"Yes. I saw you sitting on an engine block in your front yard, singing 'Happy Birthday' to yourself. Jack was inside, and I went up to you, hoping as always that you'd realize I was there. You were pregnant but not showing much yet. Still, I could tell. There was a glow on your skin, and you seemed happy."

"I think I was," she reflected. "Jack had kicked me out of the house, again." She rolled her eyes. "Said he needed to do something.

At first I was upset, him making me sit out in the yard—no chairs and three months pregnant. But then a calm feeling came over me as I sat there. On an engine block you said? Ha. I had forgotten that. Guess there are still plenty of those out there in that junkyard of a front lawn we have." She said this, waving her arm limply toward the front of the house as they sat together. They reclined back against a tree in one of their usual hidden places at the back of the house. They had tried sitting on the front porch, but the neighbors returned strange looks when she'd sit there, apparently talking to herself.

"Anyway," Lexie continued, "sitting there on that engine, I heard some birds singing, and I pretended they were singing to me. As I sang with them, I think I remember thinking of you. Maybe part of me did know you were there."

"In fact," she suddenly remembered excitedly, I started thinking of celebrating my birthdays as a kid with you. Memories of you were flooding in. I even thought I smelled you for a moment. But then," she paused, tilting her head again to think back. "Then, a loud fire truck came zipping by."

"Yeah," Tim sighed audibly. "I realized I had to go at that moment. I chased down the truck, expecting to save the day. When I caught up, it turned out they were just on a practice drill. I was only able to stop a fireman from tripping on a hose." Tim laughed sarcastically. "When I got back to your house at the end of my zone, I saw Jack opening the door for you and asking you to come in."

"Ha. No," Lexie laughed. "I remember. He opened the door, yelled, 'get in here now, Alexis!' and then let the door slam shut right in front of me as I reached out for it."

"Yeah, I guess that is what happened," Tim agreed sheepishly. "I didn't want to remind you of that part."

"It was okay though. He had made me a cake. That's why he had pushed me out, wanted it to be a surprise. We talked about the baby and what it would be like. We even laughed a little. I think we both thought that having the baby together might help us. I was a little optimistic that day as I ate my fancy lopsided vanilla cake. At least he was trying, even though I had told him before that I loved red velvet the best and chocolate second best." She smiled. Tim was glad she could find bits of happiness, despite the man she seemed forced to live with.

As time went on and the frequency of Tim's visits to Lexie increased, the randomness of their moments together seemed to decrease. Somehow their timelines had started to tie. Tim found himself aging in line with Lexie as if their worlds had become connected. With each visit to her, their comfort and expectations grew.

October 2005
Zone: October 2005

In the year of Lexie's thirty-first birthday, their lives and love for each other became one. Tim arrived in the middle of the street, just past Lexie's house. It was late evening. The sun had set hours earlier, and the full moon shimmered overhead. Jack's truck was gone.

Lexie came out of her doorway, moving gracefully like a doe. Although it was October and a slight chill stirred through the air, she wore only a short, thin nightgown, revealing her long slender legs. She stopped and leaned on the wooden railing of her front porch, alone and waiting, as if she had been expecting his arrival. Her hair glimmered in the moonlight and took on a coppery color as she leaned against the rail and turned her head upward to gaze at the moon.

When Tim saw her, his heart quickened. Part of him wanted to sprint toward her. Another part couldn't make his legs move as he took in her beauty. He watched as her gaze continued toward the moon as if she could speak to it. Maybe she could. Maybe she was asking or praying that Tim would come to her that night.

Tim couldn't wait any longer. He ran to her. As he reached the three short steps to the porch, Lexie turned, her nightgown flaring like a dancer's skirt.

"Tim?" she asked. She couldn't see him, but she felt an electrical pulse shoot through her. An instinct from deep within told her that he was close.

"I'm here," he responded. He placed his hand on her shoulder. He could feel her heat coming through the thin fabric. Lexie closed her eyes and tilted her head to rest her cheek on his hand for a moment. Then she smiled, lifted his hand into her own, and led him slowly into the house.

They said nothing to each other. For Tim and Lexie, silence didn't work the same way it worked between most people. In their silence, they communicated in volumes. They knew what the other was thinking and what was needed or wanted. It wasn't some form of telepathic link. It was love.

Lexie guided Tim to her bedroom. Once next to the bed, they stopped and stood together, still and motionless for the longest time. He looked into her incredible eyes that reflected in the dim light from outside. It seemed as if she was weaving a spell around him, for he knew what came next, and he had no power to change their course.

Lexie stepped back from Tim, releasing his hand. She slipped the straps of her gown off her shoulders and let the sleek material fall to the ground. She turned and crawled gracefully onto the bed and then lay on her side, facing him.

The moonlight etched her form against the cool smooth sheets. Her golden hair seemed haloed by an aura of silver light. She was so beautiful. Tim had admired Natalie like this before too. But this was somehow very different. Lexie was not only gorgeous and sexy, but she was beautiful, truly beautiful, from her skin down into her soul. Real beauty like hers radiates from the inside out.

Lexie did not speak, but she raised her arms to welcome Tim to her bed. He lowered himself to her slowly and let his invisible weight press on her gently. She was thirty-one, and he was thirty-three-and-a-half. It was the same age difference they had shared as children. Just as the movement of their timelines had found rhythm and merged together, they too found themselves merging as lovers. The passion and wonderment of the moment sparked a connection between them that would bind his time to hers.

November 2008
Zone: November 2008

"What is it like?" Lexie asked him one evening, three years later, as they sat at the park watching Andrew play on the tire swing. He was three-and-a-half. It was eight months before Tim knew he would be faced with either saving Andrew from the bullet or watching him die. He had not told Lexie about that future day. He wanted her to enjoy the son that she may only have for a short time. Her face glowed when she spoke of Andrew. He was the joy of her life when so much else was troubled.

The sun shown through the pine trees as the day moved toward evening. The nimbus and stratus clouds reflected the waning light in pinks, purples, and orange as the songs of nature filled the evening sky. The hum of cicadas faded to the east and then returned as strong as before as the insects took their turn in the evening chorus.

"What is what like?" he asked turning his attention away from Andrew and his thoughts toward her.

"Zoning. Traveling from your universe to mine. What does it feel like?"

"It's hard to describe, really. My senses don't seem to work correctly while it's happening. But the first thing I become aware of is darkness. It isn't like nighttime darkness or simply the absence of light. It is more like the absence of everything, even the absence of me. I have no feeling of motion, no sight, no hearing, no anything—just nothing.

"Then light begins to appear in front of me, and I feel like I am falling. I suppose it feels like falling without a parachute because I have no control, and it feels like I'm moving faster and faster as I near the light."

"Is it scary?"

"No, not really." Then Tim thought about how afraid he was the first time after the hypnotist. "I guess I should say that I'm not scared anymore. But the first time was bad. And I suppose as a little child I must have been terrified."

"That's awful! You probably felt so lost and helpless."

"Guess I'm glad I don't remember. Now, though, since I know what is happening, I feel more anticipation than anything else. Wondering where I'll be, what I'll see, what I'll be able to do, and if I'll see you." He winked at Lexie. She couldn't see the wink but smiled and rolled her eyes lovingly at him and then turned to check on Andrew.

"Just think, when you were his age," Lexie said nodding toward Andrew, "you were popping into places all over the world. No one could see you, so you probably walked around confused, maybe crying the whole time. And those boys you talk about, the scary ones, it would have been like a nightmare every night."

"Yeah, I'm surprised I wasn't severely messed up emotionally."

"Who says you aren't?!" Lexie laughed at Tim and returned his earlier wink.

Tim noticed the wink, and he wondered if she was beginning to subconsciously "see" him a little. She had once said that in sunlight, she almost thought she could see something. The light seemed to bend a little where it passed through his invisible form.

As they talked, Andrew had moved from the swing and was now sitting in the pebbles at the base of the play equipment. He was digging and making piles. Sometimes he'd throw a handful of the little stones into the air so he could feel them falling on him like heavy raindrops.

Fifteen minutes earlier, Lexie had grabbed Andrew as soon as she felt Tim arrive. "Hey, Jack," Lexie called to her hungover husband who was leaning sideways on the couch instead of getting ready for his next scheduled route. "I'm gonna take Andrew out for a walk while you get packed. It's a nice evening." Tim had watched Jack grunt slightly to acknowledge his drunken understanding. Then he slumped over completely, making it clear that he had no intention of being on time.

Usually, when Tim arrived, Jack was away on one of his shipping routes. Other times, he'd be out drinking with his buddies. The arrangement was fortunate for the development of Tim and Lexie's odd relationship. On those occasions that Jack was home, Lexie found it easy to get away long enough to enjoy their thirty-eight minutes together.

This bothered Tim at first. Jack had told her that she deserved his beatings because she was unfaithful to him. Now, Tim knew that Jack did have reason to be suspicious of Lexie's actions. Was this adultery? Was it an affair? He supposed they both meant the same thing but the word "affair" seemed much less disturbing.

It was easy for Tim to pretend that Lexie had been his from the start. He had known her long before Jack met her. She had been his first kiss, even if only on the cheek. How could it be a bad thing for him and Lexie to be together? Besides, Tim reasoned, he had no one waiting back at home for him when he returned from his zones.

But Lexie did, Tim thought, as reality had circled back on him. She was a married woman, married to Jack, even if he was a drunk, even if he beat her. This was still an affair. Worse yet, by seeing Lexie, was Tim himself indirectly causing the beatings?

Lexie had assured Tim that although she too felt guilty at times about the situation, the beatings had started well before Tim reentered her life. Tim also discovered that Jack himself was cheating. He was involved with countless women while on the road.

"I'm not even sure how or why we got together in the first place," Lexie had said as she talked about his infidelity. "I used to think that he and I were from two different worlds."

Tim and Lexie laughed at the irony of that statement.

"But really, it is strange. If he doesn't love me, and I don't love him, why do we stay together? I can't seem to leave, and he can't either. We make each other miserable. I just don't understand it."

Tim did understand but didn't feel it was time to explain. He knew that it was the screamers, the time guides, who controlled this part of Lexie's destiny. But when would she be ready to know that the script of her sad destiny was already written.

In his world, Lexie was dead, and Jack was still living in the same house in Brenham, TX. He was alone, miserable, and constantly drunk. His life was of no use to that timeline. If the screamers were really trying to merge timelines, then keeping Jack here with Lexie in this line made sense. Letting him live a drunken meaningless life with a woman who should have been dead would create fewer ripples in the timeline for them to match up to other lines.

June 2009
Zone: June 2009

But there *had* been a ripple in this line. The ripple was in the form of a little boy. Despite their dislike of each other and their forced cohabitation, a mistake led to a baby. That boy would grow up and create ripples of his own. So, the screamers guided Lexie and Andrew to the park that fateful day.

Tim arrived too, as he knew he eventually would. The sky was clear and sunny. The weather was warm and beautiful. He had told Lexie of this day during his previous visit a few days earlier. Yet she had come anyway, not realizing that the power of the screamers was even stronger than her protective motherly love for her son.

"We have to get Andrew away from here," Tim called out as he ran toward Lexie, but then stopped. She looked toward Tim but had a blank stare in her eyes. Next to her was a screamer. A second screamer stood silently next to Andrew. The truck came around the corner and Tim saw the muzzle of the gun pointing out of the window. A group of teens was playing half-court basketball. Andrew's usually smiling face was slack and distant. Then, he turned and walked toward the edge of the court, near a picnic table where three other male teens sat.

In an instant, the scene transpired as if written and choreographed for a morbid Shakespearian play. The actors, Tim, Lexie, Driver, Shooter, Teens, Andrew, and Screamers each played their own roles in the scripted tragedy.

Tim dashed over to Andrew. He hoped to move the child out of the bullet's path but was prepared, if needed, to somehow block the impending shot with his own body. The orange basketball was passed and dropped causing it to roll into the street. The screamer turned its attention away from Lexie to watch Tim. Its mouth gaped open and screeched its terrible scream. Lexie, now released from the screamer's control, realized this was the moment Tim had warned her about. She screamed her own scream, "No!" as Tim dove toward the boy. He felt his body launch but then stop in midair. Something lifted him further off his feet and his forward motion became reversed.

The shot rang out at precisely the moment the truck swerved to miss the ball. Tim thought he saw the bullet cut the air just before striking Andrew's chest. Lexie's son fell silently to the ground. His screamer hadn't let him suffer but had put him directly in the path of the bullet. The ripple was over. The boy who was not meant to live was gone.

A terrible sound of wrenching sobs tore from Lexie's throat as she scooped up her son in her arms, his body already limp and lifeless. Her sound was guttural and deep, almost primal as if she was reverting to some kind of animal. Her grief was unlike any Tim had ever experienced himself. It was the grief of a mother. Tim wanted to stop her from making that terrible sound, but all he could do was hold her and rock her back and forth as she cradled her lost child.

Tim now understood that this was what the old and wise Lexie had meant when she told him, "You can't change everything. Some things just happen. Some things must happen." He could only imagine the pain she had wrestled with to come to that conclusion. Old Lexie had understood fate in a way that up until now he couldn't. Now he saw clearly, fate was the grim reaper. It was not kind and did not show respect to those who loved.

Chapter 37

UNDERSTANDING FATE

IN THE DAYS and weeks between Tim's "Lexie Zones", he continued to serve as an invisible angel to the world into which he zoned. He was allowed to help in many situations. "Allowed," he decided, was the correct word since it seemed he could not go against the screamers. Even in times when they were present and did not stop him from acting to help a person, he realized it was because he was not interfering with their underlying goal. Some things just happen. Some things must happen.

In his own world too, Tim acted as a quiet hero. He felt a warm feeling of pride knowing he was making a difference in both worlds. It was hard but rewarding work; work that was bracketed by his frequent visits with Lexie. Somehow, it seemed, he was given those moments with her as a reward for his work. He would arrive to find her waiting, always waiting for his return.

July 2009
Zone: July 2009

"How do most people die?" Lexie asked one evening a month after Andrew had died. She was distraught over his death but oddly accepting of it too. Tim wondered if the screamers continued to somehow comfort her because of the way they forced the incident and kept her so isolated.

Unlike most people who lose a child, she had been forced to go through the pain mostly on her own. Jack refused to talk about it when he was home, and she had lost contact with her father after he had married a third time, shortly after Amber left him.

Maybe she was better off not having to talk about it with a lot of people. People never knew what to say in a situation like this. They would have tried to comfort her with words like, "Oh, what a shock, you must feel awful," or "We're so sorry, it's terrible, what a dreadful thing to happen to such a young boy," or "Our days are numbered, you know, that's just the way it is."

Tim had learned that there really weren't any words available to counsel someone stricken with grief. So during his brief visits over the last few weeks, he had done his best to hold Lexie quietly and just listen. Today, however, she seemed to want him to talk. So Tim thought carefully about her question and then answered.

"There seems to be a lot of variety in the causes of death," Tim said. She had always enjoyed hearing of his work, but he realized this question cut straight to the loss she was feeling. Did it cause her pain to know that when he was away from her, he was helping and saving people, sometimes children, but had not been able to protect her Andrew?

"Tell me some of the things you've saved them from," she coaxed, weaving her arms through his as they sat side by side under the shade of their "Talking Tree" where they were sheltered from the view of neighbors and even Jack if he was home.

"Well, a lot of people seem to die while on vacation. I always try to save them. Sometimes I'm successful and sometimes . . ." He let the sentence speak for itself. No need to remind her of the times he failed to help. "I've saved three from shark attacks, five from a roller-coaster accident in Britain back in 1972 and, strangely enough, four from falling coconuts."

"Really? That actually happens?" She laughed, but Tim didn't think it was a joyful laugh. It was more a laugh that came from the joy of being distracted from pain.

"Yeah, it really happens."

"What else?" she asked.

"Well, drowning seems to happen a lot. I've lost count of the number of children I've pulled out of pools." Tim watched Lexie for a moment to see if he should continue. "One guy," Tim laughed lightly trying to lighten the mood and get the subject away from children, "I've saved three separate times from falling off a ladder."

She surprised him again and laughed too. "You'd think he'd learn!" she said. She had a beautiful laugh and Tim smiled.

"No kidding," he agreed and then continued again. "I think the most common ways are the ones I can do the least about. Cancer, heart attacks, strokes. But in those cases, I think the best thing I can do is help get families together to say good-bye, or sometimes to help them move on. It's strange how in my world people will open up to me, a complete stranger, when I tell them that I know what happened and would simply like to listen to them."

"You are a good listener," she said, leaning her head on his shoulder.

"Not so much today. I've been talking the whole time."

"I asked you to. I think right now, I'd rather hear you talk anyway," Lexie smiled with her mouth, but sadness still filled her eyes. Then she asked, "What about lightning?"

"Uh, yes, there was this one golfer. He wouldn't listen to me, wouldn't stop the best game he said he had ever had. And there was also a teacher on the roof of his school trying to set up a weather station for his students. Here in your world, I was able to save him after he was struck by lightning by dragging him back down into the school where another teacher found him and called 911. A week later in my world, I was able to convince him to get out of the lightning just as his equipment was struck."

"Have you saved babies?"

"Many times." Tim tried to read Lexie's face to see if she was still okay with such a conversation. "In some ways, they are the easiest to save in my world because usually it just takes being in the right place at the right time for them. Most parents are so happy that they don't question how I knew to be there. Which is a good thing because it's hard to explain why I sometimes have to break in to rescue a baby from scalding hot water or wake up a young mother in her bedroom when she falls asleep and starts to roll over onto her child.

"I've also tried leaving notes and warning them ahead of time, but the events still seem to take place unless I'm there at that moment. But most of the time with kids, all I have to do is say, "Hey is that your kid?" And the parents look up, see the danger, and help their child. Not very dramatic, but it still makes me feel good.

"Honestly, a lot of the time, it isn't dramatic. Usually it isn't even saving a life. Sometimes it's just helping someone make a decision. I have talked teens out of drinking, robbers out of breaking into houses and businesses, husbands out of cheating, and all kinds of other life issues.

Lexie smiled, still resting on Tim's shoulder. She liked to lie against him with her eyes closed. It was easier to believe he was really there when her eyes weren't disagreeing with what she could feel. "Those are all still important," she said. "Maybe guiding someone's life positively is even more important than stopping someone's death."

"I never really thought of it that way. I suppose the dramatic events just seemed more important."

"Like the plane?" she asked.

"Yeah." He nodded even though she probably couldn't tell.

"So what are you going to do? If the screamers wouldn't let you save them here, why would they let you save them in your world?"

"I haven't figured that out yet. But I have to try."

"I know you do." Lexie smiled at him, her eyes searching for his. "That's why I love you. You never give up!" She kissed him tenderly. Oh how he loved the way she kissed.

"Do people tell you 'Thank you'?" she asked, still holding his face with her hand after the kiss.

He thought for a moment. "Well, not usually. The people in your world can't see me. And in mine, well, I think they are so caught up in whatever just happened that they forget I'm there."

"Aww," she pouted sympathetically.

"It's okay. I've gotten used to it. At least you know."

"Then I'll say 'thank you.'"

"For what?"

"For everything," she said. "Thank you for the families you've helped. Thank you for the men and women you've saved. Thank you for the young people you've given guidance to. Thank you for the babies and children you have saved. Thank you for trying to save my child. And thank you for lifting me up every time you come. You remind me of what it feels like to be with someone good."

Tim didn't know what to say. He knew she felt pain for the loss of Andrew, disappointment in the life she had, longing for a different future, but through it all, acceptance.

"You shouldn't thank me for all that. I wish . . ."

"Shhh," she interrupted him with her hand over his mouth. "Just say you're welcome and then kiss me again."

He did. After a time, Lexie ended the kiss, smiled, and asked, "What about snakes?"

He laughed. "Does your mind never stop?"

In this way, their romance continued for the next eleven years. Tim would arrive suddenly, and Lexie would be ready and waiting. He helped her laugh and cry and get through the loss of her son. Together, they learned that some things could be changed with his influence, but other things had to occur just as fate had written.

They also explored life and the world together through Tim's eyes, since so much of it had been closed off to Lexie. And over the years, they mixed conversations of time and existence with passion and lovemaking and generally made the most of their thirty-eight minutes together.

August 2020
Zone: August 2020

"Time must slow down while I'm here," Tim wondered aloud to Lexie one morning when he was forty-eight years old and she was forty-five. She was snuggled up into his chest under the sheets. They had already made love and were wallowing in the afterglow together, mostly talking about nothing.

"Are you saying you dislike being here with me so much that time seems to drag on?" Lexie replied in mock shock and poked at his belly.

"No, no!" Tim laughed and playfully squeezed her tighter against his body. The morning sun was shining into her bedroom window, shimmering against her hair. "It never seems long enough when I'm with you, but at the same time, it seems like we have more than thirty-eight minutes."

"Nope, we just pack a lot into your visits. I usually check the time after you leave. You are here for thirty-eight minutes and forty-one seconds, every time. But we're good at making up for lost time."

"Lost time?" Tim asked, his hands wrapped around her and caressing her smooth bare back. "Wasn't I just here yesterday at about the same time?"

"Yep, but that is twenty-three hours twenty-one minutes and nineteen seconds apart." She laughed into his chest. Her warm breath tickled the hairs on his torso lightly, and he chuckled with his chin resting on the top of her head. "In a few minutes, we'll be apart again, and most of my day will pass without you."

"Maybe I'll be back tomorrow," Tim hoped.

"It would be wonderful if you were, but you probably won't. You have already been here four times this week. Odds are you'll be pulled to some other place so you can get some hero work done."

Tim noticed for the first time a little resentment in Lexie's tone. Wasn't she proud of the work he did around the world? Didn't she realize that he couldn't help others if he was here with her every time?

"And sometimes," Lexie continued, "you show up down the street or several miles away, so our time together is even less."

"I still have no control over when and where I go. But I pray every night that I will end up here!" he assured her.

"Me too," she whispered cutely as she lifted up her head and stretched slightly to give him a peck on the mouth.

Then she shrank back down to lay her head sideways against his chest again. She let out a sigh, indicating that her thoughts had suddenly become more melancholy.

"What's wrong?" Tim asked, recognizing her change in mood. She was usually in a good mood while he was there, rarely complaining or worrying about when he'd be back. She had long ago accepted that his visits were sporadic, even if they had become relatively often.

"Oh, I was just thinking about what you said will happen when I'm in my fifties," she answered after a time. "You know, your first visit to me?"

He remembered that visit well. He had been only twenty-three then, and it was the first time he had seen Lexie in the zone. She had seemed so sad.

"I was thinking about what I said, or I mean, what I *will* say to you when that day comes."

Tim knew what she was referring to but remained quiet and only listened as she sighed again.

"You are going to be gone for a long time, aren't you, Tim?" It wasn't really a question. He had told her that she would say, "I've been waiting so long," and that she would cry tears of joy that he was finally there again.

"I don't know when that will be. It may be a long way off," Tim finally said.

"I know, I know," she sighed. "But every time you leave, I wish you could take me with you. Just stick me in your pocket and take me with you."

"I wish that too. Though I don't have any pockets right now," he tried to joke. He saw she wasn't in a joking mood so changed his approach.

"Maybe it will be just a few weeks or a month that I don't see you," Tim offered hopefully but knew in his heart that Lexie wouldn't have called that "waiting so long." He also knew that the Lexie he had met that first time looked very different than she did now. This Lexie he held in his arms was as beautiful at forty-five years old as she had been in her twenties and thirties. Jack was hard on her now, but how much worse would he be to her to cause such a dramatic change over the next ten years. The older Lexie, who had cried in his arms, had all but given up on life. She had given up on Tim, too, wondering if he would ever return.

"I'm afraid it may be years. What if I go crazy in all that time without you? Will you still love me if I go crazy?"

"Of course. I have loved you as long as I can remember."

"No, really. My mom went crazy, and my dad left her. If you are gone many years and come back to find me crazy, will you still love me?"

"These questions are *crazy*. Besides, it couldn't be that long. God has let me come here so often. I think maybe he is rewarding me with visits to you since I work hard to help people. Why would he punish me?"

"How do you know it is God controlling all this? Wouldn't he have found a better way to merge timelines than a bunch of invisible screaming boys and you?" Her tone was hard now and carried years of frustration and anger with the words.

"Why would he have allowed the lines to split in the first place?" she continued. "What about me? How is any of this fair to me? He keeps me trapped in this house, miserable except for when you're here, and let's be honest, you aren't here often enough or for long enough."

Tim felt tears on his chest. It had been a long time since she had cried with him. He realized that she put on a brave face for him during his visits, but most of the time, she was on her own, facing a life that seemed to have no meaning.

"You are right. It isn't fair, Lexie. But I still think it is God. Who else could have created everything? You can't explain screamers in natural selection or evolution. You can't explain a grand purpose of merging split timelines either. Even Doc agrees that there must be a God."

"Doc? Doc is a quack! No one will publish him, no one will accept any of his theories. I think he should just give up trying to scientifically explain your ability, and accept the fact that you are a . . ." She stopped herself. She couldn't believe what she had almost said.

"A freak?" Tim asked, completing the awful sentence for her. He pulled his arms out from around her. She sat up and looked at where she sensed his outline.

"Is that what you wanted to say, Lexie? That I am a freak?" He stared at her, surprised at what had just happened. Just minutes before, he was with his trusted lover and best friend. Now, it was as if he was staring at a stranger. She looked small suddenly, like a child, her face sulking. Her eyes were red and swollen as they peered downcast toward the bed. She didn't bother to cover herself or to adjust her long tousled hair as it lay haphazardly over her shoulders and chest.

Then he felt the familiar tug from somewhere inside his mind as if his world was beckoning him to return. His harsh stare lessened, and he understood that this wasn't just Lexie complaining; it was years of pent-up frustration and sadness pushing to the surface. He had been a fool to not realize how much harder all this was for her than him. He got to return to his home, near his loving parents, and feel the constant reward of patting himself on the back. She was lonely and abused. She was being forced to go through life alone without that support he was provided. But it was too late to say any of that as he slipped back into his physical body that lay in his bed at home.

August 2020
Zone Year: 2026

As Lexie had predicted, the next night Tim did not slide into her world to be with her. He wanted to tell her he was sorry. How could he have let such a simple word cause him to be so angry? As a child, he had been terrified of being labeled a freak. But now he was a grown man. Being different hadn't bothered him for years. He had accepted it as a gift. But hearing the word almost slip from Lexie's lips had been the trigger. Of all people in either world, she was the one whose acceptance mattered the most.

Oh how he wanted to take her back into his arms and tell her how sorry and childish he had acted. Instead he awoke, far from her home, to the sound of odd squeals and whistles. The sounds made no sense as the colors blurred around him.

When he stood up and the world around him slowed, he saw that he was downtown in the bustling city of Billings Montana, the new energy capital of the world. His dad, now retired, had often marveled at the shift from light crude oil to deep deposits of energy-rich tar buried beneath the Rockies. "You watch, Tim," his dad had said over twenty years ago, "some little town up there in the north is going to explode with people as soon as they figure out a way to make that tar into an economic energy source!"

The sound he had heard, Tim now realized, was that of sirens and yelling. He stood in front of the Energy Dome and fans of the Billings Capitalists streamed out of the baseball stadium's emergency exits. Firemen and police tried to push through but could not get past the flooding tide of frightened people.

"What happened here?" Tim thought as he too tried to push into the building. The people instinctively separated around him, creating a gap that allowed him to pass through. A few observant firemen also saw the gap and followed closely at Tim's heels. Tim heard random words from the crowds and rescuers. "Dead," "Scary," "Out of nowhere," "Bombs!"

Tim thought back to his father's words, "town going to explode." He was sure his dad had just meant a population explosion, but this seemed to be a literal interpretation. He knew what he had to do. He had to find out as much about this event as he could. What had caused the explosion? Who was responsible? How could he stop it from happening?

Suddenly, the ground beneath his feet shook, interrupting his thoughts. The screaming intensified, and people began pushing harder, making their way toward the exits. The gap that usually formed around Tim closed in, and the scared mass forced him back with them.

Tim felt another shutter and then realized what it was. The stadium was collapsing. He pushed through the people to the edge of the seating area where he could see out across the field. For a moment, he thought it looked like a crowd of fans cheering on their team with a stadium-wide wave. But he realized that instead of fans standing and sitting in rhythm, this wave was generated by the structure of the stadium itself. It seemed as though the entire support system was twisting. Beams of concrete and rebar were shifting off their support posts one by one. Entire sections of the stadium were coming down, and the collapse was growing toward him. "I'm not going to be able to get out of here," Tim thought out loud. He knew the destruction would be complete in just a few more seconds as the wave of collapse reached him. He needed to find out what day it was.

Tim looked back at the crowds running for their lives. He tried to stop a man wearing a watch, hoping to see the time and a date. But the man subconsciously fought Tim off in his futile dash for escape. The crowd all seemed to be fleeing in the same direction toward the exits that could not accommodate the surge. All, that is, except for one man.

A fat man, dressed in Billings's colors was walking calmly toward the field. Maybe he had the right idea. The stadium was collapsing, but out there, everything looked as it should.

The bioengineered grass almost glowed with a green tint that reminded him of algae. The bases, chalked lines, and dirt looked to be perfectly in place as if the game had never even started. Yet Tim knew thousands of people were being crushed on the other side of the stadium as the wave of collapse grew.

The man stopped for a moment and pointed up toward the far end of the field. Tim looked to where he pointed and saw nothing but the fountains, sky, and scoreboard past centerfield.

"The scoreboard!" Tim yelled to himself. He realized that if it was still working, it should have the date on it.

Knowing he had only seconds left, Tim ran out through the seats to get a better view of the board. The four-story high plasma screen still flashed a 3D view of the first and only play of the game; a fly ball to left field caught easily by the Billings outfielder Blas Perez. It was inning one, game one of the series with the Dodgers.

Tim read the date just in time as the wave reached the scoreboard sending a shower of sparks to the ground as the screen flickered out. New explosions echoed from the scoreboard as it seemed to sink down toward the ground.

Tim saw the fat man again. This time, he was standing still and had turned to look directly at Tim. He had a hot dog in his right hand but seemed to have forgotten about it as it slipped out of his grip and fell to the ground. Then, he lifted his left arm and pointed toward a section of the crowd. Tim looked in the direction of the fat man's finger and saw another man sitting in one of the sections that had apparently been a source of explosion.

Tim had already considered who may have been behind the destruction but was still taken aback when he recognized him.

"Jeffrey!" Tim breathed and then ran toward him. When he arrived, he saw a thirty-something-year-old Jeffrey holding a small child on his lap. The girl had blood across most of her side, and it was clear that she was dead. Jeffrey was crying and whispering to the dead girl.

"I am so sorry. I didn't know. It wasn't supposed to be like this."

Before Jeffrey could say more, the wave completed its orbit of the stadium. A block of concrete fell from a beam, killing Jeffrey instantly. Then Tim looked up and the last thing he saw was the rest of the concrete beam above his head crashing toward him as he let out a short scream of terror.

Tim awoke with a start, still screaming. He jumped to the floor and felt his body with his hands. This was only the second time he had experienced death in his zone. Though the terror of that moment had lasted only seconds and he experienced no pain, it left him completely unnerved. He felt sick and threw up violently as he struggled to clear his vision.

Chapter 38

TIME UNMERGED

August 2020
Zone: August 2020

"ARE YOU POSITIVE it was him?"

"Yes. I have no doubt. It was him. It was Jeffrey."

"But he is supposed to go to prison for the bombing, right?"

"I know, but he died. He won't be in prison now."

"You know what this means, don't you? There has been another reality split."

Tim and Lexie lay out on a large polycarbon mat near their hidden spot behind her house. It had been 2:30 in the morning when Tim arrived next to the single bed in Andrew's room. She slept there whenever Jack was home, since they hadn't shared a bed since Andrew's death. Tim had gently stroked her hair and her back to rouse her from her deep sleep.

Even before she opened her eyes, she smiled a welcoming grin as if she had anticipated his arrival at just that moment. He hadn't known what to expect from her when he arrived. Would she still be mad about their argument from his last visit four days earlier? His heart felt healed by her grin. As always, she had forgiven him.

"Jack's here," she whispered.

"I know, I already went in there and tried to kiss him awake," he laughed quietly even though she was the only one who would hear. She laughed too, opening her eyes, and reaching out to pull him into bed.

"Wait," he stopped her. "Come with me instead." Tim pulled her covers down past her knees and then tugged gently on both of her hands. She smiled again and asked him where he was taking her.

"Outside," he responded, not saying more to clue her in on his plans. She slid her legs down to the floor and reached for some clothes.

"Your nightgown is fine. It's August in Texas. You'll be warm enough!" She obeyed and followed him out into the hallway and then out the back door, careful not to let it creak or slam as it closed. The moon was new, but the stars were bright, providing sufficient light for Tim to lead her to the mat that stayed out under their tree.

Tim pulled the mat out from the tree and into the open part of the yard where the stars would be most easily seen. "C'mere," Tim said as he motioned for her to step over to him. She followed him to the edge of the mat. Tim took her into a standing embrace and then lifted her gently from her feet and laid her onto the mat.

Had any of her neighbors been peering over the fence, they would have been amazed to see her body float placidly up off her feet and then drift down horizontally onto the mat.

Next, Tim knelt down on his knees and lay down beside her. Feeling him next to her, Lexie turned her head and kissed him. Just then, a shooting star flickered into life above them and traversed the sky getting brighter first and then dimming out. "Wow!" she exclaimed in an excited whisper. "Did you see that?"

"Of course, why do you think I brought you out here?" He marveled at the way Lexie's features remained so youthful. Her face lit up again as another meteor flashed above them. "Remember the Perseid Meteor Shower we watched together as children? This is it again!"

"So beautiful," Lexie whispered as two more faint streaks of light shot across the sky in unison.

Tim wanted to do nothing more than cuddle up with Lexie and watch the light show, but he knew they needed to talk. He had questions to ask and needed answers that only Lexie could provide. The zone in Billings had occurred three nights earlier. Then both zones after that added to the challenging mystery around Jeffrey. All three had taken him farther into the future than he had been since his timeline had locked onto Lexie's. Something was very different.

"Lexie, I need your help," he said finally, deciding he had enjoyed the wonderment on her face as long as he could. "Something happened in my zone a few days ago that I can't explain."

Tim proceeded to explain the horrific scene of violence he had found at the Billings stadium. He described Jeffrey and reminded her of his previous encounters with the younger Jeffrey of both worlds. He told her how the fat man with a hot dog had directly pointed out Jeffrey to him. He also described how for the first time in years, his slide into her world had skipped ahead multiple years. He had arrived in Billings to see the destruction in 2026; September 22, 2026.

"But isn't that the same day as the plane crash," she recalled.

"Yes, it is. How am I supposed to stop both? And how did the man know I was looking for Jeffrey? How did he even know I was there?" Tim asked.

Lexie thought. Tim loved the way she still bit at her lower lip while she thought. It was something she had always done. Then after what seemed like minutes, she said, "There must have been a screamer controlling the man. That's the only explanation. Unless he has some deep emotional bond to you like I do." She was smiling again and Tim let out a playful growl to indicate she wasn't taking this seriously enough.

"Okay, okay. Let me think," she said. "Did the man seem normal or in a trance?"

"I don't know, I guess he seemed to be in a trance. He was moving slowly and didn't seem panicked like the rest of the crowd.

But I didn't see any screamers. Though I suppose it all happened so fast that I wasn't looking for them."

She thought again and then asked, "And you are sure of the date?"

"Yes, I recognized it immediately. That has been a day I've been thinking about for over twenty years. I have to somehow stop the plane crash that same day."

"And you are positive it was Jeffrey?" she asked again, still biting her lip as she processed all the information.

"Yes. I have no doubt. I have seen him as a child, a teen, and five times as an adult. Other than you, I've never seen someone so often."

"Wait, five times? You told me about him as a sweet little boy who had trouble talking and liked planes. Then you saw him at the mall. But as an adult, I only remember three times: building the bomb, prison, and now the stadium, right? What am I forgetting?"

"You're not forgetting anything. I never told you about the last two zones because they just happened. That's what's weird. I watched him three nights in a row. I saw him die at the stadium, but then saw him last night celebrating Christmas as an old man. He was married to a widow with lots of children and grandchildren. I heard him tell the whole family how thankful he was that they all loved him and were willing to forgive him of his past.

"The night before that, I witnessed his funeral. He was even older than during the Christmas celebration. And the same large family circled around his open casket. They were all very upset at losing him. They spoke about him like he was some kind of hero to them. One of the sons said over and over again how great of a role model he had been to all of them.

"After I watched him die in the stadium collapse, I assumed that the prison zone must have actually been at a time in his life before the collapse. But seeing him alive again as an old man, a changed man, makes no sense at all."

Lexie did not say anything at first. Tim could tell she was pondering his observations as her eyes watched the stars above.

Finally she spoke again. "It seems clear," Lexie thought out loud, "that you are supposed to do something, something very important either for Jeffrey or through him. Why else would you keep running into him?"

"But what?" Tim pleaded. "I don't see how these zones can possibly fit together."

"Tim, there has been another split. Another split in reality. I believe that the screamers have shown you what the future is supposed to be. Jeffrey is supposed to go to jail, not die. They have shown you how he gets there. But somehow, something else changed, and now there are two timelines splitting from this one."

"Two timelines?"

"Yes, it is the only simple explanation. You have seen Jeffrey die in two places and times and under very different circumstances. You have been shown the path that they want you to influence. You say he was an old man, living happily with a new family. If we assume the stadium event still happens before your zone in the prison yard, then that means he eventually gets paroled from prison, makes peace with himself and all of those inner demons, and starts over with a new family. For that to be true, he can't die in the collapse, and he can't have killed all those people. Something about his path has to be changed to avoid splitting the lines."

Tim thought out loud, "So, I need to get into a zone before the bombing and convince Jeffrey to break the law in some other minor way. That way he will still go to jail but not for life."

"Maybe," Lexie said uncertain. "Except, this is a trickier case. You've already seen what happens in his life later on. So to avoid another split, you'll have to get it just right."

"How will I know?"

"I don't have all the answers, Tim."

"You usually do. You're the smartest person I know in *this* universe," he teased.

"Oh, so you know someone smarter in *your* universe?" Lexie poked him in his side.

Then, speaking seriously again, she thought through it all for him again. "What you saw at that stadium is not the ultimate future for him or those people. Maybe that is true for the plane crash too. You need to fix what went wrong so the lines can merge again. There is something crucial about that date in the future. The screamers seem to be willing to help you now. Or at least willing to let you help them. Keep your eyes open for them."

"So I have to stop the bombing of a bunch of baseball fans in Montana and stop a flight from crashing in Massachusetts, both at the same time and in two or three different universes?"

"Yes," Lexie answered matter-of-factly. "Have you figured out how yet?" she asked with a smile again.

"No, you still haven't told me how."

"I told you, I don't have all the answers," she laughed again. Then waving her finger at Tim like a scolding mother, she said, "And it's not my job to figure everything out for you! You're a big boy. You can do this!" Now Tim laughed. "Tim, it's 2020 now, so you have six years to figure it out!" Then Lexie's eyes changed from mock serious to seductive. "But it's already 3:02 a.m. here, so you only have six minutes left to make out with me. So, get started!"

Their time together was short as it always was, but the shooting stars above them created a spectacular visual backdrop as Lexie looked through her invisible lover toward the sky. It was a moment she would hold onto for years to come.

When Tim's weight and his passionate kisses ceased, she knew he had silently slid back into his world as she was left alone watching the shower of lights above. She thought again of Tim describing the first time he had met her in his zone.

He said her house was a disaster, and he had jokingly said that he thought her living room had thrown up! She smiled remembering that comment and wondered how bad it really was. Then her smile faded. He had also said she looked old and broken down. She would be bruised and badly beaten.

But what worried Lexie the most was how Tim described her reaction to that visit. She was always joyful when he arrived. But Tim told her that she had broken down in tears when she realized he was finally back. She had said that she had been waiting for a very long time for him to come back. Why couldn't she stop thinking of that now? What kept forcing that terrible thought into her mind? Was it some kind of warning or just a random thought?

Lexie shivered under the warm starry August night. She stood up and made her way back inside. She paused in the doorway and looked back into the yard at the spot where they had just been. She saw the tree where she and Tim spent so much time together and the mat that they had left in the middle of the grass. But she didn't see the screamer that stood with its arms at its side, staring at her stoically and silently. She had no way of knowing that Tim's frequent visits to her were over, and that it would be many years before she saw him again. All she knew was that she was alone now and something suddenly felt different. She was alone with a cruel husband; a cruel and brutal husband who had watched her through the back window. He had watched silently as she spoke with and loved another man under the stars. It didn't matter to him that it was a man he could not see. Or that he did not love her and never had loved her. What mattered to him was that she paid the price for her unfaithfulness. And he would see to it that she paid dearly.

PART III

Time Has Come

Your will is as free as that of Eve in the Garden, child. "Go where ye list" has always been God's way, but this is what God wants of you. Be true! Stand.

–Mother Abagail from Stephen King's
"The Stand" *1994.*

Chapter 39

LIFE AND DEATH

THE NEXT FEW nights were non-Lexie zones. Tim rescued a cat from an elderly man's trunk, stopped a racecar from crashing into a crowd, and calmed a store clerk down as an armed robber took several patrons hostage.

He still wasn't sure how he would accomplish all Lexie had suggested. But she believed in him, and somehow he would find a way to save the people of flight 4612 and stop the stadium explosion. Her encouragement was the biggest reason he got up each morning, ready to face the challenges of each new day. But what about her? Were his short visits really enough when everything else in her life was miserable?

He knew she had tried to leave Jack and his abuse, but the screamers kept her there. She justified it as a sacrifice she was willing to accept so that Tim would always be able to locate her. But Tim felt that if she was allowed to leave, he would still discover a way to find her. He believed that the bigger reason behind her inability to leave Jack was due to God's determination that since she was dead in his world, she might as well be dead in her world. But why was that his plan? It didn't make sense.

Tim and Lexie had talked a lot about God over the years. Both strongly believed in him and put their trust in him to watch over them, keep them safe, and bring them together as often as was in his plan. Lexie had often encouraged Tim that as long as he was in line with that plan, he would accomplish great things. Tim knew that he couldn't give up and had to continuously seek out that plan.

But why did Lexie have to suffer just because the universe had split in two? Why would God let that happen in the first place? And why was the solution in the hands of a bunch of creepy invisible boys?

He knew these questions had no easy answers. But he also knew that Lexie was being forced to suffer the most. His time with her was never long enough. She put on her brave face for him, but when he left, she was alone in a universe that thought she shouldn't exist.

Two more weeks passed. Tim realized something had changed. Why hadn't he been back to see Lexie? He was still rescuing kids from floods, stopping bad men from doing bad things, and helping old ladies across the street.

As always, he prayed each night that he would return to Lexie. But instead of finding her, he found others in need. There were so many people around the world who seemed to need a little help.

The timing of Tim's forays into Lexie's world had also changed. As his visits with Lexie had become more and more regular, the link in time between their worlds had matched more closely. For the last ten years, it was common for Tim to find Lexie in a time that was less than one day ahead of his own. This had made communication about events in their lives easier, but it had become increasingly difficult to help people in both worlds. How could he reach a person halfway around the planet with only a days notice?

Now, however, the time difference was increasing again. Four days earlier, he had slid into a college campus. The large holographic clock tower hanging over the central commons confirmed that the slide was about a week into the future. Then, last night, his slide was to a time twenty days ahead.

Weeks without Lexie became months, months turned into a year. Tim tried everything he could think of to get back to her; different sleeping positions, vitamins, sleep aids. He also focused on the memory of her face, her laugh, and her eyes in the minutes and hours before his zone, all without success.

Knowing that Lexie rarely left her house in Brenham, TX, he temporarily rented a bungalow two doors down from where she resided in her world, hoping that proximity might increase his chances of getting to her. Still, nothing worked.

After two years in Brenham, Tim moved back at the urging of his mother. "Your father is sick. He isn't going to make it much longer, Tim. Please come back," she pleaded to him.

She had not been exaggerating. Tim was shocked to see how feeble his dad had become suddenly as the newly mutated degenerative disease, Malleosis, a variation of Parkinson's, attacked his body. His mind was still strong, however, and Tim was grateful he had a few months with his dad before he was gone from this life.

June 2023

"I feel it coming now," John said softly to Tim on his last night. It was 3:00 a.m., and Tim had stayed with John in his private hospice room.

"I'm here, Dad," Tim said as he slid his chair next to the bed and put his hand on John's arm. "Do you want me to call Mom?"

"There is no need. I already said good-bye to her, Tim. She and I knew this was our last night."

Tim thought of Lexie. Had that night under the stars been their last night? If only he had known. If only he could have said good-bye to her instead of forcing her to help him think of solutions to his problems.

John coughed twice. The coughs were weak. His breathing was shallow, and Tim knew that talking was not easy for him.

"Just rest, Dad. Don't try to talk."

"It's okay. I want to talk to you, son. I want you to know how proud I am of you."

"I know, Dad."

"And I know you will see Lexie again," John said quickly. Tim looked up. Had it been that obvious that on his dad's own deathbed, he was thinking of Lexie.

"I know you are worried about it, Tim. But you will see her again. You knew there would be a gap. She told you there would be a time when you were separated, remember?" John coughed again, but then continued. "For whatever reason, this is how it is supposed to be. You are part of something much bigger than any of us can understand. Trust God to use you well. Use this time away from Lexie to accomplish big things."

Tim reflected on his first visit to Lexie again. He remembered how surprised and overjoyed she was that he had returned. He knew his dad was right and that he was now experiencing that period of time that she had told him about. Lexie was forty-five, almost forty-six, the night they talked beneath the stars. That had been three years ago. When he saw her for the first time, she had looked fifty-five. He didn't want to do the math but it was pretty easy to guess that it may be another six or eight years before he saw her again.

"I'll try to be patient, Dad. But I miss her."

"I understand. It is difficult to be away from someone that you love. But there is a purpose to all this. Maybe I'll get to find out that purpose before you do," he said coughing again, struggling for breath.

"Then you come back and tell me what it is!" Tim ordered his dad kindly.

"I'll see what I can do," John tried to laugh. Then his tone changed. "Tim?"

"Yes, Dad?"

"I was watching you earlier when you slipped into your zone."

Tim had thought his dad was sleeping while his consciousness slid to and from Lexie's world. Even after all this time, he felt embarrassed when someone saw him zone. John seemed to read his mind again.

"Don't worry. You shouldn't be ashamed. And no one else came in while you were . . . away."

The tension in Tim eased and John continued.

"I still think it is incredible what you can do. As I watched you, I wondered if dying will be like what you experience every night."

"I don't know. I've wondered that too," Tim said, considering his dad's idea. "People who have been near death describe seeing a light and separating from their body. Maybe it is similar."

John wheezed slightly and then coughed again.

"Do you want some water, Dad? Or some more medicine?"

"No," John answered weakly. "Son? I think it may be happening now."

Tim slid his chair closer and grabbed his dad's hand.

"I feel strange," John said. "It's like my mind is in two places. Is that what you feel?"

"Yes, that is how my zone starts if I'm awake. Like I don't belong here anymore."

"Exactly," John whispered. "I have had a good life, son. I have no regrets. But I don't belong here anymore. I just want you to know how proud I am of the man you are."

Tim took in a deep breath. His dad had said that many times before, but he never could truly accept it until now.

"It is happening, my son."

"I know, Dad," Tim whispered through a held-back sob.

"I'll watch over you, Tim."

"I know you will, Dad. Dad, I love you."

His dad smiled peacefully. "I love . . . you . . . Tim . . ." John closed his eyes, the smile remained on his face. He breathed low, as if only a small part of his diaphragm was able to move.

"Dad?" Tim asked, despite knowing that his dad could not respond. "Dad?" Still no reply. John's low breathing stopped completely.

Tim lifted the hand and arm that he had been holding and folded it gently over John's chest. John's eyes were already closed, and his smile had slacked some but still left an expression of peacefulness. Tim knew John was free of the disease now, but his dad was gone. Off to another world.

Could entering Heaven be similar to entering his zones? Was his dad seeing the light source ahead of him? Were there beams of color and sparks leaping from the center? Instead of having to stand up to link into the parallel world, maybe he would awaken in the arms of God.

These were questions he was not yet meant to know the answers to. But his dad had reminded him that he had a purpose in life—one that was significant. Even if he didn't understand the details, he knew it was time to get back to work.

Tim turned his attention to the plane and the bombing. He studied aeronautics and explosives. The previously known World Wide Web had been broken up by governments and sectioned off into virtual islands of data. They had splintered the free network to better control the flow of secret or dangerous information. Still, Tim found easy step-by-step instructions for building bombs of tremendous power using common, modern household supplies. Didn't the government realize that the Splinternet was still being used maliciously?

He learned that new polymers and plastics were being developed by private terrorists that were largely undetectable and easily assembled. It was a wonder that bombings were not a more common form of protest. Maybe it was simply because they had become too powerful. Only the most die-hard terrorists could sanction the destructive force.

For Jeffrey, all it would take was a little patience and planning. He had probably found the same type of plans on the Splinternet that Tim had found. Maybe someone gave the plans directly to him. He would easily be able to build the components of his bombs in that little apartment of his and then assemble them inside the stadium once through security.

If only Tim could find him and stop Jeffrey ahead of time. But Jeffrey was off the radar. He had gone into hiding and was probably using a different name now. Even if Tim could find him, he knew that he had to be careful. The chain of events had a way of persisting if he interfered with a link in that chain too soon. Stopping Jeffrey from building the bombs or going to the stadium may change how the bombing took place but wouldn't stop it. Another bomber would take over and kill thousands, or some other devastating event would take place to cause the same outcome. Time was a stubborn creature.

Tim bounced around from place to place in his zone. The lead time he experienced while in zone to the actual date in his world continued to increase. Though he understood this meant his link with Lexie was slipping further, he also recognized that he was able to do more for others. Having weeks or months to prepare to act on something he experienced in his zone was much easier than when he had just a day or so.

At home, Tim helped his mother adjust after his father's funeral. She missed him greatly but was not unhappy. Still, only a year after they had buried John, Sarah was ready to join him. She died suddenly, but peacefully, in her sleep on a Thursday morning, four years after Tim had seen Lexie and two years before the critical day of September 22, 2026.

Tim found it difficult to mourn the loss of his mom. He knew she wanted nothing more than to be where John was waiting for her. It seemed appropriate to him that she had passed so quickly as if to follow him. Their love and their marriage had connected them in a way that Tim admired. Had he and Lexie been able to be together, he would have strove to create that same kind of lifelong connection.

Chapter 40

TIME TO CHOOSE

AS THE PLANET celebrated the New Year on January 1, 2026 and people preached of New Year resolutions, Tim thought of his own responsibilities for the year. He had a list of fifty-seven separate life-saving acts, forty-two life-changing events and a host of helpful moments he would squeeze in where possible. And of course, he had to stop the plane crash and the Billings bombing. It would be a busy year.

Sometimes, the list helped him stay focused and not dwell on his longing for Lexie. Other times he wanted to rip his volumes of notes to shreds. Yet part of him believed that if only he could successfully perform all the duties on that list, he would be rewarded and return to her.

Three of the rooms in Tim's home had transformed into laboratories. If the police ever raided, it would be hard to explain the assembled and disassembled bombs he had made. The piles of materials, schematics of airports and airliners, as well as notes of future events would lead to an immediate arrest for highly suspicious behavior. Yet Tim persevered. He knew that to stop the flight from crashing and to stop Jeffrey from killing thousands, he had a lot to understand.

By the morning of September 22, Tim knew his time was up. He had a plan; though he wasn't sure he liked it. So many things could go wrong. Whatever the outcome, he would probably end up in jail. Maybe he'd be seriously injured or even killed. Was it worth it? Was it worth dying to save thousands?

"Yes!" Tim reminded himself whenever he had doubts. His purpose was to help others. Saving their lives would be worth it. Even prison was worth saving so many lives. And if he did well, he believed he would be allowed to see Lexie again. The bars of a prison cell in this world wouldn't prevent him from zoning to her world.

Tim was ready. He had packed up the supplies and equipment he needed two days earlier and started the long drive to his first destination. It had been a tough decision. He couldn't be in two parts of the country at the same time. He couldn't be at an airport in Boston, Massachusetts trying to stop a flight to Maine and at a stadium in Billings, Montana simultaneously. Even with his amazing gift of sliding through time and space, that was still impossible.

At first, the answer seemed obvious. The plane had only one hundred and thirty or so passengers and crew. The stadium had thousands of people, most of whom would die that evening if he didn't stop Jeffrey.

However, stopping the plane would be fairly simple compared with disarming the many bombs that Jeffrey must have carefully positioned to bring down the stadium. How could he find them all? What if he missed one? Just one could still cause the death of hundreds. He realized that there was no simple answer.

As he struggled for months to find the best solution, his faded Magic 8 Ball had been of no help. "A lot more people will die at the stadium, so I should stop Jeffrey, right?" he had asked his silent wise friend.

"Concentrate and ask again," it replied.

"Should I stop Jeffrey?"

"Reply Hazy. Ask Again."

Tim didn't ask again. He decided it was time to stop believing in the wisdom of such an old children's toy. The flight would be easier to stop, but the stadium had many more lives at stake. He knew he had to think like Lexie if he was to come up with the best solution.

September 22, 2026

As he completed his drive to his destination, he hoped his complicated plan would work. He pulled into the parking lot and looked around. People of all walks of life were whizzing by, heading toward their futures. We all have a future, he thought. He was just the only one who knew part of it.

Finding an open space, Tim parked. He was early, so he would have to wait. As he sat, he again pondered the flow of time. He had learned long ago that if he acted too soon, events would deviate but restore to the same outcome. Time seemed to move like a swift current in the river of life. One could divert it momentarily, but it would find a way to continue on its course.

If Tim had warned the passengers and flight crews of the impending storm long before the flight's scheduled departure, they might take some kind of action at that moment, but when the time came, events would transpire as if he had never existed. If he warned the city of Billings, the police, security at the stadium, even the media, some events may be changed, but the devastation would still occur. Jeffrey might simply change his target. Or the security may miss the bombs.

The change in events had to occur just before or during the event itself. That was the only way to affect the prespun fabric of time and the only way to change the current of time's stubborn flow.

Tim waited. He watched families pass by. Children held on to their daddies and mommies. One dad lifted his kids up by the arms to help them jump over all the cracks in the sidewalk. It was a game he remembered playing with his own dad as they'd walk to and from their church parking lot each Sunday morning.

"Don't step on a crack!" John would say.

"Or I'll break my mother's back!" Tim would laugh back to John. Sarah would give them both a dirty look that morphed into a smile.

That memory melted into another childhood memory of those carefree days. He remembered his church pastor, standing at the pulpit. So much of what he said went over Tim's head. But one day the pastor had yelled out, "Who will stand?" Tim had been startled by the sudden outburst, but he remembered the words now.

"Who will stand?" the pastor had repeated. "All that was needed was one man among the Israelites to stand before God, to be courageous enough to lead the people from ruin and destruction. But he found none among them. None worthy enough to stand. None willing to petition on behalf of ancient Israel."

Now as Tim waited, he could not remember the context of that sermon. But he suddenly felt encouraged. He would be that man today. A man who would stand against the destruction that he had witnessed in another universe. The screamers wanted to merge timelines, to match events. The screamers wanted all those people to die, but he would stand against them in his world. He would show them a better way to align the universes. A way in which people didn't have to suffer. The time had come for Tim to stand.

Chapter 41

TIME TO STAND

TIM OPENED HIS door and grabbed the bag that sat next to him. It contained all he would need to attempt to change the unchangeable. He was ready to take on the world, starting with flight 4612 to Bangor, Maine.

Tim hurried along with the other passengers up to the entrance and through the corridors toward his gate. Stopping at security, Tim watched as his bag was examined and then passed through the gamma scan.

He was ushered into the glass-walled body scanner, and though he knew he had been careful, he still felt nervous. What if his plan was stopped right here? He realized that as much as he had planned, everything hinged on many small lucky breaks. He needed to get on that plane.

Tim looked back nervously at the security examiner as a red light flicked on and a whirring sound began. Past the security station, Tim saw a group of flight personnel hurry through their own security check. Three were young women, dressed in stiff flight assistant uniforms. They trailed quickly behind two older women; one also in a flight assistant uniform and the other dressed as a pilot. Behind the women two men followed, one, a flight assistant, and the other, a second pilot with his captain's hat low on his head.

"Head straight, Mr. Caston," ordered a gruff voice from the speaker above the scanner chamber.

"Sorry," Tim mumbled, looking ahead again, realizing he was acting too nervous. He had been through the scanners many times before. It always tingled slightly as his molecules were analyzed for traces of carbon fiber explosives, the new explosive of choice for all terrorist. But overall, there was very little sensation and no excuse for being so nervous.

The speaker above Tim clicked and he heard the officer order him to step on through the chamber as the glass door opened in front of him, allowing entrance into the standby passenger room. He had passed the test.

Entering the passenger room, Tim marveled at the feeling of déjà vu. It was a feeling he should have been used to, but it still always surprised him. The room opened up into the large waiting area that he had observed so many years before. Only now, the large flat glass monitors and personal communication occipitals with flashing green and blue lights were commonplace to him, no longer futuristic or impressive.

The old man was at the bank of antiquated pay phones, arguing with his family. "I have a weird feeling," the man argued to the son or daughter on the other end of the conversation. "I've been around much longer than you. I've learned to trust my feelings."

The old man was right. His feelings or intuition were sharp, despite his age. If he boarded that flight, he would be in serious danger.

"Report any unattended packages or baggage . . ." the loud intercom rang out. It was a message Tim was now very familiar with as it had become the standard air travel warning for almost thirty years. "Do not accept bags from strangers, do not leave bags unattended, do not stand near gate entrances and exits," and on and on. When had air travel become so unattractive? Yet surrounding Tim were over one hundred people ready for a flight from Boston to Bangor.

The rain outside pounded against the windows of the terminal. A little girl finished talking to her daddy and put her pink phone back down onto the seat next to her. Then the intercom chirped loudly as the gate supervisor picked up his mic and stated, "Attention passengers. Flight 4612 to Bangor, Maine will be delayed due to weather."

Tim recalled that same message long ago. It was no surprise to him that the message was restated by the same supervisor only seconds later. "Attention passengers. Flight 4612 to Bangor Maine will leave on time. Please prepare to board." His voice was confident. There was no hint that the supervisor or any of the other gate officers even noticed the odd reversal of caution.

Lightning struck outside. The storm was getting closer. It appeared very dark outside even though in normal weather, several hours of daylight should have remained. Passengers began lining up to board. Many of their expressions were dim. Tim couldn't see them but he knew he was surrounded by screamers. If there was one assigned to him at that moment, he could not sense it.

Tim lined up too and waited to board. The gate officer quickly scanned the boarding cards, one by one, as he matched them to the retinal images that were displayed for each passenger, before allowing them to walk through the secure entrance. When Tim got his approval to pass the officer, he again felt a sense of relief that his plan continued onward.

Walking down the enclosed ramp, Tim saw rain dripping through seams in the movable walkway. He looked out the plastic window and saw two baggage handlers carelessly tossing luggage off their motorized cart and onto a lift. They did not seem pleased to be standing in the harsh rain, lifting heavy bags into place.

Tim found his assigned seat by the window and put his bag down carefully at his feet. He looked out and saw the handlers again. They were lobbing the final pieces of baggage onto the lift. Just as the last bag and a small box were about to be hurled from the cart, a third handler, whom Tim had not seen before, stepped in and grabbed the box from his younger colleague. Tim watched as the older handler reprimanded the others for their carelessness. Once finished with their scolding, he placed the box under his raincoat and personally carried it to the lift.

Tim looked around inside the cabin and waited until no one was looking toward him. Then he opened his bag and pulled out three small containers. He headed to the rear bathroom compartment and locked the flimsy door behind him. Inside the tiny room he assembled the device quickly. It looked good and he hoped that it looked authentic enough.

Now he had to wait. The plane began moving back and then out toward the runways. Tim could feel the powerful engines whirling fast enough to gently push the plane along the tarmac. Soon, he knew it would be time to act.

"Welcome to flight 4612 to Bangor, Maine," he heard the captain's voice call out in the speaker overhead. "The runway is clear, and we will be in the air momentarily. Flight assistants, prepare cabin for takeoff."

Readying himself, Tim took in a large breath and then burst out of the bathroom, causing the door to fly open and slam against the partial wall that separated the passengers from the assistants' kitchen area.

"There's a bomb in the bathroom!" Tim called out. "It's going to explode!"

There was a sudden commotion. Tim was grateful that the passengers had heard him. What if the screamers had already been calming them? He hadn't even thought of that until now! They would have all remained calm and oblivious and ignored his warning.

As it was, the commotion erupted into panic, but the passengers were slow to react appropriately. Tim had seen this response many times. People who were panicked rarely thought clearly. Their reactions were disjointed and confused.

"Flight assistants!" Tim ordered with authority, "I am a trained marshal. Get these passengers off the plane! Now!"

The head assistant seemed confused at first but then seemed to comprehend. "Corbin, check the bathroom and confirm the situation," she ordered the young male assistant. Despite having to squeeze past passengers that stood in the aisle, he was able to reach the rear quickly.

"It's there, Ma'am!" he confirmed looking first at her and then at Tim suspiciously. "We need to get everyone off the plane."

The head assistant picked up the intercom mic. "All passengers please exit the plane through the nearest emergency exit. Stay calm and orderly." Then, pressing a different button on the mic, she reported to the pilots the situation while simultaneously punching in a code on the wall that allowed all doors to automatically open.

Upon receiving the report from the head assistant and seeing the emergency code she had punched into the computer, the pilot immediately applied the plane's breaks bringing the massive ship to a stop. Several people in the aisles fell forward, but no one was injured by the suddenness of the stop. This was going too easily, Tim thought.

The doors finished opening, and emergency ramps were inflated out into the storm. The passengers next to the exits began jumping out and sliding down the rain-slick ramps. Flashes of bright lightning illuminated the scene around them.

"I can't believe we were going to take off in this weather," Tim heard several passengers commenting to each other.

One of the pilots opened the cockpit door, stepped through, and closed it behind her. Tim recognized her as part of the flight crew he had seen stepping through security. That same crew now acted quickly and efficiently as they guided the passengers out. Their professional authority kept most of the passengers surprisingly calm.

Tim moved up the aisle toward the pilot as the seats emptied. Corbin followed him, still watching him closely. Tim knew he wasn't done yet. A lot could still go wrong if he didn't play the next role perfectly.

"Pilot Wells, the back of the plane has been evacuated," stated Corbin, only taking his eyes off Tim for a moment to address the pilot.

"Good. What do you know about the bomb? Where did it come from? Is it going to go off?" Wells asked.

"It is on a timer," he replied. "A digital green display was counting down."

"How much time?" she asked. The other flight assistants heard the conversation and turned to hear his answer.

"It was less than five minutes when I saw it. I'm guessing we have just two more minutes left. This man here saw it first." Corbin nodded at Tim. "Says he is a marshal," he added with a look that Tim knew was to alert the pilot and head flight assistant of his suspicions.

Wells spoke directly to Tim. "Anything to add, Marshal?" she asked, probing him to clarify both the bomb and his role. She was the first officer on this flight. Had there been a marshal on this plane, the captain would have told her about it.

Tim looked around and saw the last of the passengers deplane. Only he, the three assistants, and Pilot Wells remained in the cabin. The captain remained in the cockpit as Tim had hoped.

"We don't have much time," Tim spoke truthfully. "The device's timer is a fake," Tim said directly to Pilot Wells.

"What? How do you know?" Wells asked.

"I know because I put it in there," Tim said, almost surprising himself by the absurdity of it all. Yet this was part of his plan, and he couldn't back down now. He needed the plane.

One of the flight assistants, the youngest by the look of her, gasped at Tim's words. "What do you want from us?" she cried out.

"Right now, I want you to stay calm," Tim replied. "I need you to listen to me and do exactly as I say." The young assistant continued crying. Corbin, the head assistant, and Pilot Wells seemed to be considering their training and watched for a moment to strike against Tim.

Tim saw the strategy building in their eyes and realized he needed to up the threat. "The device is controlled by me," Tim said calmly. "I have placed several others in the cabin." This threat was false, but he felt he needed to keep them on edge and obedient to his demands.

"Two will explode if I push this button," he lied showing them a plastic cylinder switch. "The rest will explode if I stop pushing this button on the side," he lied again. The truth was that it was all a bluff. Tim could not bring himself to actually put anyone in danger. At least not more than they already were just by being on that plane. He also couldn't figure out how to get explosives through security. So instead, he packed some wires and some broken parts of a clock along with some innocent but ominous looking silly putty. Then he assembled the parts into a replica of a bomb he had studied. He just hoped the bluff would be strong enough to force obedience.

Tim caught a glance from Pilot Wells to a control monitor. He had seen her do it earlier too but hadn't understood. He looked and saw that at some point in all this, she had activated the intercom to the cockpit.

"I assume the captain in the cockpit is aware of the situation and has alerted security," Tim stated, already knowing it to be true. The young flight assistant gasped again. It was hard to tell if she was relieved at this news or if she was afraid it would set this crazy terrorist off.

"Are you going to kill us?" she asked still crying.

Tim knew he needed them to fear him, but it went against his being to create undue terror. He decided to simply tell the truth.

"I do not want to hurt anyone. I've already gotten all the passengers off this plane. I am not a terrorist, but I need you all to do exactly what I tell you." It seemed that his threat with the fake trigger had worked on the three women. None of them seemed willing to make a move that might cause him to either push the button or release the other. However, Corbin still seemed ready to try something. He looked like he was strung as tight as a crossbow, ready to leap at Tim if the moment allowed it.

"What is it you need us to do?" a voice called out as the door to the cockpit opened.

"I need this plane to start moving, Captain," Tim said not looking at the new arrival but keeping his eyes on the loaded Corbin.

"Let my crew off first. Then I'll do whatever you need," the captain suggested forcefully.

"No, Captain," Corbin shot out, turning his gaze from Tim for the moment. "There are five of us! We should . . ."

The captain cut him off. "No, I will not endanger you four. How about it, Marshal?" The captain asked, intentionally stressing the false name in an attempt to exert his own authority. "Security is on their way now. Let my crew go, and I'll get this plane off the ground."

Tim looked up at the captain, but now it was his turn to gasp. How could *he* be the captain? It was impossible. What did this mean for the rest of his plan? Getting everyone off the plane except the captain had been Tim's plan from the start. He wanted as few lives in danger as possible. He needed the plane to take off but knew there was still a risk of it crashing.

Confused, Tim nodded and then said, "Yes, you four may leave. Please go now."

The crew looked at each other, surprised by this apparent gesture of goodwill by the terrorist. Then the young assistant said, "He said we could go! I'm going!" She ran at the exit and jumped onto the slide.

"Go!" Tim and the captain ordered to the rest at the same time. They studied each other's expressions. The captain had seen Tim's look of surprise when he had looked up at him. It had been a look of recognition. Did he know him?

"Captain?" Wells pleaded, but he only reaffirmed his order for her to leave with the rest of the crew. Then he seemed to nod to her, to indicate that he thought everything would be all right.

Corbin, the head assistant, and Captain Wells jumped out of the plane and slid to the bottom of the ramp.

"Security is coming," the captain said, seeing flashing lights approaching in the distance. "I can't take off. My orders in a situation like this are to do everything I can to get the passengers and crew off the plane safely but to never allow the plane to be seized by terrorists. A terrorist could hurt far more people with a fueled up plane than just the number of passengers."

"I know. But that is not my intention," Tim pleaded.

"You are not a terrorist, are you?" the captain said. "And that bomb back there? And the others on the plane?"

Tim could not believe the situation. So much of his plan had worked out perfectly. Yet he knew now that this captain would not believe any false threats.

"Not real," Tim admitted. "The bomb in the back is a fake. I lied about the others too." This was no longer part of the plan. He was supposed to force the captain to take off by threatening his life. Instead, he was giving up his power with his honesty. But this was someone he knew. It was impossible but true. And he somehow felt that his only hope was that the captain would help him. And of all captains, this one would.

"Jeffrey," Tim said, still amazed at this confluence of events. "Jeffrey, my name is Tim Caston. I beg you to trust me right now and get this plane into the air."

Captain Jeffrey Mitchell looked narrowly at Tim. He thought he recognized him too but couldn't place the memory.

The emergency vehicle lights were approaching quickly. Tim knew that if security reached the plane, it was all over. He'd be arrested, Jeffrey would be a hero for keeping everyone safe and stalling the terrorist.

At least Tim had stopped the plane. No one would have to die on flight 4612. Also, since Jeffrey was here, maybe there would be no explosion at the stadium. Maybe he had done enough, just keeping the plane from taking off into the storm with all the passengers.

No, he knew that wasn't the way it worked. The universes were too closely linked. He had seen the stadium explode. If he didn't continue with his plan now, thousands would die at the stadium in just a few hours. Jeffrey wouldn't be the bomber, but it would still happen. Stubborn time! He couldn't give up.

"Jeffrey, we have to take off now. You must trust me," Tim pleaded.

Jeffrey had also seen the lights getting closer. He felt something inside him wanting to obey the familiar man. But he knew his training. He was the captain. This was his dream job. He had wanted to be a pilot all of his life. Life had started out on the wrong track, but then, something had helped him change. Not something, someone! He did know this man, he thought.

Shaking his head, surprised by his own actions, Jeffrey suddenly punched a code into the control panel on the wall. The doors automatically closed as the slides were released.

"Come on!" Jeffrey called back to Tim as he stepped toward the cockpit. "I can't believe I'm doing this," he mumbled to himself.

Tim followed. "Sit there," Jeffrey ordered with authority. An outsider would have assumed Jeffrey was hijacking the plane! "We'll be off the ground in a few moments," he said as he released the breaks and started accelerating. "It is going to be close!" he said, pointing out the vehicles that were cutting through the grass between the taxiway and runway. Tim said nothing. He looked at Jeffrey who was pushing the throttle up as far as it would go. Why was he so quick to trust him? Why was he here and not at the stadium?

The first of the emergency vehicles reached the runway. The plane picked up more speed as a large roll of spikes was ejected from the truck onto the concrete pad ahead of them.

"We're not going to clear it!" Tim exclaimed, knowing the spikes would puncture the tires and keep the plane from accelerating to takeoff speed.

"It's going to be close, I said. Hang on!" Jeffrey ordered. He pulled back on the rudder control causing the tail to dip slightly and the nose to lift up. More trucks with bright flashing lights reached the runway.

The nose lifted further and then the rear wheels bounced twice and lifted just over the spikes. Shots rang out, one bullet ricocheting off the reinforced front window.

"They're shooting at us!" Tim called out.

"I know," Jeffrey stated matter-of-factly through gritted teeth as he continued pulling back on the rudder.

The plane started climbing fast, forcing Tim back into his seat. Within a few moments, they were out of range of the small guns. "We made it," Tim breathed.

"No, not yet," Jeffrey replied. "Got two warbirds on my tail." He flipped a switch on the control panel causing the cockpit speakers to come to life.

"Attention flight 4612. Repeating. Level out to 5000' and circle clockwise for landing approach. Do you copy?"

Static hissed for a moment as the voice in one of the tailing fighters waited for a reply.

"Flight 4612, we have been ordered to shoot you down if you do not comply," came the voice again over the radio.

"Will they really shoot us down?" Tim asked, looking over at Jeffrey.

Jeffrey made no response. His eyes seemed locked forward. Tim had seen that look many times.

"Oh no," Tim breathed out. He looked forward and saw the intense lightning ahead. They were flying directly toward the heart of the storm, just as the flight had done in Lexie's world. There was no way to deny what was happening. The screamers had Jeffrey now.

"Flight 4612, this is your last warning. We have been ordered to fire. Will you comply?"

The sound of static hissed again. It was clear that the pilots in the fighters did not want to shoot down a civilian passenger jet. However, they knew that all passengers and crew, aside from the "terrorist" and one captain, were safe on the ground. That would make it an easier decision.

Tim had known that this scenario was a possibility. But he couldn't accept that it would end here. He had only accomplished half of his plan. Though the passengers were safe, the stadium was still doomed. And now Jeffrey was doomed as well.

"Please, God," he pleaded aloud.

As their plane lifted toward the heart of the storm, Jeffrey remained in his screamer-induced trance. Lightning lit up the black clouds all around them, and the plane shook violently in the turbulent storm. A master alarm on the navigation panel begged for attention. If the fighters held off long enough, the plane might crash on its own, just as it had before.

Tim knew he needed to act. He reached for the copilot controls, ready to try to fly the plane himself. He had studied cockpit flight controls during his preparation for this day. He believed that if it was necessary, he could fly the plane. He would pull up and get above the storm. The fighters may still shoot him down, but at least he would have done everything possible.

"Here we go," he said to himself, pulling on the control wheel.

"Don't!" Jeffrey's voice suddenly called out. His voice was firm and in command. Had the screamers released him?

"Fighters, this is the captain of flight 4612, Jeff Mitchell." Jeffrey looked over at Tim and then continued to speak to the fighters behind him. His eyes were clear and focused.

"There is a bomb on this flight. If we return to the ground, many people will be hurt. Please escort us away from all populations so that the explosion will not cause casualties on the ground."

Tim was confused. Why was Jeffrey lying for him? He had already told him that the bomb was a fake. There was no immediate response from the fighters. Would they accept his explanation and request?

Finally, a somewhat relieved voice rose from the cockpit speakers again. "Copy, Captain Mitchell. Please climb to ten thousand feet and adjust heading to two-one-niner and await further orders."

Jeffrey looked at Tim again. He didn't seem relieved by this news. He looked terrified!

"Mr. Caston, I know you are here to help. You have helped me before, haven't you?"

Tim started to answer, but Jeffrey went on. "There is a bomb on this flight and it will explode in less than six minutes. If we are going to survive long enough for you to explain why you are here and what you are doing on my plane, you need to do as I say." The tables had completely turned, and now Tim was being ordered to obey.

"I already told you the bomb in the bathroom was a fake. The others I just made up," Tim said.

"No, there is a very powerful bomb in the luggage compartment. I don't know how I know it is there, but I do know that it is. This plane is about to explode. You have saved over one hundred and thirty passengers, but all we can do now is get this plane out of the city so it won't kill anyone on the ground when we crash."

"Someone just told you about the bomb?" Tim asked, thinking of the blank look Jeffrey had displayed a minute ago.

"Told me? I don't think so. But I saw a vision of the explosion. And I felt . . . something. I have felt it before. A long time ago, I almost died in a fire. I felt the same feeling, only that time, it calmed me in a way that put me to sleep. Then someone rescued me . . ." Jeffrey seemed to be thinking again, but not in the screamer-induced daze as before.

Lightning continued striking all around the plane as it lifted them higher through the storm.

"I felt that feeling again at a mall. I felt it after . . ." He paused again and looked at Tim.

"You!" Jeffrey exclaimed. "It really was you. I'm sure of it now! I felt it after you told me to follow you. I felt, something, something told me to follow you. Something inside me pushed me to follow. Then, that same feeling caused me to get down below the escalator. Before I even understood what was happening, I looked up and saw the boy falling. I put my arms out without really thinking about it. And he fell onto me. I don't know how it happened. All I know is that something inside me was different from then on.

"I had been angry. Angry about having no real parents. Angry about bouncing around from foster home to foster home. Angry at the whole world.

"But then you showed up, and the next thing I knew, I was being called a hero. I liked how it felt, catching that boy and being a hero, even if only for a moment. I think I would have turned out very different if it hadn't been for that day.

"One of my friends got arrested for shoplifting just after I caught that boy. I would have been with him if you hadn't said to come. I never got to thank you, but I've thought about you ever since. And I've been trying to help people ever since."

Tim was always amazed at how events looked from different perspectives. He had known that he kept Jeffrey from shoplifting that day but hadn't realized the lifelong effect it had had. He also now understood why the screamers had forced this flight and the one in Lexie's world to take off into the storm. They knew of the bomb and knew of the destruction it would cause on the ground. They were using the plane to protect an even greater number of people.

However, Tim had found a better way. The passengers hadn't needed to die. So, he saved them all. Now, only he and Jeffrey were in danger, and as a continuation of his plan, he had hoped to force the pilot to turn away from the storm and reroute toward Billings. The threat of a hijacked plane jetting toward the stadium should have been enough to force its evacuation. But now, everything had gone suddenly wrong. A real bomb was on the plane, and fighters would never allow them to come anywhere near Billings.

"Mr. Caston," Jeffrey ordered, waking Tim from his thoughts. "We need to get that bomb off this plane. I need to stay here and get us out of this storm so you must go down below and find that bomb."

"I don't know where it is," Tim argued but realized Jeffrey was right. None of his plans could continue if the plane exploded and killed both of them.

Jeffrey thought. "I know it is in the hold, but I'm not sure where."

"They showed you, didn't they?" Tim asked remembering Jeffrey's trance and thinking about the screamers' involvement in the situation. "Think back, Jeffrey. What did it look like?"

"They? Who?" Jeffrey asked, confused.

"That isn't important. Do you know what the bomb looks like? Did you see the suitcase?"

Jeffrey wanted to question it further but decided to focus on the task at hand. "Yeah, I think so. But it wasn't in a suitcase."

Jeffrey described the box that the screamers had shown him. Tim realized now that he had seen it too. The handlers had been about to toss the box onto the lift, but the third handler took it carefully onto the plane himself. Had he known what was in the box? Tim knew that question would have to wait. He needed to find that bomb.

Jeffrey quickly explained how to get down into the luggage hold. Then Tim gave his own set of instructions to Jeffrey. He had not forgotten the stadium. His plan hadn't included removing a real bomb from the plane, but the situation was the same. He had a fully fueled plane that was heading straight toward Billings. He wasn't sure how much time they had or if they would succeed, but now he had Jeffrey to help him. There was still a chance to save all of them! It might be their last act of heroism.

"You understand?" Tim asked his new sidekick after explaining the situation at the stadium.

"Yeah, got it," Jeffrey responded affirmatively. "You ready?"

"Yes, going now."

Tim raced to the back of the plane and found the set of tools Jeffrey had described. The electric ratchet easily turned the bolts securing the hatch to the floor in the middle of the aisle. Once below, Tim made his way quickly to the secure bins containing the luggage. The ratchet didn't fit the lock on the bins so Tim tried another attachment. It didn't fit either.

"I don't have time for this!" he yelled out in frustration and fear, knowing he was standing just feet away from a ticking bomb, capable of taking out a city block if on the ground.

"Tim!" he heard his name called through the intercom.

"I can't get the lock off!" Tim yelled back toward the speaker on the opposite wall.

"Don't get it off, just push the release button on both sides!"

Tim couldn't believe his foolishness. It wasn't a lock, just a latch to secure the luggage in place. He squeezed the release levers and felt it click loose in his hand. The gate opened, and the cube-shaped cabinets lay before him, full of bags, strollers, and suitcases.

"I don't see it!" Tim shouted.

Jeffrey answered, "Look at the bottom left corner, Tim. Then count up from the floor, two rows. Now move to the right three columns. It is behind a hot pink soft sided case."

Tim started counting but then realized he could see the pink case directly in front of him. He pulled it out and let it fall to the floor.

"I see it!" Tim yelled exuberantly!

"Good, now set it beside the load door behind you," Jeffrey ordered. "You see the door?"

"Yeah, it's there!"

"Ok, hold onto something, Tim! This is going to be rough!"

Without waiting, the door blew open, and a forceful gust blasted the air out of the cargo hold. Tim grabbed onto the bulkhead and yelled as his breath seemed to explode out of his lungs, and another bolt of lightning lit up just outside the door.

Then a second flash filled the sky. Only, that flash was not caused by lightning and was almost immediately followed by a forceful shock to the side of the plane. Tim lost hold of the bulkhead and slid across the floor toward the open door. Just in time, he caught hold of the belted netting that was in place around some empty animal crates.

"Hold on, Tim!" Jeffrey shouted through the com. "We've lost part of our tail! We're going down!"

Chapter 42

NEVER GIVE UP

Date: Unknown
Zone Year: Unknown

TIM WOKE TO see the world flying past him in odd colors and sounds. What had happened? Where was he?

He stood up, the movement slowed, and his senses attached to the world around him into which he had just zoned.

"What . . ." Tim said, trying to understand what had just happened. The plane had been falling. He had been running out of oxygen and hanging on for his life. Before that, fighters had been threatening to shoot them down but then agreed to lead them out over the old Appalachian hills, west of Boston. Now he was in a zone? What had happened to the plane? What had happened to Jeffrey?

Tim looked around. He recognized this place. He was in Utah, just outside Moab. It was a hot, dry day, probably in the middle of summer. The desert-like environment blew specs of sand at him, causing him to turn away and shield his eyes.

When he opened them, he saw a man lying on the ground, barely conscious.

"I've been here before!" Tim said, remembering not only the location, but the situation as well. He had witnessed this same man many years ago in this same place. He was a hiker and, while exploring the rock canyon outside Moab, was bitten by a rattle snake. He had tried to climb out of the canyon back to his jeep, but as the heat and poison took hold, he lost consciousness.

Tim hadn't known what to do for the man in zone but had been able to find him and rescue him in his own world. Why had he been brought back here again? This event was long in the past now. Was he being given a second chance?

Tim decided to act quickly. The man was passed out, so he lifted his arm up over his shoulders and dragged him up the ravine. The man's limp weight made the task difficult, but Tim persevered. He reached the jeep ten minutes later and found the keys hidden under the floor mat. The jeep started easily and the unconscious man was taxied back to town by the invisible driver. Tim knew where the hospital was, since he had driven this same man to the emergency room in his world.

The man opened his eyes about two minutes into the drive and took notice of the jeep's new ability to steer and shift on its own before he passed back out against the passenger door. His recollection of the event, however, would be easily dismissed as a hallucination caused by his delirium.

A few minutes later, the jeep made a dramatic approach as it hopped the curb and came to rest at the emergency room doors. A nurse and doctor spotted the unconscious man in the passenger seat and pulled him onto a gurney. They believed the man must have been thrown out of the driver's seat when he hit the curb—though they could not explain how he had ended up in the passenger seat with his seat belt buckled securely around him! Regardless, he had arrived in time for them to save his life. He would be okay.

Tim faded from the zone, expecting to wake up with irritated eyes at 12:13 a.m. But he didn't. Instead, he awoke to the oddly rolling clouds overhead and noises that seemed to echo rather than emanate from the sources around him.

Tim stood up and found himself zoned yet again. Like the last time, the location and situation were familiar. He had been here before. "What is going on?" he thought.

In this place in his world, he had helped a man find his missing twin toddler boys who had wandered out of their urban apartment. But in this parallel location of Lexie's world, he had not acted quickly enough. One of the sons was hit by a car just before he located them. He had another chance now to save the boy. Was he going to be given a second chance at all the zones in which he had failed? Why hadn't he awoken from the last zone?

After saving both boys and reuniting them with their father, the pattern continued. He used his thirty-eight minutes to correct mistakes, but as one zone ended, another began. Frustration mounted. Why after so many years did the rules suddenly change? How long would, or could, this continue?

After stopping an accident involving a school bus full of children, Tim awoke directly into another zone, surrounded only by trees that stood tall and straight against sloping hillsides. Somewhere in the distance, a motorcycle without a muffler echoed through the valley.

"I'm done!" he yelled to Heaven and to the trees that towered above him. "I can't live trapped in this world if I can't see Lexie! I refuse to keep doing this!"

However, just as Tim finished declaring his bold statement, he heard a girl's scream echoing through the woods. "Lexie?" he thought for a moment, strangely hopeful. No, the cry was not from Lexie. This voice was different, he realized. Still, the voice sounded young, and the girl was pleading for help!

Tim saw movement ahead of him through the trees. He squinted and could see the girl trying to run as fast as she could. She was struggling through the thick brush below the trees. Two, no, three men were closing in fast behind her. The one in front was tall and lean with short cropped hair and a thin reddish mustache. The second man was like a beast from the days of gladiators, with long straggly hair and solid muscles bulging all over. The third man, a short, heavy man, trailed behind the other two. All three men looked liked their clothes and bodies had not been washed in weeks.

The girl had light brown hair, fair skin, and Tim guessed she was in her late teens or early twenties. Her shirt looked torn, and she seemed to be running without shoes.

Like the previous zones, Tim immediately remembered the situation. He had been here before, surrounded by the trees in this North Carolina woods that skirted the southeastern edge of the Smoky Mountains. The last time, years earlier, he was just twenty-three years old and the girl hadn't seemed so young to him. He was much older now and realized how much time had passed since he first stumbled upon her plight.

During that first encounter in his zone, he had been unable to rescue her from her pursuers. First, he was slow to find her and then slow to react as he tried to figure out what to do in his zoned state. But just like the past few zones, once back in his world, he had been able to change the outcome.

He knew what to do this time and sprinted left, even though the girl and her pursuers were heading to his right. He remembered that she would change direction and start running back toward the large clearing that he could see through the trees.

As Tim pointed himself toward the clearing, he looked back. Sure enough, just as gladiator man closed in on her, she stopped running and turned around. The huge man grabbed onto her shoulders and held her as the other men circled in.

"I got something for you, pretty lady," the thin man hissed next to her through a broken front tooth as he began fumbling with his belt. The girl spat at him. He was the leader of this backwoods trio and had been the one who promised to deliver her safely to town when her car overheated somewhere along Route 194. Instead, he brought her to his hunting cabin where she was gagged and tied to a chair while he and his gang argued over what they would do to her first.

The knots had been poorly tied, however, and as the men argued outside, she worked her way free, losing her shoes in the process. Her silent escape was short-lived, and the men had easily tracked her through the rough terrain.

Now, seemingly caught again, her bare feet bloody and her clothes torn, she wasn't ready to give up. The girl looked away from the thin leader and back up at the massive brute that held her. Unexpectedly, she raised her knee as fast as she could against his groin. He was caught off guard by her quick and forceful action, and the shock and pain to his nether regions provided her just enough distraction to twist out of his grip and begin her run toward the meadow where Tim was heading.

Tim readied himself as the girl caught up and darted into the open field. His instinct the last time had led him to try to take her by the hand and lead her away from the rapists. But he had quickly learned that with her bare feet so badly bruised and cut by the forest floor, she was unable to keep up with his guiding hand, and the men quickly overtook them. This time, Tim let her pass by, knowing that his tactic had to be different.

As the girl passed, Tim could see that she was exhausted, having already run for several minutes through the thick branches and undergrowth. She had tripped twice already, and her ankle was screaming at her to stop.

The men were close behind her as she darted along the edge of the clearing. Tim leaped toward the thin man, the fastest of her pursuers, and nudged him hard to his right, causing him to slam into the center of a large pine. He recoiled backward and slammed onto the ground but unfortunately seemed unhurt.

Then Tim turned back and dove to catch the legs of the slowest man as he huffed past, out of breath. Husky's pinned legs caused him to fall headfirst into a log. He was stunned by the sudden fall and collision, but Tim knew that he too may be on his feet again soon.

Up ahead, the girl screamed out again. Tim ran toward her cry, but by the time he had reached her, Gigantor had already grabbed onto her again. He held her arms back as he pressed her, face forward, against a tree. Then pulling hard on the back of her shirt, he ripped it off brutally, sending buttons flying. He tied the torn fabric around her arms to hold her hands behind her back.

Tim didn't hesitate. As soon as the man threw the girl to the ground, Tim grabbed him by his hair and spun him in a clockwise direction toward a large boulder. He struck it with his back and bounced partially over the rock. By the time he got his feet back under him and started for the girl again, the thin man had caught up. No sign of Husky. Tim grabbed onto thin man's loose belt and flung him on a collision course toward Gigantor.

Knowing the men would only be confused by the sudden attack for a moment, Tim pulled the girl over his shoulder and ran in the direction of a road he had spotted earlier. She cried out briefly and then seemed to understand that she was being helped.

Tim crossed quickly through the open, grassy meadow and then leapt over a small brook. He did not need to look back to know that the men would be on their tail shortly. Despite his ability to fight the men off one by one, his aging body was slower than he had anticipated. The road was still too far ahead in the distance. He knew he needed to put the girl down and find a way to defend her.

Darting into the thick forest on the far side of the meadow, Tim hurried toward a large oak tree. The tree had massive exposed roots on the edge of the hill leading down toward the road. He pulled the girl off his shoulder and let her fall into the protected space behind the roots. Her face looked confused and scared but calm.

Tim scanned the ground around the tree and then picked up a strong bat-sized log. As the two men caught up and came around the tree, Tim used the log to slam them both to the ground with repeated strikes. His blows were quick and sure, forcing the thin man to flee and Gigantor to curl up protectively into a ball.

When Tim was satisfied that the men no longer posed a threat, he lifted the girl back out of the protective roots. "I think they are finished messing with you," he said as he untied the shirt from her arms and wrists and put it into her hands. He helped her up onto her feet and gently pushed on her back, guiding her in the right direction toward the road. Though his assistance was continuing to cause the girl confusion, he persisted and led her quickly down the hill to the road and to safety. Once there, he retreated back into the woods to stand guard until a car could come by and take her to safety.

As he guarded, Tim reflected on the similar events from his world that had taken place almost thirty years before. His rescue of that same girl had occurred soon after he found out about Lexie's death. That girl had called him her hero and then broke down into tears as the realization of what had almost happened to her started to sink in. He never knew her name but had comforted her with a protective embrace and held her until a car came that could get her to safety.

At one moment, while they waited together, the scared young woman had looked up at the young Tim. She gazed longingly at her rescuer as if expecting a kiss from her hero; like a princess in a fairytale. But as she looked into his eyes, she saw that he was not looking at her in that way. He was looking at her as if he wished she were someone else.

Disappointed, she had said, "You have someone, don't you. Someone you love?"

"Yes," he had responded sadly, thinking of Lexie. "I am in love with someone."

"Then why are you here in these woods rescuing me? Why don't you go to her?" she had asked.

He had thought about Lexie and the sadness he felt having learned only a few weeks earlier of her death. "I can't. It is impossible. But I will always love her."

The girl had hugged him one last time and thanked him again as a car arrived; its two elderly occupants promising to take her to the police. Then Tim remembered something else she had said to him. "Never give up," she had whispered into his ear as she gave him a parting kiss on the cheek. "Nothing is impossible."

Tim awoke from his memory of the past as the same car pulled over next to that same girl in this zone do-over. An older couple had spotted her standing alone, with the tattered shirt still clutched against her chest. They asked if she was okay and offered to help. He knew that they would get her to safety, just as they had back in his world.

He had helped her now in both time lines and in both worlds. It seemed clear that he was supposed to help repair all the timelines where he had only made changes in one.

As usual, Lexie had been right. The screamers, or the higher power that guided them, did not want the timelines to split. Tim knew he had a lot of work ahead of him.

The old man opened the door for the girl. She was about to get in but then stopped and looked back into the woods. Tim wondered what she was doing. Suddenly she looked almost directly at Tim's invisible form and spoke.

"Never give up!" she called toward the trees where he stood. "Nothing is impossible!"

She hadn't just spoken those words toward the empty woods, she had spoken to Tim. He knew it to be true. She got into the car and closed the door. As she was taken away safely, Tim thanked God for the reassurance this stranger had provided. "Never give up," she had said to him in both worlds. He would not give up. He would be with Lexie again. Nothing was impossible.

Chapter 43

TIME TO WAKE

Date: Unknown
Zone Date: Unknown

AS THAT ZONE faded out and the next began, Tim accepted the task of continuing to correct the discrepancies he had caused. He took comfort in knowing that the number was fixed and relatively small considering how many people he had tried to help. Usually, the screamers limited his ability to act when it would have been difficult or impossible to do the same in his world. It seemed that there must be thousands, or even millions of those freaky boy-like things watching and guiding history. But for what purpose? And for whose purpose?

Tim accepted that he too had a purpose. He was now helping those in Lexie's world that he had first helped in his. In many ways, it was easier than the other way around. He already knew the situations and the expected or intended results. He found that the screamers, when they did appear, already knew how he was going to act and so supported him.

In this way, he slid from zone to zone, never sleeping, eating, or meeting any of the body's normal needs. Tim decided that he must be dead. His body hadn't survived the plane crash, but his consciousness lived on in the zone. That was the only explanation he could think of as to why he no longer woke up. His entire existence was confined to the zone. He was in limbo.

Yet if that was true, why were his zones still limited to thirty-eight minutes? And what kind of afterlife was this? Why were there always so many questions? His whole life had been questions, and now it seemed that even in death, those questions continued.

Zone after zone, Tim set right where at first he had failed. He lost count after one hundred, thirty-eight minute zones. All back to back without a break. He estimated that he had reached two hundred by now. Maybe three hundred. Somehow, he kept going. He believed that Lexie was waiting for him to finish. She would not want him to give up. He would not give up.

Then, something happened. At the end of another thirty-eight minute zone, this time having rescued a child from a pit bull that had mistaken the boy for lunch, Tim opened his eyes and they hurt! He tried to focus and saw that he was lying on a bed, in a room filled with medical instruments, test tubes, and microscopes. He felt very sleepy and wasn't able to move. After only a few seconds, Tim slipped back into the zone.

Several zones later, it happened again. His eyes opened to the sight of that same medical laboratory. He had seen this room before, but his sluggish mind was not able to piece it together before he drifted back into the zone.

A few zones later, it occurred again. This time a voice accompanied the vision. It was a familiar fatherly voice yet one he could not put a name to.

"Wake up, my friend," the male voice said. "You have slept long enough."

Tim tried to respond but could not. He was too weak. He tried to look around to find the source of the voice, but too soon, the blackness circled in on him again. Once inside the zone, he found he was healthy and strong. His body did anything and everything it should. Yet it was becoming clear that in his world, his body was in very bad shape. But he was alive!

Tim closed his eyes to the zoned world and tried to recall the image of the lab he had seen and the voice he had heard. Here in the zone where his mind was sharp, the reality of where his body lay became clear. He needed to finish his job here and then force himself to stay conscious when he returned.

Tim stood up, ready to lock into the zone, and found himself in another very familiar setting. He was standing outside the Megadome in Billings.

"What day is this?" Tim thought as he ran up to a child that had just dropped her ticket. "September 22, 2026!" he read. "This is it!" he exclaimed.

Tim rushed into the stadium, not sure what he was looking for at first. Then he remembered that he already knew the possible outcomes. Here in this world, on this timeline, Jeffrey was on the verge of committing a terrible act of murder. Tim had been shown two possible outcomes: one where Jeffrey dies along with thousands of others, and one where, somehow, Jeffrey serves his time in prison and then goes on to live a new life.

In Tim's world, Jeffrey had turned his life around and become a successful pilot. That was a third line to the two that were possible here, but maybe there was still a way to merge that one as well? Could he somehow help this Jeffrey to become a pilot? No, Jeffrey was too far along at this point on his path for Tim to change such a major part of his life. Maybe that wasn't the point here. Thousands would die or not die, depending on Jeffrey's actions today. Tim had been brought here again to make it right. And whatever he was supposed to do had to happen right here in the next thirty-eight minutes.

Tim knew that Jeffrey needed to be arrested for his part in the stadium bombing if he was going to fulfill the future. But he needed to avoid a life sentence if he was to end up living happily with a new family. And if the Captain Jeffrey back in his world had somehow successfully completed Tim's plan, then to match that timeline, most of the people here had to be saved.

Ultimately, saving as many lives as he could had to be Tim's first priority. And hopefully, he would do it with Jeffrey's help. It was time to find Jeffrey Mitchell.

Tim scanned the crowd that was flowing into the concourses and filtering out toward the field. He realized that his search for Jeffrey was like that of a needle in a moving and churning haystack.

There were fathers and mothers buying nachos, hot dogs, and popcorn for their kids. Groups of men argued jubilantly over who would make the first big play of the game. Women, dressed in Billings Black and Green, laughed together. Kids ran excitedly from concourse shops with armfuls of souvenirs. They all moved quickly and with excitement.

Tim was astonished at the way baseball could still bring people together. Outside these walls, most people had withdrawn to their occipitals, where they communicated and watched the world around them through direct-to-brain constant input. Out there, they rarely bothered to interact with the people right next to them. Yet here, those marvels of modern technology were switched off and the excitement of real life reigned supreme.

A team of little league boys swarmed past with giant, green Capitalists foam fingers. One boy barely swerved fast enough to avoid the invisible Tim, almost tripping over his own feet as he shifted his direction. Everyone was on the move. All, that is, except for one man.

Tim could only see part of the man's large body as the crowd surged around him. He stood completely frozen in the middle of the concourse. When the crowd parted enough for Tim to get a better look, he realized that it was the same fat man that had pointed Jeffrey out to him the last time he had arrived at the stadium. Tim sprinted through the crowd. As he neared, the blank stare in the man's eyes made it clear that the screamers were once again using him to provide information.

For a moment, as the sea of fans moved and shifted, Tim lost sight of his target. "Where'd you go?" he asked.

Then he spotted him again farther up the concourse. "There you are, Fatso!" Tim laughed in relief. The man had somehow covered a lot of distance and had made it about two hundred yards ahead of Tim where the stadium curved. "Stay there!" Tim ordered as he ran again.

Finally reaching Fatso, Tim considered the situation. What were the screamers going to reveal through him this time? He continued to stare blankly past Tim. The stare and unnatural stance indicated that a screamer must be close by.

Tim looked around but didn't see anything unusual. Kids, parents, husbands, wives, girlfriends, boyfriends, and plain old friends continued to laugh. They moved freely and happily. None of them had any inkling that this entire stadium would begin to collapse shortly after the game began.

Tim looked at Fatso again. He had a round, jolly face, thin, straight, wispy hair, and wore the standard Billings green and black apparel, just like most in the crowd, though his apparel was several times larger. He held a hotdog carelessly in his right hand. It was loaded with mustard, ketchup, and relish, and seemed dangerously loose in his limp hand. Some of the mustard and relish was already seeping off the bun and onto his palm near the inside of his thumb.

Then, the hand lifted up as if pulled by a transparent wire. The motion caused the hot dog to slip completely out of Fats's hand. The meat struck Tim's foot, and the bun released the toppings onto Tim's toes before coming to rest between his feet.

Tim cared little about the mess on his skin. He knew he would wake up clean. He was only concerned about finding a way to stop the impending explosion.

"I need to find Jeffrey Mitchell," Tim said to the unhearing ears of Fats. "Can you help me find him like before? I need to stop the explosion." The man's arm continued to slowly rise up. Tim followed the motion with his eyes. At the end of the man's arm, his hand, covered in mustard, moved. His index finger raised as the others closed. He was pointing at something. Tim looked but saw nothing. "What is it?" Tim asked. The man did not respond. His stare remained blank and motionless, even as a passerby bumped into his outstretched pointed hand and arm.

Tim looked again in the direction of the pointed finger. He saw a vendor's booth, surrounded by kids, begging their parents for anything that lit up or made noise. Behind the booth were restrooms. Next to them were black and green drinking fountains with arcs of green tinted water.

A teenaged girl with green painted hair bumped into Fats's outstretched hand as she and a group of friends walked past. She recoiled from the blow as his hand struck her face and pushed up over her head. Her hand shot up to her face and hair, and she yelled in disgust to the girls next to her as they continued walking on. "Awwwg! Mustard! In my hair!" The girls laughed. None of them, including the mustard coated girl, thought to look back to see where the substance had come from.

After they passed, Tim took a step in the indicated direction toward the vendor booth. The crowd separated for him as usual. The man didn't move, his arm still out and finger pointing.

"You want me to buy you something?" Tim asked facetiously. He was frustrated by the unclear guidance. Then Tim's eyes caught movement behind the man. He saw the sudden turn and vanishing of a screamer. It had been standing there, out of sight.

With the screamer gone, the man suddenly dropped his arm, blinked and then shook his head as if to clear his thoughts. His gaze dropped to his empty hands and then to the hot dog and bun on the ground near his feet. He started to bend to pick it up but thought better of it and turned instead toward the nearest food stand. He stepped back into the flow of human traffic and licked the mustard off his hand, wondering why there had been a green hair in his mustard.

Tim looked back at the vendor cart. A little boy was pointing out a large color-changing foam hat to his dad. Behind the cart, an elderly woman worked her way out of the women's restroom and then stopped to get a drink of green water. After she slowly walked away, Tim saw the men's bathroom door inch open. A face peered out through the small opening and inspected the crowd behind Tim. When the door opened fully, a man in a green jersey and

Billings Capitalists ball cap slipped out. A black duffel bag hung from his shoulder.

The man's covert exit from the bathroom morphed into a nonchalant strut as he tried to merge into the crowd. At first, his hat concealed most of his face, but as he stepped past Tim, he lifted his head slightly to scan the crowd again.

Tim knew at once that it was Jeffrey. His face looked the same as the Jeffrey who piloted the jet back in his world, only paler. How long ago had that day on the plane been? Tim was no longer sure. His zones had been back to back for so long that it seemed impossible to guess how much time had actually passed in his world.

Tim supposed that it didn't matter. The Jeffrey that had heroically flown the doomed plane away from Boston and this Jeffrey were not the same man. This Jeffrey wasn't the innocent boy he had saved, or the Jeffrey at the mall who had caught the falling boy. This was a Jeffrey who had let hatred build in his mind. Hatred and loathing that had festered and grown for so long that he was willing to destroy many thousands of lives. Abhorrence so strong that it was enough to create two alternate futures. But which future would manifest today?

Tim looked at Jeffrey's face as he scanned the crowd. He didn't have a crazed, angry look, or the look of determined action. Instead, he seemed to be afraid.

"J, what are you doing?" a voice called from behind Tim. Tim spun around and saw another man in a Capitalists Jersey walking quickly up to Jeffrey.

"I'm just not sure this is the best way, K," Jeffrey responded, looking directly through Tim to the man called "K."

"This is the only way, J. We're in this now. If we don't go through with it, they'll kill us."

Tim listened. He realized now that he had been right about Jeffrey. He had made many mistakes in his life to bring him to this point in time, but he was not evil. He was being forced into these actions.

Jeffrey turned away from K and looked at a father and mother guiding a stroller across the smooth synthetic tile. They smiled at each other and made cooing faces toward their baby. Behind them, Fatso had a new hot dog and was happily taking his first bite.

"You listening to me, J?" K stopped his forceful whisper and looked around before continuing. He stepped around Tim and said to Jeffrey in a softer voice, "You plant them all? Put them where they told us?"

Jeffrey glanced at K sheepishly and then down at the black duffel bag.

"No way! They're still all in there?" K unzipped the bag a little and quickly counted six devices. "You didn't plant any of them? What were you doing this whole time?"

Jeffrey said nothing at first. He absently wiped at his mouth. He had spent the last forty-five minutes in the restroom throwing up. His insides felt like they had been turned upside down.

"I changed my mind," Jeffrey finally said. "I can't do it."

"Too late, J. It's done. I did my job. My six are placed. My side of the stadium is coming down! I just hope you didn't screw it up. They said we had to plant them all. So if this place doesn't come down completely, it's on you, not me."

Jeffrey said nothing. K looked up to see if anyone had been listening to them. Subconsciously, he wiped sweat from his forehead. No one seemed to be paying them any attention. "C'mon, let's roll," he said grabbing onto the strap of Jeffrey's duffle and giving him a slight pull.

Jeffrey followed K. Tim followed Jeffrey.

This wasn't a Jeffrey halfway between good and evil like the twelve year-old boy that Tim had seen trying to shoplift. But this wasn't a Jeffrey who wanted to kill either. Someone had tapped into Jeffrey's anger and pushed him in this direction. He had let his revulsion for the world build inside like the bombs that he had helped put together. But now that the time had come, could Jeffrey be turned from this path? He seemed to be following orders from K right now. K needed to be out of the picture, Tim thought.

As the two men and Tim headed for the east exit, they came upon a security guard. He stood tall with his broad shoulders back as he eyed a pretty brunette in a short skirt. The men lowered their hats and quickened their pace, hoping the guard's attention remained on the woman.

Tim had an idea. He ran up along side of K. Then, just as they passed the guard, Tim pushed K as hard as he could into the guard's solid chest.

"Hey!" the guard yelled, forgetting the brunette. "Is there a problem here?" K's eyes were big. He was unsure what had just happened. He stared blankly at the guard's chest where he had just landed. A badge was clipped to the uniform. It read, "Bruce."

"Uh, just, uh, t . . . tripped," K stuttered. He looked up at the guard's face, still in shock. Jeffrey walked on but slowed. He was just as surprised as K had been, and was glad he hadn't run into the behemoth named Bruce.

As Bruce looked into K's face and K stared back, Tim grabbed K's fist and launched it forcefully at Bruce's face. The thrown punch was awkward and slow since K subconsciously resisted Tim's action, but the effect was successful. Bruce caught K's fist with his hand and immediately locked his arms around K.

"Guess we do have a problem," Bruce smirked, glancing back toward the brunette, hoping she had seen him in action. K struggled to get free, but his strength was nothing compared with Bruce.

The brunette, startled by the commotion, had turned and now rewarded Bruce with a sultry smile. Bruce nodded confidently at her and then dragged K off toward the security office.

Jeffrey stood in shock as K was taken for questioning. He stepped backward against a tall, white steel pillar, unsure of what to do next.

He took a step forward, then changed his mind again and slunk back against the pillar. "What do I do, what do I do?" he murmured to himself. "K's caught. Gotta get out. Gotta run," he convinced himself. After all, the stadium was set to explode a little after the game began.

As Jeffrey stepped out again and turned toward the exit, Tim leapt out in front of him. Jeffrey tried to veer right to avoid the obstacle, but Tim moved again to block his way. Jeffrey turned the other way and tripped over something small at his feet, causing him to stumble.

When Jeffrey looked, he saw a little girl with blonde curls, sitting next to his feet, crying. She was alone and looked only four or five years old. "Out of my way!" Jeffrey snapped harshly. The girl cried harder. He looked around and thought about the situation. He had to get out. K was caught, but only half of the bombs that he had built were placed. Maybe the destruction wouldn't be too bad. Maybe only half the stadium would collapse.

No, he thought. He knew he was kidding himself, trying to appease his guilty conscience. The stadium was doomed. Even if it didn't completely collapse as planned, the destruction would be colossal. And if he didn't get out soon, he would die along with all these people, including the stupid little crying girl.

But even if he did get out alive, if the stadium didn't come down as planned, *they* would kill him for his failure. He had failed his mission. He had frozen when the time came to place his set of explosives. Worse than frozen, he had hid out in the bathroom!

Jeffrey's hands were digging at his scalp. His inner turmoil was evident. He thought he was going to throw up again. The girl was still crying at his feet, sitting on the floor with her arms around her legs.

"Shut your mouth!" Jeffrey screamed. He hadn't meant to yell at her. He hadn't meant to do any of this. He was scared. What would *they* do to him if he failed this mission?

At first the Order had welcomed him into their anarchist organization. He was young and longed for the acceptance of a family. The Order offered that. He was bothered at first by their rationalization for retribution and revenge against perceived injustices, but soon, he accepted it as part of the price to fit in.

Over time, the ideas and philosophies had started to make sense. It wasn't his fault that he had been alone all those years. It wasn't his fault that he needed drugs to be happy. It wasn't his fault that to pay for the drugs, he needed to become a petty criminal and end up in juvie for seven months.

It was the fault of the system; the system governed by money and greed. It was the fault of the rich capitalists of the world. The Order had taught him that. And this was his chance to prove his worth. What better target to make such a point as to bring down the beloved Billings Capitalists.

At first, the Order had just asked him to build the bombs for them to use against an undisclosed target. He wasn't going to have to actually kill anyone. But then they charged him with the task itself. He balked at first, but they convinced him that it would make up for all the pain in his life. And if he didn't go through with it, his death would be the price.

Yet this little girl had nothing to do with his problems, he thought as he looked down at the child's pretty curls. How could he have gotten into this so deeply? How many children like this one would die today?

Jeffrey temporarily postponed his plan to escape. Saving his own messed up life seemed less important for the moment. Instead, he looked around in search of the girl's parents. If he was about to cause the death of this little girl, he would at least get her back with her family first.

Tim, who had been watching the turbulence in Jeffrey's emotions, suddenly saw something in his eyes that reminded him of the little boy he had first met so long ago. Jeffrey still had a chance, he thought.

Looking around, Jeffrey saw fathers carrying their children through the fast moving crowd and mothers holding onto their kids, trying not to get separated in the river of jubilant people. But none seemed to be searching for a lost child.

Then Tim spotted a woman in her early thirties, scanning the crowd about a hundred yards down the wide curving corridor. She cupped her hands around her mouth in the shape of a megaphone. She called out over and over again. Over the noise of the lively crowd, Tim couldn't hear her calls but recognized the look of panic in her eyes. She was the girl's mother.

Tim grabbed Jeffrey's shoulders and forced him to turn in the direction of the searching mother. The confusion caused by Tim's touch faded instantly when Jeffrey saw her.

The mother stood in the opposite direction that Jeffrey needed to go. He was torn again, this time between helping the girl and getting himself out. But recommitting himself to the task, Jeffrey grabbed the girl's hand.

"I am sorry I yelled at you. Is that your mother over there?" he asked gently. She looked in the direction Jeffrey was pointing but could not see over the crowd.

Jeffrey lifted her up onto his shoulders and pointed out the woman again.

"Momma!" she cried out with joy, her fear gone the moment she saw her mother calling out for her.

Jeffrey fought through the crowd toward the girl's mom. "Prisha!" the mother exclaimed, seeing her daughter and reaching out for her child with tears of relief.

"Momma!" the girl cried back. "This nice man yelled at me! And I was crying and crying. But then he picked me up and helped me!" she reported with innocent truthfulness.

Jeffrey tried to smile as he passed the girl off to her mother, pleased with the reunion that he had been able to ensure. Then, on instinct, he warned, "Ma'am, you need to get your daughter out of here."

"What?" the mom asked, not sure of what he had said as she snuggled her baby in her tight embrace.

"Something very bad is going to happen here," he warned.

The mother couldn't imagine anything worse than the fear that she had just recovered from. She gave Jeffrey an odd look and simply said, "Thank you," and stepped into the flow of people heading for their seats.

Chapter 44

RECONNECTING HISTORY

JEFFREY WATCHED HER go. The girl and her mother were still going to die, but at least they'd be together. That was more than he had ever had. His family had been taken from him. He couldn't even remember what they looked like or even their names. All he knew was that his mom was dead and his dad was either in jail or dead, too.

Thinking of himself again, he made up his decision to run. The transition in Jeffrey's demeanor as his focus changed from the girl back to himself was apparent to Tim. And letting Jeffrey run to save himself was not part of the plan.

As soon as Jeffrey picked his direction and tried to get into the flow of the crowd, Tim leapt in front of him and locked his arm out straight against Jeffrey's chest. "Where do you think you're going?" Tim yelled. Jeffrey seemed confused by the invisible barricade that had just blocked his path and he tried to run again. Tim stiff-armed him a second time.

Jeffrey stood stunned and then felt his body being pushed backward. He turned to flee but slammed into a vendor cart. Recoiling from the cart, Jeffrey once again was met with Tim's force, this time from his fist. Tim knew there was no time for gentle persuasion.

"Who are you?" Jeffrey screamed. A couple of twelve-year-old boys with corn dogs looked at him but then walked away, unconcerned about the crazy man.

"Who am I? Who are you?" Tim responded even though he was certain that Jeffrey could not hear him. "Are you really a killer? Or are you a hero? I've seen two versions of you, so I know you are capable of either. I saw the look in your eyes, Jeffrey, when you brought that mother and daughter back together. You know what is right. You can feel it. You are meant to be a hero."

Jeffrey remained still as Tim held him back against the cart. Tim knew that this wasn't the same Jeffrey who had caught the baby. Instead, this was the one who had been caught lifting games from the store. This was also the Jeffrey who would be thrown into solitary confinement sometime in the near future, after breaking Smith's arm in the prison yard.

Once again, it seemed to Tim that the future was already written. But that future for this man also included redemption. For it would be that while in that confinement, Jeffrey would wrestle with and then defeat the demons within. He would serve his time and have a new chance at life.

"You are going to jail, Jeffrey," Tim said more quietly, deciding what he was going to do. "You are going to jail, but not because you killed thousands. I've already seen that future and it is not the one for you."

Jeffrey looked as if he was listening, but Tim knew that it was more of a subconscious consideration of the words Tim was laying on him. Still, it seemed that somehow, he was getting through to him.

Then something happened, something that had never happened before. Tim felt a current shoot through his body, down his arm, and into Jeffrey's body. It was as if his stiff arm against Jeffrey's chest was completing an electrical circuit. Jeffrey felt it too, and his eyes opened round and large.

Tim had been staring intently into Jeffrey's eyes, and at the moment of the sensation, he believed he saw an image reflected from inside the eyes. The image moved and seemed to drift like a window into a dream.

A small toddler aged boy is playing in his yard in front of a sprawling home with white pillars. His mom and dad watch from decorative chairs on the large front porch. Then a sporty BMW pulls up at the house next door, and a very attractive young woman steps out and waves. The dad smiles and waves back and then watches as the woman glides, like a model on a catwalk, from her car to the front door. She looks back and smiles at him again as she enters the large home next door.

Tim jumped back, severing the connection that seemed to start the vision. The woman had been Natalie and the house she had entered had been his own before he left her. He remembered the family, too. The dad's name was Steven. He was a successful and good-natured surgeon who had worked hard to put himself through school. He knew the wife, too. Her name was Melinda, he remembered. She had a difficult pregnancy but in the end, delivered a healthy baby boy. Tim leaned in again, with his head close to Jeffrey, and put his hand onto his shoulder. The vision continued.

A young man, Tim, gets into his beat up Ford truck and drives away. Steven is peering out from his window. Then the scene shifts and the surgeon is now being guided through Tim's front door by a seductively smiling Natalie. She closes the door and the scene shifts again.

The boy, Tim realizes, is a baby version of Jeffrey. He cries from his crib as his mom and dad fight outside his room. Melinda knows of the affair and wants a divorce.

Another shift, and Tim sees Natalie embracing the surgeon in the bedroom that Tim had once shared with her. The arrangement of furniture makes it clear that this is after Tim had left her. Steven is crying now, his face buried against Natalie's naked chest. As she strokes his hair and comforts him, she is looking past him with a grin.

The vision floats back into the surgeon's home next door. Some more time has passed. Blood stains cover the floor of the hallway and bathroom. Police are there snapping pictures and collecting evidence as Jeffrey's mother's body lies motionless against a wall. Outside, Steven is forced into a squad car, his wrists fastened together by steel hand cuffs. The small boy is being whisked away by a social worker. He is on his way to his first of many foster homes.

A shift in vision at the same moment displays Natalie smashing a vase to the floor in the home in which Tim had allowed her to stay. Somehow, Tim knows that the botched murder was part of a plan concocted by Natalie to acquire the surgeon's riches for herself. But something has gone wrong. Now, the surgeon is going to jail for the rest of his life, she is out of money, and no longer has any way to continue funding the lifestyle to which she had become accustomed.

Tim felt a jolt of energy pulse through him again and for the first time, he became aware that it was a screamer that stood between him and Jeffrey creating the connection. A second joint pulled Tim back into a new vision.

Blood pours down the stairs of the Billings Metrodome. The stench of charred flesh and smoke fill Tim's mind. This is the vision of devastation that Tim witnessed, just before his night under the stars with Lexie. And this time, the vision is coming from Tim and passing to Jeffrey.

Jeffrey observes the vision of the stadium collapse. He sees his own face of despair as he holds the dead girl, Prisha, across his lap, her curls wet with blood. Then, he witnesses his own death as the concrete beam falls from above.

The vision ended and Tim saw the screamer step away, turn, and disappear. Tim looked back into Jeffrey's eyes. Jeffrey was stunned and unmoving.

"Jeffrey, can you hear me?"

Jeffrey did not respond.

"Somehow, I think you can hear me. You just saw a vision of your past and then of your future. What's past is past, but the future can be changed. That future that you saw will happen if we don't change it right now."

Tim waited for a moment but there was still no recognition of acknowledgement from Jeffrey. Tim knew there was no time to waste. He grabbed Jeffrey's jersey and pulled him back in the direction of the security office. Jeffrey didn't protest.

When the two arrived at the office entrance, a short, stern policewoman stopped Jeffrey. She looked at him, questioning the strange posture caused by the way Tim pulled at his shirt.

"You need to move along sir," she said to Jeffrey dismissively.

Suddenly, Jeffrey seemed to come alive again and pulled the invisible hand from his shirt and turned toward Tim. "I understand," he said in Tim's direction. Was he speaking to Tim or to the woman? She thought he was speaking to her and responded, "Ok, glad you get it, now move out."

"No," he said, turning now directly to her. "I saw the future. I saw what I did."

"What you've . . . ," she started but then stopped in confusion.

"I will not let that happen," he said, ignoring her now.

Jeffrey pushed passed her and marched into the office where Bruce was still questioning K.

K looked up in horror at his partner, but Jeffrey looked only at Bruce and then back at the woman. Jeffrey was ready to stand.

Three minutes later, Jeffrey and K were being escorted out of the stadium in handcuffs. As they walked ahead of Bruce, the public address system came to life.

"Attention, attention," a loud burst of sound flooded the stadium. "This is an emergency announcement," the voice said. "All guests are ordered to exit the stadium at once. Repeating, this is an emergency announcement. All guests are ordered . . ."

Tim saw the crowds stiffen and stop moving as their jubilant conversations and banter were replaced by questioning glances. Slowly, the crowds began moving again, obeying the order to evacuate.

"It worked!" Tim shouted to Jeffrey. Tim knew Jeffrey would go to jail for his part in the plot, but now, due to his heroic change of heart, his path would hopefully lead to the redemption Tim had seen in Jeffrey's future. He and K exited the stadium with Bruce and were met by a police wagon.

As the doors to the wagon closed behind Jeffrey, Tim caught a conversation between two of the arresting officers.

"You're kidding!" one said. "There was no one on board?"

"Just the pilot," the other officer said. "And he jumped out just before the explosion, parachuted down. Pretty badly hurt according to the news light. But he will be okay. Says he doesn't remember anything. Doesn't remember ordering the plane's evacuation or taking off in time to get the bomb away from the city."

"Weird. What's going on today?" the other replied, shaking his head.

"Don't know. Guess this place would have gone up like that plane if this guy hadn't spilled his guts."

"Guess that makes him a hero, eh?"

"Maybe, though I bet he still does time. You can't plot something like that and just expect an 'I'm sorry' to get ya off the hook. Seemed kinda messed up too. Not sure why he spilled, but glad he did!"

"You and me, both, man. Glad I get to go home today. Could have been a lot different, you know! Makes you appreciate . . ."

Tim smiled. More of his own path was suddenly becoming clear to him. He guessed where he would be heading next as the colors of the stadium faded, and the sounds of the officers' reflection on life slipped from his ears. As the light came back, he found himself exactly where he suspected.

The Boeing 737 slowed and then stopped at the head of the runway. Inside, all the familiar passengers were seated quietly. The crew was the same, too. Only the captain would be a different person, since here in Lexie's world, Jeffrey had not become a pilot.

Lightning flashed all around the plane and the speakers above the aisle chirped as the captain's voice ordered the passengers to deplane. Tim laughed as the pilot seemed unable to come up with a good reason for his unusual order. He stammered slightly and then simply said, "Exit now . . . because . . . well, because I'm the captain and I said so."

A screamer, just one, looked up from the captain in the cockpit as Tim entered. It then turned back to the captain and continued to guide his actions. The captain got up and ushered out the final confused passengers and flight assistants. Then, once the plane was clear, he closed and locked the cabin doors before returning to the cockpit.

Moments later as the plane sped along the runway, the tower screamed at the captain to return to the gate. He did not respond, and the plane lifted off into the storm.

Tim knew what came next and prepared himself for the impending explosion. He knew that whatever condition his body was in, back in his world, it was safe. He pulled a parachute out for the pilot and set it onto his lap. Still unaware of his actions, the pilot pulled the chute onto his back and opened the emergency hatch. He jumped, and the screamer glanced at Tim before disappearing, leaving Tim alone on the doomed flight.

Tim wondered what the pilot must have thought as he suddenly became aware that he was falling from the plane above him. Would he pull the chute immediately? Or would it take him some time to register his situation? Why had the screamer acknowledged Tim's presence before leaving? Had he detected a tiny hint of approval by the screamer?

Tim wasn't sure why he had been brought to this event again. Had he only been here to help the pilot get off the plane safely before the explosion? Maybe the screamers had just wanted him to see the outcome, to see that they now agreed that no one had to die on the doomed flight. They had guided the event to match the outcome he had caused in his world. Only, in that world, the pilot had been Jeffrey. This pilot was someone else, since at that same moment, the Jeffrey of this world was explaining to the security guards and police that six bombs he had built were set to explode all around the stadium.

Tim's thoughts were interrupted as the explosion tore through the underside and rear of the plane. He closed his eyes, and the zone was finally over.

Chapter 45

AWAKE

February 17, 2029

WHEN TIM AWOKE, he recognized a change immediately. "Ohhh!" Tim groaned. Not only did his eyes hurt, but also his entire body screamed out in pain as he tried to move. Sunlight was pouring in from a window somewhere outside the peripheral of his blurry vision. Tim squinted.

"Hold still, my friend," the familiar voice said near him. It was a man's voice. A voice he had known since he was eighteen. Then Tim heard the hum of automatic blinds stretching slowly over the light source.

The room dimmed and Tim opened his eyes again. He was wearing a clean hospital gown. Medical instruments were neatly placed on a tray that could be moved along the length of his body. The room had a distinctive medical smell, but he was certain that he was not in a hospital.

"Doc?" Tim tried to say through tight, dry, and scratchy vocal cords. Forming the word with his mouth seemed to take extraordinary concentration.

"Yes, it's me. But don't try to speak yet, Tim. I'm here with you, as I have been for the last twenty-nine months."

"That's . . . ," Tim tried to clear the fog in his head, "that's over two years."

"Yes, Tim. You have been in a coma. Yet as is common with you, it seems your coma was nothing like any I have ever witnessed." Dr. Bruin lifted the sleeve of Tim's gown and held up a pressurized syringe. "Sorry, Tim, this will sting for a sec."

Tim instinctively tried to pull back from the needle but could not move. "I can't move," he said surprised. "It hurts."

"Hush," Doc responded gently. He finished the injection and took Tim's pulse on his wrist. "You have barely moved in all these months," he responded to Tim. "Your muscles have partial atrophy. I kept your body nourished, but your brain has hogged most of your energy. You still have plenty of healing to do, but you'll be okay."

"What happened, Doc? Was it the crash?" Tim thought first of the crash he had just experienced in his zone, but then remembered that he had been in an actual crash with Jeffrey after he threw the bomb out of the plane. Could that have really been almost two-and-a-half years ago? Had he really zoned to almost nine hundred moments in time to repair the split lines?

"Yes," Doc answered him, "and what a crash it was! But don't worry about that yet. I am taking care of you. Now that I have finally woken you up today, I need to make sure we keep you awake for a while. You have slept long enough."

True to his word, Doc continued to care for Tim in his private laboratory at his home. He had retired from his practice in Tulsa in 2024 but had continued his research into the human mind. When he brought Tim's unconscious body to his lab in September 2026, his primary attention had been focused on nursing his young friend back to health. But Doc had also used his personalized home lab to delve deeper into the human mind than had ever been achieved before.

Over the next few months, Tim gained his strength back and only slipped back into his apparent coma at the expected time of 11:35 p.m. Doc continued monitoring Tim's slides into Lexie's world at night, and during the day, he filled Tim in on the events of the past two years.

"The group, now known as the Order," Doc told Tim, "had recruited many young men and women to see the new world capitalist movement as the cause of pain and suffering across the globe."

Tim listened as he lifted his leg up and down, trying to learn to use the rebuilt femur and mechanical hip that Doc had inserted during his coma. "What about Jeffrey?" he asked.

"Jeffrey Mitchell," Doc reported to Tim, "used his last moments flying that plane of yours to report that other bombs like the one on his plane had been delivered and placed at the Billings Metrodome. His credentials as one of the top captains for Uniworld Airlines had earned him enough respect to be taken seriously. His authoritative warning started the complete evacuation of the stadium only minutes before the explosions began. Thanks to you and Captain Mitchell, not a single life was lost from the stadium."

"But what about Jeffrey? Did he survive the crash?" Tim asked again.

"The bomb that you ejected from the plane over the uninhabited mountains exploded, sending a massive shock wave outward in all directions. That bomb was one of the most powerful anyone has seen since the nuclear age ended fifteen years ago. It wasn't meant to just kill the passengers on the plane. It was designed to take out most of a large city. Had it detonated anywhere near civilization, massive casualties would have been sustained."

Tim had stopped moving his leg up and down as he listened. Doc grabbed his foot and pulled on it, reminding Tim to keep working. "Your plane," he continued, "sustained fatal damage from the shock wave. But Jeffrey was able to guide the plane down the mountain slope and into a field. He had refused to parachute out, knowing that you were still in the back hanging on for your life. He was badly injured when the cockpit tore into the trees and field, but he remained conscious, unlike you, my sleepy friend."

Doc laughed and then continued, "From his recovery room, he reported that a heroic man had learned of the bomb and pretended to be a marshal in order to get the passengers off the plane. He also said that the same man had warned him of the stadium threat.

He was pushed hard by media and the FBI to reveal your identity. But Jeffrey protected you. He refused to name or describe you to anyone.

"Finally, after being released from the hospital, Jeffrey made a statement to journalists, 'We can all be heroes,' he preached. 'All it takes is a heart to serve. The man who saved so many that day has such a heart. That is the only description of him that is needed.'"

Tim thought for a moment. "I never asked him to protect my identity."

"You didn't have to. I think someone or something else guided his decision to protect you."

"The screamers?" Tim asked.

"That's my theory. For whatever reason, your identity continues to remain anonymous. Think about it. You bought a plane ticket in your name, yet no airline officials could find your name in their system. You had to be life-flighted back to Boston, from the crash site. Emergency crews pulled you out of the wreckage. Doctors and nurses saw your injuries and should have related them back to the crash. But none of them said anything.

"I was called a couple of days after your crash by one of my old colleagues who had remembered my work on brain injuries. When I asked what had happened to you, he said he didn't know. Said no one could even remember when you were brought in. Even your computer records were missing."

"Someone deleted them?"

"No, it seems that someone just forgot to put them into the system. No one made the connection between you and the crash. You still have a purpose in these parallel worlds, Tim. And I feel honored to be part of it."

Tim returned to his home in Oklahoma a few weeks later. He was anxious to get back and make sure that the old place didn't deteriorate like it had before he fixed it up. Doc agreed that he could finish healing just as well from home, as long as he continued to work on his exercises and checked back in often.

Once settled in at home, Tim's zones again took him to Lexie as well. At first his visits with her were somewhat random in time again, as if the two timelines had separated and were now slowly being relinked. However, despite the randomness, all of his zones occurred at dates in her line after September 22, 2026. Apparently, those events prior to that date were now set and unchangeable.

Over time, Tim's time line and Lexie's reconnected as they had before. His visits to her matched to within only a few days from his own time.

Tim understood now that the time away from Lexie had been even harder on her than it had been for him. The Lexie he met in her late 50s and early 60s was not the same as she had been before his long absence from her life. Jack had ruthlessly beaten and abused her before his death. And without Tim's visits to replenish her, the depression inside Lexie took over and her will to live faded.

Though Tim was back in her life now, the harm was done. Their love was still strong, but lacked the carefree abandon that had characterized their younger encounters. Even his invisible attempts to encourage strangers living nearby to check in on her and fix up the house did little to reverse the physical damage caused by the beatings and depression.

Shortly after Lexie's sixty-fifth birthday, almost immediately after Tim's young self met her on her front porch, she suffered a powerful stroke. It had been the day she explained so much to him about his future, and the day that she had said would be their last together.

One of the good Samaritans that Tim had guided to her home to keep watch over her discovered Lexie in that small back bedroom. She was found clutching an old photograph of a boy and girl sitting on a log. Lexie had cherished that picture all her life.

The Samaritan paid for her care at the local assisted rehabilitation facility. But from that day onward, when Tim arrived at her home, Lexie was gone.

Chapter 46

LEXIE'S DEATH

June 9, 2042
Zone: June 9, 2042

TWO YEARS PASSED since Lexie's stroke. Bright lights shimmered over Tim as he came out of the darkness and into his zone. He stood up and shielded his eyes. As they adjusted to the brightness, he heard screaming. Not screams of terror, but of infants. He heard adult voices calmly talking, speaking of procedures. One voice, that of a woman, softly said, "So beautiful, they are so beautiful."

His eyes adjusted to the light, and he realized that he was in a hospital delivery room. The mother had just given birth to quadruplets. She lay back sleepily on a bed. The dad sat in a white carbon poly plastic chair next to the window. It was dark outside. The four baby boys were each being placed into transparent rounded rectangular capsules by RONs, roving automated nurses. As the lids were closed, muffling the infants' wailing, steam, or what appeared to be some kind of vapor, filled the boxes. The babies stopped wailing and moving.

Tim watched the procedure, staying out of the way of the busily buzzing RONs. The human nurses all wore matching white smocks and had their hair neatly pulled back by white ribbons braided uniformly into their long hair. There didn't appear to be any doctor in the room, but doctors were not needed for such a standard procedure as birth.

"DC and C procedure complete," a nurse in a white smock said happily. All four capsules opened at once and Tim saw that the babies were clean and happy. The one nearest him cooed softly as he tried looking at his own fingers.

"Your babies," the nurse went on as she began handing them over to other nurses, "are decontaminated, clean, and calm."

Tim stood back out of the way and watched as the mother and father took the four children into their arms. They looked like good parents and he decided he must be here for another purpose.

Tim was seventy years old now. It didn't take him long to size up a situation and determine if he was where he needed to be. He had been an unseen angel in this world for almost fifty years. Countless lives had been saved, thousands of children guided toward better futures, terrifying situations calmed and led toward a better outcome.

The screamers continued to allow Tim to make changes in this world as long as he could make those same changes in his world. They also continued to somehow enter people's minds and block their ability to identify the helpful stranger.

It was strange to work with the silent, expressionless screamers, of which he still understood so little. But he learned to read them and understand when to help a situation and when to back off. As hard as it was to accept, occasionally, a person was not meant to be saved. For the good of the timeline, Tim would be forced to watch as a person's own actions lead to their destruction or even death.

This had been the case for a man that Tim had come across in 2030. In Tim's world, the man lived alone in a run down house in Brenham, Texas. That same man, in the zoned world, lived with and abused the woman Tim loved. In both worlds, Tim was unable to stop Jack from drinking himself to death. Tim tried to stop him before he got into his truck on December 25, 2030. He tried to stop him before he entered the exit ramp going the wrong way on highway 290 out of Brenham, TX. He tried to warn the oncoming fuel tanker about the small truck with the intoxicated driver approaching on the wrong side of the divided highway. The driver was able to save his own life as he avoided a head-on collision, but caused the rear of the tanker to jackknife around the cab. The eight thousand gallon tank struck Jack's pickup with such force that Jack was already dead by the time the explosion of liquid fuel reached his body.

Tim understood that death was a necessary part of both worlds. So at this hospital, he wondered, was he there to help someone live or to watch someone die. Would he be able to guide a doctor toward a solution? Would he find someone who he could save from a terrible accident back in his world? What would happen in the remaining thirty-three minutes of this zone that had caused him to be pulled into this place at this moment of time?

Tim wandered down the corridor away from the nursery. He passed patients, nurses, and a few doctors. Doctors were more of a rarity now as technology had allowed most patients to be diagnosed and treated by skilled technicians. It was cheaper to teach men and women to push buttons on scanners and read outputs from biometric displays than to train doctors.

Tim passed into the neurology outpatient wing. There he heard a familiar voice call out his name.

"Mr. Caston," an old voice hummed wisely. "You have returned."

"Doc," Tim said aloud as he turned and saw Dr. Bruin sitting in a silver rover chair next to the entrance. "I haven't seen you in TL2 since 2032."

"I don't know why you and my counterpart insist on calling this world Time Line 2. Seems to me that this is TL1. But yes, it has been ten years. I guess others needed you more than I did. So whoever or whatever guides your shift transfer didn't bring you to me. Still, it's good to see you again, so to speak, my young friend."

Dr. Bruin had never been able to sense Tim as well as Lexie could, but since losing his eyesight twelve years earlier, he found his other senses were able to key in on Tim's presence. Tim had found in his travels that other blind people had sensed something too.

Sometimes even asking, "Who is here?" but never able to actually hear Tim. They would usually just assume their minds were playing tricks on them. Doc's ability to sense Tim was an anomaly, just like Lexie and Andrew. Even his own parents in this world had been unaware of him.

"Young friend?" Tim responded. "Not so young, anymore. I turned seventy last month."

"You are as young as you feel. I'm still feeling pretty good for a man 117 years into my timeline," he sighed and then finished as he rolled his eyes, "TL2. How is old saggy bottom doing in your line?"

"Good. He's doing good. It seems that your neurologic age therapy is working wonders for you both!"

"Shhh, I'm close to getting it approved for human tests but not technically supposed to have already been testing it on myself." Bruin smiled, realizing it made no sense to 'shush' Tim since no one could hear him anyway.

"I assume my counterpart would be seventy years old here also, if he was still alive. It is 2042, correct?" Even without his visits to Lexie, Tim's slides into this world had remained consistent related to time.

"Yes, it's June 9, 2042."

"June 9?" Tim asked. "That's the same day from which I just left!"

"That's not all. Have you checked the time?"

Tim looked at the wall for a holoclock and spotted one just above Bruin's head.

"11:42 p.m.? I've been here for about . . ."

"Seven minutes," Bruin cut him off.

"How did . . ."

"It's because of your anchor," Bruin said wisely.

"I don't understand."

"Tim, listen, there isn't much time. As great as it is to see you again, someone else is here that needs you even more, someone who misses you greatly. She is the reason I dragged myself out of the lab and the reason you are here."

"Lexie!" Tim said surprised. "But I was not supposed to see her again. She told me that . . ."

"She told you that *you* reported not seeing her again after she was sixty-five. All that really means is that from this point forward, you will never talk to her again before this date. But Tim, you need to hurry. She is dying, and there is nothing I or anyone else here can do to stop that now." He lowered his blank eyes to the floor and shook his head sadly. Then, pointing to a room at the corner of the wing, he said, "Go to her, Tim. Say good-bye."

Lexie turned her head sideways to face Tim as he sat down next to her bed. "Oh," she breathed weakly. "I had a feeling when I woke up today, a feeling that you would come back." She was too weak to reach out to him so he put his arms around her frail body and then kissed her lightly. She was three years younger than him, yet her body seemed to have lived thirty more.

A nurse in the room looked at her. "Who are you talking to Ms. Alexis? I come back every hour. You know that." Lexie didn't acknowledge the nurse.

"Tim, listen. There isn't much time. I know I'm supposed to say that I'm thankful for everything I've had. I'm supposed to say that the time I've had with you was enough. But Tim, it wasn't enough. Not nearly enough." She closed her eyes and seemed to be trying to catch her breath.

"I was supposed to live happily ever after, Tim. I believed that somehow my life would change. When you started showing up, I thought that was the answer. I thought I could live for those moments. But it wasn't enough.

"You should have come to find me when I was still young. You should have saved me from the pain, from the loneliness. You save everyone else, but you never really saved me." She stopped to breathe again. Tim could see that speaking was difficult for her.

"Shhh, rest Lexie."

"I will not 'Shhh'," she said with as much force as she could muster. "Tim, I love you and I am glad you are here with me, but shut it." Tim smiled at Lexie apologetically.

The nurse left the room and commented to someone in the hall that old lady Alexis had gone delusional. Tim and Lexie didn't hear or care about the nurse's confused assessment.

"I thought it was enough to be with you every few weeks or months," Lexie went on. "Even better, when you'd show up every other day or so. But sometimes, it was years. And so I spent my whole life waiting, waiting for someone who could never stay."

"I don't know what to say," Tim whispered closely to her face.

"There is nothing you can say. It's what you can do. It's what you must do."

"What should I do, Lexie?"

"Save me, Tim. Just save me."

"I don't understand what to do."

"Find a way. You will find a way. You will. I can feel it. I'm here in this timeline without you. In your line, you are without me. Somehow, you will wipe this timeline out, change it, merge it, and you and I will be together, together for real."

"What about all the people I've helped? I can't turn my back on them."

"You won't. You will save me, and still be able to save them, too. Only this time, you will do it with me by your side. You will find a way, Tim," her voice trailed off again and her eyes closed. Her breathing was shallow. She was exhausted but forced herself to go on.

"You asked me once . . . ," she breathed again. "What did I ask your Magic 8 Ball when I snuck into your room that night I was going to kill myself. You asked what answer had made me smile though all my tears."

"I remember," Tim whispered, matching the weakness of her voice. "You sat there, wet and cold from the rain outside, on the end of my bed. I wanted to hold you and comfort you but I was so afraid you would leave if I said anything. So I just stayed near you.

"I had tried the ball before you arrived but it didn't work. I thought it was broken, so I had thrown it down onto the bed. But when you used it, it seemed to give you hope. I think it told you something that kept you from leaving."

Lexie smiled. The pain and exhaustion she was feeling seemed to abate, at least for the moment. "*You* kept me from leaving. I could feel you there. The warmth of something better than just heat filled that room. It was because of you that I stayed.

"The ball didn't work for you because you aren't part of this world. It wasn't meant for you. But you are right that it gave me hope."

"What did you ask, Lexie?"

"I asked if God wanted me to live. Then I asked if it was worth it to live. Finally, I asked if God would let me live happily ever after."

Tim smiled, remembering how often she had wished to live happily every after while they were kids. "What did it say?" he asked.

"Did you know that there are twenty possible answers the ball can give? The odds of any one answer are only 5 percent. Getting that answer twice in a row is ¼ of a percent. But three times in a row? That's pretty much impossible!"

Tim smiled. Here she was on her death bed, and still her mind was actively calculating mathematical odds.

"There are only three or four true 'yes' answers," she went on. "The rest leave doubt or are 'no's'. Tim, the answer to all three of my questions was, 'It is Certain!'" Her tone was excited, but her voice and breath were weakening further.

"Do you understand what that means?" she pleaded.

Tim shook his head, desperately wanting to understand why this was so important to her. Why would she use her last breaths talking about his Magic 8 Ball?

"Tim, it means, you *will* save me." Her eyes closed again as she seemed to reach inside herself for just a bit more strength to speak. Then, she continued again with her eyes still closed. "All of this, everything around us, isn't the end. You will save me. You . . ." Lexie struggled for her next breath.

"Lexie?"

She opened her eyes again slowly. "You, Tim, you will find a way to save me." Her eyes closed again as if the weight of her lids was too much to bear.

"Lexie, don't leave me." Tim cupped his hands around her face. "I need you to help me figure this out. You have always been smarter than me. I can't find a way without you."

Lexie's eyes opened once again, and they suddenly seemed clearer than they had been in years. She looked right at Tim. Her face suddenly brightened a little. "Tim, I can see you. I can really see you." She smiled. Then she spoke her final words, pausing in between almost every syllable for a breath, "You will, find, a . . . way. You are . . . my . . . Time Slider." Her eyes closed for the final time. Her smile slackened and her breathing ceased. She was gone.

Tim wept over her. This was the second death of Lexie for him. He had given her a much longer life in this line, but had it been a worthwhile life? How much pain had she endured all those years?

She had been abused by Jack until his death in 2030. But in the twelve years since, she had been free of that pain. She had described the feeling of a weight lifting from her when he died. So why had she still died so young?

Tim hadn't seen Dr. Bruin glide into the doorway as Lexie spoke her last words. Doc answered the unspoken question. "The physical and mental damage Jack inflicted upon her body and her soul, caught up to her, Tim."

Tim looked up and saw his friend gliding into the small room. His voice had startled Tim, but having a friend there with him at that moment was welcomed.

Doc put his hand onto Lexie's shoulder. He too had been a friend to her. As an ambassador from Tim, Doc had checked in on her occasionally and was greatly saddened now.

Two RONs automatically entered the room to prepare her body for removal. As soon as Lexie's vitals were gone, the drones had been dispatched. Their protocol for sensitivity did not include provisions for a nonrelated doctor and invisible lover from another world. No doctor or human nurse was necessary as the drones mechanically unhooked the equipment and sensors that were no longer required.

"She said I could still save her. But I don't know how," Tim contemplated aloud to Bruin as he wept, ignoring the RONs. "How can I save her now that she is gone?"

Tim thought about the word 'gone' he had just used. Her body still lay right in front of him. Yet he knew that whatever Lexie had been, she was no longer there with him in either world.

One of the RONs unrolled a long white material and began covering her body. A nurse entered the room to check the drones' work. As she checked the newly draped shroud that was being lifted over Lexie's face, she saw what looked like a tear, fall from nowhere and land on the cloth. She looked at old Dr. Bruin questioningly but then quickly turned away and headed toward the door.

As soon as she was gone, Bruin answered Tim. "I think Lexie is right. There has always been a connection between you two. A connection that defies everything I have learned and theorized about your ability. If she says there is a way, then I think you will find it."

Tim's eye was caught by the holoclock on the wall. The time had just changed to 12:13 a.m. He felt his body begin the transition. Realizing his time was up and that Bruin didn't have any direct advice to give, Tim said quietly, "I have a feeling this may be it, James."

Doc understood and smiled. "Tim, time is yours now. Your anchor has been set free."

"I don't understand," Tim started to ask but the colors faded. As Tim's zone ended, he saw Lexie's body being lifted up automatically into a temporary casket that lowered from the ceiling. Then all color, light, and sound were gone.

When the blankness lifted, Tim saw the blurry image of his own calendar. This was the first time that his slide into Lexie's world had brought him to an identical moment along the timeline. What did it mean? Was he reaching an age where he was no longer able to see a future or past but only the present?

What had Doc meant when he said, "time is yours now" and what was his anchor?

He jumped from his bed with the spring of a much younger man. He should have been depressed, discouraged or at least in mourning for the loss of his best friend and lover. But he wasn't any of those things. Instead, he was encouraged. He walked quickly down the hall and went out the front door into the cool crisp air of night.

Lexie believed that he would find a way to change everything. At the moment of her death, she had been able to see him clearly, just like she seemed to clearly know that he would change their past. “I will find a way, Lexie!” he shouted to the stars above him. “I won’t let you down!”

Chapter 47

THE ANCHOR IS FREE

TIM'S INTENTIONS WERE good, but he hadn't expected yet another hurtle. The rules had changed yet again. He wasn't sure how Bruin had known, but as the old man had said, time was now his own. His anchor, Lexie, was gone from that line. And as he struggled to understand the power of having her there, he found himself randomly sliding wildly through history.

Tim felt that his slide was different the moment he first saw the bright light growing around him. Somehow, there seemed to be less organization to the pattern of light and less strength in the pull on him toward his destination.

When he stood up after his arrival, he found himself staring at a barren world of volcanic ash, scalding rock, and fumes. Had he arrived at the Earth's distant future after its destruction? Had Armageddon come and gone, leaving no trace of humankind's existence?

Maybe it wasn't the future. Maybe he was standing on the Earth at the dawn of time. The harsh surface that lay before him hissed and churned as if the crust below his feet was only a thin skin atop an ocean of liquid magma. The gasses that escaped from below seemed to quickly slip away into a dark and thick atmosphere of vapor. Could this be the planet before the creation of life?

Either way, whether it was the far-off future or past, how had he arrived here? It was a place more unfamiliar and distant from his own than he had ever experienced. Suddenly and completely, Tim understood what Doc had meant. His anchor in time to this world was gone.

The next night, Tim watched as a fleet of Roman battleships attacked a small coastal port on the edge of the Mediterranean Sea. Then he witnessed part of the construction of China's Great Wall. He even found himself standing at the base of an immense tower that seemed to stretch through the clouds. A strangely engraved monolith that stood next to the tower read, *"Smithsonian Presents - Space Tower 1 - First operational space elevator. Construction completed 2097."*

With time and intense effort, Tim learned to control the shift. He trained himself to steer his way through the emptiness of his slide and land where and when he wanted. Finally for the first time in his life, he could end up at exactly the place and moment he desired.

However, in these self-guided slides into the alternate reality, he was totally powerless. He was completely unable to interact with people and things and had no ability to alter or guide events. His anchor that tied him to the zoned world was free.

Even Lexie, who had seen him in one way or another all her life, could no longer sense Tim's presence. He was truly a ghost in her world now. But as his control over the slides became more confident, he was able to watch her at any time of her life he chose. And the hole that had formed in his heart by Lexie's death seemed to be filled, at least temporarily, by seeing her each day.

Tim watched her win the 2nd grade spelling bee and the 6th grade Math Olympiad. He saw her drop out of high school despite the counselor's appeals for her to embrace her gifts of intelligence. He was there for the birth of Andrew and again at his funeral.

It became an addiction. Every night, Tim would watch her. Every night, Tim would miss her. She knew nothing of these forays into her world. She didn't feel him or even suspect him. This was the Lexie that existed between his previous visits. This was the Lexie that was perpetually waiting for the man she loved to return. This was the Lexie that had no hope for lasting happiness. She would live and then die, alone, having never experienced her happily ever after.

Her story had already been written. How would he ever be able to change her life? He watched her every night, searching, hoping, and praying for an answer. In this way, six more years slipped past. He was stuck. Though he hadn't given up, finding a solution to Lexie's dying request seemed hopeless.

June 2048

On a Saturday afternoon in June, 2048, Tim was ready to give up. He was seventy-six years old. Unsure where else to turn, he went to see his parents.

"I'm running out of time, Dad," he spoke to his father's grave. His mother and father lay next to each other near a large oak tree in the sprawling cemetery. The sky was blue and cloudless above him.

"I promised Lexie I would find a way to change everything. I promised to help her, to save her. But I haven't figured it out. I feel like there is something I'm missing."

Tim looked up as a family strolled into the cemetery and began examining various markers. The mom and dad held hands at first as they navigated their way through the expansive memorial park, but were forced to separate as they tried unsuccessfully to corral their three young blond haired boys, who had begun running in zigzags through the plastic markers.

A girl was with them too. At about ten years of age, she seemed to be the oldest of the four kids. She looked in Tim's direction for a moment, but then turned her attention to the markers and seemed to read each one she passed with interest.

Tim turned back to his dad's and mom's monuments. Theirs were made of permanent plastic, like most in this newer section of the graveyard. Each was an identical white, three foot tall monolith that attached seamlessly to a single large flat plastic base. The words, "John Daniel Caston and Sarah Danae Caston" were molded near the top. Below their names were universal optical ports that could be accessed by visitors to see a short biography and picture archive of the deceased. Tim didn't need to access the ports. He knew their bios by heart as he had written them both.

"Dad, I'm just not sure what to do next. Lexie has always been what grounded me. She believed in me. You and Mom did too, but without Lexie, I feel completely alone. I need help."

The boys had stopped running around the markers. Instead, they now climbed them and jumped from one to the next about one hundred yards from Tim. Their parents had given up and were walking hand in hand again, away from their rowdy sons.

Tim stepped back from his dad's marker and sat down on the soft patch of grass over his father's side of the plot. Lexie and her father were also buried somewhere in this cemetery, though he wasn't sure where. He knew hers was in the older portion of the cemetery, where actual stone markers had still been used, but wasn't sure if her father was in that section too, or in the newer part.

Tim had only visited Lexie's grave once, just after he first learned of her death from his parent's. However, since finding her living and breathing in his zone, he had avoided the spot, wanting only to think of her as alive. As long as he could see her, he could almost convince himself that she was still living.

But that was before. The anchor she had been for him in his zone was gone. And as time ticked on, it was becoming more difficult to convince himself that she ever lived at all. She was only like an actress on a screen now, in the world of his zone. He could see her there every day. But was that really alive? Day after day, living her sad life, not even knowing he was there? And day after day, his memory of truly being with her was fading. Had any of it even been real? Had his mind just played tricks on him?

"Oh God!" he yelled up to the sky in mournful sorrow. "Please help me." The boys down the hill stopped jumping over the stones and stared at him. Their parents were far away now and hadn't heard Tim's lament.

"What's wrong?" a youthful voice spoke behind him.

"Lexie?" Tim burst out as he turned and saw her, wonderfully young again. The sun shimmered through her brilliant blonde hair.

But how could it be her? It was impossible for her to be here. Was she an angel, returned from heaven to help him?

He looked again and shielded his eyes from the sun. No, it wasn't an angel or Lexie. It was just the girl who had arrived with her parents and brothers.

"Who's Lexie?" she questioned with raised eyebrows.

"My friend," he whispered. "My best friend. And my only love."

"Oh." Her face warmed as she stared at the sad old man. Then she looked at the name on John's monument. "She isn't there, you know. That's a guy." Tim stared at her. Was she making fun of him? Her face softened again as she continued speaking. "So this Lexie person, what's the deal?"

Why was this girl bothering him, Tim thought. Who was she and why did she think she could just bother a grieving man? He waited for her to give up her questioning and just walk away, but she didn't. She looked fixedly at him, expecting a response.

"It's a long story," he finally replied, feeling strangely compelled to talk with her. "She . . . ," he didn't know how to continue and looked away. How do you describe Lexie to some kid who has no respect toward someone in mourning?

"You know," she said, "I had an Aunt Alexis." Tim stared up at the girl again. "She is buried over there," the girl said as she pointed in the direction that he thought he remembered Lexie's plot to be.

He looked at her closely now. Her blonde hair blew gently in the wind against a soft pretty face covered partially by pink sunglasses. Something about her face was familiar. He had, after all, confused her with his Lexie just a few moments ago. Was it possible this girl was related? Without thinking he stood up, not taking his eyes off her. "Your aunt?" he asked with his mouth slightly gaping.

"Yeah, my aunt Alexis. I never knew her. She . . . ," the girl paused and then continued, trying to sound more mature, "she took her own life."

Tim just continued to stare. He felt dizzy. "You okay, guy?" she asked, dropping the false maturity in her tone. She took off her sunglasses and he was taken aback.

"Your eyes," he whispered.

"What?"

It was true. There was no mistaking her resemblance now. "You have your aunt's eyes." He smiled as he remembered the many times he had stared into those same almond-shaped blue eyes of Lexie's. The beauty of those eyes had persisted through all her years, even as the rest of her physical beauty waned.

"You knew her?" she questioned excitedly. "Come here, I'll take you to her." Without waiting for a response, she grabbed both his hands and started to pull him. He resisted at first but then let her lead him across the rolling cemetery and up the hill. He felt he would stumble at the pace at which she pulled him, but he held on to his balance and even laughed to himself at her Lexie-like enthusiasm.

"Here," she said grinning as they arrived at the foot of the grave. She continued to hold his left hand with her right as they read the stone. "Alexis Gracen Michols, September 7, 1974-February 12, 1995. Cherished daughter. Gone too soon."

"Way too soon," Tim uttered.

"So you did know her!" the girl giggled excitedly. "And you loved her?"

"Love her still," he smiled. It was odd. All this time, he had avoided her grave, thinking that seeing it would make him feel farther from her, and force him to acknowledge that she was dead. But standing here, he felt closer to her than he had since saying good-bye six years earlier. Watching her each day in his zone seemed less real than feeling the strength of the earth above her grave pushing up against his feet. This had been his friend. She had lived and she had died, but she was real.

"That's my Grandpa's grave there," the girl spoke quietly but without any hint of sadness as she pointed to Chris's grave next to Lexie. Gracie was there too, Tim observed. "I don't remember him either," she said. "He was pretty old when he had my dad, and super-duper old when I was born."

"So your dad must be Colton. I never met him but Lexie told me about him."

The girl scrunched her face up in thought. Tim realized immediately he'd spoken of his Lexie in the alternate line. This Lexie, who was buried here, never knew of her baby brother born four years after her death to Chris and his third wife.

Tim could see her still pondering the problem of what he had said, when suddenly her face changed expressions. He watched as her face relaxed and then turned into a slight knowing smile.

"This is going to seem strange," the girl spoke as she looked up at Tim. "But I think I have to tell you something." Tim gave her a questioning appraisal that was returned by her oddly understanding smile.

"You need to go to China, to Beijing." Her smile continued and Tim felt dizzy again. He had seen smiles like that many times. There was a screamer here. He couldn't see it while in this world, but he knew there must be one next to her right now.

"You've lost your way and need to find yourself," she finished.

"Find myself?" Tim repeated. "In Beijing?"

The girl's smile faded away and her questioning expression returned. "How did you know about my Dad? I thought my aunt . . ."

"Annika!" A motherly voice called out from nearby. The girl's mom and dad had wandered back. "Stop bothering that man," she ordered as she spotted her daughter's hand holding onto Tim's and gave Tim a suspicious frown.

"He knew Aunt Alexis, Mom," Annika called back. "He said he loved her," adding a little dance to the words "loved her" for child-like emphasis.

Tim gently pulled his hand from Annika's who tried to hold on. He understood the mother's concern. To her, he was just a stranger.

"She's very friendly," the mother said looking to Tim with a false smile as she quickly stumbled up to him. "Too friendly!" she added as she turned her eyes back to Annika without moving her head. "We just came to visit Colton's dad," she said, nodding in the direction of the father trying to chase down the three boys, but never taking her eyes off Tim. "Guess we went the wrong way."

"I knew where it was," Annika said, "and I brought this nice old man to see Aunt Alexis."

Sensing the mother's unease, Tim spoke. "I was a childhood friend of Alexis. And your daughter helped me to find her place of rest." Then, turning toward Annika, "Thank you. You have helped me more than you know. I understand now, and I know what I must do."

"What do you have to do?" Lexie's niece asked.

"Something very important. Something I should have thought of a long time ago." Tim smiled at Annika again. "It is time for me to go."

Chapter 48

A NEW COURSE FOR TIME

AS TIM LAY down in bed, ready for the approaching slide into the zoned world, he felt ready and confident. He knew it would not be easy. He had seen what had happened the last time this was tried. But this time, he would be successful. He could feel it. He also somehow knew that whether successful or not, this would be his last zone.

He lay there, careful not to fall asleep. He had learned that to control the slide, he had to be conscious up to the moment that his mind transitioned into his zone. He concentrated harder than he ever had. He thought of the massive skyscrapers towering over the small storefronts that lined the busy streets of Beijing, China. He thought of the bicyclists, cars, buses, and crowds of people of the 1990s. Those crowds had been decimated by the SWK viral outbreak in the 20s. But the Beijing he needed to get to was still clouded by smog and packed by over thirteen million people.

Tim focused on the old noodle shop where, as a young man, he had terrorized Chong with floating chopsticks, just one night after the hypnotherapist had unlocked his zone world to him. He had been so young then, unsure of what his zone was or how it could be used.

Tim visualized the red sign on the front of the shop with the intricate yellow text symbols. And as he felt his zone taking him, he focused on the people, hoping to find one person in particular.

June 2048
Zone Year: 1990

A moment later after the usual light transfer, he was there. It had worked! The swarm of people passed around him and through him. He had no physical presence here. He had no power or solid form for the people to avoid. That was the norm in these controlled slides. He was only an observer.

But that wasn't the case for the person moving through the crowds ahead of him. He could see the young man darting left and right through the crowd, testing their ability to move out of his path. The young man neared the noodle shop with the red sign, leapt out of the crowd toward the door, and reached for the handle to open the door to the restaurant.

Tim yelled, "Stop!"

The young man, a young Tim, turned and saw someone who he thought was his grandfather.

"We need to talk," old Tim said. The situation seemed impossible. It was as if he were looking into a mirror, only his hair was brown again, and his skin had been rejuvenated.

"How do you see me?" the young Tim asked, still holding onto the handle of the door.

"I see you, Tim, because I am you. I too travel from my home each night and end up in this world. I am your future. And it is a matter of life and death that you listen to me now."

The crowds around them continued to buzz past, but for the two Tims, nothing else existed at that moment. Old Tim started to reach out to place his hand on young Tim's shoulder.

Just then, something grabbed onto old Tim and pulled him backward into the rush of people. It was a screamer. Young Tim saw several more identical boys arrive as the older man was pulled through the crowd. The people had at first passed right through the man. However, now as the boys surrounded him, the crowd reformed their march to detour the 10' radius circle made by their eerie presence. At the center of that circle, the man, who had said he was *his* future self, was now held down hard against the concrete. The man tried to talk.

"You must let me speak with him!" old Tim yelled from the center of the circle to the screamers. "I was led here by others just like you from my world. They guided me back to this time and place." He considered what he had just said. He had long pondered how much power the screamers had on his own life, but had thought he was somehow immune to them. However, now it was clear that the guiding force of the screamers had greater influence than he had wanted to believe. He wondered how often they had led his actions or thoughts in one way or another.

"They led me here! You have to let me speak to him now. There isn't much time left before he leaves this zone. They want me to talk to him." Tim didn't know if the screamers had the capacity to reason, or if they even cared.

Young Tim saw one of the boys disappear for a moment, then reappear. Maybe it was more like the image of the boy flickered. Whatever had happened, something was changed. The boy let go of Tim and then the others let him stand up. However, the protective circle, separating old Tim from young Tim, was maintained. Old Tim wondered if there was some fundamental law of nature that would be violated if he interacted too closely with his other self. Was that why the screamers had always kept him away from any other Tims of the past or future?

"Who are you?" young Tim asked nervously, looking at both old Tim and the strange identical boys surrounding him.

"I am Timothy Caston. I am you, Tim. Only, I have already lived my life. You still have your whole life ahead of you. You will help many people. In a sense, you will save the world. But you won't be happy unless you listen to me."

Young Tim stared again at the screamers as he thought about the situation. This was only his second zone since the hypnotist had unlocked his ability to remember the events. So much was new to him. He wasn't even sure if any of this was real. Who were those boys that all looked the same? Was this old man really *him*? How was that even possible?

"Look at me!" old Tim ordered, trying to keep Tim's attention. "I know this is all very strange, but it is real. This place is a parallel universe to our own. You will slide to this world every night, and over time, you will learn the rules of your zone. It took me too long to understand those rules. But it is not too late for you.

"I let my zone become a curse. I made choices early on that caused me to live my life alone. I thought that was the price I had to pay to help others. But I, *you*, don't have to be alone to save the world. There has always been one person who understands us. She loves us. And we have always loved her."

"Lexie?" young Tim asked, knowing she was the only possible answer. She was the only one he had ever loved.

"Yes, Lexie," old Tim nodded.

Feeling braver, young Tim argued with the man who claimed to be him. "But I haven't seen Lexie in forever. She lives somewhere in Nebraska with her dad. I haven't spoken with her since . . ."

"Since you called her Pycho Michols in front of your friends. I know. I was there, too. Remember, I am you. And I know how bad you still feel about causing her so much pain.

"Just like you, I watched her run into her house, crying because of what I said. Then you and I both stood aside silently as she and her dad packed up and said good-bye. We thought about her almost every day after that—during class, while on dates, in our dreams. Trust me, I know everything about you because I am you.

"I know that last Friday night, you snuck into Amy's house while her parents were away. And I know that just before you crashed your car into the tree and ended up in the hospital, you were thinking of Lexie instead of Amy."

Young Tim was shocked. He hadn't told anyone that he had been at Amy's. And it was true that he couldn't get Lexie out of his mind, even while with Amy.

"This is all real?" young Tim asked. "A parallel universe? I'm not even sure what that means," he said, as belief started to sink in.

"You don't have to understand everything yet," old Tim said sympathetically. "What is important now is that you find Lexie. You must rescue her from a path of misery. And if you rescue her now, you will rescue yourself. The rest of the world will always have crime, sin, sadness, and death. No matter what you do to try to fix that, those things will all still exist. But you can do it with joy and hope, knowing that every night when you wake up with your next assignment, you'll have her beside you."

"But if you are my future, how can I change anything you've already done?"

"By changing the rules. You will still do everything I have done, but you'll know why and who you are doing it for. You will have a family and a reason to live."

"What if I do find her and she has a boyfriend or she doesn't want to see me?"

"You have to trust me, Tim. She is fifteen, almost sixteen back in your time. She is at a crossroads in her life. Our dad will know how to contact her dad. And whatever her situation is when you find her, even if she has a boyfriend, she will choose you. And if I am wrong, or if she is confused, then fight for her. Don't give up. Never give up!"

"How do you know it will work?"

"It will. I used to think the rules were unchangeable and that the future is set. But now I know that isn't true. I'm talking to you right now, telling you how to change your future and Lexie's. When I was standing in your shoes, my older self tried to do the same. He failed. The screamers didn't allow him to speak to me. But I have not failed. The rules have already changed and because of it, your future has changed, too."

Old Tim hoped young Tim understood. He seemed to be trying to understand, but it would be difficult for him to believe. He was eighteen and had only discovered the realness of his zone the day before. Now he was being confronted with a vision of his own future. And that future would be completely changed because of this moment. How could he be expected to understand so much? But he had to understand. Lexie's life and his life depended on it.

"Find Lexie! Find her before it is too late for you both," Tim yelled at the young man one last time. Time had run out. Young Tim's thirty-eight minutes had expired.

Old Tim saw his young self collapse to the ground suddenly, and then phase out of this time reality. The young man would wake up in his bedroom of 1990 and have to decide whether he believed in himself enough to change the future.

Alone, Tim stood as the screamers closed in on him. Had he done enough? Would the young Tim believe him and go to Lexie before it was too late?

The screamers were upon him. Tim felt no pain as his body and his existence was obliterated by the boys. He had changed his own past and therefore, he could no longer exist. Both timelines, his and Lexie's, would be changed by the new path his younger self was on. From those merging lines, a new one would be created. His young self would have a different life from the one he had lived. And through that life, he might truly live, and finally experience the meaning of love.

Chapter 49

A NEW WORLD

Saturday, May 10, 2003

THEY TIPTOED, BAREFOOT, down the wooden staircase, careful to avoid the third stair up from the bottom, knowing it would squeak. Slipping as silently as possible into the kitchen, they began their mission. Together, the three young children, two girls, and a boy pulled the necessary ingredients from the fridge and cupboards and clumsily put them together as best they could onto a tray.

Twenty two minutes later, a bag of sugar lay half spilled on the floor next to a leaky carton of orange juice and several slices of soggy bread. A paper plate was securely glued to the counter top by Mrs. Butterworth's maple syrup. Footprints, in the shape of bare children's feet, led past the refrigerator, through a pile of corn flakes, around the kitchen table, toward a squashed meatball, and then out through the living room.

The children's father slept peacefully and soundly even as the bedroom door opened quietly amid hushed conspiratorial whispers and giggles. He lay on his stomach, next to his wife, clad only in red boxers and a green University of Tulsa t-shirt. Suddenly, little hands tickling his back startled him awake.

"Happy Birthday, Daddy!" the young children sang out to him cheerfully. "We made you breakfast!"

Tim opened his eyes and saw his wife smiling brightly at him just a few inches away. Her blonde hair was slightly tangled from sleeping, and faint lines from her pillow still marked her face. She was beautiful, he thought. He loved waking up to the sight of Lexie's blue eyes every morning. Their sparkle could illuminate a room.

"Morning Honey," Lexie whispered. "Looks like the kids have something for you. It looks . . . tasty!" She smiled with a raised eyebrow and an expression of warning to Tim.

"Think it is edible?" he smirked, his back still toward his happy kids.

"Probably not, but it's still pretty sweet," she whispered back. Then Lexie sat up and addressed the kids. "Poor Daddy is still tired. Give him a moment to wake up." She put her hand on the top of his head and patted his hair. "After all, he isn't as young as he used to be!" she laughed.

Tim laughed too. He pushed himself up onto his elbows and turned his head to the kids.

"Yum," he laughed again as he admired the blackened toast with jelly pooling up in a wet mass, slimy cereal of indiscernible variety floating in a mixture of milk and orange juice, a meatball that looked like it had been dropped onto the floor, and a glass of orange juice with a soaking tea bag. Spilled sugar garnished the breakfast display and piled up in various places on the food and drinks—so much so that some of it might actually taste okay.

"Want some music while you eat," their oldest daughter Abby asked as she turned on the small clock radio that sat on the night stand next to Tim. She didn't recognize or particularly like the 80s music flashback that streamed out of the speaker. She knew her dad liked it though, so she didn't change the station.

"Thank you, honey," Tim said, acknowledging the thoughtfulness of his six year-old.

Rolling over onto his back, Tim smiled up at his lovely wife again. The sun was shining in through the open window and cascaded through her golden hair and onto her face; a face that had never been beaten or abused. She glowed like an angel above him.

Recognizing that he was staring at her again, Lexie leaned in over Tim, letting her hair fall around his face like a curtain. "Happy Birthday, Timmy," she whispered as their lips met gently.

"Awww, Mommy and Daddy are kissing again," their five-year-old son, Andrew, complained.

"They are supposed to kiss," Abby said. "That's what Mommies and Daddies are s'pos ta do." Lexie and Tim parted lips, but let their noses and foreheads stay together for a moment longer.

The bed shook as the three children climbed up onto their parents, having put the food down on the nightstand. Playfully they made kissing sounds and wrestled to pull Lexie off her husband. Lexie reluctantly slid out of Tim's embrace and then teamed up with Tim for a well deserved tickle fight against their happy children.

"Give, give," the kids laughed when they had enough.

Tim and Lexie stopped their barrage and sat back victoriously.

"So what should we do today for Daddy's birthday?" Lexie asked the kids.

"Daddy needs to make a wish. Make a wish, Daddy!" Andrew yelled out, bouncing on the bed.

"I can't make a wish. You didn't put a candle on my toast," Tim laughed.

"I'll go find one," Andrew said excitedly, jumping off the bed.

"No, no," Lexie laughed, stopping him. "You aren't old enough to be finding and using candles."

Abby jumped off the bed. "I have an idea," she yelled back as she ran out of the room.

She returned with Tim's Magic 8 Ball in hand. "Here, make a wish with this." Tim took the ball and turned it over a few times.

"Will we all live happily ever after?" he asked, beaming at each of his kids and then toward Lexie.

The answer inside floated up to the surface quickly. Tim smiled and showed it to Lexie. "It is certain," she read aloud.

"Tell us about your dream, Daddy!" their youngest daughter said. All three children loved to hear his stories. "Did you rescue a kitty cat from a tree?" she asked.

"I think he stopped a bank robbery!" Andrew suggested.

"Maybe he helped a beautiful princess! Or a damsel in distress," Abby offered.

Tim smiled. He enjoyed telling the stories of his zone adventures to his kids, always disguised as normal, vivid dreams of course.

"It *was* a damsel in distress," he said, nodding toward Abby.

"Of course," laughed Lexie. "You always help the pretty girls."

"Hey, I'm an equal opportunity rescuer!" Tim said, smiling faithfully at Lexie.

"Go on," she said while rolling her eyes and smiling. "Tell us about the damsel."

"So" Tim began as his family lovingly curled up around him on the bed. "In a future, not too far from now, a young woman was lost during a snowstorm. Suddenly her little white Nissan IO slid off the road and into a snow bank. A few minutes later, a robotic automated plow piled snow up against her car. It was piled so high that no one would ever be able to see her."

Andrew interrupted. "Wait, snow plows don't have robots."

Tim and Lexie smiled. Then Tim gave his standard response that the kids had heard many times. "Oh, but they will."

The 80s flashback continued on the radio next to them. Cyndi Lauper sang along softly as Tim continued his story.

"If you're lost, you can look and you will find me, time after time. If you fall, I will catch you, I'll be waiting, time after time. Time after time. Time after time."

Epilogue

THE ANCIENT BEING arrived from the void, ready to meet the overseer. His form was that of an adult human man, but his mind was far more than that of any man. As he moved out of the void, the image of a forest expanded fluidly around him. Bright light reflected and shimmered all around the being as if transmitted through a wall of water. The trees that towered over him seemed to lack color due to the brightness, but they still possessed a sepia-toned beauty that was indescribable with human words.

The being followed a sandy path that lay beneath his bare feet. The path was familiar to the being, as he had traveled it many times to report to the overseer. His steps were soundless and his golden hair and pale cloak appeared to blow in the wind, though no wind was present.

He reached the part of the path, where a clear stream moved in close and formed the left edge of the trail with its smooth water-worn rocks. Laminar flowing water passed effortlessly around the rocks and in one place, a fallen leaf spun around and around in a moss-lined pool.

He closed his eyes as he walked along the stream, imagining the sound of the water cascading over the rocks and of the breezes blowing through this same forest back on Earth. He had never been to Earth himself. But his purpose was greater than those who labored there.

The path turned left and led to a wooden bridge, designed and built long before the first human picked up the first stone tool.

The being crossed over the ageless bridge and entered the clearing. An eagle-like creature with a white head and brown wings circled overhead like a sentinel.

As the being passed into the clearing, he saw that the overseer was already there, waiting with eternal patience. His robes were as white as the shimmering light that surrounded them both. His face was old and wise.

"I see you have returned," the overseer stated without expression.

"I believe my task is complete," the being responded. "We have found the dominant line."

"And what of the anomaly?" the overseer asked.

The being expected the question and also suspected that the wise overseer already knew the answer.

The anomaly that the overseer referred to was a human man, a slider. At first, the man had complicated the being's purpose. He had caused rifts and divisions to form, but in the end, he had created the solution for them all.

"The anomaly has been appeased. I believe that he too favors the dominant line. He is content now and willing to serve our purpose." The being hesitated slightly and then continued, "We have allowed him to have the woman. It would seem that together, they offer more stability to the line than apart."

The overseer slowly nodded in agreement. "And what of their children?" he questioned astutely.

"They will be laced into the texture of the line. The weaver has found a gap that is neatly filled by their new existence."

The overseer nodded again. He did not appear at all surprised to learn of the gap in the fabric of time that had existed. Nor did it seem to cause him surprise to learn that the same gap could be perfectly filled by the actions of the anomalous human man.

The being continued his report, "The children do not exhibit the capability of the anomaly. His gift was not passed to them. However, they have their mother's intellect. They will surely learn of the anomaly's ability. They will study it and will expose it to humankind."

The overseer slowly nodded yet again. "The humans will attain knowledge, but they will still lack understanding. The created will create, but only within the bounds set for them. Each generation will assume they have discovered a great truth in the universe. But only in the end will the Master's plan be revealed to them and to us."

The being understood. The new children and this newly stitched family would be allowed to exist unhindered. Their lives were part of the chosen thread onto which all other time lines would be woven.

"Be on watch," the overseer warned. "Humans with such a gift will appear again. It has already happened, both in the past and in the future of this created world."

The being understood. The overseer was not bound by linear time. He knew of the past, present, and future as if they were one.

"I will continue in my charge," the being answered, "to discover the will of the Creator and Master, and to keep the line pure."

"As will I continue to intercede on the Master's behalf," the overseer agreed.

"Do you believe he will be satisfied with the primary line's new direction?" the being asked.

"Yes. The Master has already made that clear to me. The dominant line you have chosen is pure. His will has been met, despite the substantial deviations that were tested. The fabric was frayed but now has regained stability."

"The anomaly was persistent," the being admitted. "He did not give up and therefore fabricated this new line for himself. It has not been done in such a way before."

"All things are possible, and even this was foreseen by the Master. Clearly, the Master is not surprised by the outcome. He has assured me that he is satisfied, as he is always satisfied when we perform our purpose."

"Then I shall return and wait until we are needed again. Will you be here when that time comes?" the being asked, knowing it was an unnecessary question.

The overseer spoke eternally, "I am already there." Above them, the winged creature continued its slow flight overhead. And beyond the glimmering forest, the Master was pleased.

Made in the USA
Lexington, KY
05 October 2012